THE LIVING LABYRINTH

Ian Stewart and Tim Poston

ReAnimus Press
Breathing Life into Great Books

ReAnimus Press
1100 Johnson Road #16-143
Golden, CO 80402
www.ReAnimus.com

© 2016 by Tim Poston and Joat Enterprises. All rights reserved.

ISBN-13: 978-1535298421

First edition: August, 2016

10 9 8 7 6 5 4 3 2 1

This is as strange a maze as e'er men trod
And there is in this business more than nature
Was ever conduct of: some oracle
Must rectify our knowledge.
—William Shakespeare, *The Tempest*

To Odysseus, who made it.
To Magellan, who didn't.

Contents

7:	Chapter 1 Karmabhumi Weather
23:	Chapter 2 Simquake
29:	Globe of Squill III
33:	Chapter 3 Downfall
49:	Chapter 4 Gold Bones, Violet Blood
49:	Map of Shaaluy
63:	Chapter 5 Munication
67:	Chapter 6 Pilgrims to Magog
75:	Chapter 7 Ni Porbleem
85:	Chapter 8 Two Mountains
95:	Chapter 9 Sacred Growth
107:	Chapter 10 Dividing the Body
119:	Chapter 11 The View from the Groin
127:	Chapter 12 Tidal Stress
137:	Chapter 13 Abomination
147:	Chapter 14 Gold Lightning
147:	Map of Samdal
155:	Chapter 15 Beast Mistress
163:	Chapter 16 Captives of the Slavestone
163:	Map of Lamynt

177:    Chapter 17 Show Business
185:    Chapter 18 Displaced Persons

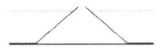

195:    Chapter 19 Vulcan's Anvil

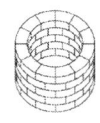

207:    Chapter 20 Water Empire
217:    Chapter 21 Reinventing the Wall

227:    Chapter 22 Botanical Warfare
227:    Map of Wevory
241:    Chapter 23 The War in the Air
242:    Lamynt-Wevory warmap
251:    Chapter 24 Plan B4

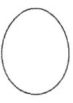

261:    Chapter 25 Cavern-Dwellers
271:    Chapter 26 Egg Flower

283:    Chapter 27 Only Connect
291:    Chapter 28 Word of the Prophet
299:    Chapter 29 Crowd Cuckoo Land
309:    Epilogue
313:    Glossary
317:    Warning

See www.syntei.com for richly detailed background information on the characters, the planet and Concordat galaxy, as well as a community where you can check out and share fan-supplied art, science, engineering, and more stories.

1

Karmabhumi Weather

My leaving-home present was a knife.

"A *knife*, grandmother?" It was long, straight, and weirdly heavy. No modern material I knew. "What is it made of? Some alloy of iron?"

"It's called steel, Samuel Grey Deer." I'd heard of that. "This one has been in the family since before the first powered flight on Old Earth."

"It doesn't look like the beads and stuff you've showed me, from our Iroquois ancestors."

"We didn't make this, Sam. We took it off the guy who tried to give us smallpox in blankets." The look on her face was somehow right for those 'we', two thousand years dead. "He died without showing courage, but we kept this knife. It always passes to a grandson who is going out to face those who took our lands. The knife keeps safe the grandson. The grandson keeps safe the knife."

"Grandmother, we're hundreds of light years from those lands, and the family genes are from all over Old Earth. I should be facing tech school with a *knife*? I won't even build machines; navigation is about star jumps. Tensor sheaves, not sheaths."

"And I have a doxorate in shaded nucleonics, Sam. Take the knife."

I did get fascinated by the thing. It's an 'Arkansas toothpick', perfectly balanced for throwing as well as thrust and slash. Most knives rotate clumsily when you let them go... inertia tensors have to be just so, like with spacecraft. Would you believe it improved my gut feel for orbits? There are training clubs for anything, and I got my Black Belt in 'artistic' knife fighting the same day as my in-system navigation licence. I always carry it.

You're right, that's the other thing. Somehow it does attract smart people. Like you.

—*Message on a dating site, Sam Wasumi*

Suufi was a tiny moon of a gas giant, roofed over with a sphere of impact-proof plastic and pressurised. The doctor looked out of her fifty-sixth storey window at one of the dome's supports and sighed. She knew the routine by heart. Another group of ill-assorted trainees from all corners of the Concordat, assembled on a small moon, bound for Starhome and qualification as galactic citizens. If they made it.

The medical records showed excellent physical health for all six. A couple of bones broken, the recommended childhood diseases. No body mods from their genomes, all close to human baseline: no gills, no fur, no Schrödinger catspaws, no prehensile testicles. Sensible mods for endurance and rapid muscular recovery from stress. She ran her eye down the list:

Irenotincala Laurel. Age 21 standard years. Waylander. Tall with characteristically lopsided hands, index finger longer than the rest, thumb curiously extended. Brown eyes, brunette hair in scalloped bangs. Keeps her head when all about her are losing theirs. Accomplished pilot, can fly pretty much anything in or out of atmosphere. High levels of physical courage and mental strength, but brittle under extremes of stress.

Jane Bytinsky. Age 24 sy. Not as tall as the other two women: typical slender build from mid-gee worlds like her home planet of Ebisu. Unusually fast reflexes. Xenologist — expert on alien worlds, habitats, and critters. Paired with Felix Wylde. Starhome doesn't usually put matchpairs in the same group. Wonder how...? Read on.

Felix Wylde. Age 26 sy. From Daikoku, around the same star as Ebisu. Tall, muscular, hair cropped short with a typical Daikoku gengineered silver streak. Quiet personality, taciturn. And — well, well. Another xenologist. That explains it. Starhome must have kept them together for professional reasons.

Next, the last-minute replacement for Amberdon Lorimer: this one's a doozy.

Lady Elzabet of Quynt. Age 22 sy. Third daughter of a Duchess, spent all her life on Hippolyta. Spoilt brat, most likely. *Third* daughter... ah, that explains why she's in this group. Willowy blonde, physically striking, must drive the boys crazy. Quick reflexes. Doxorate in rock dynamics. Physically up there with the best of them. Mentally: mild instability, occasional mood swings. Impulsive and unpredictable. Nothing pathological, but a potential flashpoint for trouble.

Samuel Grey Deer Wasumi. Age 22 sy. Born on Buffalo; family moved to Wounded Knee when he was six. Martial arts qualified, and looks it. Prone to snap decisions from little information, prefers action to discussion. Despite which, he's the group's navigator. Interesting choice.

And finally:

Marco Leontevich Bianchi. Age 22 sy. From Inferno, the dark side of a close-in planet named Dante. Engineer, a very good one by the look of it, aced all the tests. Short and stocky, with a mop of black curls in a bonsai topiary style once fashionable on Inferno; now almost a brandmark of graduates from the Inferno Institute of Technology. The joker in the pack, in and out of scrapes all the time. *Mostly* minor. Has difficulty taking anything seriously. Impetuous, like Sam: ready, fire, aim. Another possible flashpoint.

She closed the file, half horrified, half amused. A mismatched bunch of overqualified Babes in the Wood. *They always were*: that was the main point of the exercise. Teach them to work together as a team. Start with one extended voyage to the boondocks, out in space where all they could damage was themselves and a very expensive Da Silva starship. Then an exacting mission under the eyes of competent professionals, where they might just make themselves useful once they'd climbed the learning curve. If they made it, back to Starhome for galactic citizenship training. Maybe, in a century or three, some would get to be essential.

Time to call in the first pair.

~~~

The doctor slapped yellow paste over Sam's wrist with a broad, flat brush. "This'll sting a bit," she said, "but only for a moment. New one'll sting more, till you get used to it. Purely in the mind — but then, isn't all pain in the mind? No nerves, no feelings. Lift your arm just a wee tad, *there's* a good—" her fingers found the groove in his wristcomp, pulled hard and diagonally. It unzipped from his skin like a used stickyaid. She held it up to the light, inspected the registration code. "Obsolete." Into the bin.

"Hey! I only had that fitted two years back!"

"On Wounded Knee."

"Yah."

These backworlders. "It was obsolete the day you printed your thumb on the creditpad, Wasumi." She grimaced. "Five gigachannels, ten petawords, node speed of Zeno's tortoise. Not parallel enough, no expansion capacity, and *slow*. Definitely not acceptable for the navigator of a passage team."

Lifting a slightly broader band from a gel-bath she rinsed it, let the optics sense his wrist colour and tune the liquid-protein surface membranes to match. She slapped the 'comp on to Sam's wrist, wrapped it tight. It faded to match his skin.

"Chameleonics," she explained. "The quiet mode is unseeable, but this setting is more interesting."

Sam wriggled his hand on the end of an invisible wrist. "Active cloaking? Must take a lot of qbit-crunching. Can they do this for the whole body?"

"Yah, but you need special hardware over the eyes and other openings — not practical for embedware. It's mainly restricted to uses where stealth is critical, not just fun. But the main new feature is a direct hook-in to your central nervous system, Grey Deer, assuming you have one. I don't expect allergic reactions, but watch out for symptoms anyway — rapid pulse, swollen fingers, stiffness in the elbow joints. The 'comp will monitor you, but it can't detach itself if you hit trouble, because of the synaptic connectors. Takes the power of a stand-alone to decouple those safely."

Tinka Laurel had been assigned to act as Sam's second — partner, confidant, back-watcher, and often back-scratcher. "I get the same treatment?"

"Pilot gets a better upgrade — harder to learn, easier later. Starcharts and karm-abhumi field solvers, like Sam. Plus flight data, comm codes, Starhome regs, Da Silva topographic imaging... Same allergy warning, dah?"

"Yah. Same interface?"

"No point reinventing the pyramid. Comp: init code 'araucaria'." She turned to face him. "That's 'monkey-puzzle' to you, youngster. Now it's all yours. Feel anything yet?"

"It's tightening — yow! It's burning me!"

"That's the nerves hooking in. Like fire, only if you concentrate you realise it feels *cold*. Tiny icicle teeth gnawing at your soul."

"Just feels sore."

The doctor pretended to consult Sam's file. "Yah, it says there's no poetry in you, Wasumi. Pain easing off now?"

He gritted his teeth, then started to relax. "A bit. Getting used to it."

"This is just the opening lovebite. Still feeling tight?"

"Nah, it's kind of loosened off. Can't really feel the band at all, any more than I can see it. Just feels like I've had my wrist rubbed with sandpaper."

"It's digging in. Down to the mesoderm by now. Don't worry, it'll stop once it's properly bedded." The doctor cocked her head slightly to one side, watching his face. "Hear anything?"

"Nah. Wait — kind of internal whispers. Not making sense. They disappear when I focus attention on them."

"Fine. It's subvocalising. You'll hear it clearly in a day or so, once it correlates external sounds with your neural responses, so it can give you quick answers silently. But it'll take longer for you to command it that way."

"*Command* it?"

"Much faster. You don't talk to it, like a conventional 'comp. You *think* at it. But you have to learn to think its language. It'll teach you, over a few days. Unless you're incompat. If so, we find ourselves another navigator."

"Why wasn't I tested for this in nav-school? Mother of a time to find out I'm not up to the job *now*."

The doctor emitted a mirthless chuckle. "Sensitive technology, only available to galactics or candidates. Don't worry, you'll be fine. In six months it will show you visions, but the visual cortex takes longer than Broca's area: that's why it has a visible mode, for display to your eyes or to other people's. It can even project on a white wall. Now, go sit down while I get Irenotincala fitted out, then you can go back to the waiting room while I process the other four. You'll find everything you need is already there. Induction, pre-flight training, and briefings start tomorrow."

~~~

Three more Starfolk waited in the outer room.

"What's keeping Elzabet?"

"Dunno, Jane," said Marco. "Her private cruiser, courtesy of the Duchy of Quynt, landed hours ago. Probably trying to decide which dress to — "

The door swung open. So did Marco's mouth. The sixth was slim, dark skinned and stunningly shaped, with long blonde hair braided into three flictails, as befitted a Third Daughter. She had a face to die for — fine bones, flawless eyelids.

The vision of loveliness spoke.

"I do not belong here! I was not told I was on the candidate list for diplomat training until two days ago. I see no reason to become a galactic, just for access to the worlds of uncouth persons who can perfectly well come to Quynt! I did not volunteer for this assignment, and I have not been given adequate time to prepare for it. I have instructed the Hippolytan Ambassador to register a formal protest!"

She can *register* it, Jane thought. And Starhome will ignore it. Once you've signed up for induction, only sickness or death can reverse your decision. And once you recover from either, they shove you into the next available slot. But what she said was: "You must be Lady Elzabet. I'm Jane; this is Marco, and Felix is over there in the corner. Tinka and Sam are in with the doc — nah, here they come."

The two trainees emerged, and the doctor poked her head round the door.

"Ah. I see you have arrived, Elzabet of Quynt."

"*Lady* Elzabet of Quynt."

"Yah. Hippolytan. Never mind, you'll get over it eventually. Come this way."

"Fringe world," said Jane, "Let's not pre-judge her, After all, first passage is all about getting along with other people. If everybody in a team had compatible personalities, it would be too easy. First passage is a social ritual, a coming of age. We grow together and we grow up together. *Then* we're ready for galactic re-education. Would Wounded Knee want free travel from backworlds like Fort Purity? Would you want to run a *visa system* to let in just the ones who don't blow their noses on their neighbours? If you can't be polite to a snob you're not flexible enough for galactic citizenship."

~~~

Six weeks flew by in a blur…

~~~

"Marco," said the instructor, "do you approve of male enslavement on Hippolyta?"

"Mmmm," said Marco, looking at Elzabet less eagerly than usual, "it's not up to me to *dis*approve of the way a world is organised. If they're not trying to export it."

"A typical Core world attitude," agreed the instructor, "nearly the Starfolk view. Now, Elza, how do you see Suufi?"

"Rather gross. It's not the free-roaming males, I was braced for that, but the general lack of respect. You can't expect me to approve of the casual way everybody treats authority."

"I don't, but as Marco said, it's not up to you to *dis*approve. People here do respect expertise, but I'm not here to defend them to you. I'm here to help you learn respect for difference."

Elzabet nodded, deferentially, thinking *but maybe I like disapproving of things.*

~~~

From nowhere, Elza's bare foot flashed at Sam's head. He ducked, and felt it brush his hair. He made a grab for the other foot: it wasn't there. As he whirled to defend himself against the next strike, she flipped over in mid-air, smashed him to the floor, and landed astride his diaphragm. One hand was at the pressure-point at the side of his neck.

"Yield!"

The *hai ganzai* instructor pushed the hand aside. "He's too winded to yield. Where did you learn how to do an *ibukuro-summasshu*?"

"Madame Lollengass's Academy, self-defence classes. To avoid unwanted attention from males."

Sam, staggering up, managed to breathe "Defence? All-out-attack, you mean."

"Best kind. *Ibukuro-summasshu*? Is that what it's called? We never learnt the names, just the moves."

"Let me show you one more." The instructor squared up. "Try that again. Yah, I know it's coming, but so would any *meijin*." There was a glitter in his eyes.

Without warning, Elza launched herself. He swayed, extended a leg—

"Yield!"

The instructor looked up at a fine-boned face. "How did you—?"

"They taught us the *subaskhikoi-touben* countermove, too," Elza admitted. "And I lied about the names."

~~~

"I see why Duchess Arabella would like a galactic in the family," said Tinka, "but how come she let you train to meddle with rocks?"

They'd been told to be informal and open with each other, to build team spirit. Elzabet no longer complained openly about lack of respect, and was struggling to unbend after the Hippolytan Ambassador had engaged her in a frank, private conversation.

"I am a *third* daughter. I was special, but I bowed to my elder sisters, and even mother bowed to the Queen. And of course all males had to bend the knee to everybody important, even me.

"When I was seven, my mother took me on a special wilderness trip. She brought a lot of servants, of course: perfectly safe. There were wild beasts, and massive, fat trees like nothing I'd ever seen. But the best bit was the cave. It went in forever, or so it seemed to me then. It was dark and gloomy, so I had to be very brave.

"The men working in the cave used strange machines, gigantic. It was so noisy I had to wear earmuffs, lovely furry ones. My mother told one of the men to show me the jewellery made from the rocks, golden and glittery. Mother let me try some on, but what really fascinated me was the big white crystals in the rocky walls. She gave me a gold necklace, and I begged a crystal from the workman when she wasn't looking.

"That was my first visit to what I soon knew were 'mines', and the first of many rocks. One day, on the side of a cliff where the rocks formed thick layers, I split open a lump, and inside was a seven-pointed star. Mother said it was a fossil, a living creature from long before people arrived on Hippolyta.

"I'd never been told that people hadn't always been there.

"Mother would have wanted to discourage a first or second daughter from collecting rocks, but a third daughter goes into the family business. So when I finished basic education, off I went to the School of Mines. I loved it. The passion for rocks and fossils has never left me, but even more I love the moving earth that makes them.

"Eventually I realised that Mother never does anything just for happiness or curiosity. Right from the start, she'd been grooming me to manage the mines. But she was so busy getting me interested in mining that it never occurred to her that I wouldn't be interested in management.

"I think that was the moment I began to rebel. Nah, I don't hate her, she's my mother. But I lost all respect for her. She could have asked."

~~~

"I'm glad we did sims of emergency evac to a planetary surface," said Jane, "or we might not have made it down alive." That evac would give her nightmares for years. "But what are we doing *here*?"

"We'll be heading off to Starhome, on our own in a Da Silva starship," said Tinka. "That alone is a test. At Starhome there will be more tests, then a training mission. A tough one, always. Consider this a gentle warm-up, training for survival."

"Right now I'm dubious about that," Sam put in. "Cliff-tops are unnerving, more so with no shelter. See that storm coming?"

"Yah, but we can see the pickup point already," said Jane, pointing to the depths of the valley. "We just have to get down there."

"Seven hundred metres down," said Sam, "on a four hundred metre rope."

Elzabet lay flat to look over the edge. "There's an overhang over a ledge, about half way down. We can attach a pulley here, rappel down one by one."

"And getting down from there… oh," said Marco, "The pulley has a remote detach widget."

It did have a remote detach, but by the time they were all on the ledge, freezing rain had sealed it in place until sunlight returned. The one tent they could set up held off the cold, almost enough for the six muttering bodies heaped inside.

"Do you sincerely want to be a galactic?" asked Sam. "They could stop this now. I want to get off."

"Step off the ledge," said Marco. "There are training bots hidden out there. They'd grab you as you fell."

"And park you," said Jane firmly, "back at the top of the cliff. Without a tent. Nah, we get home by our own efforts or…"

"Not," said Sam, "at all."

"You know," said Tinka, "I don't much like heights, when I don't have wings."

Jane didn't feel in danger of falling, with Felix settled on top of her, but she did want to change the conversation. "Tinka, when did you decide to be a pilot?"

"Some are born to fly, I guess, but according to my family, I was born flying.

"Most people on station opt for low-gee delivery, for comfort, but fashion comes and goes for microgee, 'from floating in the womb to floating in air'. Sounds dreamy, but childbirth isn't a dream: my mother was wide-hipped with powerful muscles, I was small, and when the pelvis softeners got to work I shot out like a glider launched from a bungee, trailing the cord. My gene-fathers fumbled the catch, and I sailed across the birth chamber, bounced off the carrier-bubble they had ready, and flailed every limb I had. Newborn muscle fibres are far stronger than adults', so that flight took several turns before someone grabbed the cord.

"I was using tiddleywings before I could stand. Resentment that in stan-gee I couldn't get into the air at all delayed my toddling; I would just beat on a father until he took me somewhere I was lighter.

"When I was five stanyears the family moved to a small, fast-spinning station, where the low-gee varied across the flying chamber and the Coriolis forces were stronger than wing beats. It's quite easy to zig past males and make them barf, but it's not a good idea, because making small sick boys flit around and collect their gobules takes persistence. Worth it when you're feeling mean, but usually not.

"Age seven I learned that the word for what I wanted to be is pilot. Age nine they told me how much mathematics I was going to need. It turns out that inertia tensors are less scary when you need them to think about docking with a tumbling starship."

~~~

"But what comes *before* Plan A?" Seeing their baffled faces, the Instructor for Strategy and Tactics expanded her theme. "Plan B is usually an improvised alternative to Plan A when Plan A goes wrong, not an integral part of the planning process. There needs to be a plan that *precedes* Plan A — something to fall back on."

"You mean, the planners should leave themselves some kind of back door in case of trouble, not abandon their primary plan?"

"Excellent, Bianchi!"

"But there isn't a letter before A."

"That's because whoever designed the alphabet forgot to make it backwardly compatible," the Instructor replied. "Which proves my point."

"Dah. So what comes before Plan A?"

"Isn't it obvious? Plan B4."

~~~

"You're taking this better than I expected."

Elzabet gave Marco a measured, unblinking glance. Just before he decided she wasn't going to reply, she did. "On Hippolyta, the nobility are trained not to show their emotions. Except when it is to their advantage." Marco realised that her quick shake of the head wasn't just 'no', but also a reflex flick of her 'tails as a sign of displeasure.

She shrugged. "Better or worse, I have to deal with whatever my family wants. With a mother like mine, I've had plenty of practice."

Eleven days into their pre-flight training period, talk could be casual. The others were relaxing in the lounge after a long day; Elzabet was with Marco in a cubicle. Talking. Just talking. They did a lot of that. Perhaps they both felt that in some sense they didn't quite belong.

"What's it like to be one of the privileged few?" Marco suddenly blurted.

Elzabet raised her eyebrows, finished untying her second braid, and ran her fingers distractedly through the tassel of the third. "On Hippolyta? Not what you'd think if you've not been born to it. It's how we've always done things out on the

Fringe. Until recently, life there was too hard to take democratic decisions. Someone had to decide quickly and irrevocably. Someone who knew what they were doing."

"I'm not making any value judgements, Elzabet. Just wondering what it's *like*. Inferno is egalitarian. Possibly to a fault. I'm seeking perspective."

She made a half-hearted attempt to explain.

The next time he saw her, her hair was short. What did that mean?

~~~

Elzabet hadn't admitted it to anyone, but she was feeling lonely and abandoned. Getting rid of her symbolic 'tails declared independence from Family, but it hurt. Despite their differences in social standing, in Marco she had found a friend and a potential ally. Here he was, inquisitive again.

"There are a lot of pressures on the nobility, Marco. Being rich isn't such a chore, I admit, though you do have to work hard to stay that way. But sometimes it's poor compensation for having your life laid out before you like a cowfish on a platter from the day before you were conceived."

Marco nodded. "Like being the third daughter of a Duchess?"

Elzabet sat up and stared at him. "How do you know what *that* entails?"

"I researched your background. Everyone's. Don't look at me like that, we all did. Hippolyta is a hereditary monomatriarchy. Only one in the Concordat. Named for the queen of the Amazons. Symbolic, yah? Now, correct me if I'm wrong, but: there are rigid conventions. First daughter of a Duchess inherits the title and property, when the time comes. Second goes into politics on behalf of her family. Third—"

"Management. Or if she's *lucky*," in the selection lottery her family had entered her for, "Starhome when she reaches the ripe old age of fifty. Twenty-two standard. Or whatever else the family decides will best keep her occupied, help advance its standing, and prevent her kicking up trouble. Same for any younger girls. That's OK, family matters more than anything, but *do I matter to the family*?"

Marco let that pass. "You didn't want to go."

"I still don't want to — oh, Marco, I'm so *scared*!" She started to sniffle, then broke down in tears. "I don't understand how anything works, I miss my maidservants — not their service, their companionship! I miss my home and my family and my snow-leopards. But no one at Quynt House seemed to care! They just—"

"Popped you on a private yacht to join a bunch of ill-mannered peasants on a trip into the great unknown. Curse of the third daughter. That's why you got rid of those braids, of course. Good idea. But it's a wrench, right?"

Elza's facade had crumbled completely now. "Please, Marco — promise me you won't tell the others."

"My lips are sealed. Come on, tell Uncle Marco."

Through the tears, she saw a well-built and cultured young man, strong in mind and body, not too musclebound. You could see from his face that he — alone among her companions, she was sure — was on her side. The others thought she was a stuck-up snootypants, and — oh, plebspit, they were right. But Marco hadn't been repelled by her inbred selfishness. He accepted her as she was.

So she clung to him, and he stroked her hair and calmed her fears. She felt *safe*. And he never once made a move that might seem improper. He didn't even try to kiss her, not even on the cheek. He respected her vulnerability.

She wasn't sure whether to be pleased or offended.

~~~

"I hope they'll get round to telling us why we're here."

"You've been on about that for days, Marco. It's got us exactly nowhere."

"It's still a good question, Elza."

He was right. Candidate galactics always got intensive training: a bonding exercise, preparation for the responsibilities of citizenship. That was common knowledge. But as *their* training progressed, they'd realised it was different. Physically harder, technically more specialised, and often plain weird. They were being prepared for something unusual, but they couldn't work out what.

"You're here to be trained, Bianchi." It was a new voice, not one of the regular instructors. Their heads turned towards the source, a stocky woman with clipped grey hair, now standing just inside the doorway. They'd never seen her before. Her clothing was informal, her bearing not. She looked formidable.

Elza was the least intimidated. "With respect, Citizen — I don't know your name, rank, or role — that's the answer to a different question. Our training isn't the generic stuff we've heard of. It's tougher, it's more specific, but also more diverse. So, Citizen, stop giving us the runaround and tell us our *real* mission."

"Who said anything about a mission, Quynt?"

"No one, Citizen. That's the problem."

The woman inclined her head, motioned them to squat, and joined them. "Dah, some of you are ready, at least. Vance, CSE, doesn't matter what rank." She leaned forward, looking at them in turn. What she saw seemed to satisfy her. "This is confidential, highest security level. You will *not* discuss anything I tell you outside the group. If you ask for more information now, you won't get an answer. Part of your training is to work things out for yourselves, to avoid getting trapped by groupthink.

"You'll be told everything you need to know after you reach Starhome. Be advised that you won't be landing there: you'll be diverted immediately to a new destination. Your assigned tasks will be explained when you get there. Not before."

"Since it's all so top secret, why tell us this now?"

"Because, Laurel, you all need to be mentally prepared for something far more challenging than entry-level work in Starhome."

Marco looked thoughtful. "We're not the only trainee team with this mission."

Vance shot him a sharp glance.

"You said 'groupthink'," Marco explained. "And you weren't referring to this little group, because anything we work out for ourselves will be done *as* a group."

Jane had been thinking, too. "We've got *two* xenologists. I don't believe Starhome wanted to keep me and Felix together. Duplicate roles are very unusual in training groups. So —" her nose wrinkled with concentration — "what sort of aliens have you found?"

"And why do you think they might be sapient?" Felix added.

"Towers of conjecture on a foundation of pure guesswork, people." But Vance was visibly taken aback.

"Very *solid* guesswork... Citizen."

"No comment. Just *wait*. You'll get answers." She rose. "I'll say no more."

As soon as Vance had left, everyone except Felix started talking. Marco's voice rose above the rest. "I was right, we do have a mission."

"Yah, you're a genius," Elza grunted.

"What bothers me," said Sam, "is what all that was about. Basically, all she did was to tell us to stop worrying and keep quiet."

"Yah, but she did it with *authority*. They want us to take this seriously. Be mentally prepared for the unknown. Kick us out of our comfort zone."

"It worked," said Marco.

"What agency do you think she's with?" Elza asked.

"She *said* CSE."

"Yah, and you're Queen Francesca, Sam. The Concordat Special Executive is a civilian bureaucracy."

"What, then?"

"SS."

"You really think they'd send an SS operative, just to give a vague pep-talk to a piddling bunch of amateurs like us?"

Elza gave a mirthless laugh. "I've been to enough diplomatic functions to recognise the smell of Starhome Security a light year away. Vance poked her nose in because someone very high up told her to."

"Why?"

"Because something is making the Concordat distinctly nervous, and we are among those lucky souls chosen as its eyes in the dark."

"Makes sense. They need a lot of people to handle it, so it must be *big*. We're useful extras, no more than that."

"Yah. But that makes me... look, I don't want to worry you; maybe you don't want to hear what I'm thinking."

"What we *want* to hear is irrelevant," said Tinka. "Maybe we *need* to hear."

"Dah. Whatever this is about, it's sensitive and dangerous. So why is Starhome involving a bunch of space cadets like us?"

Felix looked blankly at Jane, then they saw it together. As usual, it was Jane who spoke. "Oh, Mother."

"Exactly," said Elza. "We're expendable."

~~~

It was ironic that the faster-than-light Da Silva drive had led to more, not less, plain old action-and-reaction flight between planets and moons, but Tinka liked it that way. If there's matter nearby, a Da Silva ship still leaves, but what arrives is hopelessly scrambled. So to make sure that a ship and its crew still resemble a ship and its crew when they arrive at their destination, everything has to start from a near-vacuum.

So you keep a starship in space, in a spot you can stabilise, and free of accumulated dust. Suufi's Lagrange-2 point was ideal. The six trainees rode a reaction-drive shuttle, slow and cramped. Tinka took pride in her minimal-energy ballistics and ignored the grumbling. After three days, a small, shiny dot on one of the screens grew into a regular spiky shape, festooned with other pieces of technology. Soon it filled the screen, as the shuttle made its docking approach.

"*Valkyrie*," said Sam. "Our home for the next few months."

"I hope that's not an omen," Marco muttered.

"Sorry?" They'd all learned from their training that hardly anyone understood Marco's obscure Old Earth references, but they sometimes led somewhere.

"I'd prefer not to be given a wild ride."

Elzabet's mouth clamped in disapproval. "That junk-heap's already had one."

"Good," said Tinka. "That means it has survived everything that the universe has thrown at it. I *hate* them when they're shiny and new.

"It looks like a throwing-star or a caltrop," said Elzabet. "Doesn't seem as solid as *Star Pyramid*."

Star Pyramid had been the first Da Silva ship, nigh-on two millennia back. Old Earth's last and greatest gamble secured an extensive supply of mahabhavium and opened a path to the stars for humanity. Though not, ironically, for Old Earth. Concordat cultures still felt a twinge of guilt about that, but the quarantine had been inevitable. Still, Old Earth had supplied nearly all of the Colonists for the long Diaspora that had created and expanded the Concordat of Habitable Exoplanets.

They each had the use of a tubular room between one spike of the caltrop and another. The ship's control area was further inboard, along with communal spaces. The Da Silva drive was in the centre — it had to be, to carry the ship with it. The rest of the machinery and equipment, mainly life support, was scattered throughout the remaining crevices of the ship.

"Our lives will change completely once we get off this ship," Jane observed. "All of us have left things we value. And people, though I'm lucky I still have Felix with me. But my parents, friends... everything's going to change, isn't it? It's the price we have to pay. As galactics, we start over."

"If we qualify," Felix reminded her, since nobody else had said it. Felix didn't use one word when none would suffice.

"We will," said Sam. "But only if we can function as a team. Like it or not — and I do — we're all in this together. Whatever we want to be galactics *for*." His eyes flicked towards Elzabet.

The others murmured agreement. Even the third-born daughter of the Duchess of Quynt. Reality was starting to sink in.

~~~

Like every spacecraft in living memory, *Valkyrie* pretty much ran itself, but rules required a human pilot for lateral thinking and emergencies. The navigator's main task, and the only predictable one, was making the flight plan. A Da Silva drive could relocate a ship by ten light years in a split second, but it took anything from a day to a week to decide where to jump.

"I'd have expected a trip to Starhome to be routine," Jane wondered out loud, as Sam ran yet another simulation. "Why is it taking so long to set up a route?"

"No Da Silva trip is routine," Marco broke in. This was a mathematical engineering issue. "The problem is the weather."

"In a vacuum?"

"The k-weather in the karmabhumi landscape."

Ouch. "What's that when it's at home?"

"You know how a Da Silva works, in broad terms?"

"Yah," said Jane. "It grabs quanta of spacetime and shifts bunches of them around. Any physical object whose wave-function peaks in that region gets shifted along with the spacetime it's sitting in."

Marco nodded. "And how do the bits of quantum spacetime move?"

"They don't. One moment they're here, the next they're there. They… jump. But without passing through anything in between. Like quantum tunnelling"

"A bit, yah. What *causes* the jump?"

"Mahabhavium." He nodded, inviting more. "Superheavy element 126. What *Star Pyramid* brought back."

"Yah. Its atoms are so heavy that they act as a catalyst for the sort-of-tunnelling effect, and there you are."

"Where?"

"Not here. So the next question is harder. What *controls* where the lumps of spacetime go?"

Jane laughed. "They never even tried to explain that to us."

"Dah. A twelve-dimensional karmabhumi field isn't something you can sketch on a graphics pad. It's a bit like wind, which has a size and a direction, but this has more. The k-size determines where you *can* go: it has to be the same at both ends of the jump. But the direction determines where you *do* go."

"Not sure I get the picture, Marco."

"Remember that ledge where we were stuck overnight?"

"Remember how we smelled," said Jane, "when we got home?"

"If those mountains were a k-landscape, the only places we could shift to would be similar ledges on a similar cliff, at a similar height. But we can't get to *all* of those similar points. Masses act like lenses for the k-field, and we can only get to a focus. Lots of stars and planets mean lots of focal points. Which one we end up at depends on fluctuations in the k-field, which are hard to predict.

"When we tune *Valkyrie* towards a star, and push the 'go' button, the most likely number of *Valkyrie* at our current position drifts down. In compensation, though, the number drifts *up* somewhere far beyond the star, where the k-geodesics come to a focus. So we stop being *here* and turn up *there* instead."

"*Number of?*"

"There's a quantity that measures how plausibly we exist in a given location. If it's small, we don't; if it's big enough, we do. But sometimes… well, in theory that number could be bigger than one. There can sometimes be multiple foci, like a mirage for light. We *could* end up in two places at once. But that's controversial, never been observed — sorry. All you need to know is that it *feels* like a jump, and it goes to a new focal point. A planet can sometimes form a focus too, but it's a weaker lens, so we end up further away from it."

Jane shook her head. "Marco: why didn't you just tell me that to begin with?'

"Because I only just thought of that way of saying it. Anyway, now I can answer your original question."

"I've forgotten it."

"Why is it taking me so long to set up the jump?" said Sam.

"And the answer is," Marco jumped in, before Sam could grab his punch-line, "the chaotic nature of the karmabhumi field. It's like predicting the weather: climate is simpler, but showers are hard. Those local variations bend the geodesics. There's a prediction horizon, soft but implacable. Even to get near it, the calculations are ferocious."

"Tell me about it," said Sam. "But what this all means, Jane, is that I have to keep running very complicated simulations until I get a favourable forecast — one that lets me pick out a feasible jump, with good options for later jumps. Planets when we're nearly there, for finer aiming."

Jane now had the picture. "You mean it's a bit like an old-fashioned sailing-ship, where you know which port you want to go to, but you have to spend ages in the harbour waiting for a favourable wind."

"Yah — but we need a weather forecast for which the wind is favourable for the entire voyage, landfall included. And the karmabhumi wind blows at about 3.5 zettaklicks per hour. Without actually *going* anywhere."

I was right to choose xenology, Jane thought.

~~~

The *k*-weather was unusually unpredictable, holding them up for days. Sam spent many tedious hours debating options with the ship's computer, trading brain-signals via his new wristcomp, and talking out loud whenever the voices in his head made no sense.

Finally, a potential route struggled out of the on-screen garbage. Tinka as a pilot quickly agreed that it was as good an option as they were likely to get.

The first seven jumps went smoothly. So did the next, and the next. The tenth jump was even smoother, a tribute to Sam's choices and Tinka's growing familiarity with *Valkyrie*'s quirks. But the eleventh —

~~~

"*Valkyrie* calling Suufi," for an hour, "*Valkyrie* calling Suufi, please respond," thought Sam to the Da Silva communicator, and passed its silence on.

"It's that *k*-storm you were worrying about, two jumps back," said Tinka. "It's fragging the comm link."

"It's also screwed up my flight plan. Filed when we left. We'll have to recompute, find an alternative, and file that one. If I can raise anybody to tell them of our change of plan." *They trained me not to sound worried. I hope it took.*

Tinka looked no happier. "Can you contact Starhome? Anyone?"

"Nah. It's not a storm, it's a swarm of tiny k-showers, even less predictable. I've never heard of k-weather like this."

When signals don't get through, sometimes ships don't get through.

"What should we do?"

"Two options. Wait for the swarm to pass, or hit the sims and find a clean new route. If at that stage we still can't raise anybody, we can break all the rules and take it *without* filing a plan."

"How long until the swarm clears?" Felix asked.

"Weeks. A month. No idea."

"It's like being on the ledge again, with no bots," said Tinka. "We do have supplies for half a year. Prudence says, wait."

"We'll be judged by how we react," said Elzabet.

"Yah, but which way? For caution, or for using our initiative?"

Elzabet was obviously losing what little patience she still possessed. "We took the wrong route. Highly unorthodox, way off the usual star-lanes."

"We'd still be at the Typhon-Suufi L2 point if we hadn't taken the only option that was open," Sam said, in a deliberately neutral tone.

"No offence meant, Sam, we all agreed with the decision. So now we have to deal with the consequences, as a team. I propose that in view of the communications blackout, we stuff prudence *and* the rules and find an alternative route as quickly as Sam can do the sums. Then we *go*. If the comm is back, file a new flight-plan. If not, too bad. We can argue the case with the Regulator when we finally get to Starhome."

"Motion seconded!" said Marco, who never voted to wait.

Tinka looked dubious, shrugged. "Fair enough, Elza. But I just hope we don't run into a problem. Because if we do, no one will know where to look for us."

Felix had been listening silently, but saw a hole in her argument. "The risk is real. But if anything goes wrong, there won't be enough left to be worth rescuing."

"Dah," said Tinka. "We're all agreed? Sam: find us a new route."

"Well, actually…"

"You've already computed one."

"I didn't want to lose time. But I need another hour or two to test if it'll work."

"Soon as you're satisfied, we'll be on our way."

~~~

Elzabet seemed tense, even for her.

As they strapped in for the first jump along Sam's new route, her hands moved tightly, without grace. Marco leaned across and touched her shoulder. "Don't worry. We'll all be fine."

"I'm not worried!" Elza snapped.

"Good, because there's nothing to worry about. Nothing can possibly go wrong. Believe me, I'm a mathematical engineer."

2

Simquake

> Colonists must learn to cope with whatever their new world throws at them. But the first Colonies, to Lalande, Tau Ceti, and Groombridge 34 (now New Earth, Owemgee, and Kevin), kept touch with Earth. That proved disastrous. Colonists from aging-infrastucture slums spent most of the time moaning how terrible Exoplanet Z was, and wishing they'd never left home. The catastrophic loss of morale, both in the Colony and on Old Earth, almost killed the entire Colonisation Programme.
>
> The Agency for Exo-Development took an agonising decision. New Colonies lose all contact with Earth soon after confirmed safe arrival, to drive home that they must solve their problems themselves. Contact is re-established only after a hundred years of quarantine, via a robot beacon — a stripped-down Da Silva communicator. To prevent premature attempts, the beacon lands somewhere highly inaccessible.
>
> —Xanthippe Jones-Wyrn, The Colonial Imperative and the Emergence of the Concordat

One moment, all was normal. The next — *Valkyrie* snapped into local existence impossibly close to a planet, headed straight down. All Hell broke loose.

Tinka acted barely in time, flaring the emergency reaction-mass. A violet blast slammed the ship sideways into an elongated orbit — the best she could manage. She shut down the routine autopilot before it misjudged, in such a critical state.

"*Valkyrie*?" Had the computer survived whatever broke them into normal space? "Damage report!"

A long pause loosened their bowels.

"Simpler to tell you what's *not* damaged."

"Go ahead."

"The life-support pod and unpleasantly little else," the computer chanted. "The Da Silva drive is out. Permanently."

"Repairs?"

"A shipyard job, and even a shipyard would junk everything and fit new. The re-action drive would work if it had anything left to spit with, but that was all used up scraping us into this apology for an orbit. Begging your pardon, it was a nice piece of piloting and no one could have done better, not even me. But still."

"Where are we?"

"Spectral triangulation identifies star as SQL7812 in catalogues, provisional usename Squill. Nearest Concordat star, 213 light-years. No record of a visit."

"How long can we stay in orbit?"

"Seventy-four hours and twenty-one minutes. Too messy for more precision. This long ellipse keeps dipping us into denser atmosphere. So it's decaying. Fast."

Oh, Mother. Not good news. Tinka felt her muscles tensing.

She made a failed effort to relax. "Can we change to a more stable orbit?"

"Nah."

So much for saving the mission. Now it was about saving lives. The emergency capsule should get them down intact, but at best in a controlled crash.

There'd be no way back.

The other five had joined Tinka in *Valkyrie*'s central space.

"Have you notified?"

"Nah, Jane," said Tinka. "No contact before we jumped, and now the comm is wrecked. There's one positive, though. The planet has breathable air and near-normal gravity. Humans could live there."

"That's a *positive*? We're about to be shipwrecked on a desert island where no shipping ever comes, and nobody will know we're there. Wonderful."

"So much for galactic citizenship," Marco grumbled. "I was looking forward — in an apprehensive sort of way — to unwrapping our top-secret mission. Now I can't even look forward to a decent breakfast."

"One thing at a time. At least we get to live."

"Air and gravity don't guarantee we can live there, Tinka," Felix warned. "The plants could poison us. The fauna could eat us."

"This couldn't be planned?" Jane wondered. "To test resilience and initiative?"

"Nah," said Marco. "It's not a sim. That drive is most definitely trashed. Even the Concordat wouldn't wreck a Da Silva deliberately, just to put the wind up half a dozen trainee galactics. This is a *real* disaster."

Elzabet took a deep breath. "Or a real opportunity?" Heads turned. "A third daughter spends her time doing what she's told. Yah, I had nice clothes and jewels and things that don't matter, but I never had choices. Now, in a weird way, I will."

Tinka stared. So did the others. This side to Elza, nobody had seen before.

"I didn't learn a lot from Mother that was useful to *me*, rather than to her plans. But she always told me that when life throws something unexpected at you, you change what you can and make the best of what you can't. Our sole chance of survival, and our only hope of a future, is down there under our butts. Just be grateful the nanacurst thing isn't a gas giant."

Sam broke the shocked silence. "Damn right. Elza, I've been underestimating you. Apologies."

Tinka found herself in efficient pilot mode. "*Valkyrie*: will the emergency landing capsule get us down to the planet in one piece?"

"In six live pieces, provided it launches as intended."

Good old *Valkyrie*. Pedantic to a fault. But the confirmation was reassuring… or was it? Weasel words. Why did the computer think the descent might not go according to plan?

"*Valkyrie*: are you feeling functional?"

"Imprecisely," the computer intoned, "I'm not feeling so good."

Tinka tried not to panic. "Damage report on your core functions. *Now!*"

"Circuit failures in six hundred and forty-four modules. Some memory loss, most of it irrecoverable. Control systems erratic, not sure why, probably damaged optic cables. Intermittent faults in all major units. The sooner you evacuate, the better."

Tinka cursed in three languages. "Sorry, *Valkyrie*, not your fault. But can you hold together long enough for a planned, well-equipped evacuation?"

"Think yes. Exist work-arounds can use. Am using now." Mangled syntax did little to reassure an increasingly nervous pilot.

Sam looked around at them, uncomfortable. "My fault," he said. "Trying to be too clever on my first flight."

"The plan was sound, Sam," said Marco. "You weren't to know something would dump *Valkyrie* back into the normal universe, deep inside a piddling little planetary system. It's crazy."

Before Sam could respond, Elzabet jumped in. "That's not all that's crazy. What caused all this damage?"

"Has to be the navigator's worst nightmare," said Sam. "A simquake."

"Which is?"

"Kharmabumi catch-up time. k-size doesn't increase at the same rate everywhere. k-fields glitch when a big enough difference builds up. Low-k areas catch up with high-k areas, like stuck plates of a planetary crust in an earthquake. We call it a simultaneity-quake. Simquakes don't do much damage to ordinary matter — trigger conventional earthquakes, flip magnetic field polarity, create the odd new sunspot. But they're a menace to navigation. Geodesics jump about, focal points are all over the place. There can be aftershocks as it settles down, and a planet can have years of being out of Da Silva contact, k-simultaneous with nowhere."

Contrition wasn't really Sam's line, and a different emotion asserted itself. "But I *checked* this region for simquakes! And *Valkyrie* accepted my orders!"

"So *was* it a simquake?" asked Tinka.

It was a rhetorical question, but the computer assumed otherwise, unusually obtuse. There was a disturbing crackling noise, followed by a flat "Nah."

"What *was* it?"

"Nah idea."

"*Sure* it wasn't?"

"Nah."

"Trash it, what else can go wrong besides a 'quake?" Sam wailed.

Marco's mind was racing. "Nothing you could have calculated — or miscalculated. Something dumped us out two thirds of the way along our path, right?"

"We're not even *near* our intended path."

"So whatever, it interacted with our wave-function *while we were in transit.*"

Sam shrugged. "So?"

"People, as a mathematical engineer with too damn much training in these matters, I have news for you. With a Da Silva drive, there is no such thing as transit. You are here, you are there: you are never in any sense *between*, and nobody can follow our path to look for us. Nothing actually travels *along* the paths, they're just mathematical abstractions that we humans use to compute jumps. Mother Nature doesn't know they exist. She just swaps wavefunction peaks between conjugate points in the karmabhumi landscape."

"Whatever it was," Sam insisted, "we're a hundred klicks from the third planet in the system. That's very close — *way* too close for normal Da Silva operation. The weirdest thing is our own atoms still nicely playing at being Us. Something must have created a rogue focal point here, one that the simulator couldn't compute. And the one plausible something is the planet itself."

"Perhaps," said Marco. "But even granting that, how could a little ball of mud bring us into focus so close? Do *you* know why?" he asked the computer.

"Nah."

"Then give us a view of this planet."

Jane felt every breath in her body being sucked out. "It's *beautiful!*"

The blue, green and orange globe of Squill III spun serenely below, fleeced with grey-white vapour clouds. Even from orbit it looked habitable.

Sam told the computer to stop seeking the navigational trap that had sprung on them, and concentrate sensors and analysis on the planet. In the short life left to *Valkyrie*, they needed to learn as much as they could about their future home, to decide what equipment to take. Space in the landing capsule was in short supply.

~~~

While the others ransacked the ship for anything that might prove useful, Elzabet had been watching the computer watch the planet. Once certain it was showing her what she thought it was, she called them over.

"News?" Tinka asked.

"It's inhabited."

"*What?*"

"*Valkyrie* agrees, Tinka. There's intelligent life on this planet."

"Aliens?" Felix asked, by reflex.

Elza frowned. "That would make more sense, Felix. Nah; the natives seem human."

Everyone shouted at everyone, no one listened. She waited for a pause, then shut them up. Even third daughters are accustomed to command.

"Let's take it one step at a time, dah? The spectral data says there are Old Earth crops down there. They're mixed up with all sorts of alien vegetation I can't identify — native bush and forest, I guess — in shades of orange."

"What society type?" Tinka enquired. "Primitive or advanced?"

"Don't know yet," said Elzabet. She addressed the computer. "What's the energy use on this planet like?"

There was a pause. Too long.

"*Valkyrie?* Are you there?"

"Sorry, bypassing break in retrieval. No activity in electromagnetic spectrum; no neutrino emission; no temperatures above — *whine* — above 1300°K heat points. Clearly associated with open-air meta*zzzzz*—" The words were drowned by an ear-splitting howl, suddenly turned off.

The Starfolk shot each other worried glances. If the computer failed, they'd have to abandon ship under manual control, which would make planetfall distinctly hairy.

Abruptly, the computer resumed in a normal tone, as if nothing had happened. If anything, that was even more worrying. "—metal working. No petroleum-based pollutants."

"So we can't contact them, nor they rescue us — not in the Iron Age," said Elzabet. "Are there *any* indications of high-technology artefacts down there?"

"Two," said *Valkyrie*.

"Why didn't you tell us that straight away, you steampunk idiot?" Elzabet was getting angry now.

"You didn't ask."

"Residual solitronic fields are typical of inactive Da Silva drives or communication equipment."

"How the freaking plebspit did—" Elza began, but Tinka interrupted.

"Colony Vessels? That would explain a lot. But why two? They didn't normally send them out in pairs—"

"Only one source will be a CV," *Valkyrie* replied.

"Of course," said Marco. "During the Diaspora, they let Old Earth supply emigrants, in huge Colony Vessels. Each CV hid a Da Silva beacon and comm station on the planet where it landed, far from the landing-point. It was purely for Starfolk use, not for the colonists, during their quarantine century."

"Confirm," said the computer. "These emissions match an unactivated rescue beacon and a damaged Da Silva drive."

Marco, brimming over, explained that CVs used Da Silva to approach a world, but plasma drives to land — strictly one-way, by design. The Colonists couldn't just turn for home if they didn't like what they saw. A CV was stripped bare by its passengers, but the impregnable beacon was to last indefinitely. "In this instance, either the Colonists never found it, or they never used it. Either way, it should still be functional," he concluded.

"Does anyone know how to operate an obsolete rescue beacon?" Tinka asked.

"I do," Marco told her. "Probably."

"We've found our ticket back to civilisation."

Everybody's breathing relaxed. Then Elzabet asked: "Which source is which?"

"Cannot compute."

"*Valkyrie*: put up detailed images of both sites," Tinka commanded.

"Eye-spy *crackle-spit* malfunction. Substituting low-res." Images appeared side by side. One showed swamp in variegated oranges and browns; the other, high-contrast light and shade, snow and rock.

In neither could they see anything man-made, let alone a ship or a beacon.

"Overgrown and buried," Sam said in disgust.

"Too small to resolve, even if not," said Tinka. "Frustrating. But after this long, hardly a surprise. But that's no problem: *Valkyrie* can interrogate both sources."

"Uh — nah — can't," in a staccato chirp. "Can receive signals, with difficulty. Can't transmit."

It was a few seconds before anyone ventured to speak.

"So we study Squill III from orbit as long as we can," said Jane, "learn as much as we can, see if we can deduce which source is the beacon—"

"And go down there," Sam finished for her. "Deduce it or not."

"I wonder how long ago these people arrived?" Felix mused.

Elza spoke to the computer. "*Valkyrie*: you said that after some time, both a drive and a beacon would give the fields you detect. Can you use that to get a rough estimate of the time since they landed? I don't want precision, dah?"

For once, the computer replied without hesitation. "Between sixteen and eighteen hundred years."

~~~

They needed maps, terrain reports, geological and environmental surveys, weather patterns, clues about social activity — as much as their wristcomps could hold. The 'comps couldn't link to the global galactic grid, so most functionality was lost — so much for nebular computing. No intercomp comm, no global positioning, no public infobanks, and — a negative with teeth — no real-time natural-language translation. But they could record, remember, and perform low-level data analysis.

They would sleep at most twice more — if at all — before the increasingly erratic *Valkyrie* would scatter across the planet in blazing fragments. Tinka, the only one of them with a real rapport for the ship, relieved Elzabet at the consoles. Several times the image flickered crazily as *Valkyrie* dealt with a new glitch. Every time, Tinka felt her heart skip a beat. But the computer soldiered doggedly on.

A tap on her shoulder made her jump, but it was just Sam. He always did that. She always jumped. He slid on to the neighbouring seat as she froze the screen view.

"Hi, Sam. The wonders of Squill III."

Sam squeezed her free hand. He looked strained. "Those are really oceans?"

"About eighty per cent of the surface. One covers more than half the planet. Water with dissolved gunk — not a lot, nothing outlandish, but not drinkable. The land divides into four big chunks and a gaggle of islands.

"The biggest continent is this one, straddling the equator. Provisionally named Aleph. About forty-five per cent of the dry land. Beth has about fifteen per cent, Gimel has twenty, Daleth has ten, and the rest is islands. There are plenty of rivers, and a thriving CHON ecology."

Her hands slid deftly along the computer's touchbar. "Now, take a look at a blow-up. I'll be a little selective to save time... ah, yah, *there*, look you."

She pointed to a region of oranges and browns, speckled with clumps of green. A river passed across the lower left diagonal of the screen. Near the mid-point was a hazy, more structured area. It looked like irregular cross-hatching.

"A town?" said Sam. Tinka nodded. "Fits a Colony world, I suppose..." He scratched one ear. "A bit bothered about all this, Tinka. What's it doing way out here? Two thousand years ago the Concordat was barely a hundred light years across."

"Simultaneity-mapping wasn't as good back then," Tinka reminded him. "If they met a 'quake front, they could have been reflected, reappearing just about anywhere. As it happened, they crashed here. Enough survived to start some kind of colony, maybe missing a lot of the usual equipment. So they'd have had to improvise. Ever since, they've been lost to civilisation. Until now."

"That may continue. If we can't get to the rescue beacon, or it doesn't work, we'll just have to sign up to join the Lost Colony of Squill III."

"You know, Sam, that might be safer than our mysterious mission beyond Starhome."

"If I were you, Tinka, I'd keep that particular thought to myself."

She grimaced. "Yah."

By now everyone was in the parlour except Marco, who was checking the emergency landing capsule. Until he finished, it was hard to plan. "Plenty of work down there for Felix and me," said Jane. "After nearly two millennia the natives will have drifted a long way, culturally. Alien enough for xenology training to be useful."

Tinka stared at her. Jane was actually enjoying the prospect.

Squill III continents (provisional names), showing residual solitronic fields (☆).

~~~

With attention now on locals, the xenologists took the lead. Felix knew most about low-tech inhabited worlds, which forced him to talk more than usual. At first, Squill III looked very much like any of them. As more fine detail came in, it started to look very strange indeed.

The rocky desert of the North-East tip of Gimel contained, apparently, the continent's textile industry. Elza took chemical spectra, which gave a close fit to typical effluent patterns: dyestuffs, flax rotting down to fibre, jute. The level of activity was well above cottage industry; possibly water-driven mechanical. But no higher.

The siting of the industrial area displayed considerable forethought, for here almost any wind took the effluent out to sea. Primitive textile production is a fouler smell than any other human industrial achievement.

That all made sense.

However, there were no highways leading into the area. Only a few narrow tracks, suitable for a man on horseback, but too rocky for a cart, and empty. No canals, and the only river in the area joined the factories to… nothing. The rivers showed a few boats, all going downstream.

"It all goes by sea," suggested Felix. "They must have some kind of distribution system. The raw materials alone have to get there somehow. And food for the workers. And who'd build a factory complex if they couldn't ship the goods out?"

But the scans showed no wharves, no ships, no large boats, and no stockpiles. A quick study of transit patterns revealed nothing that looked remotely like a warehouse. In fact, there were very few towns by the coast, and those few lacked anything resembling a harbour or docks.

"With that enormous moon," said Tinka, "tides are brutal. You'd need heavy engineering to cope."

"Yah, but how did they spread across four continents?" Marco wondered. "And scattered islands? CVs didn't carry aircraft. They'd be fabricated along with the infrastructure to fly them. There must have been boats once."

"What I can't understand is why there are so many towns in the mountains," Elza said, pointing at buildings huddled tightly on plateaus and perched dizzily on precipices. Farmland plains had smaller towns, more geometric in plan, and villages in plenty. Every large farming settlement had its tall, thin tower.

"Those must be religious," said Felix, "Probably for a call to prayer. That at least suggests a unitary planet-wide culture."

"Even if we get down in one piece, what are we going to find?" Sam sounded tense, the uncertainty was the worst bit. "There may be humans down there, but we've got to deal with an alien world until we contact them."

"Possibly after, too," said Felix. "Eighteen hundred years is long enough for them to lose everything we expect of civilised people, but not long enough to rebuild it. They've probably reverted to primitive social patterns."

"One of which is sometimes to slaughter all outsiders on sight," said Jane.

"Great, thanks."

"We have to be aware of potential dangers, Sam."

"You think I'm not?"

Felix tried to calm them. "You're being too pessimistic, Jane. They won't have sunk that far, it was a well-equipped colony."

"Yah. Which crashed. Who knows what they managed to salvage?"

"Enough to have a flourishing society, even if it is low-tech."

"Enough to have deadly weapons," said Sam, his hand resting lightly on his knife, "even if they are low-tech."

"Whatever they're like," said Felix, "they're in their own space, and we deal with it. Don't judge. Even if they are like Old Earth was, killing a species a day and a million people a year on their roads—"

"They don't have roads," said Sam, "but yah, I get your point. We're Starfolk."

"They don't have roads?" asked Marco, returning from his landing capsule check. Felix showed him the scans.

"An underground transport system?" Marco suggested.

"The level of technology we can see in the textile factories just isn't capable of building a planetwide network of tunnels."

"Of course not, Felix," said Marco. "The tunnels date back to an earlier age, when they could still do it. The local civilisation has regressed, but still uses the original transport system." Even Marco sounded tentative, and Jane squashed it.

"Don't be silly, Marco," she said. "Just to maintain that kind of tunnel system needs fancy tech. And it's not just one anomaly. The whole trashed planet is an anomaly. No bridges over the rivers. Nothing but footpaths."

"Do they use horses?" Jane asked. Colony vessels had usually been sent out with a package of useful Old Earth flora and fauna in the form of seeds, eggs, sperm and mechawombs. Horses were high on the list.

"Horses, oxen, yaks — anything that can carry a load," said Sam. "Valkyrie's seen them. And dug up some odd transit patterns. Very few coastal towns, hardly anything like a port. If they're not up to ships, how did they colonise all four continents? And ocean islands? But there's lots of activity on mountain slopes. In fact, that's where the majority of the towns are, not fords or crossroads. The slopes are packed with traffic. Not just animals and people, but carts too. Laden. There's plenty of traffic in goods. But not in any sensible place."

"The craziest places," said Jane. "The highest mountains are on Aleph, taller than anything on Old Earth— really hard to even breathe, at the top. But they're lugging great loads up there, on llamas, from quarries and iron works lower down. Way lower down."

"It makes sense for heights to be sacred," said Felix. "Are they building a temple up there?"

"They're not building anything. There's a few solid buildings, half covered in snow and ice."

"The geography's weird, too," Elza said. "There's a huge rainforest on Aleph where there's no rain. I can't spot any major waterways running in or out. But the geology all looks conventional, mountains aligned with plate boundaries and clear signs of continental drift." She sighed with frustration. "It's got *me* beat."

"Any luck on the rescue beacon?" asked Jane.

"Well, we know a lot more about those two sites," said Tinka. It didn't sound encouraging, and for a moment no one reacted.

Sam broke the spell. "Still fifty-fifty?"

She sighed. "*Valkyrie* still finds no useful difference in the residual fields. The decay-pattern tends to converge on the same thing after a while, independently of original capacity. So we have to go on circumstantial evidence." A full planetary map appeared on the screen, with two widely separated glowing dots. She pointed. "This trace is near an uninhabited coast of Beth, with a seven-hundred-kilometre desert belt inland. The coastal region is swampland. It's crossed by a river — a big one, but the only one. I can't think why anyone would ever go there, which makes it a good place to hide a beacon. The other is up near one of the sharpest, craggiest peaks on Daleth, *but* it's surrounded by fertile country. It's actually pretty much in an inhabited area, though that may be just the Squillian thing for mountains. They seem to *like* living on precipices.

"That's the evidence. Not a lot to go on. Now we have to choose."

3

Downfall

> A mistaken belief in Magog as a physical entity, rather than a supernatural being, persists in some outlying rural areas. Credulous folk imagine allegorical statements such as 'descending from the heavens' and 'bearing his people into the world' to be literal truth. Nowhere are these errors more engrained than in the divisive teachings of the hidden sect known as Descenters.
> — *The Path of Righteousness,* Patrick Aloysius de Vere Harmsworth Nasruddin

An unpowered landing capsule can descend almost anywhere, given a few hours' choice of when to leave orbit. But once down, their only means of transport would be local ones. And imported feet.

Emergency/evac for real. Tinka, in overall command, keeps the ship alive until the capsule's ready to launch. The navigator preps the capsule, the engineer checks out all systems and — if necessary and possible — repairs defective ones. Sam and Marco hit capsule storage.

Valkyrie's computer they had to leave, along with most of its valuable data. In less than two days a firework display across a few thousand kilometres of sky would leave nothing to access via a radio terminal, either. Their only resources would be what they could carry. They transferred the most important items of information to their wristcomputers. But 'comps are a narrow window for images, so they printed hard copy of anything with fine visual detail — especially maps.

Food was probably no problem. They had five months' supply of concentrates and supplements, and they could presumably eat whatever local humans ate. They'd have to: concentrates guarantee vitamins, trace elements, and energy, but no roughage.

The Da Silva burnout had destroyed most medical supplies. That left first-aid kits, a small stock of drugs in the landing capsule, and whatever the locals had in the way of medicine. At least Starfolk biotech simplified a few basic requirements. All three male chins, permanently depilated, wouldn't grow hair; nor would six female legs, but this was a closely guarded feminine secret. The women had been hormonally stabilised, and until further medical intervention they couldn't conceive or menstruate.

"*Valkyrie*: give me a quick checklist of what's in the capsule," Tinka asked. She knew what should be, but followed procedure in case the computer knew better.

"Food, water purification tabs, meds, first-aid kit, airsuits, tents — *crackle*."

Pause.

"*Valkyrie?*"

Crackle.

"Is that everything? Any weapons? *Valkyrie*, talk to me!"

She exhaled loudly as the computer answered: "— flechette rifles and ammo, stunbeams that work on ionic nerve impulse systems. That's most animals on most planets, but be wary: on some biotas they're lethal. The lightweight welding laser makes a mean weapon in a pinch."

Tinka nodded. The Concordat's risk-mitigation experts had planned for three main scenarios. Brief escape from a crippled ship, in deep space or a stable orbit, to await rescue. Backup for the normal atmosphere shuttle, at destination. Emergency landing in a remote region of a Concordat world, in a thriving ecology with deadly predators. That's why there were weapons. They hadn't planned for potentially hostile humans, but weapons would work against those too, if it came to that.

The capsule was no more than a lifeboat for controlled descent, not flight, too small to hold or power its own Da Silva communicator. An accident should either kill you, or leave the main ship and its communicator working for long enough for an emergency call. And of course everyone files a flight-plan, so when they go missing, the Concordat knows where to look. Up to now.

The capsule's repeater for the global galactic grid was a radio synch to their 'comps, for on-planet comm on a Concordat world. Nothing that could phone home from a low-tech lost colony world.

It would be the rescue beacon, or nothing.

Tinka looked quickly round the control room. Under stress, people nearby are a distraction. Even with Sam and Marco off in the capsule, she suddenly felt crowded.

"Jane! Felix! Hunt down anything that might be useful. Take it to Sam and Marco and stow it if there's room. Spare food and medicines. Tools. Useful gadgets. Think laterally, improvise. Elza's making maps and we'll collect all the information we can get about this world."

~~~

Tinka gathered them all to run through procedures. To reassure them. Well, the Concordat's psychlists thought it should do that. Theoretically.

"We'll do this by the book, people." *If the ship hangs together that long.* "When I give the word, and not before, I want you all inside the capsule, in your allocated crashcoons, and strapped down." Ordinarily Tinka hated to get in an impact protection sac, like squirming into a squidgy coffin. But right now, it would be a flying womb. "There's a launch window in seventeen minutes, and I want to grab it while *Valkyrie* is still functioning. Marco, you checked the gel?"

"We checked everything."

"I want us all in place ten minutes before launch, to get the life-support up and running without wasting air. *Valkyrie* will track the trajectory, and launch us on time. If all goes to plan, I do absolutely nothing and we touch down on target using only autoguidance." Noticing Felix shaking his head, she added, "If we have to deviate, Felix, *Valkyrie* recomputes and redirects us. Or, in a worst-case scenario, I fly the capsule manually."

The others nodded, calmed by Tinka's cool.

Then every light on the ship went out.

"*Valkyrie*? What happened?"

Silence. Then somewhere, machinery whined into action.

"Power loss," the ship sang, off-key and hesitant. "Restoring emergency backup power. Not as easy as I — *crackle*. You don't know what a mess this trashpile is turning — *crackle* — into. It's a struggle." Dim lighting came on. "*Uh*-oh."

What evil coder put *that* into the vocabulary of a spacecraft's controlling intelligence?

"*Valkyrie*, what now?"

"Air-pump failure. We have air *supply*, but it no longer *crackle* where it should. Attempting — no, sorry, not work. Think this one fatal. If you pard—*crackle*—expression. Losing more subsystems as failures cascade. Advise immediate evacu—" *cracklecracklecrackle*.

Hiss.

Nothing.

Into the silence, Tinka dropped a quiet statement, hiding the uncontrolled thumping of her heart: "You heard, people. Let's go!"

The dim emergency lights made it a tricky squirm into the cramped crashcoons, like six large bright orange silkworms, heads poking out the top until the cocoons sealed themselves. They had audio and visual links. Tinka's had the capsule's controls, Sam's had backups. Tinka looked at the tiny command screen, grunting in surprised satisfaction when it told her it was hooked into to the capsule's systems. *Something* was going right.

Green across the board, and just eight minutes from an acceptable launch. She rehearsed the planned procedure in her mind. *Valkyrie* had lost its voice, but she still had contact by text codewords over the local grid. The computer claimed enough control of the launch automatics, but warned her the links were disintegrating fast.

Five minutes.

Four.

"Trash it!"

Tinka cursed, at last showing her frustration. She could see the others in her screen; they could see her. No one looked remotely happy. "Sorry, people, but *Valkyrie* just went down. Completely. Don't worry, this crate is autonomous. But I'm going to have to fly it myself.

"Fortunately, you just happened to ship out with the best pilot in the entire Concordat." She looked at the clock. "Three min—"

A tremendous wailing noise grew in pitch and intensity at alarming speed.

"Incipient Da Silva collapse!" Marco shouted. "Radiation haz—"

Tinka's reaction was unthinking. Even through the sacs the launch bay opening blasted their ears, as an entire hull segment exploded in a controlled fury. A tenth of a second later the capsule followed it into space, sudden acceleration transmitted by the protective gel of the crashcoons.

It was like being sat on by an elephant. The only good thing was that the pressure was so heavy, it was impossible to scream.

Tinka's mind went crystal-clear. This was her job, it was what she had been born to do. Getting the capsule down would be routine. Unlike *Valkyrie*, now awash with deadly radiation, the little vessel was functioning exactly as it should.

She reviewed the capsule. It had super-radiant re-entry shielding, and limited use-once landing capability. Some powered flight, not a lot. Small control surfaces for unpowered gliding once shielding and the 'chute had killed most of its speed.

Yes, getting down would be routine. The capsule was on its way already. The problem was to get it down in the right place.

The Da Silva collapse had forced her to detach early. On their current path, they would hit ground about 200 kilometres short of the target.

Too far for comfort, and most of those kilometres were swamp or ocean. They needed to conserve resources, reach the beacon as quickly as possible. The fewer days stuck on this planet, the better.

How many of those 200 klicks could she stretch the flight across?

If she followed safety rules, hardly any. This left only a riskier angle of attack for re-entry, late parachute deployment with early ejection, in a vessel that glided marginally better than a cheese. Using more fuel than she'd have liked, making the final landing harder than it should have been.

The target area *was* swamp, after all. A lot softer than rock. And that meant...

No time to consult.

The capsule howled through the upper atmosphere in a sheet of flame. It slowed violently as the parachute opened, and juddered down through thunderheads, trailing streaks of steam as hail struck its ultraviolet-glowing hull.

The 'chute detached, and stubby winglets peeped out. The nose lifted as the control surfaces began to bite, and began a long slow swing to the north-east.

The ground beneath was brown rock, then orange patchwork — some dull, some brilliant, some dark, murky water. The capsule dropped lower, until it was almost skimming the surface of the swamp. Fire erupted from its nose as the retrojets started burning what little fuel was left.

It slowed, and dropped like a cannonball, still almost horizontal as it hit the swamp. It slalomed across thick, slimy mud, through tall groves of plants like giant bullrushes, torn stalks scattered by a huge V-shaped plume of water in its wake. Its sonic boom overtook it, knocking panicked flocks of flying creatures from the skies.

Trees fell as waves tore their floating root-mats. The whole swamp shook.

The capsule continued to slow, and come back to Tinka's control, until one side hit something hard.

A submerged rock sliced the hull like a can-opener, and flipped it over.

That saved them from drowning. No water came in through the rip. At first.

~~~

Six scared, battered, bruised, but unbroken Starfolk sat on a sticky mound in the middle of one the largest swamps on Squill III, their mud-covered olive-green airsuits matching their surroundings. They had saved some of the contents of the capsule before the water sank it.

Tinka consulted her 'comp again. "Eight kilometres short of target." Her speech was thick with disappointment.

"Don't be so hard on yourself," Sam comforted her. "You did well to get us down at all, let alone so close."

"Yah. We even managed to salvage one pack of rations. Pity about the flechette rifles and the welding laser, though," said Marco.

"Yah, yah, yah," Tinka muttered. "I should have remembered they were fragile when I decided to flip the capsule on its back, but I was unconscious at the time, dah?"

"Nah, Tinka, I didn't mean — trash it, you know. You got us down alive, and pretty much intact, which is *amazing*. I'm just a bit sad to—"

"Have lost the flechette rifles and the laser."

"Yah."

"We've got this," said Sam, holding up his knife. "It doesn't fire flechettes, but it *is* reusable. At least for the last two thousand years."

Jane was dangling something between her fingers. "Would this help?"

"What is it? A pendant? Pretty stone."

"Rhodochrosite?"

"Yah, Elza. Also a laser. It's a laser medallion. Felix bought it for me on vacation on Smedley, just in case. It's as light as a feather, hangs round my neck looking innocent. I carry it everywhere."

Marco pointed at his chest, nodding urgently, and she passed it to him. "Oh, great! One of those rechargeable ones! With that neat little two-stroke MHD shockwave reactor for fusion and lasing. Compact, lots of power, but limited until you recharge it." A thought struck him. "Aren't those illegal?"

"Not on Smedley. That was kind of the point, you know?"

"Oh. Right. But how did you smuggle—"

"That's why they make it look like jewellery. No one expects a respectable xenologist to be carrying an illegal weapon."

In one direction the desert spread out in stratified oranges and greys, with sharp triangular hillocks and eroded gullies. In the other, the scrub gave way to dense foliage and waterlogged undergrowth. It was humid and hot in the white sunlight.

Elzabet grimaced and shook her wrist. "Trash it, my 'comp's lost its direct neural link!"

"We've been disconnected from the grid since the crash," Marco reminded her.

"So?"

"The neuroprocessing software for your visual and motor cortex was too big to copy over from *Valkyrie*. It only ever worked in the nebula. Now that we're out of contact with the ship, not to mention the Grid, the 'comps have defaulted to touch, speech and screen only. It can't see what you're mentally pointing at. It will still talk to you in your head, but it can't receive your thoughts."

"You mean," Elzabet replied with some heat, "that all that time we spent training to use the direct neural link was wasted?"

"Some, but you *can* still talk with it. Mental command line: you have to formulate words and subvocalise."

Elza remained unimpressed. "And what about tools?"

"Sam's knife again," said Felix, "and the laser is more than a weapon, too. Then there's this thing."

"An aer-O-web?" said Elza, "what's that good for, beyond spinning kitschy fuzz? Maybe we can trade singers on velvet for food and transport?"

"It can spin *anything*," said Marco, "if you feed it carbonaceous matter. Nanotube filament, rope... it's my favourite toy."

"That's it? That's all our tools?"

"That's it," confirmed Sam. "Better look out for more."

They made camp well before sunset, because it was the first time. They had to set up the tents on a mat of decaying vegetation, the driest patch of ground they could find. It took longer than it had in training, but that would soon improve.

Felix took one tent, for him and Jane; Sam and Tinka another.

"Hobson's choice," said Marco, opening the third's flap for Elzabet.

"Who was Hobson?" she asked, as Marco followed her inside.

"Someone who gave people exactly one choice. Which is none at all."

"I know exactly how they felt."

~~~

They travelled in single file. Sam, as navigator, took the lead. Next Tinka, Elzabet, Felix, and Marco. Jane, with the most sensitive hearing and an accurate shot with a stunbeam, brought up the rear.

Small froglike beasts flopped away across the mud, at their approach. Tiny insects, equipped for biting, rose in clouds, but didn't actually *bite*. Human sweat seemed to jam their chemical hunter-seeker programs. The travellers' slick olive-green spray-on airsuits protected against leeches and small animals; each separately hoped that Squill III possessed nothing of the order of, say, a crocodile. There was an abundance of birdlife in brilliant plumage.

Felix found himself automatically cataloguing the ecology. Plant life was endlessly entangled, with no chance to stop and separate plants, but the bird song fitted as usual into audible-call space: mating calls and warnings had to be species-specific, as usual, though only persistent observation told him which was which. Persistent observation kept his mind off endlessly dragging a foot out of the mud, and squelching in again a step further along, making maybe two hundred metres an hour when they weren't climbing through vegetable tangles. The "my turf!" morning chorus was the loudest he had ever heard, waking them still-exhausted each morning to face another punishing day.

~~~

"I wouldn't mind so much if the rain was *cool*," Jane muttered. "This just makes me sticky and miserable. And we can't see where we're going."

They had woken to a monotonous warm drizzle, with occasional sudden downpours that did not clear the humidity. The airsuits kept the rain out, and their sweat in.

Tinka tried to break the sullen mood.

"A good landing is a landing you can walk away from," she said to Jane, as they reached a welcome patch of open ground where plants didn't drip all over them. "A good relationship is a relationship you can walk away from, and don't."

"You and Sam?"

"Yah. For him, piloting came second to nav, but he needed to certify on both. We were both on Bwawa-kubwa flying six-seaters for Melonhead."

"Who?"

"Elmon Hedd."

"Oh. Gridbot billionaire with a hunt fetish? Built himself a safari planet?"

"Yah. Pilots logged a lot of hours ferrying tourists between camps. The pay was be-cheaper-than-AI, but it was a quick-and-dirty way to get an atmosphere certificate. We kept meeting.

"I was three hours toward an outlying camp on a cargo run. Sudden electrical storm: humidity, not enough satellites for warning. Melonhead always cut costs. Anyway, a lightning strike took out both engines. I coaxed the Caat down on to a strip of sand — they glide pretty well. Hairy landing, though, cracked the door open.

"So there I was in the middle of a game reserve, no radio, no gridnode within hailing distance. No one knew where, but they had a rough idea where to look.

"There'd be predators galore; Melonhead had imported pretty much all he could think of, insane ecology. So I opened the stunbeam box, and what did I find? A card with HUMAN SAFETY DIRECTORATE: REMOVED FOR COMPLIANCE INSPECTION.

"Anyway, five hours of nothing much until the storm cleared. Then a leopard spotted the wreck and got curious. I scrambled out and up the nearest tree. A leopard can climb carrying a gazelle twice its own size, but I'm small. I reached a branch *maybe* too thin for the beast, while it prowled the ground, tail twitching.

"Then I heard another plane hit the sand. Made a pig's breakfast of it, too, almost flipped.

"By that time the leopard had started up the trunk. I screamed, but it didn't take much notice. I was crawling along my limb, when—"

"*Look out!*"

With a sucking sound, an arm-thick snake poured itself across the mud just in front of Tinka. Well, it looked like a snake, except for the eyes and the crested head.

As Tinka retreated, the others turned to see what had caused the outburst.

Jane aimed her beam: better safe than sorry, and this was just a stun.

Only it wasn't even that.

She tried twice more. The snake slithered on as if nothing had happened, disappearing into the slime.

"Oh, Mother," said Felix, as the others started paying a bit more attention to their surroundings. "Good job it didn't notice us."

"Oh, it *noticed* us well enough," said Jane. "Just didn't give a spit. Had business elsewhere, I guess, lucky for us."

"Pity you missed it. I thought you were—"

"Felix, my love: *I didn't miss it*. I hit it in the head. Three times. With the power maxed out for the second and third shots."

"Oh, Mother."

"Oh, Mother, indeed. Our only wide-beam weapons are useless, at least on big, calm snakes. And I don't know why."

After that they walked closer together.

Eventually the clouds began to melt and the rain stopped. Vapour rose from the swamp as the sun's rays penetrated.

They squelched on dejectedly into a thickening mist.

~~~

On the second night the strident cacophony of the frog-forms kept them all awake, except for Felix, who slept — as always — like a sandhog. During Tinka's spell of guard duty she saw, down against the Northern horizon, the fiery passage of the disintegrating *Valkyrie* through the lower atmosphere.

She went into the tent and held Sam close against her, against the planet.

"I feel like I've just lost an old friend."

"We have."

Pilots and navigators often got close to their ships. They were truly alone, now. Their survival was in their own hands...

So, after gently detaching her and kissing her, he sent her back outside.

~~~

A katascope, jury-rigged as a solitronic field detector, led them to the area where they hoped to find the beacon. It took four days through knee-deep slime and insect clouds, until the solitron source was too close for its field to be directional. The small sun was once more reddening the sky, the horizon was streaked with purple, and they still hadn't spotted the beacon.

They made camp on an outcrop of grey shale. Sam and Marco stood guard duty as the others squatted, brooding. Landing on Squill III had been better than burning up, but now that the euphoria of survival had evaporated, the planet was a nightmare.

Tinka looked especially shaky. "You never finished telling me about the leopard," said Jane, in an effort to lighten the pilot's mood.

"Nah."

"Want to?"

Tinka took a moment to answer. "Yah. Where was I?"

"Out on a limb, screaming your head off, with the leopard on its way up."

"Ah. Well, I was eyeing the ground, wondering if I could drop without breaking a leg. Then there was a solid *thunk!* and the big cat started yowling like crazy. It had been Sam in the plane. He'd thrown his knife, pinned the cat to the trunk through the fleshy part of its back leg. He shouted, and rushed off again. The leopard bit at the knife, but it was deep in the wood.

"Sam came right back with the medikit. The cat clawed his face, but he sprayed something, and it was out cold. Then he climbed up and helped me down. Once I was standing, we got the knife out and the leopard down. Sam said 'Not the cat's fault,' slapped some degradable biogel on its wound, and we ran back to his plane.

"And a wheel broken off. And doors a beast could smash.

"Sam was panicking about getting off again, but I had him cut a straight branch with that knife of his. I tied it to the landing-gear like a ski. 'That won't hold,' said Sam, but we got in and I opened up, with a lot of rudder to compensate for the drag. Within seconds the speed lifted the wing on that side, kept the branch off the ground. Pretty much a normal takeoff.

"Turned out, Sam had helped himself to the plane as soon as he heard I'd gone missing. Flew along my flight path, spotted where I'd ditched, then my tree. Same HSD inspection card, but anyway, he preferred his knife.

"We were half way back to base when he suddenly said: 'You landed your plane intact in a thunderstorm with no power. You got this one up with landing gear that I managed to break, landing a good plane in sunlight. I'm a crap pilot, but I can stick to my major after this.' He became the best navigator I've ever met. Oh, and he's a sucker for cats. I found later that he'd uploaded the beast's chip ID, and then spent hours every day checking its condition. I'm not sure if he keeps that scar on his forehead to remember me up the tree, or the leopard.

"We each felt saved by the other, but it was teamwork. And we've found a lot of uses for that."

"Lucky, the two of you being in the same training group."

"Yah. Well, lucky we were both selected, and at the same time. There's no way to influence decisions that close to Starhome." She licked her lips. "But allocation is a lower level of dingbeaucracy, often sloppy." She stared at her fingers, avoiding eye-contact. "I have well-developed computer skills."

A flicker appeared at the corners of Jane's ample mouth. "Don't worry, I won't tell him. But aren't you feeling guilty about getting him into this mess?"

"Nah, missions are assigned randomly. Anyway, it was his idea."

~~~

The sinking sun turned the sky a glowering red. Jane would mount the first watch—favouring her laser rather than a stunbeam.

Marco lit a small portable lamp. After four days... well. Give it a try. "We need to get these airsuits off, Elza. Give our skin a chance to breathe."

"Sure. Let's save energy." She turned the lamp off and burrowed into her sleeping-sack. After some wriggling about, she extracted the suit and tossed it aside. "Good night, Marco."

Frustrated beyond measure, Marco did the same.

~~~

In the dawn light, it was Elzabet who spotted a glint of curved metal among a towering grove of twisty green ferns. Old, but only slightly corroded. Tilted away from them was a partly submerged doorway beside etched instructions in Galaxic Standard. The curve suggested that it was vast, and mostly under the swamp.

It didn't look at all like a beacon.

"We're in trouble," said Elzabet. "This is a ship — a big one. Four days to cross eight klicks to get here, and now we're *twelve thousand* klicks from the beacon?"

"We always were," said Sam, "since we landed."

"That," said Tinka, "is true. It is also no comfort *at all*."

"Men," said Elzabet.

"Men," agreed Jane.

Marco took a closer look.

"This hatchway seems space-tight to me. It's not the main airlock — one of the side airlocks, maybe. There's a code down here — something OG... yah, CV23 MA-GOG. Right. Colony Vessel 23, one of the earliest. Name: *Magog*. Every group, of language or skin or religion, wanted a few of its people off Old Earth back then.."

"This must be the site of the original landing. I bet they hit the edge of the desert, and the swamp has encroached further inland since then."

"If so, it got a lot deeper," said Marco. "I wonder if the vessel was right way up when it landed?"

"But why land here at all?" said Jane. "It's a lousy spot for a Colony. That's why I voted to look here for the beacon. My mistake. Trash it."

"Don't blame yourself," said Sam, who had favoured the mountain site. "Our collective guess was based on logic, but it put down where it could; no logic to it." A thought struck him. "Maybe Squill III did its thing to them, too."

Tinka, who had been feeling around in the mud beside the hull and was only half-listening to Sam, suddenly stopped groping. "If the *drive* still has a residual field," she pointed out, "possibly the *communicator* still works."

"Fat chance," said Felix. "There'd be a short period after the landing when the communicator could be used for real emergencies. Then it would've autodisabled, and recycled its parts, leaving only the rescue beacon. And that was interdicted. They must never have contacted base, because this place isn't marked on the charts as inhabited. We'll just have to hope the beacon is still in working order when we get there."

"Halfway round the forsaken planet!" said Sam. "When they knew they were crippled, why didn't they have the ship put it down beside them, for a rescue call?"

"There's an easy answer to that, Sam," said Tinka. In Gregorian chant she intoned, 'Instructions in non-operational mode cannot be implemented.' Then, in her normal voice, "You've had enough arguments with *Valkyrie* to see it for yourself."

"Oh. Right. The CV's automatics placed it as they'd been told, regardless. So no one knew where it was."

"At least *we* know that," Marco observed. "Now we just have to get there."

"If it's in working order, after eighteen hundred years," said Elzabet bitterly.

"Oh, come on, Elza. While there's life, there's hope."

"You know, that's not really encouraging when you think about it." The others looked blank. "The operative word is '*while*'."

Marco began digging in the mud. "May as well see what we've got." He found a handle, just below the surface and struggled with it. "Looks like a postern lock. Maybe the early colonists left something we can use.... Say, it's moving!" The door squelched outwards. A torrent of silty water, scum and vegetation poured out. Marco lost his balance and sat in the swamp.

Sam peered in the opening. "Yah, Marco: they did leave something."

"What?"

"They left an airlock open. *Magog*," he spat, "is full of mud."

Hope breathed out of them, like life itself departing, It had been stupid even to *imagine* the vessel might still have a working Da Silva communicator. But it hadn't been stupid to hope to call the beacon, which was long past its vow of silence. No.

No.

"Just our luck," Elzabet snapped, more upset by the workings of the universe than by the failings of anyone in particular. "We might *just* have been able to save ourselves a tramp halfway round this nanacurst planet!"

"*If* there was still a functional comm of some sort in there, *if* we could reach it, and *if* we could make it work," said Sam. "That's a lot of ifs."

"Here's a historical if," said Tinka. "If they'd had a functioning Da Silva comm right after the crash, they'd have been free to use it at the time and scream for help."

Marco followed her lead. *Someone* had to say the obvious. "Some of them survived, and they didn't contact Old Earth. So their comm must have been wrecked before they crashed; in fact, before they even realised they were *going* to crash. Like what happened to *Valkyrie*."

"Sure, they crashed in the same place as us, but that doesn't mean —"

"Elza: if the comm had been live before they hit, *Magog* would have sent a distress signal. That might be wrong, but the same goes if the comm was live after. Yah, the computer was programmed to deactivate it, to stop the colonists whingeing about the terrible world they'd just been dumped on. But it wouldn't have self-disabled until after a safe landing, with the rescue beacon successfully deployed. Then it would send a final report to Colony Central, and shut itself down."

"Couldn't they have used the beacon's comm *before* it was deployed?"

"Nah. Absolutely inactive for a century was the only hack-proof rule."

"Could the beacon have been wrecked too?"

"Thank you, Tinka, for that encouraging thought. It's possible, but unlikely. I can think of half a dozen ways to ruin a live Da Silva. I can't think of any that would damage a dormant one without obliteration. And beacons are *tough*. Actually, *Magog* wasn't damaged as badly as *Valkyrie*. We had to drop in a capsule; *Magog* made it down safe and they walked away to colonise. The clincher is, the only way to explain the signature *Valkyrie* spotted is that the beacon got away intact."

Elzabet grunted, possibly in assent. "So you don't think there'll be anything useful inside."

"Probably not. The colonists would have cleaned the ship out, taken everything that wasn't welded down. Most of what was, too." Marco threw a stone into the scummy brown goo that blocked the entrance. It made a soft splattering noise and left an expanding ring of slow ripples on the surface.

Felix was the first to take the bad news at face value and consider using it. "Marco, you said just now that we might find something we can use. Agreed, not a working comm. But shouldn't we at least make an effort to look? Just in case?"

Marco paused in the act of prying another stone loose from the dried mud at his feet. "Well, what I had in mind was... Despite everything I said, there's a faint possibility the beacon's still in there. *Very* faint. Don't get your hopes up. It wouldn't fit what *Valkyrie* told us, and I have no idea what that other solitron source can be if it's not the beacon. I'm clutching at straws."

"If it's not there, we'll know they launched it," Tinka pointed out. "It's got to be worth our while to find out, either way."

"How deep is the mud? How thick?" Felix asked.

"Not sure. They left one airlock open... but what about the bulwarks? Maybe it's just this part of the ring that's full of mud. It's not *quite* up to the roof of the outer airlock." Marco found a stick and poked it into the scummy mess, stirring up bubbles of marsh-gas. "Hmmm, it's quite liquid actually; no surprise with all this water about, I guess. It just *looks* thick. We might be able to force our way through it. Bit slimy underfoot, but hey."

Jane had a sudden vision of the snake that had slithered across their path, and repressed a shudder. "No knowing what that mud hides."

"It's probably safe," said Felix. "We've only just opened up an airlock. It's not like we're bearding a cave-bear in her den." When Jane looked unimpressed, he tried another tack. "Look, we can't just *assume* there's nothing worth having inside this thing, and go traipsing gaily across a potentially hostile planet without making sure."

Jane shook her head, but slowly. Tinka broke the impasse. "I'll buy that. We can't just *assume* there's nothing hostile inside this thing, but we ought to try. Anyone want to volunteer?"

Felix's hand shot up. After a few seconds, Marco gave her a wave. "I know the layout of these things."

~~~

The two Starfolk had pushed through the stagnant water to a junction. Inside their suits they were sweating. Marco, now in the lead, muttered something under his breath, but when Felix started to reply he turned to face him. "Nah, you were right. Keep going." He scraped mud off the wall, revealed a stencilled sign. "Climb up here. It would have been a higher corridor in flight, and it gets us out of the water."

In the cold blue light of the glowbands round their heads, *Magog*'s interior looked like something out of a holvix space opera — metallic struts and panels draped in sludge and scum, with strange creeping vines twining round them, rooted in the gluey mud that hampered every hand- and foothold. The acoustics echoed emptily.

The wall they were travelling on was now more level: climbing was replaced by scrambling over a deep, tangled growth.

Here and there, the remains of things that had once been living looked vaguely like the exoskeletons of overgrown woodlice, about the size of a human foot. They exchanged worried glances, and Marco grimaced, looking down. Felix took pictures of it all with his 'comp. He and Jane had already decided not to collect samples, for the no-brainer reason that they had too much to carry as it was. He shook his head sadly, wishing they'd had a choice. Squill III was his first real research opportunity, and it was going to be frustrating, because he couldn't do it justice.

The further they penetrated, the thicker and more tangled the surface became. "We need to find a passage that's not blocked," said Felix.

Marco gestured with his head, eyes flicking upwards. "We're in one."

"Can we — oh, there are micrograv D-rings in the floor."

Marco hitched himself up the side of the wide tube, grunting. "Be careful not to lose your grip, they're slippery."

Ring by ring, they climbed along the floor. Mud slid down their airsuits and dripped off in glutinous lumps. Marco said the wall signs matched usual CV layout. In the angle where a supporting strut met the core's shielding, he noticed something.

"Hang on, Felix, just let me prise this loose." He pulled off a small disc. "A souvenir. Bit damaged, wouldn't come off easily. Look at the writing."

Felix held it up, tilted it until shadows showed the embossed letters.

UMAN SAFETY DIRECTORAT
UBLIC LIABILITY CONFORMITY CERTIFIC
ILVA CORE #0003347821QQ46
23 MAGOG

They came to a doorway, now on its side, and peered into a large expanse of very little. In the light of the glowbands, there was nothing to cast a shadow. Whatever this vast, curved compartment had once held, it had been stripped bare.

They were well above water level now, with merely difficult floors. Every room told the same stripped story. They passed a sign saying 'main airlock', that led to a large vacuum-tight door, shut tight and overgrown by roots.

"The rescue beacon would have been stored in a bay by the main lock," Marco said, "for easy release just before landing. But it might just still be here, if you want to claim the galactic record for unwarranted optimism." He studied the walls. "There should be an access way for the engineers. But it wouldn't be used often, if at all, so — yah, this must be it. A crawltube. Wait here, I won't be long." He slithered out of sight.

Soon he was back. "Sorry, Felix: it's empty. But you can see that's where the beacon was. They cut away most of the cradle that held it, but that proves they launched it, so it wasn't damaged. Which is good news."

"It says something," Felix said, "when it's good news that our goal is half way round the planet."

"Yah. Especially when *Valkyrie* saw no ships crossing the oceans."

"Trash it, there must be *some* ships. The colonists spread across this entire world, islands and all."

"Must have been ships once. No sign now."

"If necessary, we'll build our own. After all, as a mathematical engineer —"

"What was next to this? The door looks undamaged."

"That's the alternative to beacon launch — launch blister for the deathpods."

"*Deathpods?*"

"If a CV wasn't going to make it, if a crash or starvation was 100% certain, they'd scatter those as widely as possible in local space. Just 'we're vanished, but not into night' closure records, and something to help investigators find them."

"So they'd have insystem communicators?"

"You're right… if they're still there. Pretty useless for colonists to carry off, but they *could* signal to the beacon."

"They might be behind that door?"

"Might, I guess," Marco was coming alert. "But it's a blast-defence door. Strictly senior crew access. We couldn't get it without a command key."

"Which would be where?"

"One in the bridge, for sure, but that's way below swamp level. No way could we ever reach it without pumps. They probably went off with it, anyway."

"And?"

"One in the emergency control space. Near the lock we came in by, not much loot there, could still be closed up. Maybe we could burn our way in with Jane's laser…"

"But?"

"If I have the layout right, it's under two metres of mud."

~~~

When they had splashed their way back through the airlock to solid ground, Jane wrapped Felix in a bear-hug. "Don't you ever volunteer for any damn-fool thing like that again!"

Marco almost drowned in questions from the others.

"Did you find anything?"

"Yah. They did launch the beacon. It has to be the solitron source *Valkyrie* spotted, up that mountain."

"Now that really is worth knowing," Tinka said. "Gets rid of our biggest worry. Good work."

"Anything else?"

"Just a maybe," said Marco. "Right about there," he pointed into the mud, "there *could* be a key that *could* let us into a space that *could* maybe hold pods that would let us call the Beacon." He explained.

"No way," said Jane, "will this laser burn through a lock, underwater."

~~~

By nightfall, they had gathered about half enough rocks to start building a coffer dam around the area where the emergency control space should be, and returned to their tents, exhausted.

On his pad waiting for sleep, listening to Elza's measured, deep breaths, Marco became dimly aware that he had missed something. Sleep refused to come, despite the weariness in his limbs, until he figured out what it was.

When he'd opened the postern airlock, water had poured out. Quite a lot of water must have accumulated inside, a metre or so *above* the present waterline. Fair enough: at some time in the past, the level of the swamp had been higher. Or there had been a flood, or a thunderstorm, or even a series of them, causing water to pour in through the open main airlock.

Problem solved.

Except... he and Felix had reached the main airlock, high above the level of the swamp in the dry parts of the ship, and... *it had been shut.*

Yes, *Magog* was full of mud, water, and plants, to a level way above the swamp. But the colonists hadn't left the main airlock open to the rain. So *how had the water got in?*

Maybe one of the other side airlocks had been open? Hidden under the swamp? Water that got in that way, in a flood, would drain out later. Same problem for a hole below the waterline, even if a crash caused a breach. *No open side airlock either*, he suddenly realised.

So how had the extra water got in?

And why did it have vegetation growing in it, in total darkness?

Maybe there had been a hole, and then it got plugged with mud. Maybe some Squill III vegetation didn't need light, but got energy another way. By eating giant woodlice? Neither hypothesis was likely, but both were more plausible than any alternative he could think of. There had to be *some* explanation. But right now...

Aching all over, Marco drifted into a troubled sleep.

~~~

Gathering enough rocks should have been two days' work. In the swamp, posting guards, it took five.

Constructing a dam took three, sealing gaps with a sticky goop that Felix created by boiling down marsh plants.

Then they began to bail.

What should have been a volume they could empty in two days, took six. As they worked downward, exposing more of the dam, they saw no problem with Felix's sealant: but the level was always higher in the morning than they'd left it at night.

"Maybe it flows through these roots?"

"They're not hosepipes, Tinka," said Jane. "Anyway, only one thing we can do."

"Keep bailing."

"Right."

On the ninth day, the edge of a door appeared that Marco swore would be the right one. By nightfall, they had exposed a notice that proved him right. At mid-day on the tenth, the lock emerged. It took an hour to burn it out, with pauses to re-charge the laser, while they still kept bailing, to keep it clear.

When they got the door open, the level of muddy water did drop, as some of it came in with them to the tilted room.

Another day's bailing found the key cabinet, and more burning got it open.

Nobody could now believe the deathpod key would be there, but —

"This has to be it," said Marco.

Together, they struggled to the beacon launch area. At first the lock jammed. They had no oil, but a long sluicing with near-boiling water cleared it enough to open. It took the strength of all of them to move the heavy door with its hinge now above them, but they shifted it a little, and jammed it open with a rock. Cannibalising the dam, they brought up more rocks, and step by step opened it wide enough to enter. The light of their wrist comps showed forty-two ovoids, each as tall as a ten-year-old child.

"Deathpods," said Marco.

Opening one did not turn out to be easy — nobody believed in the existence of easy, now — but he got one opened up.

The interior was full of... something. Purple-grey, like a fungus. Mould.

"How," he murmured in a flat voice, "did this grow in total darkness? With no nutrients?"

"Perhaps it eats wiring?"

"I don't think so," said Jane, feeling fibrous remnants between her fingertips, "but it certainly destroys it."

"Let's eat something," said Tinka, "before we check the other pods."

~~~

By nightfall they knew that not one deathpod would work for them.

~~~

In the morning, carrying the remnants of their food and what little was left of their survival gear, they set off to cross the planet.

4

Gold Bones, Violet Blood

It isn't what you don't know.
It's what you know that ain't so.
—*Folk Wisdom*

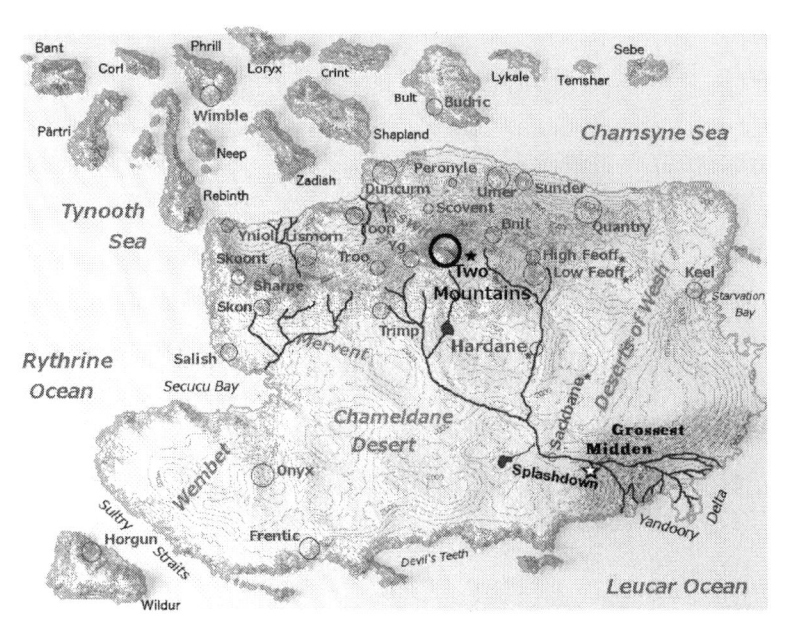

Shaaluy ('Beth') Stars (★) mark Starfolk-visited sites.

"It feels really strange, navigating with a *piece of paper*."

"Yah, Sam, I know what you mean. I keep waiting for my 'comp to tell me what to do next."

"At least we've *got* a map," said Jane. "Where are we now?"

"Near the edge of the swamp. This river will take us up through this gorge, across the desert."

"Why not some gentle rolling countryside, with pretty flowers and birds singing?" Marco grumbled.

"You've had flowers and birds."

"The flowers *stink*."

"The local insects seem to like the smell."

"The smell sucks, just like the ground. I don't appreciate birds when each step is against suction."

"No other way," said Tinka. "There's nothing on the coast, and we have to stay near to drinking water."

"And near to bulk food," Felix reminded her. "No way we can survive for long on just the concentrates we have left."

Despondently, they set off upstream. The narrowing river became deep and turbulent. Soon, walls of dark rock enclosed them, but at least the footing was firm, carpeted underfoot with a springy moss-like growth. For city-dwellers, they made good time.

Occasionally they heard movement in the forest around them, but saw only the planet's version of bird-life. The rustlings seemed like natural sounds of small animals. Lulled by the sense of peace, the travellers became less apprehensive, though still wary. Two kept to the front and rear of the group, where the danger was likely to be greatest. The others walked between them in pairs, keeping an eye open but not so fully alert.

From time to time, they swapped places, so that they got a chance to relax.

As the sun reached its zenith, Tinka and Felix were walking a dozen paces behind Marco. Next came Sam and Elza, another dozen paces back, chatting about nothing in particular; then Jane with the laser. Felix had spoken even less than usual.

When they were crossing a stretch of bare rock, unlikely to conceal anything nasty, Tinka decided it was safe to ask why.

"You always seem very quiet, Felix."

He looked up, nodded, looked away.

"I won't bite, you know."

He gave her the faintest of grins. "Dah." He hesitated, glanced behind them. "Jane knows why, but I don't want her to know that *you* know. Promise not to tell anyone else?"

"My lips are sealed even more than yours usually are."

"Well... I used to argue. A lot. But then..."

~~~

"My solo xeno field trip will be to *Gamut*? You're sending me to Gamut? My father's solo trip was to Gamut. My great-aunt wrote the book on Gamut, the one on my freshman reading list. I might as well stay home, and read it again. I don't even need to do that, I could recite it. What can I learn by going to Gamut?"

"You know all about Gamut, Mr Wylde?" There was something about that "Mr", from Professor Doxor Smythe, that got up my nose.

"It's all in *Running The Gamut*, isn't it?"

"Please summarise it, Mr Wylde."

"Alternate pollination. The early plants developed motile gametes, which turned multicellular, and when animals started to develop, they ate them. External fertilisation, like Old Earth frogs, but more so."

"Go on, Mr Wylde."

"The usual Self-complicating Theorem of Ecology still applies. Everything that moves is a pollen grain with teeth, or an ovule with fins or wings, whatever, but opportunity space fills up. You get herbivore jism, you get carnivore jism — jismivore jism, I guess — but everything is born out of a pod. You get ovule guarding, a group of male gametes protecting a female and taking her to a nice patch of soil. Then she puts down roots, sometimes eats the males. You get ambushes, you get camouflage, you get smarter gametes, because smarts is a dimension of opportunity space.

"Give it long enough, you get sapience. You get the people Aunt Kro wrote the book about. And you want me to go confirm her observations *again*?"

"First, Mr Wylde, we like to have data to check students' reports against. Secondly, we like to know what to protect or at least warn them against: we send only *qualified* xenologists to truly unknown places. Dead seniors don't pay tuition fees. Thirdly, you will never qualify as a research xenologist if you think your textbooks are always right — even, Mr Wylde, a textbook written by one of your illustrious relatives.

"You will go to Gamut, Mr Wylde. And if you expect more than a $B_\flat$, you will report a serious error in your aunt's book. And prove it, to the satisfaction of your committee."

So, I had argued an easy $A_\sharp$ into the assignment from the hot place.

So far, so good...

"You are here again."

Tooloo looked like a metre-tall land squid, obviously a scout-male as he was alone. He had eleven arm-legs, and seventeen manipulatory palps around his mouth, in the mottled maroon colouring that Aunt Kro had recorded as typical for this region (though the Hkoo have pentachromatic vision, so how they looked to him, who knows?). I could have accepted his statement.

"I have never been here before," I said, with my wristcomp supplying some of the stridulated vowels.

"You have been coming to this valley for a face of faces of years, as some tell it." I didn't suppose he meant exactly 172, two hundred eighty-nine — more like an Israelite saying forty, or a Chinese *man*, 104 — but with the short local years, it would vaguely fit.

"That was kin of mine, and then others." No word for 'students', or 'xenologists'.

"And none of them planted, but you keep coming. Are you edible?"

"Only to close relatives." Earth life could digest me, but he couldn't.

"You don't smell edible, so I will believe you. You will not eat from the fruits of my mother."

"No, I carried my own food." The bot did, anyway.

"You did not come for food. You came for land. There is no open ground for your female."

"I came to know things. My females do not grow roots."

Tooloo gave a series of hoots that my wristcomp subtitled [laughter], attracting another Hkoo. "T!lo, his females never settle!"

It is hard enough to explain mammalian biology to human children, never mind xenos, but I found myself trying. I'll spare you my analogies.

T!lo asked "What do your females even look like?"

"Much like me: two legs each, empty face, but a bit wider just here, and here they have the feeding glands I was just telling you about. They can grow quite large."

"And that is enough to tell the difference?"

"Maybe," said Tooloo, "they go by scent."

"Can you show us one?" asked T!lo.

"Not on this side of the mountains, but I have a friend" — just a classmate, but no way to say that — "ten days walk from here, on the high plateau." I didn't think sharing that would complicate my life. I didn't think.

"I hear there is good soil there," said T!lo, "maybe we should take Sister and go. Her root tips are itching."

In just half an hour, seven brothers and their sister — lower and solider, with a couple fewer legs — were on the march, with myself firmly in tow. They accepted Bot as a baggage carrier, and even loaded their reserve arrows on him.

It took more than twelve days, with some scary climbs (for me: the Hkoo held on more easily), but we got there. The orbital Advisor objected to the breach of student separation, but passed a message to Jane to expect us.

"Jane?" Tinka interrupted. "Our Jane Bytinsky?"

"Our Jane Bytinsky."

"And what," said Jane, "are you doing here? Messing up my observations?"

"My observation subjects wanted to look at you, and they brought me along. 'Unexpected travel suggestions are dancing lessons from God.'"

But just now, Tooloo and T!lo and the guys weren't looking at Jane. They had eyestalks only for a local who looked pretty much like Sister, maybe a bit bigger and greener, with her own protective males around her. Those males were gazing at Sister. The two groups flowed into each other, with a lot of sniffing, and then apart, with an exchange of centres. Perfectly following the script in *Running the Gamut*, each female reared up with the males circling around her. Taking turns in some non-obvious way, each flattened himself and offered up one arm/leg/tentacle. She wrapped an opening around it, it separated from his body, and she sucked it in like a giant strand of spaghetti. According to studies on non-sapient relatives, she would keep it as a long-term store of his genes.

When all the males had contributed, the females retreated to opposite sides of the clearing, shifted earth like a dog burying a bone, and settled into the resulting hollows, with their males resting around them.

And looking at Jane and me.

"You have watched us," said Tooloo.

"Now," said T!lo, "we will see how you do it."

I looked at Jane. "That is not according to our customs," I prevaricated.

"You are on our ground," said Tooloo. "We will see how you do it."

Jane looked at me.

"Perhaps," she said, "only fair. This will be the first double mating of Hkoo, for Institute files, and should really help our field trip grades. These guys don't even have recording equipment."

"We're a bit camera-shy on Daikoku. You're very attractive, but..." I wasn't rising to the occasion.

"There are ways to handle that," said Jane firmly. "Just lie down on that tree trunk." There are times not to argue.

She made something of a performance of unwrapping my anatomy, rather completely, for the budding Hkoo biologists. Nice to see that Kro *et al.* was definitely incorrect about their lack of intellectual curiosity, but I still felt inhibited, until she took me into her mouth. Call me a slut (I do), but I always come to attention when a lady takes charge that way.

Once she had me ready she got astride, taking care to show the Hkoo what was going where, and rode me all the way. Then she did a limber booty dance that somehow made particularly clear that she was not taking root.

"That," said Jane, "is how we mammals make new ones."

"Is he yours only, now?" asked Tooloo. "I was so interested in what you did with your mouth!"

"Feel free," said Jane, with the happy smile of a researcher whose plans are not disrupted with impunity.

Well, slut, dah, but if you haven't survived a seventeen-finger blow job ... you haven't lived.

"Tastes nice," said Tooloo. "And in you, that stuff makes new ones, even if you keep walking around?"

"That stuff makes new ones," confirmed Jane. No need to mention that she certainly had the standard hormone fix, and the stuff wouldn't work unless she planned on it.

"So how long does it take?" They all seemed fascinated by the way that she didn't seem any different, while the Sisters were already changing colour and looking settled. They would barely notice that she had a big sappy grin on, and nothing else.

"Just over two years," said Jane, in terms of Gamut's orbit.

"We can wait," said T!lo. "Would you like help building a winterhouse?"

...It took some negotiating before we could get on the Advisor-shuttle in time to graduate, and we had to promise them replacement subjects. You can get volunteers for just about anything.

That's why Gamut now has a small breeding population of humans, as well as a somewhat specialised tourist trade. And Jane and I went to graduate school. And, whenever possible, I keep my mouth shut.

~~~

Tinka gave her head a wry shake. "I've never heard a more eloquent case for silence."

"I swear it on my great-aunt's ashes."

"I'll keep my mouth shut too, then. But you might find it easier to open up if you told Sam, Marco and Elza. Secrets are a luxury on this world."

Felix wiped sweat from his forehead. "Dah. I'll think about it. Talked out, for now."

~~~

Towards evening, Tinka spotted a grove of trees. Implausibly, they grew on a bare, greenish escarpment like a stain across the reds and browns of the valley walls, away from the moist strip by the river. Like huge dumpy pineapples, dazzling orange with a spray of spiky leaves on top, they seemed to have sunk themselves in the bare rock.

"Maybe there's some special nutrient in the green stone?" Jane hazarded. "But where do they get *general* nutrients, and the water to dissolve rock away like that?"

"Not from below," said Elzabet. "That's a thick stratum of igneous rock, solid and insoluble. No way it has water channels. They must exude acid to penetrate it."

Tinka showed more interest in the clusters of fruit around the base, like lavender-blue pear-shaped cherries. "Don't know about you, but I'm getting tired of concentrates. I wonder if these blobs are edible?" She reached to pluck one.

"Whoah, hold it! I wasn't trying to categorise these out of mere curiosity, dah? Those *blobs* might very well kill us. Or worse." Jane smiled to take the sting out of her criticism. "However, I'm probably being over-cautious. Felix?"

"Probably. Plants won't bite your head off, at least."

"Right. I wouldn't be surprised if these things contain some sugars and starches that we can digest. But I doubt we'll be able to eat any native animals. More's the pity: I could do with a nice juicy steak right now."

Felix's eye flicked up to meet her gaze, and he cocked his head to one side. She recognised the look. "Right. Less talk, more action." She rummaged through her pack, found a small flat probe, stuck it into the fruit. Its thin-film chemistry lab performed an instant analysis and displayed the results. "Not too bad," she announced. "The amino acids won't do anything for us either way — not even an immune response, so no allergies — but most of the carbs are just like those at home. Provided there are no hidden nasties, they'll provide natural fibre too, so we can save on concentrates *and* keep our digestive systems in good shape."

Testing for poisons, allergens, and the like was simple, since the biologists got the bugs into it. Now, anyone out of their native ecology — in particular, off-planet — carried a phial of genetically modified bug eggs incorporating their DNA. Faced with any new food, insert the phial's ovipositor. If in five minutes a green bug clambers out of the foodstuffs and flies off, that traveller can dig in with no further questions.

Their bugs flew.

They dug in.

"These are tasty," said Elzabet. "Hah. "You know, I used to hate state banquets. Excesses of food as a cover for politics. Push it round your plate, let the servants throw most of it away."

"Could've let 'em take it home," Marco mumbled.

"Nah, bad form to let servants eat above their station. But now — oh, what I'd give for a plate of six-fowl *scaloppini en croûte* with a marmalade glaze, stuffed gulley-pears and a diced bush-crab garnish! I'd even be willing to put up with Parminder Bindraginder whining on about her latest stallion."

"That's a horse, right? Sorry, just asking. I'd settle for good old cow pie and root-beet hash. With marmalade glaze, of course, we're *civilised* on Inferno."

"Don't be facetious."

"I'd sell my mother into slavery for a decent meal. Even *without* marma—"

"I'd sell *my* mother into slavery for a friendly smile, except that you don't do that to family."

"Well, we don't get the option, Elza. It's a limited menu today. And you're right, these are *good*. Not too sweet, not too sharp. At least there's *something* palatable in this dump!"

"Pippy, though," said Sam.

"Stop moaning. No worse than cherries," Elzabet answered. "Just one small stone. You can easily spit it — oops!"

"What happened?"

"You can't easily spit it out and talk at the same time. I just swallowed one. Good job the bugs tested the pips too."

They cut several bunches of the fruit, and went to camp on softer ground near the river.

~~~

The river drained the higher land, and swamp gave way to firm gravelly soil and rocky outcrops. Paths through the vegetation, presumably animal tracks, made them more wary, but faster. They still had to pick their way across rough terrain, and more than once a blockage forced them to backtrack. Mostly there was a river bank on their side, but sometimes the water came so close to the cliff that they had to rope together and scramble along bare rock. There was usually local food, but they sometimes went a long way without seeing any. For security, they took to adding three days' supplies to their packs. Undehydrated vegetables and fruit are not light, and their backs were weary. They had to compromise.

Late one afternoon, they came to where they could not continue on that side. The giddily distant canyon rim, past tilted orange strata that had split almost vertically when the softer rock beneath had eroded away, decided them they couldn't climb out either. The alternatives seemed to be to go fifteen klicks back down the river to a point where they could climb up to the desert, or to find a way to cross to the Eastern side.

Felix noticed a dead tree, fallen half into the water.

"That's crooked enough not to roll," he said. "I think the current should bring us near the other shore if we launch it from here."

"Rubbish!" snapped Marco. "I did endless courses on fluids, I know instinctively how they behave. We'd just get in the middle and float for ages. Look, I'll show you." He borrowed Jane's laser and burned through the base of a smaller tree, which fell into the river with a hissing splash. Murky shapes approached it in the muddy water and confirmed their decision not to swim.

The tree moved out, followed an odd undertow swirl in the middle of the river, and fetched up neatly on an Eastern sandbank, about a kilometre downstream.

"I think that confirms it," said Elzabet, as Marco began to prove that Felix couldn't have correctly deduced his lucky prediction because the visible indicators were all the other way. "Let's launch the big one and get on board."

They passed the middle without incident. Their tree grounded fifty metres upstream from the first, about its own length from the wide, sandy bank. Beyond that was a sparse green-leafed grove, so like birch trees that Jane suggested they'd come with the human colonists.

"Shallow enough to wade ashore safely," Elzabet observed. "and nothing big is on the prowl. As our *hai ganzai* foremost, I hereby volunteer. Marco, come with me? Thanks."

Sam handed Marco his Arkansas toothpick. "Nah, *take* it! The stunbeams can't be relied on; you need something that can. Don't let go of it: you haven't practiced throwing and you don't have a reserve weapon. Jane? Cover them with the laser."

They scrambled down from the tree, ankle-deep in wet sand, and made their way ashore. Then a sudden sound came from the bank, and they froze.

From between the trees stepped the first animal they had seen outside the swamp. Stippled green and brown, about a metre high, it somehow combined a hog's solidity with the graceful movement and delicate face of a red deer. Behind it trotted two young ones, in whom the same markings were green and orange. They shared their mother's wide, nervous eyes.

"Oh, look at that," Marco whispered, not to disturb the beautiful sight. "Let's not assume they're harmless, just because they look that way to our eyes," Elzabet warned him, also in a whisper. She gripped Marco's hand.

"Eyes at the side, look like herbivores," he muttered under his breath, half to himself. "Still, so was the Old Earth hippo, one of the most dangerous animals ever before it went extinct. I agree, we have to be careful, but I'd be surprised —"

All at once, from a knee-high bush on the bank that rose behind her, a hand-sized creature darted like a flash of scarlet and black. Elza grabbed Marco's arm, suppressing a cry. The deer-hog mother squealed as the creature leaped upwards to set golden teeth in her throat. Before the humans knew what was happening, she and the little ones were each half-buried under a writhing heap of red and black carnivores. Violet blood oozed towards the river. Golden bones began to show.

The carnage had come from nowhere. Fast. From idyll to abattoir in a moment. The Starfolk recoiled in horror. None of them had met this kind of violence before.

"Shaven Lily! They're a sort of land-piranha! Look at those teeth —" Sam stopped, too late. At the sound of his voice, some of the beasts had jumped from their dead prey and were heading straight for Elza. "Elza! Look out!"

She didn't need to be told. She raised her stunbeam, took aim, and fired. The beam didn't even slow the land-piranhas down; they just kept coming. *Hai ganzai* wasn't going to hack it with these things. She screamed.

By then, Jane had the laser in hand. She cut down a dozen of the beasts in a single burst, but it was no sharp-shooter's weapon. "Elza! Get down! You're in the way!"

But there was nowhere for Elza to go except the river, and the creatures had surrounded her.

Marco didn't stop to think. He waded into the pack of land-piranhas, slashing to left and right with Sam's hunting-knife, which quickly became sticky with violet fluid. Several sank their fangs into his calves and ankles, and he sliced apart those he could reach. He grabbed Elzabet, slung her over his shoulder, and waded back into the river, heading for what he hoped would be the safety of the tree.

To the watchers' horror, the beasts dived into the river behind him. Jane could not aim accurately, but as Marco passed Elza to Sam, and clambered out of the water himself, she pointed the laser at the nearest. In seconds the water nearby heated to boiling, and a steaming lump of scorched meat floated downstream. The beam moved to the next, but more of the things were leaping into the river.

"Elza! Are you hurt? I—"

"Marco! You're bleeding!" Elza yelled. "Look out! There's one on your leg!" Marco slashed with the knife. Elza hugged him tightly. Despite the danger, he grinned.

Jane kept up the attack. "Where are these Motherhumpers *coming* from?" Tinka cried, scared and exasperated in equal measure.

Felix had broken off a branch and was standing by to repel. They all knew that wouldn't work. It was all up to Jane.

Soon, she got the knack of keeping the mid-channel boiling while making time for quick sweeps over the pack on the bank. Nothing seemed to diminish their numbers, or deter their shrill yipping attack, until she had reduced the whole bank to burnt earth. Suddenly there were no more live ones scrambling over the roasted corpses. The boiled ones floated out of the shallows to where invisible mouths rose to swallow them. All was quiet again.

"Mother of Galaxies!" Felix broke the silence. "That must have been close! How much left in the laser, love?"

Jane's brown face went grey as she looked. "Three more pulses and it would have been out of hydrogen! Then I'd have to override the safeties to get one last pulse out of the residual charge." Fully discharged, the laser could not have restored its hydrogen supply by the usual electrolysis of water drawn from the air. Its reactor would have been out of action until they next had access to a high-civ power supply. "I move we stay on this tree until the laser reloads." To speed the process, she dipped it in the river.

They sat looking at the carnage on the bank; cowed, shocked, and horribly aware of the unknown. This world was at its most dangerous when it looked benign, luring them into lowering their guard.

Sam put it into words. "Will we ever be able to relax?" He took a deep breath, started again. "Sorry. Negative thinking, should have kept it to myself. Doesn't help, I know. Couldn't stop —"

Tinka put a finger to his lips. "Sam: shut up. If it's any comfort, our Starhome intended mission might have been worse yet. Crashing here could be a huge stroke of luck. Anyway, we can discuss defensive tactics this evening, when we've all got our wits back. We've dealt with the menace, but we do need to move on soon."

Elza shuddered occasionally in the crook of Marco's arm as he murmured comfort into her ear. Eventually she regained a degree of composure. "Thank you, thank you! You risked your life to save mine!"

Marco shook his head. "We're a team. We do what's necessary." But his eyes were moist.

Before they headed upstream, Jane stuck a probe into what remained of the deerhog. "Yah, as I thought," she said, as the data flowed to her wristcomp. "We can't eat that! Violet blood, golden bones — too much cadmium, iron missing... Marco?"

He stopped gazing into Elza's eyes. "Yah?"

"You'll be delighted to know that you're just as poisonous to the native fauna as they are to you. Their cells have a pathway that ATP would block solid."

"Great. We can kill them by letting them eat us alive." A moment later: "So why did they attack us?" Before Jane could react, he slapped himself and answered his own question. "Because they didn't have time to test us for biohazards, I mean, sniff us. It moves, it's food. Silly me. Too tired to think straight."

Nobody voiced what was on everyone's mind. When their food ran out, hunting wasn't going to be an option. They just had to hope the locals were friendly.

As the others prepared to move off, Jane made a quick inspection of the area where the land-piranhas had emerged. "You know, I *still* can't see where those horrors were coming from," she shouted. "I thought there was a tunnel behind that bush — " she pointed to the burnt woody stump where she had seen them first appear — "but it looks like solid rock." Stepping back, she pulled up the stump's shallow roots, and kicked loose earth from the rocky slope. "Maybe the laser fused the tunnel shut."

But the others were anxious to be gone. She hurried to join them.

~~~

They stopped to make camp beside a rockpile. Elzabet always looked at rocks, and these didn't match the local geology. Investigating, she discovered chisel-marks. More dressed stone turned up nearby.

"It's got to be a ruined village," she told the others. "Someone tried to make a living here, early on, but failed."

"Stone walls? It must have been a terrible time." said Jane. "This inhuman wilderness looks pretty, but the sooner we reach a real live village, the happier I'll be."

That night they stood guard watches again, except for Marco and Elza. He'd been hurt and she'd been terrified. While the others kept watch, passing the laser earnestly from guard to guard, they returned to their tent.

"Airsuit off, Marco!"

"Uh?"

"Time to wash blood and Squillian gore off your leg, and treat your wounds."

"Oh." He stripped off, disappointed by the reason. Still... He could have cleaned the wounds himself, but he'd have died the death of a thousand cuts rather than say so. Her fingers on his skin were electrifying as she rubbed ointment into the wounds and stuck the edges together with sterile strips.

Then the fingers moved higher up his leg. Without a word, Elza slipped off her airsuit as well, and this time she didn't hide under the covers first. Her eyes gleamed.

"Elza, love — you don't have to feel any obligation, just because you think I saved your life when —"

"*Shhh*. No obligation. You *did* save my life. Risked yours. Gift horse, teeth, don't, dah?"

"Some horse." To his incredulous delight, her fingers moved higher still. "You have my full attention," he told her with a sharp intake of breath.

"I have you *at* attention, certainly," Elza said, stroking.

"I'm not wounded *there*," he gasped.

"Marco, stop being so noble!" Then, realising what she'd said, Elza giggled. "I suppose it's really *me* who's — anyway, wound or not, I think I need to check this out," she whispered in his ear, sticking her tongue in it. "*Very* thoroughly. To make sure it's still in working order."

"I wouldn't dream of — of stopping you —" he managed to reply.

"Marco, my love, when those things attacked, my entire life flashed before me, just like they say it does. And you know what? I didn't like what I saw one little bit. And I vowed then and there to do something abou — *oooh!*"

Marco's fingers had begun to repay the compliment. "I think we need to check *everything* out," he whispered. They clung together and merged.

~~~

From then on the Starfolk stopped fretting each other about whether the planet *might* have monsters in store. Somehow they took strength from it. They had survived so far. Alert for danger, they walked on.

After nine days on the East bank, they reached a place where the river narrowed to a white-water torrent, pouring from between sheer cliffs of bare red rock. The tilted strata gave the optical illusion of the water flowing slightly uphill. A collapsed section of cliff allowed them a steep scramble up to the desert, where they pressed on upriver, paralleling the cliff edge. A dust-storm stirred up clouds of fine windblown gravel, which cut at their flesh. They trudged doggedly on.

By next evening, the dust-storm had abated, and they were looking down into a wide, shallow lake. From a broad wedge of directions, the water converged on a deep waterfall at the lake's narrow exit, crashing down with an earsplitting roar. Spray hung about the cliff-tops like a grounded cloud.

While the other four prepared the camp-site, now a routine task, Jane and Felix stood side by side at the top of the falls looking into the spray. A rainbow so bright it seemed solid formed a three quarter ring enclosing cloudy brightness, making the ordinary white of sunlit spray outside it seem glowingly dark in comparison. Above the endless thunderclap of the falling water Jane shouted to Felix: "You know, I'm beginning to *like* this place!"

"Me too!" Felix's tenor shout competed with the bass of Mother Nature. They scrambled over the rocky shore to rejoin the others.

They found Elzabet lying unconscious, with Tinka and Marco squatting panic-stricken beside her. Sam was rummaging in their packs for medicines.

"What's the matter?"

"I don't know, Jane. Sam just looked round and saw her collapse."

Jane reached for Elzabet's wrist, and her fingers flickered over the touchpads that now became visible with Elza's 'comp. Symbols began to flow. Jane took a medipack from Sam and injected a mild stimulant. Elzabet's eyes opened.

"What happened?"

"We're hoping," Marco gently took her hand, "you might tell us." Her skin felt cold and clammy.

Elza grimaced. "I'm not sure. I was feeling a bit tired, then nauseous. Next thing, I'm on the ground and you're up there."

Jane was still taking readings from Elza's wrist. "No external poisons, just fatigue and stress toxins — but in nasty quantities. You remember, we had to override the wristcomps two weeks ago about those, because Felix's and Sam's 'comps got worried about blood readings that weren't what they would have been sitting around in Silicon City! So we missed a genuine draw-down in Elzabet's. There are other shortages, too..." She lapsed into inaudible muttering.

Elza's metabolism was in a strange mess — too little iron and calcium, too few vitamins, prothrombin deficiency... Beyond all this, came the sudden realisation, she was *thin*. And her blood count was low.

The best the wristcomp could come up with was maladsorption syndrome. It was no good pining over *Valkyrie*'s lost information-banks, so they followed the 'comp's instructions, giving her a double ration of concentrates. The 'comp put itself in standby and vanished again.

~~~

Next morning, she felt better, but after half an hour's travel they had to halt.

"It's no use," she apologised. "I just don't have the energy to go any further. I feel fine when I rest, but my legs don't seem to hold out."

"It can't be the land-piranha bites," said Jane. "Marco got more of those."

"Don't worry," said Tinka, looking worried sick. "We can carry you on a litter until you feel better."

If I feel better, thought Elzabet, which we can't predict. *While* there's life there's hope. There are enough litter-bearers as long as no one *else* is infected. She kept her thoughts to herself and gave a weak nod, as Tinka went on: "The map shows villages not much further upriver. We'll soon get you to rest and shelter." They all knew locals could be a whole new can of worms, but it needed opening. "We can travel nearly as fast with a litter," Tinka concluded brightly. She was a hopeless actor.

Despite the brave words, they camped at noon, finding it hard to move on. Dragging the litter — or carrying it, which they also tried — slowed them more than they'd hoped.

~~~

Sam noticed some fish in the river. Now rested, and lacking anything better to do, and seeking distraction, he spun some aer-O-web line and caught one on a hook trimmed from a thorn. It looked remarkably like an enormous trout. It bug-tested as edible, and Felix built a fire to light with the laser. Cooked, it tasted like trout. "Trash it, it *is* trout!" Sam declared, and the collective mood improved markedly at the prospect of fresh, edible meat. "Must have been bred for size from frozen ova, by the colonists. More, anyone?"

"What do you think, Wasumi?"

"Right. Just checking." He headed for the riverbank at a trot.

It was peaceful, he was within easy earshot of camp, the others were preoccupied with Elzabet... So, seeing an especially likely pool just past the next bend in the shoreline, and then an even better one... Accumulating fish, Sam wandered slowly upstream.

5

Munication

> Communication [Lat. *commūnicāre*: to share]. The meaningful exchange of information between two or more participants, such as persons, animals, or computers.
> —*New Revised Dictionary of Galaxic, Version 5*

Birajaro had a hard calculation to do. He always found it easier to slip away from the village into the woods across the river, where nobody would disturb him counting on his fingers. While his feet trod the moss of their own volition, he ran through the figures again. Three sow grunters in pod, the commonest litter was five, that meant — uh — five-and-ten new gruntins come Leafdrop. One gruntin consumed about two sheaves of boloona stalks daily, so over next Frost he would need — he would need more fingers — he would need to plant out at least three quarters of the fallowland. Now, that would take some help from the Coperativo, so he would be debited one tenth by the priest. On the other hand, if he sold half the gruntins at the next Grand Market, he could expect a profit of —

By the beast-with-seven-heads, what is that fellow doing? It looks like *fishing*. But why doesn't he use the barrel in the village, like any other traveller? The best fish always come there for the scraps the women drop in.

Birajaro hurried to the riverbank. Approaching quietly, so as not to disturb the stranger, he came close enough to utter a polite "Strabyen, Sab!"

Sam Wasumi dropped his fifth trout as if it had suddenly glowed red-hot, and spun rapidly in a half-crouch. *Shaven Lily, it's a native!* He saw a short, bronzed, wiry young man wearing a lopsided mauve kilt, calf-high leather boots, and a plumed hat like an inverted gravy-boat. The effect should have been comical, but with his dignified bearing the youth looked curiously natural, though none too bright.

Birajaro had never before seen clothes like those worn by this blond, dark-faced man, who towered over him as he rose to his feet. Had he been dipped in shiny green mud? He must be from... uh. No idea.

"Donday ven*gi*, Sab?" he asked.

Sam knew the main colony planet languages, which added to his confusion. If this one were European-based, the intonation would clearly make it a question. But tone in most languages in space distinguished words, not grammatical forms. Well... whether he had said "Who you?" or "Give back those fish", the native was visibly expecting an answer.

"I am sorry if I have caused offence," Sam said in a solemn voice. "I am a traveller, and I was trying to catch some fish to eat. I did not realise they were yours." Birajaro's brow furrowed. Sam thought it was anger, and got ready to run.

Actually, it was perplexity. The stranger's speech was even weirder than his looks. Even Cityfolk were more comprehensible than this. Maybe this *hoom* was from Crosswit Beyond the Mountains? It was said the folk of Toon could not understand even each other. Was the stranger talking about the fish? But why? Even a Crosswit would know he had only to declare himself to the priest and take what he needed; there was no need to discuss it with Birajaro, or to fool around in the open river.

"Peesh," he said, gesturing at the trout. "Ni porbleem, Sab, ni porbleem. Donday ven*gi*?"

By now Sam had remembered his wristcomp's 'always-on secure record'. That would provide something for Jane and Felix to work over when he got back. "I am sorry, I do not speak your language." Now what? It had to be the old standby. He thumped his chest and declared "Samuel Grey Deer Wasumi!"

Four names! Truly important personage! Birajaro was relieved that the chest-slap had been with the open palm, in greeting, and not with the clenched fist. He had no wish to engage in mortal combat with someone so well-connected. Bowing *sideways* from the waist, he named himself: "Birajaro."

"Pleased to meet you. I hope we will soon understand each other."

Understand! Ondrestend? Birajaro's mind came as close as it could to racing. That was Holy Talk. Could the stranger be a wandering Pilgrim, vowed to speak only the Holy Tongue? Every few years one would come downriver, seeking the mystical Footprints of Magog, who was rumoured still to walk the swamp. Birajaro carefully framed a question, screwing up his nose with the effort.

"Use pig laxative?"

"What?"

Now I'm finished. I've annoyed him. Hastily Birajaro tried again, correcting his speech to the Holy pattern.

"Yü, spig, G'laxitiv?"

Click! went something in Sam's brain. *He wants to know if I speak Galaxic Standard. Maybe his language is derived from Standard.*

If so, it's derived a forsaken long way in eighteen hundred years.

"Yes. I — uh — spig G'laxitiv."

Well, it was progress of a sort, Birajaro thought. "Birajaro ni spig. Ni porbleem. Venven *ki*, Sab." Sam looked across the river where he pointed. Around a small bay was a group of orange stone houses.

When in doubt, consult higher authority; in this case, the village priest. "Venven *ki*, Sab," Birajaro repeated. "Sackbane. Vigáro spig G'laxitiv."

He set off towards the woods, gesturing at a group of silvery trees to show Sam how to get there. "Wyzand, strut Sackbane. Venven *ki*."

"Uh, wait a bit," said Sam, as the small man again beckoned him on. "I can't leave my companions."

"Com-*pans*? Meegis?" Birajaro hadn't heard of Pilgrims travelling in a group, before. "Porbleem ni tenk. Venvenven ki *tote*!" He made an obviously inclusive gesture. "Strabyen, Sab."

To Sam's surprise the native bowed again, this time in the normal direction, and departed, once more heading for the trees.

Unaware that relief was mutual, Sam grabbed his fish and hightailed it back to camp. Breathlessly he described the encounter, ending up with: "I'm not sure I understood — Jane and Felix can maybe tell by running through the recording — but I think we're all invited to the village to meet someone who speaks Standard. Felix, how far will their version of Standard have diverged from ours in two thousand years?"

"Not much. The old holvix records—"

"*You raving lunatic, Sam!*" yelled Tinka. "You could have got yourself *killed* going off alone like that!" She paused for breath. "Though why I let it bother me, I sometimes wonder."

Sam looked crestfallen. "Sorry, Tinka. I never thought."

"Nah, you never do. *And* you've come up smelling of roses, which will only encourage you to do some silly small-boy thing again. Sheer forsaken *luck*! I ought to paddle your behind!"

"Time for that later." Levity aside, Marco sounded irritated. "Sam's unharmed. It's Elza we need to be thinking about." Realising she was awake again, and could hear them, he added, "Isn't that right, love?" Elza grunted something inaudible, and Marco hurried over to kneel down and comfort her.

Tinka grimaced in embarrassment. "Sorry, Elza. Marco's right. We need to get you over to the village, to get help."

It was Felix who asked the obvious. "How do we get across?"

Sam pondered, unconsciously gripping the hilt of his knife. "Well... Birajaro was taking me to his canoe. Or something. Through the woods, I think."

"How convenient! Could have been a set-up. I wonder how many of his friends were waiting in the woods?"

"Don't be so paranoid, Tinka! If that was what they had in mind, they could have nabbed me while I was catching trout. Anyway, because I couldn't wander off *completely*," said Sam, with a sulky look at Tinka, "and didn't go with him, he must have assumed that we have our own transport. He'll have taken the canoe by now, though, so there's no point us looking for it."

"It *might* be safe to swim, here," Jane mused. "But with Elza... I guess we make a raft."

"Is it sensible for us *all* to go?" Marco wondered.

"I think so," said Tinka graciously. "I hate to admit it, but Sam's right. We can't cross two continents by dodging from tree to tree. We have to meet the natives some time. They know we're here, and it will just look suspicious if we appear in ones and twos. Anyway, there's strength in numbers. Let's get the raft made. With luck, we can get across before nightfall."

Upstream, they felled and trimmed some waist-thick grey trees with the laser, lashing them securely with aer-O-web ropes. On fine beam the laser also shaped them some rough paddles, sooty but serviceable. Here, where the river was so wide they could just make out the houses on the other bank, and very shallow, Marco and Felix could agree that the current did nothing complicated; they would drift down slowly while paddling across.

After carrying Elzabet's litter on board and securing it with more ropes, they pushed off.

6

Pilgrims to Magog

> Magog the giant!
>   Hair of midnight!
> Tall as mountains!
>   Wide as ocean!
> Sky-stride giant!
>   Stars on shoulders!
> Stricken was Magog!
>   Fell to the World!
> Deaf, blinded, dumb!
>   People of Magog!
> Go to the forests!
>   Lowlands and highlands!
> Greenlands and brownlands!
>   Build you a city!
> Glorify Magog!
>   —*Edited extract from* Magog the Father, *an epic poem*

The sun was setting as their crude but serviceable craft neared the village on the far bank. When they were most of the way across, they came into the shadow of the valley side and could begin to make out details.

"Well-made buildings," said Felix. "That big round one is probably a temple."

"You characters always think *everything* is a temple," said Marco. "Why not an observatory? Or a supermart?"

"Do you see the braided circle carved over the door?" said Felix. "A symbol of unity, of wholeness, I'd guess."

"Planet," muttered Marco stubbornly. "Company logo..." His voice trailed off at a sudden movement. They had at last been noticed. Within a minute three hundred people were watching from the shore.

"I hope someone *does* speak Standard," said Marco. "Pity our 'comps can't access automatic translation."

"Not safe to use them, anyway," Sam warned. "No knowing what effect they'd have on these people."

"Or what they might do to us if they knew," Felix added.

"It won't take long to learn the local speech, anyway," Jane replied. "Judging by Sam's sample it seems to be a mix of Old Earth South American forms, though there's odd stuff from Shaven Lily knows where, and it's moved a good bit."

"My arms are dropping off," said Sam. "Why couldn't they send a boat to meet us?"

"What boat?" asked Tinka.

"Birajaro must have had use of one — I met him across the river." He shaded his eyes, saw a low shape in the water. "There's a boat!" But when they looked, it was obviously just a rotted skeleton, not used for years.

The people were slipping back into their houses, wary of lunatic Pilgrims — especially when, by Birajaro's account, they might have four names each. When the raft reached the shore, just one man was standing in the dusk. Pale and lean, dressed in a soft dark robe, he had to be a priest.

He looked up at them and spread his hands. "Please follow me." His Galaxic Standard was clear, despite a droning accent.

As they entered the building, the priest bowed sideways to the circle above the doorway. They thought it tactful to do the same. A dim, round chamber was lit by a patch of brightness the dead white of noon sunlight, centred in another circle motif in the roof.

"I wonder what the energy source is," Marco whispered to Jane. "No sign of electrical power in the village. Underground cables?"

"Nah, *Valkyrie* said no electromag—" She stopped. The priest was talking.

"Seating yourselves, be welcome. Name Keli hep Brundo to me. In name from Undivided Body there is greeting."

Like all Starfolk, they would have preferred to squat, but local custom clearly demanded chairs. They sat, not entirely comfortably. The priest gave Elza a sideways glance and gestured towards a low couch. "Put sick lady there." Within seconds she was asleep again.

"You Pilgrims travel seek Magog?" the priest asked, without preamble.

"Yes," Jane replied. "We have seen *Magog*."

"Have-seen?" The priest was confused. "Foy? *Did* seen Magog? Ondrestend, already time?"

"We saw *Magog* about... forty days ago. Almost buried in the marshes."

"Not ground marks only, you did seen Magog all self?" There was an awed expression on his face.

"Well, not exactly *all*," said Marco. "We saw the front end."

"Looked how like? You speak is not wrong, I priest from Church of Undivided Body, to me stands hearing."

"Like a mighty wheel in metal," Marco replied, keeping it simple. When Keli still looked confused, he pointed to the circle motif above them. "Like that."

"Fffff." The priest bowed to each of the Starfolk in turn. "Now is ondrestending why water you cross on sticks. Pilgrim vow to walking most limit to walking paths, weakness from flesh. You vow whole, *undivided*, yar, see Magog." He paused. "Yar, forty-one nights ago did come Night from Omolu, all faithful did seen fire in sky falling. Sign from vision of Magog that was to you be seen."

They were starting to get used to his scrambled grammar, and Tinka's puzzled look disappeared completely when she realised what he was referring to. This was her territory. "Oh. Yar — I mean, yah — uh, I was standing watch. I saw *Valkyrie* come down. At just the time the computer had predicted."

"Walkylie... is oracle?"

"Sort of. Until... those lights in the sky, they were caused by — " She stopped as Elzabet slid unconscious from her seat.

As they squatted around her, Jane's fingers moving anxiously on Elza's wrist, Keli stood up. "Did see pilgrim lady was sickness. I bring Sackbane doctor-man. Skilful in means, yar, training Great School in Two Mountains. Munto." He hurried out.

"I don't want some primitive medicine-man to touch her!" Marco objected. He looked miserable. "He'll just anoint her in jellied toads' glands, or — "

"Marco, don't be a snob. There's nothing *we* can do for Elza. I've been running regular analyses on her blood. I'll pull up the latest — oh, pigshit."

"What?"

Jane beckoned them out of Elza's earshot, and whispered. "She's dying! the 'comp gives her less than three weeks to live!" It was the first time it had even hinted that the disease might be fatal.

"What *is* it?" Marco was close to tears. They all were. "What's *causing* it?"

"The 'comp still can't assign a cause. Something local and external. Her epigenome's on record, so the odds are massively against some pre-existing problem suddenly showing up just when she meets a new planet. Whatever it is, it came from this world. But it's not a bug or a chemical in the bloodstream.

"The 'comp has no cure suggestion. The natives are her best chance, Marco. If it's local, the locals should know about it. They might even be able to cure her. Folk remedies are based on experience, and they sometimes work. We lose nothing by trusting the local quack, shaman, witch-doctor — or medic. Even if he kills her."

The Starfolk fell silent, lost in their own thoughts.

~~~

"Yar. Thought so." The doctor's accent was harsh but his grammar was more conventional than the priest's.

"What is it, doctor?" It was funny how easily they had all accepted the wizened old man with the big nose and beaded loincloth as a *bona fide* doctor. Partly it was his air of competence and authority, partly his bedside manner. But mostly, they *needed* to accept him. Even very small groups of humans tend to throw up universal figures: the priest, the hunter, the teacher, the decision-maker, the fool... and the doctor.

"She eat vunbugula fruit?" Dr Beni Salu asked, giving them a sharp look.

"We all ate a lot of plant stuff," said Felix. "The main fruit was a blue thing, hung in bunches on a rounded plant with spiky leaves. Growing on bare rock."

The doctor nodded, and pulled a stick of graphite wrapped in paper from his handbag, together with a notepad. He sketched rapidly. "Vunbugula."

"Yes, that's it. But — we *all* ate it. Is it poisonous? Are we *all* going to come down with these symptoms?"

The doctor inspected their eyelids. "Nar. Symptoms show quick. You clear. But lady — she must have swallow stone."

"We tested the fruit and the stone for allergens and poisons," Jane protested.

"You test?" asked the doctor, puzzled. "Nar, no matter. Tell how later. Is not poison. Is kind of — fah! Best old word: *parasite*. Embed in wall of gut, feed on nutrients direct from intestine, blood."

"Yuck. Like a tapeworm."

"Nar, not worm. Yar, is *like* worm."

Jane was fairly sure she'd understood that, and she still had no idea what sort of parasite it was. "What's the prognosis?"

The doctor stood up, and settled his feathered cloak back round his shoulders with economy and dignity. "Fatal if untreated. Sixteen days. Maybe two more if she strong."

"How do you treat it? Surgery?"

Dr Salu looked shocked. "Nar! Nar! No good. Catch early, then, yar, surgery may work. Like cancer. But by now, vunbugula stone grow long fine branches, infiltrate gut wall. Impossible cut out everything. What leave behind just grow new vunbugula."

"Then—"

"Operation not recommended anyway. Hardly ever benefit outweighs risk. Usual cure simpler, less invasive."

He did sound as though he knew what he was talking about. "Some good news for once," Jane said to the others. Turning back to the doctor, she asked: "How *do* you cure an infestation of vunbugula parasites, then?"

"You not know?" He gave them a curious look. "You Pilgrimage, but not know base survival techniques?" His brow furrowed, then cleared. "Ah. You grow adult hidden in mountain Holy House, I think. Eat Old Food. Learn only Old Knowledge. Pah!" His contempt for Old Knowledge was palpable.

"Something like that," said Jane. "Can you cure her?"

"Depends. Cure simple, sometimes but not feasible."

"Why not?"

The doctor, still unable to credit these people's ignorance, eyed him as if he'd crawled out from under a rock. "Every child know cure." He pointed downriver. "Burn vunbugula tree."

~~~

"He definitely told us, burn a vunbugula tree," Jane said for the tenth or eleventh time, playing it back out loud from her 'comp. "There's a grove just where he pointed, at that bend in the river."

"Yah, but when we asked why, he went off Galaxic Standard with a bang. 'Vunbugula syntelic parasite, feed by strint.' All we got was mumbo-jumbo!" It was remarkable how quickly their faith in the doctor had evaporated.

"Maybe. It *is* a local phenomenon, Tinka. Otherwise Elza's wristcomp would have given a sensible diagnosis, it knows about parasites. So 'parasite' isn't even the right word, just the closest one that the doctor knows. It's an alien ecology, probably there are no words in Standard for how the nanacurst thing works."

By now Tinka, under the relentless barrage of bad news, was even less flexible than Marco. "What a feeble excuse! This is a primitive dump and he's just a bloody witch-doctor! It's all an act and we get taken in like the yokels. 'Yah, doctor. Nah, doctor. Bah-bah-bah, doc—'"

"Sorry, but I think Tinka's right," said Felix. "Jane, you can see as well as I do that all the signs point to it. Sympathetic magic. To harm your enemy, hurt something like your enemy, like crushing the arm of a monkey to break his. This parasite is inaccessible, but it is represented by the tree, which is easy to get hold of. To kill the parasite, kill the tree."

"He knew about cancer, though," said Marco doubtfully. Ironically, he was now the only one of them to express any faith in the doctor. "He had paper and a sort of pencil. He gave the impression he could operate if necessary. And he knew about 'Old Knowledge', even if he didn't think it was worth knowing."

"The ancient Romans could write," said Felix. "They *named* cancer. Throughout history, primitive cultures performed trepanning and amputations. We didn't see any hard evidence he really knew what he was talking about."

"His diagnosis was spot on, though," Marco persisted. "She *did* swallow a vunbugula stone, remember? She was the only one of us who did, and the only one who's ill. *That's* not a coincidence! And his prognosis agrees with her wristcomp. Eighteen days, max!"

There was a hysterical edge to his voice. Jane couldn't meet his eyes. "Marco, we all want her to recover. But burning a vunbugula tree is ridiculous."

"Seems to me," Sam tossed into the silence, "we've got nothing to lose by trying it."

None of them could find an answer to that.

"And," he went on, "I can think of at least one possible rationale. He said burn the tree, not kill it. Why?"

"Search me."

"Perhaps something in the smoke kills the parasite."

"That kind of thinking is perilously close to magic too, Sam—"

"I say it's Elza's decision." He turned to the patient. "What do you think, love?"

Elza's reply was barely audible, but firm. "It's hard to see what harm it could do — though that's what I thought after I swallowed the stone. I say we burn a tree, see what happens."

~~~

They awoke with the sunrise, habit from their weeks in the open. The village was as quiet as a burial in deep space. They decided to try the experiment at once, in the vunbugula grove where they'd seen the doctor point.

At the bend in the river, Tinka had new doubts. "These look cultivated, Sam." She pointed to a drying rack with bunches of the little fruit. The stones had all been cut out.

"We'll burn this small one here, downwind. No one will miss one little tree."

They laid Elzabet's litter on the ground, where smoke would surround her. Sam collected dry kindling and piled sticks around the chosen vunbugula. Jane lit them with her medallion. The root was sappy, but the brittle leaves began to catch fire almost at once. They threw more brush on the fire. The heat drove moisture out of the root, which bled a sticky blue resin, hissed fiercely, then burst into apple-green flame.

Smoke billowed around Elza, who started to cough. Tinka, coughing just as violently, gasped: "This baby burns *too* well. Ugh, this is foul stuff, I can hardly see!"

Eyes watering, they dragged the litter out into fresher air, trying to keep it close enough for Elzabet to continue inhaling the smoke. And to cough.

It was Jane who noticed a thin trail of smoke rising from a nearby vunbugula in the plantation. Then another. And another...

"The whole *grove* is catching fire!" she shouted in alarm.

"That's crazy!" yelled Sam. "They're all sitting on rock. How could the fire spread like that?"

"Upwind, too. They must be linked by a common root system."

"Yah, sure. Roots that penetrate solid rock and burn underground."

"There must be holes in the rocks. Perhaps the roots are hollow."

"I hate to interrupt the inquest," said Elzabet between coughs, "but we seem to have started a major conflagration. Don't you think we should get our forsaken arses out of here, before anyone comes along to investigate?"

They grabbed the litter and set off downstream, along the narrow path that wound around the grey-green rock of the vunbugula grove. As they emerged from the smoke, they saw a distant figure approaching at a trot. Behind him came a dozen more.

It seemed wiser not to stay for negotiations. They beat a strategic retreat along a narrow ledge in the valley wall. Struggling to carry the litter without shaking Elza too much, they saw another group approach from downriver. The lead figure, his face bright with exertion or rage, delved into his handbag and came out with a green tube.

"Sam! What's he holding?"

"Looks like a blowpipe. *That* won't do him any good at this range!"

The tube's owner raised it to his lips, aimed it at a tree growing near the path above them, and bit down. *Something* shot past them with the unmistakable *crack!* of a small object going faster than sound. There was a muffled 'Whoomp!', a flash, and a cloud of smoke. In a dignified fashion the tree collapsed, blocking the path.

Tinka was first to restart her wits. "Sam... Are we *sure* it will do them no good?"

~~~

"Kay faki?" hissed Keli hep Brundo. Then he remembered that the strangers didn't speak Yandoory dialect, and tried again in Galaxic. "What doing you?"

"What the doctor told us," said Jane, truculently.

"To me he tell it too: *tree* burn. *Grove* burn he tell not. Each man know, other trees wetting. But in all good sense, why *that* tree burn? Is wrong tree."

"Wrong tree? Why—"

"Not fruit to that tree eaten."

Jane looked baffled. "Eh?"

"Tree must burn fruit was eaten."

Tinka's eyes blazed. "We did, Keli! It was a vunbugula, just like the one she ate the stone from! And we didn't set fire to the grove. Just one tree."

Keli gripped his left thumb at her. "Nar, tree false. Burn tree, burn grove *same thing*, wetting not others."

"But—"

"Tree not *like* must burn. Tree *same* must burn, fruit was eaten." How could anyone be this ignorant? "Tree *same*. Sky same. Place same. Root-branch-rockhole same! *All* same!"

"You mean," said Felix, "we have to burn the tree that we got the fruit from? The exact selfsame original tree that Elzabet picked the fruit from? All that way downriver?"

"Yar. So say I, not? Doctor say, not? Doctor down river point, not? *Crimba gatbi!* Doctor words exact: syntelic parasite. So why burn you tree here? Donday ven — *aachi!*" He spat, on the ground because he couldn't spit at six people at once.

Felix murmured to Jane: "See? Magic. The stone knows which tree it came from?"

"Maybe it's chemically tree-specific," said Jane. "Lock-and-key enzymes."

"No, that would be an unstable evolutionary pathway. It's ridiculous. You'd have to—"

"Silence!" bellowed Keli. "Diculous is *not*. Diculous is ignorant Pilgrims, think selves so holy can village fruit burn. Elementary is: vunbugula syntelic tree. Stone is tree, tree is stone. Tree is grove, grove is tree. Different place all same..." He reached up, and pulled Felix's ear, hard, saying to Jane "That *you* hurt?"

"Well, no. I feel sorry for Felix, but it has no physical effect on me."

"Just so. But *him* hurt good. Ear part of fool, stone part of tree. Tree part of grove. Now village whole hungry, eat patto root whole season, gaaaah! True Pilgrim not just speak holy: *act* holy. Holy act harm not."

Jane didn't like where this seemed headed. "But Keli — we didn't know."

"Must know. Everyone know. Child know this. Even holy Pilgrim know this."

"But —"

"Nar! To you stands quiet! Holy Pilgrim act all fortune good, increase crop and child. *Tree* burn..."

Suddenly the hot anger and confusion drained from his face, to be replaced by a cold, hard expression that gave his small figure a terrible dignity.

"Pilgrims not," he said flatly.

This was definitely taking an ugly turn.

"We never said we were Pilgrims," Marco pointed out, but it was a weak argument. Jane glanced over her shoulder: more villagers. Even with the laser, their chances were poor. Killing or burning a few villagers would be unlikely to improve their plight.

Keli started ranting at Marco. "Say you vision from Magog! Holy only Pilgrim see. You did *not* seen! Lies! Now accusing time: Pilgrims not, Church of Undivided Body not. Lie binding lie. *What master you serve?*"

"We serve no master. We come from far away —" Marco began.

It was the wrong thing to say. "Perverts from Ocean beyond! Wevorin undermines! Vain Vaimoksi! Exchangers in Abomination! Dividing and subdivided filth! Blasphemers against sacred Unity!" The priest gestured to a dozen of the small tough villagers. "Holy inspection inward parts to determine fate!"

Felix and Jane grabbed their stunbeams, Sam his knife. They had five villagers unconscious, one badly cut about the arm, before their darkness came down.

7

Ni Porbleem

My father was a priest.

You may think that helped my acceptance into the Seminariu, but when young he was an acolyte of the Prelate of Vanduul, who liked to take his acolytes to bed. That can be well enough — we are blessed to give comfort in all ways to those set over us — but the Prelate was one of those who turns against his loves, so my father became a humble cleric in Wembet, coming never to Two Mountains.

Nevertheless, his time at the Holy left him with more books than is usual in Wembet, and I grew up among them. Like my sisters I made syntelic fountains and played with half-wheels, but the books held me. I asked my father difficult questions, but when I was eleven I found in my father's desk a rare copy of the *Apocryphon of* FORTRAN. It is a text much forgotten, for the language is obscure even for ancient documents, and some phrases suggest that this lore was archaic even to those who were first Cast Down, but my eye was drawn to the statement

MAGOG IS INTEGER, UNLESS DECLARED DOUBLE

in the holy script of that mysterious text.

It echoed as a voice deep in my mind, a truth for me personally, and for a twelveday it haunted my dreams. Then I woke for the Day of Knots, knowing that I knew the truth, and the truth had bound me forever. Magog *is* integer, integral, whole and perfect, and we the Church, we the people, we the descendants of the first Cast Down, are whole and must be whole, if these be not broken by double-tongued declarations in denial of the roots of unity, divided by schism and heresy. Those who divide the body, divide the body of the Church. All must be One, all is won when all is One, all is lost when declared double.

My questionings of the Church fell away, for flawed and temporal though its ministers here below must be, yet is it the voice of unity for Qish, the integer voice of Magog's self. Heresy hurts us all, divides the body of us, even under the guise of a different path to finding moral truth, for morality is integer, and not to be declared double.

> At the Celebration of Knotted Space I vowed myself to the service of the unity of the body, of the people, and of the Church. I would understand ever deeper, I would explain ever more clearly, I would integrate those who spoke double. Where possible I would resist those of the divided self with words, but should unity require it, I would constrain them.
>
> Much indeed did I learn in the fiveyear that followed, and my Statement Of Purpose won me my place in the Seminariu despite my lack of patronage. Magog is never to be declared double, and with the integral blessing of Magog I have risen high in the Diaconal Palace. Even here one may be disturbed by hints of division, even here are those whom one fears to be DOUBLE and suspects to be FLOATING, but the path integrals will circumscribe the singular points, as it is written in the *Handbook*. To this I dedicate my mind and my body, despite all temptations that may arise within and without, knowing that within and without are the same.
>
> —Veridical Testimony of Acolyte Sadruddin A.T., Church Archives

"You say they burned down an *entire vunbugula grove*? How remarkably clumsy of them." The voice from the temple communicator had the languid tones that come only from generations of fierce grip on the reins of power.

"You speak truth, Sab," Keli replied in the city dialect. "Clumsy — but even more, *ignorant*." The priest, nervous and frightened, chose his words with care, hoping to deflect criticism. "I thought their ignorance might be betraying them as blasphemers, and had them placed under arrest and confinement, Sab."

"Be calm, you did well. Have you enquired of neighbouring villages, to know when these strangers came down the river?"

"Sab, yes, yes. No person has seen these folk, or heard tell of them. They appear to have come *up* the river, from Grossest Midden. How they got *there* — I have no idea. It is baffling."

"Indeed. Equally puzzling is why they could possibly have wanted to go there in the first place."

"They claim, Sab, to have seen Magog!"

"Not the usual footprint rubbish? Magog *himself*?" The voice suddenly had a sharp edge. "How did they describe the giant? Tall as a mountain, with hair like the dark before dawn?"

"No, Sab. They said —" he concentrated — "like a mighty wheel of metal."

The silence went on for so long that Keli broke it, unbidden. "Sab, I allowed myself to be deceived into imagining them Holy Pilgrims. I will make penance, I will stand and tell of my foolishness in every town along the river, I will —"

"You will not. You will speak to none of this. You will hold your tongue or lose it to the Quizitors. You will stay in Sackbane, and pray to the Shaper that he grant you the intelligence to find your buttocks with both hands. You will forget everything the strangers told you about Magog. Most importantly, as a matter of the utmost urgency, you will have the strangers conveyed *here*, to Two Mountains, by continuous relay. They will say *nothing* as they travel. I will issue instructions for fresh ponies along the route. No syntowers: too many, too public. Take the prisoners to Low Feoff: I will send an authorised official to meet you and escort them from there. How many days will the journey take?" A Two Mountains question, belittling Keli and his town: why keep track?

"Sab: thirteen days. But—"

"But I should have asked a commissary officiant, not a two-named priest."

"Sab." Keli was hurt; 'hep' was not quite a third name, but his cousin Gorgi Brundo was green with envy nonetheless. Humbly, he raised one pertinent issue that he had not yet mentioned.

"Sab: one of the females has a syntstone infestation. She will die within eighteen days if the tree is not burned."

"You know which tree?"

"No, Sab. Somewhere downriver of Sackbane."

"Ah. Well, if we decide that they should live, there may be sufficient time. If not, it is the Will of Magog. Ask the doctor for advice on how she should be fed during the journey, and see that it is followed. She may have that much. But if the woman does not survive —" the voice shifted sardonically into river dialect — "*Ni porbleem.*"

~~~

*Across two oceans from his sin, they had found him and brought him back. Bare moments seemed to pass from sitting at peace by the river to helpless paralysis, facing the dead eyes of the priests in the Great Temple of the Church of the Undivided Body. A wall of eyes, hundreds of eyes unseparated by faces, surrounding his dru*g-*limp body, glued into place. Looking into his soul.*

He had confessed, of course. But only to Abomination. Not to hearing the voices deep in the rocks that plotted the closure of those eyes.

Not yet.

But now the Quizitors were back with another cup of the drini *juice to keep him from merciful shock with half his small bones broken. Soon, they would start on the large ones.*

Disciplines whispered from the caverns gave him strength to cross the herbal barrier into waiting darkness. As unconsciousness enfolded him, he willed and knew that he would not wake again.

Next day, they threw his body to the dogs.

~~~

A Deacon's burden, DeLameter ruminated sourly, *can never be put down. Not even for a second. The sacrifices I make for my Church!* The battle to combat sin and defend against crime and heresy was unending. The complexities were horrendous. This gaggle of mad strangers had turned up, along with wild rumours that couldn't *quite* be discounted. And within a day, new reports of Wevorin incursions. Were these somehow related? What game do these interlopers play, with their casual talk of Magog? Whose puppets are they?

The bird song that filled his rooms failed, as often lately, to calm him. His predecessor had preferred human musicians, but human musicians heard and remembered human words: that was one reason he was now a predecessor. But today the birds did not help his thoughts.

DeLameter usually found his own counsel more congenial than the ill-considered drivel of others. But for once, advice was an attractive option. He summoned his Chaplain, the new appointee with the oddly subtle mind.

~~~

"Sadruddin. There are reports of Wevorin agents operating in the Crosswit area. They must have come by boat, probably along the coast from Duncurm."

Augustine Tambiah Sadruddin thought more likely that agents came by concealed wyzand, direct from the caverns of Wevory. There were always rumours of covert Wevorin activity; a few might sometimes even be accurate.

The young Chaplain was more worried about *unreported* incursions, and even more by the Wevorins' web of spysyntei. All knew that the cavern-dwellers had spun an extensive net. Less clear was what they intended with the secrets they so endlessly gathered. He said only: "That is disturbing, Sab. I am yours to command."

He watched the Deacon gesture vaguely northward. "We have many enemies, Sadruddin — Vain Vaimoksi, Samdali Abominators, Wevorin infidels. But two of those are no mystery. The Vain Vaimoksi are straightforward: criminals, who can be manipulated. From time to time they can even be negotiated with, and perform services to our advantage — for do not the scriptures tell that there is no sin in dirtying one's feet in a Holy cause? Abominators from Samdal, mired in sin as they are, cannot fail to encourage sin in Shaaluy as well, but our good citizens have their own boundless capabilities for sin in any case. And we have many agents of our own in Samdal. But we have ever been unable to infiltrate those heretics who hide themselves from Magog's good light in the Wevorin caverns. It is axiomatic that they plot the downfall of the Church. It is known they recruit by temptation to unspeakable sin. But all else is enigma. And, therefore, a great danger to everything we stand for."

The cavern-dwellers weren't really heretics, Sadruddin thought. Their religion had other roots. But he said only: "Heresy must be rooted out."

"Especially heretics bearing wyzands," the Deacon muttered. "I need not relate the damage a wyzand might do that is not under the watchful eye of the Church."

"Body-division would be merely one aspect, Sab." The Chaplain well knew that given an opening, many of the apparently most stalwart in the Church would flee the continent. He wasn't entirely sure that DeLameter understood that. Like any bigot, he remained gloriously unaware of his impact on everyone else. The Deacon was probably concerned that his faithful followers might be abducted.

"Sadruddin, you are wise in such matters. Advise me."

An unusual command. DeLameter must be at his wits' end. "Sab. Were the decision mine to make, which it is not, I would dispatch trusted operatives to Crosswit, disguised as locals, have them listen to tavern talk and market gossip, and instruct them to report their findings to a competent subordinate."

"Would you undertake that task yourself, Sadruddin?"

This, long experience taught, could be a trap. It would be unwise to openly welcome the task; a mind like the Deacon's might smell ulterior motives. "Sab, I would never refuse any task that you chose to set me. But in this instance there are others who are far more qualified than I."

"Perhaps. But the Chief Quizitor is unimaginative, and the High Guards are too militant to avoid alerting half the countryside. My own agents in the region have already reported what they know, and it is inadequate. They will be dealt with, but that solves nothing. Select suitable persons, Sadruddin; females and males. Deploy them where they can be most effective. Resolve this issue with the utmost urgency."

He turned away, showing Sadruddin he was dismissed. But then he spoke again. "If this nest of vipers has introduced wyzands to our continent, Sadruddin, I charge you root them out. But never reveal your knowledge. Report all to me, and I will order covert surveillance. Then shall we apprehend those who reject Holy doctrine by choice, not merely prevent forbidden acts by their dupes. The guilty will then be punished as the scriptures prescribe. And when the time is ripe, we will use our knowledge of their schemes to entrap our enemies from beyond the oceans."

Sadruddin suspected the time would remain sour. The cavern-dwellers were much too careful to fall for any such trick. "A masterstroke, Sab."

He bowed and left the room. Next, he set the required elements in motion. The rest of the afternoon he pondered what, exactly, Wevory was up to this time. And how it might impinge on his own plans.

~~~

"What in the name of the Mother *are* these things?" demanded Marco of the world at large. They had all been leashed, with ropes glued tight around their necks, then strapped into large, awkward frames, unable to move so much as an ankle.

"Portage frames," said Jane, who had caught more of the language around them. "I think they're just waiting for a couple more ponies. Then they'll be taking us to higher authority."

"What was our big mistake?" Jane asked, returning to the mystery.

"We burnt what the priest considered to be the wrong tree," said Felix, "but that wasn't blasphemous. Our crimes — whatever they may be — must be more serious to his particular religion. Subversion, perversion, inversion, heresy… Division of the Sacred Unity. Remember the circle motif? However, we haven't actually done anything that *we* would consider terrible. We're suspects because we're strangers."

Jane nodded. "We don't know basics of the local culture. That makes us suspect, like any 'foreigner'. As soon as we weren't Pilgrims — no doubt the only outsiders they ever meet, people that require special treatment for religious reasons — it was an immediate reaction." She flexed her legs to improve the circulation. "If they hadn't assumed we were Pilgrims, we'd probably have been arrested at first sight."

"Foreign equals pervert," said Sam. "But what's the perversion?"

"It need not be anything we would see as perverted," said Felix. "We're up against a xenophobic religious cult. It's the old exchange about someone from the next village: *'Ere comes a foreigner* ; *'Eave 'alf a brick at 'im*. But the social structure must encourage that kind of reaction. The locals are an underclass, widely dispersed in small villages, semi-isolated even from their neighbours. Remember what Keli said about the trees? His village had lost its prime food supply, and would have to resort to some kind of bad-tasting root. That suggests little trade between villages.

"Now, it might just be this region that's like that, the whole continent, or the planet. To reinforce it, the usual trick is to introduce some identity-boosting taboo. We're not criminals; we're perverts. We broke the taboo, or they think we did."

"What sort of taboo?" Marco asked. "Maybe we *did* break it. Who knows?"

"At a guess: sexual. There are puritanical undercurrents everywhere. 'Undivided body', 'subdivided filth'. Now, the only common pattern to human sexual taboos across the Concordat is that most societies have them. The main reason for taboos is to keep people in practice at sacrificing their choices to the group's, even when the group's are not good for the majority. Nearly everything is taboo *somewhere*, and most forms of behaviour are acceptable, if not mandatory, somewhere else."

"So what defence should we offer, if we get the chance?"

"We tell the truth," said Felix. That was a no-brainer. "We haven't the data to fake a local background. Any attempt would just get us into even more trouble. We're in their space, we learn their rules, we fit as best we can. Starfolk."

"The truth, yah. But slightly edited," amended Jane. "Lies of omission."

"So — we fell out of the sky?" asked Sam.

"Not quite in those terms, Sam. They still retain some of the 'Old Knowledge'. Garbled, no doubt — religions tend to interpret words in ever-changing ways — but they ought to have some concept of space travel, if only myths about the first colonists. They know *something* about *Magog*."

"Yah. It's a giant."

"If we do say we came from another world, why should they believe us?" asked Tinka. "They seem to think we're from another continent, full of perverts. That's probably as distant to them as another world would be."

"We have... knowledge they don't."

"But not about vunbugulas."

"We have wristcomps and stunbeams and your laser. Concentrates. High-tech."

"Too advanced, Sam. I strongly advise against even taking a 'comp out of skin camo mode. It will look like magic and get us burned at the stake for witchcraft."

"Thank you for that encouraging thought, Jane," said Tinka.

Suddenly the area before the temple was full of men. Their cages went on to matching frames on six ponies — *they must do this a lot*, she thought — and surrounded by guards. She made a last attempt to query Keli, and he spat in her mouth.

"Heretic not speak," he said. He rattled off quick instructions to the guards. One raised a club. "You speak, he break mouth. Silent, until Two Mountains."

~~~

After a few more days, Jane would have found trial for heresy or witchcraft a pleasant break from the monotonous pain of their travel. Anything to stop moving, to stop the sun darkening their faces all day long and the cold flowing in from the desert at night, and the endless motion.

The pony lurched again, and her sphincters loosened.

She was used to it.

~~~

Felix found himself tracking bird song, again, to keep his mind from the pain of his bonds. He could rarely spot the birds, but he learned new groups of sounds: fewer species (as expected) in the desert, and harsher sounds. Old Earth crows? No, those would need Old Earth cadavers, fed on Old Earth plants, rare in this wilderness. But some raucous species was quarrelling over something long torn apart. He shuddered.

The guards plodded on, rarely speaking except at the small towns where they handed the prisoners over to the next relay, and helped in the change of ponies. The frames would be laboriously opened, the prisoners unstrapped, sluiced down, walked on their leashes around the empty town square, put back and laboriously shut in again. *Why* those long protrusions? They served as handles when hoisting on and off the ponies, but they made endless problems on the trail.

Elzabet they left in her frame. Once a doctor in his loincloth came out to look at her, shook his head sadly, and departed.

From six days (twisting for a look at his wrist) after they left Sackbane, a superior officer had travelled along with them, with a contraption that let him sometimes sleep in the saddle, as a junior led his horse. He had taken a disgusted look at them: spray-on airsuits are not permanent, and the aer-O-web was tucked away with their stun-beams in a pack on one of the ponies, with its own guard. He had ordered them re-clothed in coarse linen tunics, and the airsuit remains rinsed and put in the pack. The tunics had been a relief, while they were clean, but that was days ago.

He spoke little more than the guards, and then mostly to something held in his hand; deferential, obviously reporting in to a superior. Marco must be going mad for a close look, on this signal-free planet, but Felix strained to catch the words.

"Ni porbleem," going smoothly. "Two Mountains, five days now... no speaking, prisoners... vunbugula, yes... maybe six days more alive, maybe nine, maybe few, ride not good... yes," he made a dismissive gesture, "five prisoners left anyway, vunbugula case no use questions... bring anyway, yes Sab. Moving out now, Sab."

At the next town two more frames like theirs were standing, lashed to the temple gate, with a woman in one, a man in the other. Joining the trek? No, the guards were ignoring them. On his leashed walk, Felix passed close, and saw that each one had their left arm and leg unbound, and draped loose... loose. Like a rope. What had happened to their long bones? Oh, Mother, even their fingers and toes...

Behind him, Tinka vomited at the sight. The guards took no notice. Only attempts to speak were punished.

~~~

Jane gave Elzabet, just ahead of her, an anxious look. In spite of the special foods that the guards had been giving her, Elza was so thin that they needed to put pads under her straps. The left side of her golden hair had mostly fallen out, and Jane wept inside to see, down the flank of the pony, that the rectal bleeding had started again.

She had never lived in one of those cultures where you are reminded and encouraged to be conscious of death, and to see it gradually swallowing her friend was more than Jane could bear. What were they supposed to have done to deserve *this*?

~~~

In the eastern uplands of the continent that *Valkyrie* named Beth, whose natives call it Shaaluy, in the area Vanduul, a succulent relative of the grape ferments in vats of silver-oak and distils into a fine liqueur, with an ice-blue tincture. Bottled in small quantities, it is sold at ruinous cost.

A glass of Vanduul liqueur sat solidly in the grip of the Deacon of Two Mountains, the Revered Tanling Denison Bancroft Geoffroy DeLameter. A second rested more lightly in the hand of his Chaplain.

"These strangers of yours. They interest me," said the Revered One. "How much have you learned?"

"Very little as yet, Sab. They speak no Kalingo, or refuse to. Of necessity since leaving Sackbane they have been amid guards who speak only that tongue and the river dialect. In Sackbane itself they spoke only briefly with the priest and the doctor, who have already made their reports. They understood little." He shrugged. "Of course."

"You think it would be wise to have those two poisoned?"

Sadruddin shivered, just a slight movement, as a bird trilled. "Revered One, it seems needless at this juncture, and might attract unwanted attention. The priest is a simpleton, and I have frightened him most thoroughly with the customary threats. The doctor wants no more than the health of his patients, and would be hard to replace."

DeLameter raised an eyebrow. "Medical services for three hundred yokels? You concern yourself with trifling details, Sadruddin. Return to the strangers. Summarise what you *do* know."

"They speak fluent Galaxic. They wore glossy green clothes, now rags, resembling nothing our agents have seen in the Lands of Abomination. Or elsewhere. They carry weapons, surprisingly few but uncannily like those described in the *Handbook*. And —" he paused — "they described Magog not as a humanoid giant, but as a great structure of metal."

"Are you suggesting," the Deacon said, his green eyes looking coldly into Sadruddin's, "that a faction of the Divided has gained access to the *Handbook*, and has found the key to some of its mysteries?"

Sadruddin swallowed, but did not take the easy way out by agreeing with the Deacon. "No, Sab. But they carried metal, marked with *this*." He placed a careful drawing in front of the Deacon, who peered at it.

Eventually he said, "Holy writing."

He was clearly struggling to decipher it, Sadruddin saw, and admittedly the script was antiquated. But surely he would at least —

"The final word is the most significant, Sab."

De Lameter's voice was stony. "Magog."

Sadruddin waited for the implications to sink in. "It might not be genuine, Sab. But if it is, it lends some credence to their stories. In which case, Sab, I cannot avoid suspecting that they do indeed come from among the stars. As they claim."

He waited for the usual reaction of the High Priesthood to such peasant literalism. But DeLameter held his tongue, and his eyes were unreadable. *Not the time to press this*, Sadruddin decided. He would withhold his best arguments until more evidence had accumulated. But *something* had to back such a wild assertion. "The — uh — the Prior of Horgun does not doubt that something physical fell from the sky, not long before these strangers appeared in our midst."

DeLameter nodded. He had seen the trail of fire with his own eyes. "Lights in the night sky may be uncommon, Sadruddin, but they are not unheard of. Was anything physical *found*?"

"No, Sab. Some flames fell into the Leucar Ocean, and the rest passed beyond the horizon. The Prior did see a few pieces falling apart, though the townsfolk speak only of a fiery omen on the night of Omolu."

The Deacon seemed unimpressed, but, thankfully, not insulted.

"One other thing occurs to me, Reverence." Sadruddin had kept his best evidence to last. "The males are clean-shaven."

"It is possible to shave, Sadruddin."

"You speak truth. However, your guards seized their knife, and gave none of them time or tools to shave. Their beards simply *do not grow*."

DeLameter sat upright in surprise. "Curious, I grant you." He stared into space as if seeking inspiration. "Some taint of the bloodline."

The Deacon's mind, made up, could always find innumerable arguments to support his decision. It was a strength in the ecclesiastical disputations that had smoothed his path to high office, but Sadruddin had always considered it a weakness in threat-assessment. However, what the Deacon lacked in analytical honesty he made up for with instinctive cunning.

"Very possibly, Reverence. If so, they must be closely related, despite many superficial differences in their appearance."

"From the same small tribe, no doubt. Abominators are often inbred."

In Sadruddin's view, body-dividers were usually anything but. They tended to spread their seed around with reckless abandon. Sensing that his Chaplain remained unconvinced, DeLameter tossed out another argument. "Abominators also make use of many herbs in conjunction with their wicked rites. Practitioners of witchcraft might well have discovered a poultice to prevent the growth of facial hair."

Sadruddin nodded, choosing his words with care. "It would of course have been applied selectively, Sab, for the prisoners' hair has grown noticeably since their capture. One has a silver streak, growing from the roots."

"So have I, Sadruddin: you may have noticed this happening as humans age."

"Not white or grey, Reverence. It shines like cheap metal, but burns with no ash."

"Strange... surely copper would be the choice of vanity. No, Sadruddin, odd hair growth does not convince of otherworldly origins. Nevertheless, your hypothesis is intriguing, despite being doubtfully supported and undoubtedly heretical. I am minded to overlook unorthodoxy on this occasion, because you may just have stumbled upon something significant. If there is any substance to your suggestion, then its implications... Perhaps I shall permit your starwalkers to live. If they have not been tainted by agents of Wevory."

"When are they expected?"

"Tomorrow, Sab. The ponies have just passed Santun."

"Then you will keep me closely informed of their arrival. And any new developments. Without delay."

8

Two Mountains

The secrets of success begin with four inviolable rules. Plants need water, light, appropriate habitat, and a supply of vital nutrients. If any of those is lacking, your plants will not prosper.
— *Trudi Jellicoe, Gardening Basics for Beginners*

Jane became dimly aware, through a fog of pain and raw nerves, that they had stopped. The officer was gone. The guards seemed in no hurry to transfer their frames to fresh ponies, or to unstrap their arms to let them eat and drink. Or to sluice the filth from the sores on their aching bodies in the river.

Where *was* the river?

The pony track had ended abruptly in a dry gulley. Bone dry, yet filled with luxuriantly orange vegetation: bushes, enormous bell-like fungi, creeping moss. A winding stair zigzagged from up a steepening slope to high, hidden places. Even in the reddening light, the mountain gleamed golden, with umber in the shadows. It should have been familiar and reassuring, but the colours were garish, the play of light unsettling. This world felt wrong, looked wrong, sounded wrong, smelled wrong.

The ponies would go no further, unless winched up on a rope. The guards took little three-legged stools off them, and sat around in the evening silence.

One urinated where he sat.

The shadows lengthened.

Jane, struggling not to pass out, watched Felix's unfocused eyes. He groaned again, and his groan seemed to come from her own pain.

Suddenly, the guards scrambled to their feet, and made those odd sideways bows. A short figure in a dark blue robe had come down with the officer, to the foot of the stairs. He ignored the guards and approached the prisoners.

"Augustine Tambiah Sadruddin. How far can you walk?" It was a voice accustomed to command. Seeing their hesitation, he added "You may speak to me. No guard will harm you now."

Hearing Standard shocked Jane's senses to her own state. Dizzy with nausea, she came round to find her eyes flowing silently with tears. She remembered he had asked a question.

"If we — we are allowed to flex our limbs and... regain some strength, we can walk. A short way. But not Elzabet —"

"I have been informed that one is ill." The man turned to the guards and gave orders in a matter-of-fact manner.

Two guards unstrapped Jane, applied a liquid that freed her leash, and lifted her to her feet. She swayed, gasped, and said "I think you need to sit me down." After a time, and some experimental stretching of muscles, she ventured "If you knew we would have to walk, you should have given us more freedom of movement for the last week." There was no response. Finally, she levered herself to her feet against the gulley wall, and found she could take a step. Lurching, she took another. Her eyes followed the stair to the dizzying heights above. "If you want us to climb that thing, we'll need more time."

"Time is short," said the robed man. "Guards will support you."

Two men had removed Jane's frame from the pony, and rebuilt it laboriously into a litter. On this, they placed Elzabet. Her skeletal legs stuck out at one end.

Tinka and Sam were on their feet now, holding each other upright. Marco and Felix were swaying between their guards. First Marco's knees buckled, then Felix's. They slumped to the ground.

The little priest gave more orders. Soon they were in painful motion up the stairs: Jane, Tinka, and Sam, raising one foot achingly above the other; then Elzabet, Marco, and Felix on litters held between pairs of guards. The robed man — some sort of priest, clearly higher than Keli — brought up the rear. Below, she saw two guards leading back the ponies.

Slowly Jane's muscles began to respond to the chance to move, and Tinka and Sam followed her quickening footsteps. But the new aches of weariness set in, and feet bled against the gritty stone. She was an automaton, placing one foot at a time, seeing nothing save the next step.

The path wound up the mountainside towards the sunset. Every hundred steps, they halted for respite, but not for long. Her lungs burned.

Darkness fell, and the climb went on. She lost count of the halts, but it seemed like midnight when one respite included water and food. When they started again, her legs had almost turned rigid, but they loosened into a kind of flowing agony.

With a jolt, Jane trod on a step that wasn't there, and staggered. A guard grabbed her. They had reached a wooden platform, not far below the peak. It was barely large enough to hold them all.

"Will you look at *that*!" said Sam. Jane flinched, but he was ignored. The new guards could hear what heretics said? Somehow, even more ominous.

Facing their mountainside, the sun was just rising over a jagged skyline. The river they had followed from the marsh was a sinuous golden track in the purple twilight, merging to the west tributaries in the foothills. Strange lights flew in the mountain's shadow, sometimes swooping as if for prey.

"You will come this way." The priest pointed to an opening in the rock. From behind them the sun shone into it, without reaching its further depths.

"I hope they don't intend to shut us up in it," muttered Tinka. "A dungeon at the top of a mountain is not my taste in fairy vids. I always flew carpets!"

There was no dungeon visible when the party trekked into the rock. At intervals along the wall shone flameless lamps, like the lamp in Keli's temple. The yellowish floor was hollowed, like the stairs, by innumerable feet. Not so much a cave as a tunnel, it sloped gradually up into the mountain, enlarged and neatened from a natural fissure. A continuation of their route, and obviously well-used.

As the opening shrank to a glowing dot behind them, they reached a large, heavy door, carved with the braided circle they'd first seen in the village temple. A guard pushed in a crude but solid key and heaved the door open. Beyond it the tunnel walls were hidden beneath a thick spongy outgrowth, like a large fungus that formed a broad ring. Across the floor and roof, Jane saw with surprise, as well as up the walls. *Keep thinking.* "I'd have expected this thing to have worn away at foot level. It seems to mark the junction between two different types of rock, so perhaps cracks between the strata feed it water?"

"We could do with Elza's geological smarts to—" Marco began in a faint voice; then trailed off with a sob.

"Uh, we... Anyway, however it got its nutrients, it looks totally out of place."

The door shut with a thud behind them, and a guard locked it. The priest stepped carefully over the rubbery growth without touching it, and motioned the prisoners on. "Do not touch the plant," he said, as Tinka's foot approached it. "Safe it is not thus to act."

"Better do as he says," said Sam. "It could be poison to touch."

"Or sacred," said Jane. "They seem keen on plants."

"After what happened to Elza, I think we should just do what we're told," said Marco, sounding a little stronger. "We can find out *why* later." The guards threaded his litter through the fungus-like ring, taking care to avoid contact.

Beyond the ring they passed another heavy door, in the same manner. The tunnel became narrower and steeper now, but continued straight ahead. After a short walk they emerged, blinking, to face the sun.

They stood near the base of a tremendous chasm, that split the mountain. A great ridge ran between them and the sunset, but around to their left the now-crimson light shone into a cleft with sides decorated by a complex system of walkways, arches, pagodas, balconies, towers, and buildings of all kinds, rising up and up until the eye was lost in contradictions of perspective.

A city.

Of course, thought Jane. *Two Mountains. Where the doctor was trained.* But she was too exhausted to speak.

Marco, who had been carried up the mountain stairway, and who might have paused in the jaws of death to consider the engineering of the teeth, had more breath.

"Those buildings?" he asked no one in particular.

"Sure, buildings," Sam replied, with an effort. "So?"

"These folks really understand stone. And those cantilevered walkways... So why don't they do the obvious?"

"What obvious?"

"How do they cross the chasm? Anybody see any bridges up there?"

Nobody could, or seemed interested.

They were taken up a short, curved stair, through a crumbling arch, and across cobblestones towards a tall square building, with a turret. A few curious faces peered up from within small, deep openings in the walls; a few children scurried away into side-passages. Inside the building they came to a doorway with an amorphous outline.

"Another fungus?" whispered Sam.

The priest ushered them through; the guards lowered the litters and stood up with sighs and grunts. Elzabet gave a sudden groan, and Marco squatted beside her, muttering words of comfort. A rattling sound came from the door, and they were alone.

~~~

"Revered One, I have taken the strangers to the Shadress."

"What have you learned?" The Deacon scratched behind the ears of a large dog at his feet.

"They are currently beyond useful interrogation, Sab, until they have recovered from their pony-trek. But I have brought the objects they carried." The two guards accompanying him lowered their packs to the table and departed the room, leaving Sadruddin alone with DeLameter and the dog. "All their other possessions are here."

It was an extraordinary collection.

Maps on inferior paper — but tough — of the *whole world*, including the ocean depths. Cities marked but unnamed; elaborate colour, to no clear aesthetic scheme; innumerable tiny annotations in a brutal but perfectly regular script, spelling impossible words. What was PTRLM RESVS: NO XPLOITN, for example?

A chart of the night sky, with *numbers* against half the stars.

Bars of some sour chewy substance, in quantity. Food?

Three tents in an unwoven fabric, like — the skin of a deep-ocean fish? If so, a well protected fish. Fragmented clothes in similar fabric, shaped without seams.

Assorted fine cord, fish hooks, and other survival gear. A pack of what had to be medical supplies, some outlandish.

A necklace with a ruby-coloured pendant and a gold chain.

Six impossibly *Handbook* stunbeams.

A far more primitive weapon: a knife of unfamiliar design.

The inexplicable disc bearing the sacred name of Magog.

And a blobby object with a brown organic gleam. A plant?

The stunbeams worked: five Sackbane villagers would have sworn to it, but the Deacon tried one out on his dog, and called its handler for a second test. Then he pointed it at the wall, behind which silence always revealed scritchings: it had no effect. They brought other animals: the beams stunned only the white-boned ones. Why would the strangers choose to be defenceless against every creature that ran wild on Qish? If they were *unfamiliar* with such creatures... the implications were dangerous.

And, what was the blob? At DeLameter's order, Sadruddin pointed what seemed to be the fruiting end at the wall, and squeezed.

He nearly dropped it.

The aer-O-web was a sophisticated model, capable of generating most Starfolk fashions around a body. Pointed at a wall, it responded with tapestry. Unprogrammed, its default option was to reproduce the tapestry design it had most recently executed. Fortunately, after Marco had covered the wall of *Valkyrie*'s parlour with All Change Night at the main Silicon City groping-pool, Sam had been exploring an astronomical subject. The instrument kicked and twitched in the Chaplain's hands for several minutes. When it fell silent, so did he.

The Deacon's wall showed, in that furry illusion of depth that some claim is more convincing — because less literal — than a hologram, the breakup of a moon. Strand by strand the aer-O-web had built up the glow of its still-molten core visible through gigantic cracks, the cloudy planet *above* the viewer, the purple flaring sun to the left, and the sharp, ineffably distant points of light that are the stars. Behind these, the black was absolute.

The image blazed, incomprehensible.

"This is not what we are told," DeLameter finally said, "of what is beyond the sky. Where this heretical plant grew, I dare not contemplate."

"It does not resemble the Hell of Division, though, Sab."

"It is the vision of a lunatic," declared the Deacon. "Or of an inspired mind. Either can be very dangerous... or useful... if properly controlled."

With an effort, Sadruddin brought them back to the mundane realm. "Revered One: if, contrary to what they claim, we find that the strangers *are* from this world —"

"Yes?"

"— then they can only be from the Caverns of Wevory, where the Church's agents do not penetrate. Nowhere else could such strangeness grow to fruit unknown."

The penetrating observation, typical of this young man, meshed with the Deacon's own suspicions. "You speak truth, Sadruddin. That Nest of Abomination is beyond our control, or even covert dealing. Which means that the strangers must die."

DeLameter made a gesture of dismissal, but caught an irresolute look from his Chaplain. "Unless, of course, your fantasy about the stars is true. If these are angels, they must be properly entertained. But the nonsense must be *proved*, Sadruddin, *to me.*

"You may go."

~~~

The Starfolk, exhausted and crippled, had done no more than splash themselves in the stone basin, tend to Elzabet as best they could, and stretch out on the wide moss-filled sleeping-pads they had found in the half-darkness. They were asleep within minutes.

Tinka looped in endless nightmares of the two unknowns in the cage frames. Sometimes their eyes met hers, begging for a mercy she could not give. Sometimes their left arms writhed toward her neck, like tentacles tasting for the gummed rope that had throttled her for two weeks.

She woke with the dawn light. To suppress panic, she tried to take stock.

Think.

The room was like a large, irregular cave — trash it, it *was,* a natural cave. But... hadn't they come to a masonry building, last night?

A hole in the floor, leading to a gurgling sewage tank. Cooking smells came past a wooden flap two hand-spans across. Both were bordered by the ever-present fungus. *Sacred?* Jane's suggestion came to mind. *Surely there can't be anything holy about a prison shittery?* Mould grew down the walls, where yellowish water trickled. She went over and wrapped Elza more warmly in her pad.

And, there was the door they had come in by.

Open.

She went up to it, and looked down the corridor.

No guards.

In the gloom they had taken guards, or bars, or *something* for granted. But on closer examination, it *couldn't* shut. It was yet another hole in the wall, rimmed with fungus.

"Curiouser and curiouser!"

She jumped. "Marco, you idiot, don't creep up unannounced like that!"

"Sorry. It puzzled me, too. I wonder what's out there?" He shook off her restraining hand, ducked down to the level of the door, and stepped forward.

Tinka managed to catch him as he fell.

"Shaven Lily! What *hit* me?" He put out a cautious finger and prodded the empty space of the door. Something blocked the exit, like a totally slick surface of hard rubber. Invisible rubber.

"Trash it, I said back on *Valkyrie* that these people must have some tricky technology." He rubbed his frizzy head. "But *force-fields?* Everything looked primitive along the river. This caps everything. I wonder if someone can get me into the local engineering school?"

"What are you talking about?" Jane and Sam had joined them, without waking Felix.

"What am I talking about? I'm talking about the beta-calculus! For nineteen hundred years this trick's been possible, in principle, but no one ever has. The closest is the way you can push momentum through a Da Silva drive unit, but that effect is light-minutes across. Here, they've tuned it to millimetres!" He pulled out the metal rod that replaced buttons on his local tunic, pushed it toward the corridor, and leaned. Gradually it penetrated. The force needed gradually increased, too. Then, at about the peak of its strength, it stabilised.

"I'd say the force field is about two centimetres thick," said Marco in wonderment. "Ah, the tip's through." He went on pushing. When the rod was about half embedded in the force field, his hand slipped. The rod twisted in his grip and hurtled back out of the doorway, spinning end over end to sink itself in Elzabet's sleeping-pad, next to her ear. She stirred and moaned. Marco hurried over and cradled her head in his arms, cursing himself for his clumsiness, and muttering darkly about engineering genius in the boondocks.

With a clatter, the flap opened. A pale water-wrinkled hand deposited five plates of boiled fish, and a bowl of the broth the guards had been giving Elzabet. A night's motionless sleep had restored their appetites, and they were ravenous.

As they rinsed the lugubrious taste from their mouths with the mineral-flavoured water that dribbled into the basin, Tinka's eyes caught a flicker of movement at the door. Before she could focus, something seemed to be hurled upwards; there was a slamming sound; then silence.

Outside stood the priest, Sadruddin, with a new squad. A head taller than him, they wore hard dark leather and closed steel helmets.

"Your eyes must be covered to take the way to the apartments of the Revered One, who will either send you to the Quizitors or permit you to live unbroken. Pray it is the latter." The guards applied neat, professional blindfolds to the five at the basin. Leaving Elzabet alone on her pallet, the prisoners were herded out.

~~~

Stairs again, Felix thought, stubbing his toe for the fourth time. They'd climbed for a day, slept in a rough stone building that was little more than a big room strewn with straw pallets, and resumed their endless climbing. His knees ached, his legs kept cramping.

Why couldn't people with force-screens invent the elevator?

Somewhere behind, Marco muttered something to himself, ending in an anguished yell. He had stubbed his toe on the same unexpected step.

Perversely comforted, Felix went on climbing in his blindfolded darkness. Slow antiphonal singing faded under by the sound of quarrelling children, replaced in turn by the THUMP-*thump* and rattle of some kind of steady work. He smelled baking bread, disinfectant, acrid spices, freshly cut wood... Pushed by his guard, he continued up ramps, over courtyards, and up, endlessly, these irregular stairs.

Their eyes were uncovered in an empty room, panelled with silky green stone. Herded towards a low platform of slaty rock along the wall, they trudged over to squat comfortably beside it. The guards stood stiffly to attention along the opposite side of the room, while the priest left through a high doorway.

They waited.

From the door came the tweets and trills of birds. *Marsh birds, up here?* thought Felix, and as he listened became sure that the birds were not in cages. And these were afternoon songs. Somehow this disturbed him as much as the faceless helmets of the guards.

Nearly an hour passed before the priest beckoned them in.

~~~

DeLameter watched the strangers file into his receiving room, as the Deacon's Guards led them to the low window, where they stood in a straggled row. *A seven hundred* vij *drop always has a salutary effect on a prisoner's morale,* he thought, seeing them glance out and down. He waited. When they were thoroughly still, he said, "I am The Revered Tanling Denison Bancroft Geoffroy DeLameter, Deacon of the Church of the Undivided Body. Who are you?"

Jane began cautiously: "I am Jane Bytinsky, xenologist."

Three names? This woman surely rated higher, from her bearing.

"We are not of your world," Jane continued.

And that was the point! Perhaps these people could unravel the mysteries of Old Knowledge in the *Handbook*. But perhaps, equally, Sadruddin — who sometimes suffered from a regrettable sentimentality — had coached them in the wise thing to say. The Deacon could trust no one, should trust no one.

Did trust no one.

Time to throw them off their guard. "Then you claim to be spiritual beings?" His gaze wandered over their uncovered feet and legs. "For angels or demons, you bruise rather easily."

"No, Revered One." Felix had picked up the honorific from Sadruddin's casual use of it, but it increased the Deacon's impression of rehearsal. Or, come to think of it, Shaaluin knowledge, which these people denied possessing. "By 'world', we mean this place. Your planet. We come, as your ancestors did, from the stars. Around most stars circle worlds like yours. From one of those do we come."

The very phrasing of the *Handbook*. "Ah. You flapped your long arms and descended gracefully through the sky like angels?"

"Revered One, no. We were carried to this world in a giant machine. As your ancestors were, by *Magog*."

"Yes, that delusion has been conveyed to me." The Deacon shuffled through the papers on his desk. "You told the priest of Sackbane that you had seen a vision of Magog. You really expect me to believe that you are Pilgrims? That you witnessed a sight reserved for Saints alone?"

"We never claimed to be Pilgrims," said Sam. "Or Saints. Your people assumed that, and never asked us. What we saw was no vision. It was an obsolete Colony Vessel, full of mud."

Blasphemy! To the inner priesthood Magog was not the gigantic peasant god of thunder, but this was not the reverent way that the *Handbook* spoke of the great metal chalice that had carried its authors to this planet. DeLameter held back his anger, to provoke further lies. "Your own vehicle was a chariot of fire, I suppose?" Let them claim the omen of the Night of Omolu for themselves, and he would know Sadruddin had been advising them.

"No, a ship of metal like *Magog*, but smaller."

"I see. And when will you show me this ship?" Silence. "I can send you rapidly to any destination you specify." If this was not some fantasy designed to discredit the Diaconate of the Church of the Undivided Body — and if their landfall was not in the reach of Wevory. That started a whole, nasty new train of thought. Maybe they were both from the stars *and* agents of Abomination. The stars themselves were clean, but these folk were perhaps newly Fallen. And still not answering a simple question. "Where is your ship?"

"Broken, Revered One," said Jane, waving Sam *quiet!* "It broke in the sky and we had to descend in a capsule. It sank in the swamp."

"Capsule?"

"A small ship without power. A pod." She pointed at the ripening fruit on the vine that decorated one wall, which had much the same blunt-ended streamlined shape. "Rather like one of those, but big enough for people to enter, Revered One."

It cannot be Sadruddin who has suggested they tell lies of such stupidity. "Of what," he asked icily, "do you claim your bones are made?"

"Why... the same substance as anyone's, Revered One."

"And you descended from the sky by a synte? Yet you stand before me now with no marks, save those of a luxurious journey on my Church's ponies?" He felt that little burst of red darkness at the back of his head that always meant divine, victorious anger. "You will not be in such an unbroken state tomorrow night! In Shaaluy we do not Divide the Body even by such minor practices as cutting off heads, but we shall break every bone in your insolent bodies, beginning with your toes and fingertips and ending with your blasphemous skulls. Thus will the bone-hammers remake your words as truth, and their consequences according to the laws of Magog and Nature be seen by all men!" *How could even a lunatic from Wevory think that such a fall could ever be softened? Bones would not break: they would crumble! Well, truth will out!*

He spoke rapidly in Kalingo to the guards, who dragged them out.

~~~

The Starfolk stared back towards the Deacon, then at each other. What had they said to merit such insulted anger? He was calm when they spoke of other worlds, or of people living there. It was as though they had claimed to breathe rock.

Before they were blindfolded again, Marco caught a glimpse through the anteroom window. That building, with the curling tower... From that lunatic's office, surely it had been on the *other* side of the chasm?

9

Sacred Growth

> Newton's laws of motion and gravity did not provide an immediate understanding of solar system dynamics. Mathematicians grappled with a whole new range of questions: what do the laws imply? They struggled with the orbital dynamics of a three-body system for centuries, and replaced solving the equations by finding the shape of the solutions.
> The like is true of Muthuramalingam Anpalagan's equations for the karm-abhumi field, but the difficulties are orders of magnitude greater. At present, solutions are found only through simulation, and then only for infinitesimal mass-densities. If any single unsolved mathematical problem is preventing the advance of the human race, it is the solution of the beta-calculus for mass-densities comparable to those on a planetary surface.
> —János Schuburt, *The Great Mathematical Problems*

When she pulled off her blindfold, Tinka was alone, and thinking *bone-hammers*. Those arms and legs reduced to limp tentacles... she vomited again.

Think.

She looked at her own forearm. *Do they break it first in the middle, then break the halves, and then the pieces, and then the pieces,...? Or do they start at the wrist and work upward, keeping a big piece for clamping, as long as they can?*

No.

Think what is here.

This cave was tiny. One side was blocked by a decaying wall of rough stone; the entry she had been forced to crawl in by was at its base, the only source of light. Blocked, by the same invisible force as the other.

There was no food, and no water. A squat spot gave out the same sounds and vapours as in the larger dungeon. Either they have a cleanliness fetish, she thought, which wasn't in evidence on our trip, or they don't waste prison fertiliser. She wondered whether they made efficient use of prisoners' corpses, and trembled.

When in doubt, think. There was no rational escape from her cell, and no getting out of the city or helping the others even if she did. But when rationality points you straight at a pointless, nasty death... keep thinking.

How?

As her throat grew drier, she thought about the door. She would be no worse off outside it. Maybe she could reach a cliff and die quickly.

The trace of sunlight outside moved slowly round and disappeared. As the light dimmed, she had an idea. Sucking her thumb to make moisture flow, she considered it.

She didn't know how force-fields worked. But as a hotshot pilot, she *did* know a lot about field-effect equipment. All such gadgets have one factor in common. You can *always* overload them.

How do you overload a force that pushes?

You give it too much to push on.

Pity she couldn't bring up an immovable object. But then, it wouldn't be, would it? She giggled. One of the stones at the top of the wall, twice her height, looked loose. She climbed up — lucky the walls were so rough — and wiggled it. Right! A good heavy one. And this triangular one came free at a touch!

Maybe she could tunnel right out, directly? She banged the wall with her free stone. No: it sounds metres thick. And the deeper mortar is *solid*. Back to the first idea.

She climbed down and put her stone wedge near the door, sloped down towards it. Up again, perched with one foot in a crevice, one on a protruding stone. Wobble the big rock, like a loose tooth when she was little. The day nurse, where she went when Mummy was working, kept trying to stop her. Beast! He looked like DeLameter.

Surely it was looser. The scraping noise the set her real teeth on edge... do they want to break her teeth as well as her bones? *All* her bones — *of course* they'd go for the teeth. Why hold back? Push, pull, up, sideways — *now* it was coming free!

Suddenly the rock began to slide out, and she jumped down to squat at the rear of the cell. It slipped further, gathered speed, then fell the rest of the way to hit her wedge and bounce into the doorway. It split as it struck the mysterious force field, and almost stopped. Both parts seemed to hesitate, but one went through. The small chunk crashed back, against the rock wall behind her, but the big chunk hit the fungoid rim of the doorway, at its lowest point.

The scene outside trembled, and suddenly began to rise. As though from an elevator, she saw the stone floor rise and another corridor appear, and a new floor came up towards her. But there was no smooth, automated stop.

As the lower floor reached the level where she was squatting, her big rock fragment crushed against the threshold. For a moment the scene she was watching writhed like a subrealist holodrama, then vanished.

In the darkness, she put out her hand to the force-screen and felt only rock. She moved both hands over the wall, pulling away tattered remnants of the fungus.

Nothing but rock. And a little patch of damp earth where the doorway had been. Nothing told her searching fingers that there had ever been anything there but a roughly dressed stone wall. Where she *thought* the door had been, a long horizontal block stretched half the width of the cell.

When in doubt, find new data. She attacked more stones, but after one small rock loosened she broke only her fingernails. Stepping back exhausted, she collapsed, sobbing.

The air began to thicken. How many hours did it take to breathe — how many — litres of oxygen? She should know. Her fingers activated the touchpads on her wrist, and the 'comp monitored oxygen and dioxide levels in both air and blood, but she could not take in the flickering figures on the screen. Her wrists held her forearms, puzzled at their smooth, strong straightness.

Finally the air became so foul that she pressed her nose to the sanitary hole. There is little oxygen in activated sewage, but a lot of other gases. Slowly, inexorably, she lost consciousness.

~~~

"A cavern-dweller from Wevory might have less fear of suffocation than of the bone-hammers," DeLameter observed. "She chose it as an easy death."

As the Chaplain had noticed many times, the Deacon latched on to evidence that he could fit to his beliefs, ignoring alternative interpretations. It was a weakness to exploit when the time was ripe. "You speak truth, Revered One. I do, however, wonder why she went to such extraordinary lengths to damage the outer part of the entrance, when her bare fingers could as easily destroy it from inside."

"Agents of Abomination are not rational. All either could achieve was to trap herself between stone walls. Perhaps, if your workmen are in time, we can discover her true motives." DeLameter looked up from Tinka's wreckage to rocks being pulled from a cell door at the far end of the corridor. All at once this ended, and a slim brown shape was passed into the morning sunlight.

A doctor knelt down and examined her. "She lives, Sab, though not by much. She will soon open her eyes."

When she did, the jowly face of DeLameter was centimetres from her nose.

"Go 'way. You're a bad dream."

Sadruddin knelt by her head and shook her shoulder. When she unwillingly looked up again, he said: "One question, woman, then you may sleep. Why did you try to drive that rock out of your cell?"

"What rock? It's all so fuzzy... Oh. Yes. *That* rock. I... I wanted to overload the force that was holding me inside."

Sadruddin stared down at her, and his face moved in a strange way. Finally it seemed to split, and he began to gurgle; then he dissolved in helpless mirth. A moment later, the Revered Tanling Denison Bancroft Geoffroy DeLameter was also shaking in the kind of laughter that hurts muscles around the ribs.

The workmen, who did not speak Standard, and the woman who had said something impossibly funny in it, looked on in bafflement at the near-hysterical dignitaries of the Church.

~~~

It was next evening before anyone disturbed the others, alone in their cells except for their evil dreams. Deliberate pain, deliberate death, filled their minds. It is hard to face death bravely when there is no cause to die for, no cause even for the killing, that they could understand. No reason, and no way out.

When the guards finally came to gather them, one by one, Marco assumed they were being taken for execution. Between despair and caution, nobody spoke.

There was no sign of Elzbet. He hoped that he would see her once before they died. He hoped that her weakness would make her death mercifully fast. He hoped... no, there was no hoping left to do.

But the guards treated them almost gently, and this time they were not blindfold when a guard brought them before the Deacon. DeLameter dismissed the leather-clad figure with a wave of one hand. Waving his adopted stunbeam like a brand new dolly that says 'dada', he directed them along a passage to a balcony. There he left them.

Stretched calmly on a richly-draped couch, looking down over the carved marble railing at the vertical city beyond, was a familiar figure.

"Tinka! How — what —"

Unlike them, she was freshly bathed, and her hair had been trimmed in an unfamiliar style.

She smiled maliciously. "I'll explain all, Sam. She turned to Jane. "Do you remember telling me that they'd believe we were from the stars because of all our fancy knowledge and equipment?"

"Yah. And you said they'd think it was witchcraft. And now you're going to say 'I told you so'."

"They forsaken near *did* decide the aer-O-web was witchcraft, I gather. But I wasn't referring to that. I was referring to our fancy knowledge.

"It wasn't knowledge that saved us, Jane. It was pure one-hundred-carat ignorance."

Marco seized on the two pertinent words. "Saved us?"

"For the moment, at least, the bone-hammers are off the agenda." She stroked her forearms in luxurious wonder, and stretched them out in front of her eyes.

"Oh, thank the Mother of Galaxies!" said Sam, sagging downward against the couch.

"I'm not actually very maternal," said Tinka.

"Strabyen, Sabi, thank *you*, oh Tinka, thank you," Marco burbled, "but what about Elza? Where is she?"

The smile lost its malice. "She's in the infirmary being given the best available care, and in two days she'll be cured."

Marco had tried to face the fact that Elza was about to die. Now, when hope finally appeared, he didn't believe it, so he tried to pretend he did.

"That's a relief." He could stand up straight, if he tried. He knew he could. "Uh — what *is* the cure?"

"You won't believe me."

No, I probably won't. Just more madness. "Try me."

"Just like the doctor ordered. Burn the tree."

He stared at her. "Don't be stupid, Tinka, we tried that."

"We did not. It's just like the doc said: only the original tree will do."

"DeLameter is arranging transport. Some of us will go and point to it. Then we'll set it ablaze, nice and hot, and reduce it to a heap of smoking ashes. As fast as possible."

Marco still couldn't believe that simple answer, even though he desperately wanted to. *Dah, find the exact selfsame tree, don't ask why.* But— "Tinka, even if that really is the way to save Elza's life, it's *too late*! She swallowed the stone right at the start of the trip, on the edge of the marsh! It took *weeks* for us to get here! Even with ponies, there's no way—"

Tinka interrupted with a gesture. "There's — uh — a short cut."

"You now really believe in *magic*?" Felix protested, coming out of his own daze. For him it seemed unbroken fingers that held his mind: he kept stroking Jane's. "Magic works on *minds*. It's a mental process. How can we trust —"

Tinka laughed. "We all thought that. But on Squill III, magic isn't symbolic, Felix. And it doesn't call on deities, and it doesn't depend on ritual. It just works."

"Irenotincala Laurel," asked Jane in a quiet voice that sounded more like a scream than Marco could have imagined, "have you taken *total* leave of your senses?"

Tinka leaned back, and ran a hand through her freshly washed hair. "My senses have caught up with me and slotted neatly into place. We might have got there much sooner if we'd realised that the locals knew their stuff, asked better questions, and believed the answers."

"Oh, Tinka! What have they done to you?" Marco yelped. "Did you have to inhale?" But she shook her head, chuckled, and stared straight back at him.

"What questions are better?" Sam blurted, in obvious unbelief, but looking up hopefully. She ran a finger over his temple, along the old leopard scar, as if touching it for the first time. Even she seemed awed by simply being alive.

"Well, Sam love: while we're waiting for Sadruddin to set up the utterboat, I'll reveal all. I've always wanted to do one of those final-explanation Great Detective acts, like Shirley Combs on the holvix." Marco, who had a passion for all things Old Earth in the original, muttered under his breath but did not interrupt. Tinka crouched comfortably against the rail, licked her lips, and began.

"The elementary factor here, with which everything else on the planet is compounded, is the plants." She wriggled her toes. "These are no ordinary plants. Pop into one, and you pop out somewhere else."

"Pardon?"

"People: some plants on this planet act as natural matter-transmitters."

There was a stunned silence.

"Mother of Galaxies, she *has* gone nuts," said Marco.

"Never saner. I'll prove it." Tinka reached behind her to the vine growing on the wall. Its fruit had a curious dumbbell shape, with a kind of seam round its waist. She broke off half a ripe one at the seam, leaving the rest on the stem. "Marco," she offered, "Just pop your finger in here. Go on, it won't bite."

Tentatively, expecting something sticky and mushy, Marco poked in an exploratory finger. It went in without resistance. In fact, he realised with a jolt, it went in a lot deeper than the fruit was long.

"Over there." Tinka was staring at the vine. Marco followed her gaze, to see the tip of his finger poking out from the other half of the fruit. He pushed his finger in and out. On the vine, the disembodied finger went out and in.

"Oh my sainted giddy aunt Matilda. Mother of Galaxies, Shaven Lily. Matter-transmission by fruit and vegetables, pick-your-own tech." He walked up to the vine. "Wow! You can see right through from one piece to the other! What *are* these things?"

"A word to the wise, Marco: get your finger out before the fruit starts to die. It'll be a few hours yet, but if you leave your digit poking through when the fruit begins to shrivel, it'll be amputated when the connection collapses."

Marco quickly removed his finger and looked at it with suspicion.

Tinka laughed. "I'm teasing you. Actually, there's no danger with *small* ones. A small-bore wormhole collapses slowly, and pushes out anything trapped. But wider ones store enough energy to tear apart bone. One big enough to take your head is also big enough to chop it off. Fast. And fresh, live ones are very easily damaged, which is why you see people being careful when stepping through one. Desiccated or preserved plants are tougher, and still act as wormholes if they're not otherwise damaged."

After a few more wiggles Marco pulled the fruit off his finger and held it in his upturned palm. "How do you know all this?"

"It's a long story. Uh… pardon me for being blunt, but you could all do with a shower. And a haircut, too? Thought so. I'll call the maids, they'll take you off, freshen you up, and bring you back here." She turned to a small opening in the wall and spoke a few words into it.

~~~

As the maids returned to their duties, Tinka cast her eyes over her cleaned-up companions. They almost looked human.

It was impossible to distract Marco. "Come on, Tinka. Give."

Tinka looked sheepish. "I found out some of it by accident, and nearly got myself killed. Nah, not by these people: all on my lonesome. They rescued me, just in the nick of time, by dismantling my cell. I got the rest from Sadruddin — that's DeLameter's errand-boy, the little priest guy who met us on the stairs. Some sort of factotum, vizier, something like that. Orders people around as if he'd been born to it, but I'd bet a month's pay it's mostly an act. Actually, he's rather sweet… but I think —" she lowered her voice " — that the Big Boss is a grape or two short of a bunch.

"Which brings me back to the plant-life. One phylum of this planet's indigenous flora reproduces by budding. When the bud separates from mama, it retains contact through a wormhole. It maintains a transspatial connection, even though the pieces physically separate."

"Whoah there, wait, wait, wait!" Marco was almost dancing with frustration. "Wormholes are unstable unless there's enough exotic matter to hold them open. And there's not enough exotic matter outside stellar cores."

"Marco, these things *work*. You've just seen one doing it, dah? The wormhole — if that's what it is, I don't know — is stable until the plant dies, no matter how far apart the ends are. So either the plant provides exotic matter, or these are a different kind of wormhole, or the theory's wrong. Live with it.

"You get the effect by pulling ripe ones apart at the seams, like I just did, but you can't keep the pieces alive for long. When they bud naturally, though, any half-competent gardener can keep them growing for years."

Marco stroked his chin. "Doesn't sound like a relativistic wormhole. More like some kind of quantum tunnelling effect, how a Da Silva operates."

"If you say so. But whatever the physics, you don't follow *that* wormhole. You can't, it's full of plant. What makes the matter-transmitter is the math. The plant's tunnel through space ends at two plane discs, on two fruit bits. Each disc is two-sided, front and back, giving *four* sides to play with. The two back sides keep the plant joined, but those are still part of it, hidden from view. Now comes the clever bit. By symmetry, the two front sides are *also* connected to each other. So what you see is — well, a 'gate', linking one region of the outside to the other, and that's the obvious wormhole. The locals call it a synte."

"'*Syntelic parasite*,'" Felix muttered. "'*Feed by strint*.' Just as the doc was telling us. Not magic at all, just sufficiently advanced botany. What a fool —"

"We all made the mistake, Felix. Not your fault. Anyway, the link has huge evolutionary value for the plant, which can spread to places with resources that mama doesn't have. Like water or copper ions or —"

"Elza's gut!"

"Well done, Marco. Yah, the stone that she swallowed was synted to the tree. So now do you all see why we have to burn the *original* tree?"

"The parasite is the tree, not the stone. It has the resources to root itself fast, overcome defences. The stone is just the connecting channel."

"Absolutely. Now, once we recognise the possibility of syntei — yah, people, the plural — a lot of other puzzles make sense. Like those land-piranhas, which seemed to appear from nowhere. Actually, they came through that bush on the bank. They live round the mother-tree and watch for prey through her bushes. She gets their droppings as fertiliser in exchange. Reproduction, parasitism, symbiosis... it's a whole new ecological tactic. And on this world, it's in *everything*.

"I *bet* these natural wormholes or whatever explain the weird geography we saw from orbit," said Elza. "A rainforest in the wrong place — it probably gets its water through syntei."

"Very likely. And *Magog* was full of upriver water. Those roots inside it were hosepipes from outside.

"But what syntei do naturally is nothing to what the colonists do with them... and with breeding new varieties. Wireless without solitronics! Think about the global galactic grid... But that's not the most important use."

"Transport," said Felix.

"Right. No roads, no bridges. Hardly any coastal towns, no ports."

"They must have built ports and ocean-going ships early on, to distribute syntelic connections to other continents and islands," Jane pointed out. "But once even a skeletal synte network was established, ships were no longer economic, and became obsolete. Except maybe a few specialist uses."

A lot of things were starting to make sense. "So that tunnel at the top of the long staircase —"

"A big synte connected Golden Mountain to Two Mountains," said Tinka. "I think they put it in a tunnel, with those doors, to protect it and make it easy to defend."

"We thought it was a sacred fungus," said Jane. "We underestimated these people big time. They've turned this whole world into a vast maze. A living labyrinth. Distance, physical barriers... They're not obstacles any more."

They fell silent as the enormity of this sank in.

Tinka broke the silence. "If we'd thought a bit more coherently, we'd have wondered why we didn't see any of this —" she waved at the opposite mountain "— *before* we went through."

"We weren't really thinking at all at that point," said Marco. "We were exhausted, terrified, and in pain. We were worried sick about Elza, and wondering if every minute would be our last. Vegetable matter-transmitters wouldn't exactly have sprung to mind, even if we *had* been able to think straight."

"I *saw* that the sun had turned round," said Sam. "I thought *we* had."

"And that's another application, isn't it," said Marco. "Sunlight. The light in the roof of Keli's temple. The lights in the tunnel. They were synted from some place where it was daytime."

"But the effort of transporting syntei —" Jane began.

"What effort? Just shove 'em through an existing synte," said Sam. "There's some investment of time and effort to get a transport network up and running, but after that it's plain sailing." It was hard to take in all the implications at once.

"Not just human time," said Tinka. "You can only shove a *smaller* one through an existing synte, so the big ones — wyzands — go through immature and grow in place, with a lot of careful attention. But that's fine for plant-based societies: Earth villagers made pitchforks by growing wood into the right shape."

"What a way to travel," said Elza, "step through, unbroken, rather than being separately recreated, like the Da Silva does. I've always been bothered by that. How can I ever know that a Da Silva re-creation is *me*?"

"You can't," said Jane. "It's not a physical question, not even philosophical, it's social. As long as the re-creation has the same access to bank accounts, jumpers acquire more wealth, power and descendants than people who go the long way. A cure for religious mania changes 'you' more than a star voyage does.

"But I agree, the Da Silva moment when there's maybe one of me, or maybe I'm just a re-creation about to happen elsewhere, or maybe that happens first and I'm ever so briefly *two*, or *n* ... lucky it's so brief that we don't get time to think about it."

"So that's the short cut to save Elza? Jump through a synte back to where we first ate the fruit?"

"Most of it, Marco. But it's not that simple." It was, Marco thought, a strange new use of the word 'simple'. "Why did they bring us all that way from Sackbane by pony? Why not just push us through a synte in Sackbane?"

"No idea."

Tinka smiled sweetly. "And you an engineer, too. Why did we climb that towering staircase?"

Marco looked baffled. Then it hit him. "Energy is conserved?"

"Being snatched from the jaws of death must have woken you up. Correct. If you put two kasyntei — that's the plural for halves of a synte, dah? — at a vertical displacement of, say, two kilometres, and go through the top one to its kantasynte, you lose that much potential energy. So you emerge with two klicks' worth of kinetic energy. Seven hundred klicks per second, here. Half the speed of sound."

"So that's how that farmer in Sackbane felled a tree to stop us escaping," said Felix. "A stone up a mountain, waiting to fall through, and some way to release it."

"A really high mountain, that one," said Marco. "It sounded like Mach 2."

"What about the momentum it suddenly acquired?" said Tinka, "I didn't see a big recoil."

"Nöther's Theorem," said Marco, "time translation symmetry means energy is conserved, but what all these tunnels do to space symmetry completely wrecks the conservation of momentum."

"This explains the habitation patterns, too," said Felix. "Trash it, mountains are where up-down is concentrated. Sideways motion is easy, take the local synte. Up or down, go some other way. A mountain becomes a trade nexus, like a ford or a bridge would be on any saner planet." He paused for breath. "The river drops as it heads to the sea, so it's a string of places at different levels. They're only synteable, if that's the word, to liveable spots on the other side of the continent. If it's too much effort to grow a big synte and keep it open, for the piddling amount of produce from a narrow-valley site, it's no wonder that the valley died on the vine after the Colonists had made their way up it."

"That explains those ruins we found," said Elza.

"Yah. And it's also why it took us so long to get from *Magog*'s landing-site to anywhere inhabited."

"You know," said Felix, "We got at cross-purposes about *Magog*. We meant the ship. These guys meant a supernatural being. Remember their talk about giants?"

Marco was fiddling about at floor level. "Down through a synte is concentrated instant fall," he was muttering. "So up through a synte is a jump to the top of a wall in a split second. So what do you *feel* if you try?" He pushed his finger against the half-fruit. "Two metres of gravity squashed into a millimetre. Force-screen, trash it! I thought some genius had solved the beta-calculus, but it's just some mothertrashed *plant*! To stop us getting out, they just raised the other half of the door!"

Jane wanted to ask Tinka something else. "How did you discover all this, how did you get us out, and why are we no longer fodder for the bone-hammer brigade."

Tinka cleared her throat. "They're called Quizitors. Very nasty people. We got lucky. What DeLameter really wanted was to be convinced we're truly from off-planet."

She outlined her attack on the door, and the questioning afterward. "So there they were, the two of them, laughing like a drain. And *then* they believed me."

"Why?" Jane and Felix were bewildered, but Sam was starting to get there.

Marco could hardly contain himself.

"Why? Because, like Tinka told us, these things are in everything here. Every kid on the planet learns the basics at the age we'd start learning to code. And Tinka solemnly announced — ow, can't say it — she told them she'd tried to overload... to overload the... the law of gravity!" He rolled into a corner making cackling noises.

"Never mind the children, Tinka," said Jane. "They haven't found a cure for the male sense of humour yet. But why are they letting us go? Why not keep us prisoners? How do they know we're harmless?"

"They don't. They do know we're from the stars, and their theology says anyone from offworld is an angel. However, what DeLameter most definitely *does* know is that we can be useful. We have knowledge and skills that he doesn't — even if we haven't a clue about syntei. They have a thing called the *Handbook*. It's a compendium of knowledge from the early days of the colony. But they can't make head nor tail of it. We can."

"Should we," asked Sam, "help these bonebreaking maniacs?"

"The bonebreakers are still in reach if we *don't*," said Tinka, "but that's not the main point."

"Did you see all the stoop labour we passed?" said Marco. "Recovered tech would lift those backs — and CV-era sources wouldn't point them to fossil fuels."

"That isn't the main point either," said Felix, "We *deal with what's here*. And now we have a reason beyond survival, to get home. Starhome needs to know about syntei. Not just for the benefits they could bring — they could threaten the Concordat's very existence. For the moment, we have to cooperate."

"Yah," said Tinka. "Imagine if Old Earth got hold of them."

"I'd be fascinated to see what they have in the *Handbook*," said Marco.

"I already volunteered you for that. You help Sadruddin work through it — he'll provide DeLameter with the executive summary later — and in your spare time you do everything you can to keep Elzabet comfortable. And alive.

"The rest of us have urgent work to do to make sure she stays that way. We have to *sheft* down in a boat to a guard-station by the marsh — near where we crashed but across the river—and kill off the drop-velocity by hydroplaning a dozen or so kliks. Then we pony-trek for half a day on a vunbugula-burning spree. If we can't recognise the exact tree we burn the lot — that'll probably happen anyway, each grove is a highly connected network of syntei."

"Wouldn't the fire destroy the syntei before it could pass through?"

"Nah, sparks and hot smoke are enough to trigger a fire. Vunbugula are highly inflammable because they have a lot of resin. By the time the synte dies, the next tree along is already burning brightly, and so it goes. Anyway, we can tell when the job's done, using a falasynte. A synte communicator, one you just shout through." She waved a hand at the wall. "I used that one to call the maids."

"How will we know?"

"Elza will know." Before Marco could ask how, she went on: "This time we'll *ride* the ponies back upriver."

Marco was torn between his desire to experience long-distance synte-transport and the need to look after Elzabet. Recalling the pain of pony-trekking, he brightened. The prospect of her recovery made him even happier. Then more questions hit him.

"Tinka? Did you find out what this Undivided Body thing is all about? Why the priest accused us of being perverts? What was the taboo? It can't be merely using syntei, surely? They do that here all the time. But it must involve syntei somehow."

~~~

On a shelf in Sadruddin's chambers there sat an official effigy of the Revered Tanling Denison Bancroft Geoffroy DeLameter, carved in soapstone by the Secretary of the Society of Masons. The Deacon had presented it to his Chaplain as a mark of esteem.

Closeted now in private, after re-checking the room against hidden watchers, Sadruddin took up two fist-sized kasyntei, settling them on a small table so that they faced each other. He tipped one on to its back. Then he picked up the effigy and inserted DeLameter's head into the upright gate.

A small, disembodied DeLameter-head rose through the table and gazed with an air of surprise at the soles of a headless DeLameter-body, flat on its back with its knobbly toes turned up.

A mirthless smirk flickered across Sadruddin's face. He held the figure, divided across eternity, for a long moment.

Then he shuddered, and replaced it in its prominent position on the shelf. Returning the synte to a cupboard, he knelt to pray.

~~~

"Yah, Marco, it involves syntei. But DeLameter doesn't like to talk about it explicitly. He prefers to denounce it as an Abomination. I think we should wait until Elza is back in full health before I share my guess with you. Knowing you, you'll be desperate to try it, probably using scientific curiosity as an excuse. *Don't*. If DeLameter catches you, his Quizitors will be breaking out the bone-hammers."

10

Dividing the Body

"Much have you told of Heaven," said Uriah the Uncertain. "But what of Hell?"

"Those who obey the laws of the Church need not concern themselves with Hell," the Prophet replied. "Those who obey not, will learn in due season."

Uriah was unsatisfied, and asked again: "Tell me of Hell."

"There is not one Hell, but an infinitude. Each contains many others, these in turn contain many Hells, Hell without end. As a man or woman descends deeper in this Hell of Hells, each step becomes ever more excruciating. Yet one Hell is reserved for a greater punishment than any other. And this is the Hell of Division."

"How can that be," asked Uriah, "if the chain of Hells never ends?"

"Ask those whose fate is to penetrate ever deeper, without end," replied the Prophet. "For that is the fate of those who Divide the Body."

The Apocryphon of Manuel Volix, Precept 469

Marco reached forward and scratched himself on the back.

It felt good.

Marco felt good. Last night Elzabet had screamed, and that had turned out to be good too: she was no longer dying.

Last night, he had woken suddenly from a dream of hungry fruits in the desert to hear her call his name. Sitting up! And clutching her stomach. Pale as a corpse.

"Marco? It *hurts*! Help me!"

Grabbing a small gourd from beside his sleeping-pad — a falasynte — he yelled "Sadruddin!"

There was a long pause. Then: "I hear, Sab."

"Sadruddin? My lady, she hurts!"

"Excellent, Sab."

"*What?*"

"Be calm, Sab. I will bring the doctor immediately."

Sadruddin hurried into the room. A short man in the beaded loincloth they had learned to see as medical uniform went directly to Elzabet, opened her mouth, pushed something down her throat, and laid her back down on the sleeping-pad. Then he pulled a mask over his eyes and sat against the wall, apparently in a trance. He was clutching something in each hand, and his fingers twitched.

"Sadruddin? What is he —"

"Be silent, Sab! His mind must remain in your lady. Have patience."

Elzabet had lost consciousness again. Marco could recognise shock on top of anaemia, but every time he twitched, Sadruddin laid a restraining hand on his shoulder.

After an endless wait, something changed. Elzabet still looked bloodless, but she seemed, now, to be asleep.

"Can you help her?" Marco asked the doctor. "Is she going to die?"

"Yes, I can help her. Yes, she will die," the doctor replied enigmatically. "As shall we all, one day, when Magog takes us. But she will not die of this syntstone infestation." Marco mentally cursed the little man's appalling bedside manner. "Feed her when she wakes. Small quantities, frequently, to begin with. Soup, bread — simple food. Avoid anything acidic until the lining of her gut heals — a twelveday is normal."

"Right, yes. But — what did you do?"

The doctor stared at him. "What did *I*... oh, yes. I forgot that you offworlders lack syntelic techniques. My internal examination confirmed the treatment's success."

"But — the pain —"

"A clear sign that the stone is dead, the cure is finished."

"But nothing has happened to her."

The doctor stared, then shook his head like a dog emerging from a pond. "They did tell you, surely, how to kill the parent tree fast enough to stop its death harming her?"

Marco realised that in his worry he'd forgotten how to think. "Oh. They must have found the tree and burned it. Nobody told me that would be painful for Elza."

"That is the only cure. It must be very rapid, which requires a very hot, very intense fire, using syntelic air-blowers. Unavoidably, some heat passes through the syntstone. That was the source of her pain. But there is a beneficial side-effect: the wound is nicely cauterised. Look."

Marco put on the mask the doctor was offering, and got his first ever close-up view of the inside of a human intestine. He saw pink, red, and some streaks of black. It didn't mean much to him.

"We have excellent syndepts in Two Mountains. That probe is the best available for the digestive system," said the doctor, his voice tinged with pride. "Two syntei for binocular vision, three for diffuse lighting, two for manual control of swimming and wriggling, and one in the nose for administering medicines. All protected against reverse leakage.

"There is a bigger unit for ulcer surgery and stomach cancers, but it is slower to get into place, and not usually needed for a syntstone burn." He turned to leave. "She will be fine now, Sab. Keep her warm, give her food as I directed, and plenty to drink to restore her fluid balance. Let her sleep as long as she needs. Oh — and be sure to catch the probe on its way out, and have it returned to me. Precision instruments don't just grow on trees."

~~~

Basking, Marco looked out at night and storm. Lightning raged around the crags and chasms.

The sun shone from far to the west. Temples, and most private dwellings of the Sacred class, were lit by imported sunlight. Sunbathing syntei, though, shone only in the Deacon's House, whose component mansions glittered from the most spectacular crags on both sides of both peaks. Marco glanced through the door at the room where Elzabet was sleeping, and back across to North Mountain where her window was visible for a moment among the rippling clouds. He still wasn't sure how to get out of Deacon's House — but, as he had remarked to her that morning, one sure got *around* in it.

It was nice to be an honoured guest, and he had always been a sunshine freak, but a question had been bothering him. "Sadruddin, sun-carriers are easily moved, and syntei in general are plentiful. Why do the common people in villages like Sackbane have to burn oil to make light?"

Sadruddin, who had been transcribing some of Marco's comments on the *Handbook* in a florid Qishi script, stopped writing. "Sab, sun punctyles are imported from other continents, where times differ."

"Dah, but transportation is easy here. Just step through a wyzand." A thought struck him. "No problems when you take syntei through other syntei, I suppose? No interference between synte-fields, topological obstructions, stuff like that?"

"Indeed, Sab, there is even a Ceremony of Knotted Space in the Misty Season, when one half of an oval brasure is passed through the other and emerges from itself. It symbolises tying of the bands against sin, and rebirth of the year from its own turning passage. This is the true meaning of that section of the *Handbook* that you were telling me is just mathematics, where the knot polynomial is generated by—"

"I would never say anything is *just* mathematics," said Marco carefully, "though why your ancestors recorded all that knot theory and left out aerodynamics escapes me. But, now that you mention it, I suspect that synte-tubes can't actually knot in karmabhumi-space anyway ... Where was I?"

"You spoke truth of syntei for sunlight, Sab, and of stepping, but this House holds the single synte that may be stepped through between this continent and another. It is heavily guarded by soldiers loyal to the Church and its Deacon, and what little passes through does so on the Deacon's authority *alone*."

"But why? Surely sun punctyles —" small syntei, right? "— give the best and cheapest light. Everyone should have them."

"Sab, a lamp does not pass light alone."

"What do you mean? You don't have a dope-smuggling problem, do you?"

"A smuggling of fools, Sab? Or is my Galaxic at fault? Sab — I refer to the smuggling of wicked men."

"You've lost me," said Marco. "You didn't just tell me that wicked men can come through two-centimetre punctyles?"

"It is the wicked who *do* the smuggling, Sab. It is not men that they smuggle."
"What do they smuggle, then?"
"Whispers."
"Whispers? What *kind* of whispers?"
"Wicked whispers, Sab."

~~~

"Seventeen hundred years ago men had grown many and prosperous in this land. They forgot the sufferings of their fathers when the giant Magog stumbled and went dark, setting them comfortless to the ground." Sadruddin's voice took on a singsong rhythm. "Fat they grew, and proud, and their women showed bellies like honey loaves. In their pride and lust they turned to Abomination. It is written, 'Thou shalt not Divide the Body, for it is an Image of Me.'" He was standing now like a short, wrathful prophet; Marco seemed to hear the mountain storms in his voice. "In division did they wallow, men and women alike in sin, until Two Mountains became the twin breasts of the Great Whore that was foretold, and all the land did stink of lechery.

"But Magog in His infinite compassion sent us Patrick Aloysius de Vere Harmsworth Nasruddin: His messenger, our redeemer, leader of hosts, first Deacon of the Church of the Undivided Body. Then was there a great Cleansing, and the ungodly were smitten; they did repent of their wickedness, and in all this land did Magog rule among men. But some fled across the sea, where their children, bred in lechery, linger yet. It is prophesied that there shall come a Second Cleansing, and all this world shall return to the undivided purity of our fathers from the stars."

"However,'" Sadruddin continued with a shift of voice and a shrug, "that day will not be soon. Samdal, the continent where they fled, turned out to be considerably bigger and more fertile than this one. We are now outnumbered by seven to one, and they have higher mountains. If we were to launch a second Purification Raid we would not just get lost in the forest. We would be wiped out, and the ungodly would come after Two Mountains with a big stick."

Marco was getting it. "Trade with other continents is forbidden because it would be corrupting?"

"You speak truth, Sab. As the Holy Book says: 'Permit no part to come into contact with incompatible components.' Wise words from the prophet Manuel Volix. The lower orders are all too ready to think up Abominations of their own, even without assistance from…" His voice trailed off.

Sadruddin had alluded indirectly to this ultra-Holy Book several times, but its name seemed too holy to use. It definitely wasn't the *Handbook*. It was, the Chaplain said, 'a purer source of divine knowledge'. It seemed to Marco that Sadruddin was dipping his toe into deep waters, testing…

He must have found them too chill. He suddenly reverted to the original topic.

"We have a sealed and guarded Embassy at Sensifoy on Samdal, four *klòvij* below the capital city." Their wristcomps had worked out most of the common Kalingo units: that was about two kilometres. "It is from the roof of that building that you have sunlight in your outer chamber. Through the Embassy wyzand we carry on essential trade, but only what is really essential: tropical medicinal plants, optical crystals, that sort of thing. Absolutely no synte where foreigners can reach the kantasynte! And the space on the Embassy roof is strictly limited."

"So, the ice cream I enjoy here...?"

"Is strictly for the Deacon's guests, yes, as the ice comes from the Greywraiths of Lamynt. Nowhere on Shaaluy is cold enough. More importantly, we have no cold storage industry, though dry storage uses the desert of Wesh." He seemed to sense where this talk of economics might lead, and ended with a pious observation. "The reasons of matter join the reasons of spirit for ending the division of Qish. Heresy must end."

The way he said it was chilling.

~~~

"How are you feeling now, Elza?"

Two weeks had passed, and Fringe folk were notoriously resilient. Marco might have meant it as an innocent enquiry, but Elza sensed undercurrents and snuggled closer to him. "*Much* better — especially now, Marco. You must have been in a pretty miserable state yourself, these last few weeks. I don't suppose they laid on dancing girls, or anything similar?"

"Naturally," said Marco. "Nothing but the best for the Man from the Stars. Ice cream in bed every morning, served by luscious beauties in transparent harem pants. And that was just breakfast. For *lunch* —"

"Tease."

"Yah, you've seen though my feeble tale, though I did get lemon ice this morning. This place is in the prurient puritan stage. Not like the patriarchal setups where women are exactly property, loaned out to guests. But not like the typical high-civ world either, where people welcome strangers and are friendly with their bodies. The head of IIT would have had a fit if she'd been able to see the way these priests carry themselves. She always said that to get any decent work out of men — and easily a third of the school were men, it was Policy — to get decent work you have to keep their bodies in tune. Let them build up sexual tensions, she said, and you get all sorts of planning errors. Like that series of fission reactor accidents that nearly destroyed Old Earth before we got starflight. And you get the *damnedest* designs! Form doesn't follow function, it follows phallus."

Elza pulled his ears. "Marco, you're preaching. And I think you're quoting your old teacher, word for word."

"You speak truth, Elza. Oh, trash it, I'm picking up Sadruddin's speech-patterns now! But — well, she was so inspiring, as well as being such a great engineer... Have you looked at the way the men here walk?"

"Rigid." She frowned. "Rigid, as though they weren't getting any at all. But... that makes no sense. The race would die out."

"Nah, it's more complicated," said Marco. "Most priests are married; even DeLameter, they tell me, though I've seen neither hide nor hair of a Deacon's Wife. Strict monogamy, mind you, which must be pretty depressing. *And,*" said in a tone of voice that conveyed the impression that the remark would prove decisive, "from that room with the street-window I've seen a lot of sensible outdoor clothing."

It seemed a complete non sequitur. "Sensible?"

"They don't seem bothered by strangers seeing that their women are female-shaped. Vital areas covered, yah, but not disguised. Quite a lot of bare flesh when it's really warm. The bodies aren't exaggerated either, to say they're for sale. The clothes are just comfortable. Some are downright skimpy."

"Dah, I catch your drift."

"If it wasn't for the way people move, Elza, I'd deduce that their attitude to sex is high-civ-normal."

Elza nodded thoughtfully, she'd noticed similar things herself. "People *touch* each other — you spotted that? Not intimately and not too much, but there's no contact taboo. Even so, they all look as if there's something they want to do, but they're afraid they'll go blind if they try it." She searched for an adequate image. "The men look like... cheap toy robots with the wires too tight. And the women all have the glum perseverance of sheep in a ten-day downpour."

Marco's eyes were glazing over. "Something they *want* to do, but are too scared... Something they *could* do, easily, if they could get up the courage — so it's an ever-present temptation. *Abomination*... Elza, Sadruddin was talking as though his ancestors had invented a brand new perversion, not one of the usual thousands known to humanity, but something that offworlders could never conceive of."

Elzabet shook her head. "Marco, the subtlety of the universe is without limit, but the number of orifices and protrusions in the human body is finite. The anatomical permutations were catalogued exhaustively in pre-atomic India. These people *can't* have invented a genuinely original sin."

"Sadruddin seemed to think they had."

"Yah. And he didn't seem too impressed by the attitude of his church, either. He puts on a good show, but he *doubts*. I think he's up to something, Elza. Something that the church would not approve."

"With some reservations, I agree. He's kind of cute, actually."

"And so," she added, reaching down and stroking until Marco's flesh was hard again, "are you. Speaking of permutations, I believe I'm strong enough to climb on top this time."

Marco lay back with a sigh of gratification. But even as his body responded to her expert ministrations, she could see his mind still wandered, and wondered.

~~~

A meal, another nap for Elza; then they were squatting in a roof garden on a crag of North Mountain. Squill's stark white light was turning blood-red as the dusty atmosphere put on another spectacular sunset. The eye moved from the tangible colours of the sky, to the lit mountainside scattered with fairy-tale palaces, to the gloaming below and behind, pricked with windows of lamplight or — higher — imported sunlight. The first lightowls were flying, like predatory searchlights in the dusk.

Above, in a green darkness, were the clustered suns of the Galactic Core.

"So, since you haven't been sporting with dancing girls or disturbing me in my sleep, what *have* you been up to these past two weeks?"

Marco grimaced. "I'm not *completely* dependent on sex, Elza. Except for fine work like taming a sunspot cycle. You absolutely do not hire celibates, of either gender, for that job."

"Don't change the subject."

"Dah. I've been busy earning our keep."

"I thought we were honoured guests."

"We are... of the Revered-Tanling-Denison-Bancroft-Geoffroy-DeLameter. Even an honoured guest gets precious little for a kind face. In the intervals between soothing your fevered brow I've been working through the *Handbook* the first settlers put together. *Magog* was in too bad a state for Plan A, to support them long enough to set up a self-sustaining technological culture. So they went straight to Plan F, recording the basics in a form that their descendants would still be able to use however much technology was lost. After a few decades they had a pastoral system stable enough for an economic surplus, and they had enough spare time to make tools to make tools to make machines. A few of them tried before going off to look for ores and fossil fuels and suchlike. But —"

"Go on."

"But, the first generation were high-tech specialists. No expertise or experience in communicating with non-technicals, and without references they didn't even know what germanium ore looks like, or how to smelt iron. (That was rediscovered later.) The *Handbook* keeps assuming knowledge it doesn't provide, and the choice of subjects is occasionally half-witted. By the time the surviving settlers had got themselves a nice functional low-tech social system, a completely wild factor had entered the picture."

"Plan Z?"

"More a case of no plan at all."

"Syntei."

"Absolutely. Syntei gave them the basis for technology that in some ways is more advanced than Starhome's, but with a really nasty twist. *They don't know how anything works*. They've got the practical know-how: they can grow all the different plants, harvest them, breed them selectively for desirable traits. When *Magog* arrived there were no door-sized syntei — wyzands. Just a few rare species that kids could wriggle through. But they had to use Old Earth macroscopic breeding methods, maybe more organised and a bit more efficient. No molecular genetics, no bacterioviral DNA factories, no concept of the microscopic below the level of gross bacterial structure.

"So most of the physics in the *Handbook* has turned into religious allegory. The Uncertainty Principle is more wonderful and inspiring here than Thomas Aquinas and Saint Bernard of Mars rolled into one, but you couldn't run a quantum dot on it."

His waving arm was dark against the a pale amber crescent moon appearing from behind South Mountain. "They have no concept of pure research or pure scientific understanding. No concept *at all*. I've been called a Philistine by ivory-womb theoreticians, because my question is always 'What can I do with this?' But that's me, I'm a mathematical engineer. However, I also recognise that ivory wombs give birth in the end, and my question is what rough beast it will be this time. Compared to Qishites, I'm as ivory-womb as Euclid.

"I know in my gut that understanding is a tool in its own right. That practice without theory is ultimately a confusing dead end. But these people have had something so useful, and so incomprehensible, dumped on them from below that they can't imagine any intellectual or experimental work that doesn't lead to an *immediate* payoff, like bigger or more stable syntei.

"Anyway, I'm going through the *Handbook* telling Sadruddin how the information it contains leads to aer-O-webs and computers and stunbeams, when he doesn't want to know how things *work*! The language problem doesn't help, either."

"But Sadruddin's Galaxic is beautiful!" protested Elzabet. "A bit ceremonious, but not likely to get us burning *a* tree when we need to burn *the* tree!"

"Yah, Sadruddin's Galaxic *is* beautiful, it *is* ceremonious — he learnt it for ceremonial purposes. So anything he says in his Galaxic is automatically sacred, so he can't get into a questioning mindset. And the basis of science is *doubt*. Directed doubt, constructive doubt, but *doubt*. You have to wallow in it, but to Sadruddin, doubt expressed in Galaxic equals heresy. You can't approach science from that point of view, because then it stops developing. It stops being science. So I'm spending a lot of time with Gus—"

"*Gus*? On nickname terms?" *What's Marco getting into now?*

"Yah. He's a decent sort underneath the churchy posture: it's not safe here, to drop that. I think he's doing a lot behind the scenes to protect us from the Deacon's more paranoid delusions. He's dropped a few hints."

"Do you trust him?"

"Not completely, but more than I did. I'm getting him to teach me Kalingo, the common speech. That will help me get to know him better. I think he could be of use."

"That's a good idea, anyway. I'll join you. But I just hope he'll be prepared to talk about sacred subjects in the profane speech, and help you to invent new vocabulary when you need it. Kalingo will also be useful when Jane and Felix get back. They'll want to understand the religion. We have to work out how these people tick to reach the rescue beacon."

A long-suppressed fear resurfaced. " I hope it *is* that other solitron source halfway round the planet! What if there were *two* Colony Vessels, and neither managed to get its beacon away properly?"

Marco paled. "*Oh, Mother.* Gog and Magog."

"What's the matter? Another Old Earth flashback?"

"Yajuj and Majuj were often a two-fer."

Elza pursed her lips in thought. After a moment, her face brightened. "Don't be silly, Marco. If the ships had been *a pair* then the myth would have two giants, or some form of the second ship."

Marco ran a hand through his hair. "Trash it, the other source is in *mountains*! Wait! Hold it! Despite what *Valkyrie* said, we've all been assuming *Magog* was scattered here by a 'quake, right?"

"Sure. What else? The ship was dying, it said crazy things."

"Maybe not so crazy. How likely is two ships scattering to one star system, let alone one planet?"

Elzabet slapped her forehead. "Nil, basically."

"Yah. Unless the two ships were coupled in some way... Nah, trash it, meshing two drives is a truly *horrible* problem in beta-calculus. I agree, *Magog* was alone. Even if there were a *Gog*, it'd be half a galaxy away. So the mountain source *has* to be a beacon. Just typical of our luck on this half-arsed planet that we picked the other one."

Time to stop whining and get practical, Elza thought. "What can we offer DeLameter to get us out of this nanacurst mountain theocracy with enough diplomatic protection to cross the planet?"

"I doubt he could do that, even if he wanted."

"Then how?"

"Inside help."

"Sadruddin?"

"Who else? He sometimes seems sympathetic. We need to work on that."

"Yah. And in the meantime?"

"We learn all we can, especially about syntei. I helped myself to a fist-sized pair of kachamfrets for experiments. At first I thought I'd work on their physics, but without equipment it was unrealistic to hope for useful clues. If they do work on the same basic principles as the Da Silvas, I'd get nowhere without some way to pick up solitron field densities — so even on *Valkyrie* I'd have been stuck. You'd not learn anything significant about her drive by physical examination unless you had a pion microscope. It's the controlled *nucleus* configurations that count. So all I know about syntelics — my name for synte physics — is 'thing go in *here*, thing come out *there*, presto!'"

"So why are you experimenting?"

"Because I'm a —"

"Mathematical engineer!"

"— so my question is always 'what can I do with it?', and I will thank you not to interrupt my pet speeches. And asking that has already solved one problem that's bothered me for years. Come back to our day room, and I'll show you."

They stepped across the inside of a cave to an airy room on South Mountain, where Marco opened lamps to let in the afternoon light from three kiloklicks westward. He picked up a pair of bulbous plants and handed one to Elza.

"Hold that if you would — just so."

Holding the other in his left hand, he turned away from her, plunged his right arm into it up to the elbow, and reached out from Elzabet's plant to scratch his back.

"That's where it always itches, you never get it quite right. You were a lot better than nothing, but now thanks to Qish vegetable genius, I am a free and independent spirit, able to —"

"*Sab!*"

Sadruddin stood in the doorway, his mouth sagging with horror. "Sab, what are you doing? In front of a *window*?"

"Gus, I was only scratching my back," said Marco, pulling his hand from his right scapula as though it were red hot.

"Marco, my newest friend," said Sadruddin, "do you truly know nothing? To Divide the Body in a lighted room facing North Mountain? Put that synte on the floor — so. Stand back, do not touch it.

"Marco, pray that you were not seen. If you were, nothing I can do will save you, or your golden lady. I will not enter now" — Marco realised that Sadruddin had never been in view of the window — "and I have not come this way. If no guards come before moonset" — about half an hour, Marco judged — "nothing has happened, and I will return." The door was empty.

Elzabet broke the silence. "So *that's* the big taboo? Back-scratching?" She no longer had trouble taking fanaticism seriously: it had come so close to agonising death for them all. Clearly they had blundered into it again, somehow. Sadruddin had seemed terrified. But *back-scratching?*

"You scratch my back and I'll scratch mine," said Marco automatically. Then doubled back. "It wasn't the scratching, Elza. It was doing it *using a synte*. I was *dividing the body*."

Oh, Mother of all galaxies, they had heard that denounced, more times than she had bones in her body. More than she *would* have, when the bone-hammers had multiplied them. She stared at him in horror, trying to pretend her heart wasn't pounding, trying not to keep glancing towards the door, listening for approaching feet.

"Why didn't Gus *warn* us?"

"He didn't know I'd pinched a synte."

"Nah, but he must have realised there was a chance we'd get hold of one and accidentally ... *misuse* it."

"I guess it never crossed his mind. He just assumed we'd know."

"True. It's a very rigid society. Imagination counts little; obedience is all. Doesn't occur to them that some people might be ignorant of the belief-system. For them, it's how the world works. They've all been told as much, from birth."

"Well, he hasn't denounced us to DeLameter. He's taking a big risk by not doing that."

"Maybe. Notice how he kept out of sight?"

"Yah. But he'd be careful to do that, however he felt about us."

"Yah. *Dividing*... Not really, but I think I see. You were *partly* through a synte. I found it pretty gruesome myself... but: a *mortal sin?*"

"I wish Jane and Felix were here, they'd be able to tell us more. I do know it's typical of religions to take something pleasant, natural, and readily available, and stop people using it. It gives the priests control. And the way to stop it is to brand it as being sinful, and then to punish the sinner. Really, it's just a way to enforce your own view about human behaviour through violence. But calling it sinful puts the blame on your deity, who is of course blameless, so no one can object without committing something even worse, like blasphemy or heresy."

"Marco, everyone uses syntei for all sorts of things, in full view, even the priests and the guards. Every time someone steps through one, they divide the body."

Marco's face took on the blank look it always did when seized by a scientific problem. Though, as Elza had noticed, it might equally well indicate lights on, no one home. "Well," he said, "the priests can do whatever they want, it's only the common folk who commit a sin. But I think there's a rationale. Remember when Tinka had me stick my finger through that punctyle — Shaven Lily! Good thing there were no guards about! — after she'd sorted the synte business out?"

"You were like a kitten with a new catnip mouse."

"Well, after we got used to the shock, none of us was bothered by it. It's not the *finger* that gets chopped up."

"Dah, using a synte doesn't actually divide the body. Tell DeLameter."

"My point is: they don't think about it like that. They think about what it looks like. The locals don't hesitate about going all the way." He squatted down beside her. "It's getting off at Edge Hill that's sinful."

For once Elzabet did know that ancient railway metaphor for the sin of Onan; some of Marco's Old Earthisms tended to recur. And his stream-of-consciousness utterances sometimes gave clues to something sensible. This one suggested the final connection. "It's sexual, right?"

Marco was way ahead of her. "Well, that's how it started —"

"Wow! The great new perversion was sex using syntei! You'd *really* have to re-write that ancient Indian catalogue! So then their prophet, wossname —"

"Patrick Aloysius de Vere Harmsworth Nasruddin."

"— then Saint Paddy said it was illegal, immoral, and shrivelling. And the taint spread to *ever* letting the body be in two places. Church of the Undivided Body... right. Though you'd need the casuistry of a Jesuit to draw the line between temporary division when you pass through a synte, and the prohibited uses. And they'd *have* to draw one, because even the priests would find synte travel too useful to lose. Talk about splitting hairs... or not, I suppose."

"I think it's easier than that. Just a simple-minded, naive distinction, Elza. When you travel through a synte, you don't *appear* to be in two places. But start using syntei as sex-toys and there will be divided body-parts all over the furniture. At a casual glance."

"Yah, that fits." She paused. "Um. I — I wonder what they were actually *doing*?"

A grin settled over his face, like a lion lying down with a lamb. "Now that *is* a question for a topologically trained mathematical engineer." As they waited for Sadruddin's return, or the tramp of guards' feet, a terrified Elza watched Marco escape sane fear in the ageless self-absorption of the creative mind.

11

The View from the Groin

>   Early conditioning by parents, priests, and wider social culture are fundamental to sexual inhibitions and associated mental health problems. A small human receives conflicting signals about what to regard as normal sexual behaviour. Inhibitions stem from incompatible beliefs, childhood repression, ignorance, and myths. Both men and women may learn body shame and guilt. Closed, ritualistic societies may repress practices considered normal by the majority of humanity, using punishments that themselves seem pathological to others. Other closed, ritualistic societies that fetishise unlimited sexuality have other personality disorders…
>   — *Naomi D'Oyly-Hamilton, Sex and the Single Starperson*

Sam Wasumi didn't know much about ponies, but she had to be thirsty: he was thirsty himself, and hadn't been working so hard. He watched out for water.

He had to admit that the trek to Two Mountains was more comfortable than their first visit, but it was taking a lot longer. The season had turned, the rains had come, and the Little Yandoory pony tracks their captors had previously used were waterlogged and impassable. The only route open to ponies was up the main Yandoory watercourse, and even that was occasionally blocked by landslides.

It was going to take at least a month to get back. Still, this time there was no reason to hurry.

Their intended route stayed close to the Yandoory river, but right now there was no water to be seen. Two hours ago a collapsed cliff face had forced them to scramble up a crumbled side of the gorge into the surrounding desert. If 'desert' was the right word.

It did resemble the deserts on innumerable Concordat worlds: red and ochre rock with patches of sunbaked soil. *Some* of the plants were typical desert flora, too. Sparse, wiry little bushes and succulents like cacti, cried out by shape, habit, and tough skin that water retention was the most important thing in the world. But they had just ridden through a dried-up gulley where the air felt cool and quiet, with moisture freely released by a grove of tall and shining trees. Rather, by a part of one tree, as Kurpershoek had explained. Like the parasitic vunbugula, the silver-oak divided over different resources. A new plant began at the river, then syntseeds on the wind reached iron-rich ground. Those not too far above or below it grew to silver-oaks, rich on river water and feeding minerals back to the mother plant. Dry-living plants adapted to water parasitism made strange drab streaks on their opulently graceful trunks.

Sam was still finding it hard to come to terms with this weird planet. He knew the others had the same problem: out of place, disoriented. He tried to focus on his immediate surroundings. His hand went unconsciously for reassurance to the hilt of his knife, returned to its now-respected owner. Weird tools went into holy keeping, but the Church knew knives.

There was no track. The ponies picked their own way over the awkward ground. Sam, Tinka, Jane, Felix, Kurpershoek, and his five Deacon's Guards made a straggly bunch. Sam was far enough to the right of the rest to glimpse a small pool between rocks, and turn his pony towards it.

About two metres across, the pool looked similarly deep. Small leafiness grew around its edge, but the bottom and sides looked hard, with no established underwater plants. Filled occasionally by the run-off from a desert shower?

His pony's head bent towards the water.

The next moment, Sam was flying through the air. He lost his grip on the reins, grabbed instinctively for them, and saved his life by missing. As he hit the ground, the pony went head first into the pool.

He came to on a sleeping-pad, in an early-set camp. Tinka Laurel was squatting beside him, her face a mixture of tenderness and fury. He quailed.

"Sorry, Tinka. Uh — what happened?"

"You nearly got eaten, that's what happened, and you nearly lost your knife." She held it out to him. "What in the Cavity's name did you think you were doing?"

"My pony was thirsty, I was sorry for it. I—"

"Your pony is dead, and you can be as sorry as you like, but it won't bring her back. Jane and Felix and I haven't seen ponies outside zoos either, but what made you think Kurpershoek doesn't know how to manage them?"

Sam scrabbled to an unsteady squat. "Dah, point registered. But what happened? Nothing around that pool looked big enough and tough enough to grab a pony. It was so fast! What was it."

"Gravity."

"A tiny mascon under that pool? Only a loose chunk of neutron star could pull so hard!"

"Not a mass concentration, Sam. Can you walk a few steps?"

He lurched to his feet, and hung on to her shoulder as they walked over to the pool. As they looked into it from a safe distance, Sam threw up.

At the bottom was the pony. It had to be the pony. But it was almost shapeless, with legs like crumpled rope. The bottom of the pool was a rich translucent red, with darker strands emerging from his ruined pony. Like a soup cube dissolving in hot water.

"What *did* that?"

"The pony fell in." Tinka pulled a long creeper from a rock. "Drop in the end of this. But *don't* hold on to your end too tightly!"

Sam flicked the heavy stalk, and yelped as it dragged out of his hand. The creeper slammed through the water surface with a bang, but not much splash or waves, like a bullwhip striking molasses. Fragments pelted down over the pony's body.

"That vine," said Tinka, "just fell a hundred metres."

"Shaven Lily! The pool is a synte plant?"

"Carnivorous. Kurpershoek says he's never seen a lurepool half so big; he thinks maybe there's been crossbreeding with a domesticated species. It's a complicated monster, comes in at least three parts."

"Um. One by the river for the pool's water... Like the silver-oaks, right?" Sam frowned. "That would need to be at the same level as this, so it must scatter a good few syntseeds before it finds a suitable site and lets one grow. This one must be a fair way upriver, by the height of the water surface. Then another bit, for the bottom half. Is that at a lower level in the landscape somewhere, or just straight down?"

"Kurpershoek says most of the plant is a single piece way down underground," said Tinka. "Even a hundred-metre dig usually hits solid rock. So mother plant sets her lowest seeds to burrow deep; then she enlarges the most successful one and fuses the synte with this one. You fall directly from here into the stomach pool underground, while the other sides of the syntei still connect mama to this bit and to the stomach."

"So my poor beast, there, is being digested somewhere underground. She really hit the bottom with a bang!"

"Sam, love, you're still hazy. Her bones broke in the fall, before she hit."

"It's the sudden *stop* that disturbs my meditation, as the man said on his way down Priapus Skylon." Sam glanced at her. "Nah, wait. Tidal stresses?"

"I pronounce you cured, no dopier than usual from that knock on the head. So it will be you who sleeps without the pad you lost with your pony!"

Sam paid no attention: her own sleeping-pad was big enough for two, and his had never served for more than extra rolling space. His fingers danced over the touch surfaces round his left wrist. "Like going through a concertina. First the front end tries to accelerate at more than a hundred gee while the rest stays behind. Coming out, you get the squeeze. Say we concentrate in one tenth of a metre the velocity change usual in a hundred... S-shaped speedup... Great Mother!" He blinked slackly at the numbers. "It's a marvel that she wasn't torn to confetti!"

"There speaks your true physical scientist," said Jane from behind him. "More impressed by what's on his wrist than what's in front of his nose."

"Oh, hi, Jane. It's not the numbers, it's the *nature* of the thing. I've always *watched* varying gravity tear big things apart. This is like a black hole in your bathroom!"

"Then how come we're alive?"

They turned towards Felix. "We came down from Two Mountains. We fell at least a kilometre," he said. "Through a synte. So why aren't we shredded Starfolk?"

"Shaven Lily!" Sam instinctively reached for Tinka's hand. "I did notice that they strapped us hard into that boat. I assumed it was to protect us from the jolt when we came out at 500 kph from the drop, and hit air. That slide along the lake to slow down, we must have gone ten klicks! But now... of course, the big thump we felt was tidal, happening inside the synte. Even so... Kurpershoek my friend," he called in Kalingo, "how long is the big wyzand we fell through, inside?"

Kurpershoek passed his insect-frying to an underling. "Forty *vij* deep," he said proudly. About twenty metres. "We only have such since about ten years ago. In my childhood a fall of more than a thousand *vij* would shred you, but the new breeds of our syndepts are a wonder."

Sam paused for an internal dialogue with his 'comp. "Mmmm... yah, maximum stress about like five gee thrust, first one way and then the other, spreadeagled the way we were."

"Five gee?" asked Jane. "In twenty metres that wouldn't build up the same speed as one gee over a kilometre, surely?"

After a fruitless effort to explain 'gee' in Kalingo to Kurpershoek, Sam returned to her question. "Arrival momentum changed as if we accelerated that far at about a hundred gee, but free fall never hurt anyone. We *weren't* accelerating. We were just following the most direct curves in spacetime. The stress was from different parts of us trying to follow different curves, pulling each other off course. The farther apart along the gate, the worse it gets." He turned again to Kurpershoek. "Can fat men ride that wyzand?"

Kurpershoek looked at him respectfully. "I thought you knew nothing of syntei, Sab? Indeed, a great belly means unendurable pain in such a journey. Nor can ponies survive, since they cannot flatten like a man. Is your 'gee' some explanation of this?" Sam's answer failed. "I am a simple man, you must speak to the syndepts about this. Perhaps your mysteries will provide a way to go *up* a wyzand?"

"Sorry. Only a reason for its impossibility. If you were prevented from falling you would *experience* those hundred gee, and be crushed at once."

Tinka had been questioning her own wristcomp, and said abruptly: "Kurpershoek, what's the boat made of? The stresses must be terrific, it's fifteen *vij* long."

"Indeed, Sabi, only utterwood will serve, and it is hard to work. Such a boat is more grown than cut, and we have few. But utterboats and high wyzands we must have, to send guards at once to where they are needed."

"We're extremely grateful for that one, believe me," said Jane. "I wonder how Elzabet is feeling now?"

~~~

Elzabet was curled up, clutching her stomach, and groaning. With laughter.

"Marco, you look ridiculous."

He lurched again, just missing the washbasin. He was wearing only a mask over his eyes and an arrangement of straps around his legs.

"Nah, I'm getting the hang of it now. It's just an unusual point of view."

He was looking through two punctyles at the view from one metre above the floor. Part of his arm-waving was flailing to keep his balance, but part was simple clowning. Part was fascination in watching and guiding his hands from *below*. He looked at her along his dark length. "Time you put yours on." He pointed at the other set that Sadruddin had brought, when Marco had delicately enquired about permissible practices.

She slid off her robe and stood, putting on the mask. "Oops, I should have put the other bit on first. Now I can't see what I'm doing. Care to put it on for me?"

Marco muttered something inaudible, but his hands moved around her thighs and groin. Suddenly, he was looking into her eyes at the corners of her pubic triangle, her hips flaring beside them and her small breasts dancing at the top of his vision, above her gently rounded belly. His hands flowed up and down her sides.

Her eyes holding his, her left arm reached to bring his head to hers for a long, slow kiss. Her right hand came down, just before his eyes, slender fingers stroking until his rigidity became almost unendurable. Below her gaze, he saw a mouth water.

As she eased forward and engulfed him, he watched in dreamy clarity until his eyes could see nothing but a world of golden curls, too close for focus. As the familiar motions began, her teeth on his shoulders echoed and re-echoed from his fingertips and toes to a silent shout at his groin.

That night they re-explored all their well-known pleasures, from what Marco insisted on calling a new perspective. Then they exchanged masks…

In the morning, they slept.

~~~

The sun blazed full as they breakfasted on roast mountain fish in the roof garden, though behind South Mountain an impressive thunderstorm was gathering.

"You know," said Marco between mouthfuls, "syntei are hard to beat. Even if you *don't* go through them. Vision did, but we weren't Dividing the Body."

"That's how come Sadruddin could let us have them. With cautions to stick to the manufacturer's specified uses."

"Tinka warned me: *don't*. Not exactly don't *what*, but it's obvious now. Don't Divide the Body. But stay clear of actual Division, and maintain privacy, and we'll get away with this much even if they catch us. Gus made that crystal clear. The Church allows small private sins, to keep people feeling guilty, and avoid the lid blowing off. But publicly they have to discourage even those. People always push boundaries."

"Syntei do strange things to boundaries."

"True! I hadn't realised until Gus gave us those punctyle pants that *dormant* synte plants' wormholes stay open. That opens up all *sorts* of opportunities. I suppose you have to dry them out just so, and they're brittle. You can still damage them and lose the link. I guess it's a bit like wood: cut it and cure it the right way and you can make furniture, but treat it badly and it will crack or rot. Takes practice and skill."

"Yes. And an apple tree in winter still has a trickle of life."

"It certainly widens what — ah, strabyen, Gus my friend."

"Strabyen, Marcolo." That '-lo' seemed to be both an honorific and a marker of eternal friendship, but Marco hadn't yet worked out all the implications. Kalingo was… *difficult*. Sadruddin had started 'Marcolo' after Marco had casually called him 'Gus' and then tried to explain. Augustine Tambiah Sadruddin seemed to find being cut down to the second syllable of his first name refreshingly original, but daring…

"Strabyen, Sabi Quynt."

Sabi Quynt felt uncomfortable. "Please call me Elzabet, or Elza. And may I, too, call you Gus?"

"You do me too much honour, Sabi. By your pleasure, Els'bett" — this with a strange hiss on the 's' — "I rejoice that you call me Gus. Uh..."

"Yes?"

"I hope that my small gift gave pleasure?"

Elzabet laid a brown hand on his pale forearm. "Gus, look at my face and you will see it is so." Cautiously, she moved on. "Truly this is a world of marvels."

"Truth, Els'bett, that is also my belief, though not as I was taught. 'O Heavenly Shaper, keep me clean and whole, to be reborn among the stars where Division is unknown.' But you, Els'bett and Marcolo, have shown me it truly is unknown there, but a simple lack of awareness is not holy rejection. Falsely was I taught that without Division of the Body there will be no division among men."

The leap of logic took Elza by surprise. "Sorry?"

"I was telling Gus about the civil war on Fort Purity," Marco explained.

"Ah."

Sadruddin sighed. "Truly does it appear that we the Children are the Children in all places. But it is yet a truth that this world — " he gestured at the rainbow now shining behind South Mountain, a glowing three-quarter circle, doubled and englobing the purple crags " — this *is* a world of marvels. Not the least among which are the joys I have practised in shame and burning secret."

Elzabet realised that she hadn't changed the subject. "I hope we haven't caused you to lose your faith, Gus."

It took Marco a split second longer. "You mean, you — you have..." He suddenly found himself inhibited about those words.

Sadruddin was hushed, but spoke now without defiance or shame, as if a barrier had simply dissolved and evaporated into mist. "Truth time. Long and long have I Divided the Body, though always in the wish to act otherwise. For I was taught that Division is a sin and an Abomination, and I believed the teachings. I just... I could not forever obey them, hard as I might try. I have been careful, obsessively so. No one providing proscribed services knows my name or my face."

"You must trust us deeply, to tell us."

Gus gave a mirthless laugh. "You imagine the Deacon's minions would believe captives of doubtful origin? Against a senior priest?"

So you think. Elza's eyes flicked to her wrist, where her invisible 'comp was recording every word. If Gus did betray them, they could take him down with them. Given warning, they could play him the recording. It would be interesting to see his face... but she hoped it wouldn't come to that.

Marco was glancing at his own wrist, evidently having the same thought.

"One word from me," Sadruddin continued in blissful ignorance, "and DeLameter would march you to the Quizitors with no moment of hesitation. Or of thought."

"Even so, why did you put yourself in such a high-profile position if you couldn't stick to the rules?"

Sadruddin hesitated, and gave her a penetrating glance. Then nodded, as if whatever he had seen had reassured him. "Belief, at first. In a divided world that must unite, a man must work against division. When I discovered myself sinful — knowing what is right does not prevent disobedience, Els'bett — to retreat from my rise would have been to denounce myself. I held to truths that could redeem the world, truths betrayed by those who govern.

"I fought against Division both in the world and in my heart. But when I saw you by that window, I began to ask whether the fault was never in my heart, but with the founders of my Church. I came to think that it was ignorance, not innocence, that my fathers had left among the stars.

"I offered you my punctyle masks to know for certain. They tread a delicate line, one that is permitted, but opens endless possibilities that are not. I am sure that you have considered some of these, and that abstract contemplation alone will not satisfy the wish to *know* through personal experience."

"You can speak plainly to me, Gus."

"Very well. You, too, would Divide the Body, I think?"

It dawned on Elzabet that she had been underestimating the natives. Sadruddin had a very direct and subtle sense of psychology, even across cultural boundaries. And his confession had been a sign of trust, even though he'd tried to deny it.

The barriers between them were coming down.

"You speak truth, Gus. We know that the penalties would be excruciating beyond measure. We would never consider taking such a risk. But that hasn't stopped us thinking of possibilities."

"If you take syntei to the stars," Sadruddin said, "all will Divide the Body."

"Not all," said Elzabet. "Most worlds can find someone dead set against *anything*. But on Squamish, for instance, sexual gear would be a large chunk of a big syntelics industry within a month. Within a year it would be everywhere."

Sadruddin nodded. "What has changed — for me — is that I no longer think that your worlds would be the worse for it. My Church is a hard-built and pointless dam to prevent water from flowing down, where finally all water goes."

Elza touched his wet cheek with soft fingertips. "I fear we have caused you to lose your faith, Gus. It's called disillusion, it can hurt. But it's to be celebrated, not feared: illusions profit no one save those who promote them." She found Division intriguing and attractive, but could take it or leave it. Sadruddin obviously could not. Which set him up to become some kind of Messianic figure, an iconoclast — and history records the common fate of such people.

History. Another Augustine. Memories of her Gendercide course at the Academy came flooding back. There was an opposite danger. Gus might do a Saint Augustine of Hippo, so guilt-ridden that he switched back to his faith again in extreme form. That Augustine, whose promiscuous youth would be a one-way ticket to damnation, blamed all of womankind for his own carnality. He invented — virtually single-handed and contrary to his Holy Book — 'original sin'. The first woman yielded to the serpent, and got herself and the first man thrown out of Paradise. By the woman's fault, all women were eternally tainted. His church made Augustine a saint, and had been scared silly of sex ever since.

If Gus went confessional, he'd rat on his former accomplices, and end more extreme than DeLameter. How to head him off? Lower the emotional voltage... "Gus, you're not planning to pop along to DeLameter and enlighten him, are you? I doubt you'd convince him."

"I have long observed that his Reverence has two minds. One is given up to hate-filled holiness. The other is not truly convinced of anything — except that, if the Body may be Divided, then so might be the Church. And if the Church Divides and falls, where then is its Deacon?

"I now see the Church propagating delusions, of no benefit to anyone save those like its Deacon — and even he is being destroyed. They make him a monster, setting his Quizitors to torture anyone who question or obstruct. The Church has fallen into the Pit of Evil! It has become a dangerous obstacle to necessary change!"

With an effort, he lowered his voice and regained his composure. "I must take my own counsel in silence and privacy, and consider what actions are wise." He rose to leave.

"Er, Gus... Before you go..."

"Marcolo?"

"Um."

"What he's trying to say," said Elzabet firmly, "is that it's all a bit vague. We're not even tempted to risk the bone-hammers, or whatever tortures the Quizitors inflict. I can keep my imagination in check, but Marco would like to know some more about the actual practice of dividing the body. The — uh — biology. Isn't that right?"

"Well, yes." The tips of Marco's ears glowed. "But even that could be dangerous. Slippery slope and all that."

"True," said Elza, "but suppressing those thoughts could turn them obsessive, and that would be far more dangerous."

Sadruddin was clearly in two minds. "Well," he began slowly, "these are not practices upon which I am accustomed to lecture at length, even were this wise. There are syntelic ears, both of the Church and of its enemies — though not, I am certain, here, now, otherwise I would not have spoken as I did."

He paused, as if Marco's diffidence had made frankness less easy. "This I can do," he said eventually. "From Samdal, where there is no Church" — this was the continent that *Valkyrie* had provisionally named Aleph — "punctyle seeds are smuggled by Embassy guards. I will bring you masks that show you what is done afar off, where there are those that delight to display themselves, and delight even more to do so for gain. But these masks you must keep truly hidden. Strabyen."

He was gone.

12

Tidal Stress

> Tabby T. Macavity, there's no one quite like Tabby T.
> She's broken every human law, she breaks the law of gravity.
> —Tom Stearns-Elecat, The Wayland Book of Cute Cat Poems

They had long left the Yandoory. Large syntei exchanged the desert in turn for a forest, a grassy plain, a higher desert, an island in a sea of mud, and a strange cratered region reeking of sulphur. The sun lurched erratically in the sky at each transition.

Now they were approaching another town, and Tinka was looking forward to chewy food. The field rations dropped twice daily through Kurpershoek's grubsynte were nourishing, but...! All the usual faults of institutional cooking, plus nothing could survive but rock-hard pemmican or slop. Mostly, slop. Even slop struck the iron catchbowl like the hammer of Thor. At each campsite they left a deep dent in the soil. But at Hardane they would get (she began to salivate at the thought) fresh trout, roast vunbugula (deseeded!), and, maybe, *sweetapple pie*... Just around the bend in the river! She could see the syntower from here — pity the wyzand at the top still wouldn't get them off these lowlands.

They turned the corner on a riot.

The central square was filled with people running, arguing in clamorous groups, or yelling in Kalingo at the temple doors. Two active types were climbing its sides, for no reason she could detect. The doors remained obstinately shut.

They rode right into town, just reaching the square before heads began to turn. Kurpershoek spoke louder than seemed possible for the unamplified human voice.

"*Jawaharlal Megiddo Ataulfo Kurpershoek!*"

He announced his quadruple name, gripping his right elbow, right fist raised. All voices fell silent; nobody moved, save for a few edging behind others. Tinka noticed a man on the temple roof, frozen, trying to be inconspicuous on the skyline.

Kurpershoek turned to the nearest townsman. "How are you called?"

"Kirlian, Sab."

He made a motion of disgust. "Who is here with two names?"

Kirlian silently pointed to a dark-haired man in green jacket and kilt, who reluctantly came forward. With both palms against his chest, he made a formal sideways bow of respectful greeting. "Thomas Sokagai, Sab."

"Twice-named and bearing the kilt of a syndept, you run and shout like — like this Kirlian?" Kurpershoek spat at the man's feet.

"Sab, it is not because a man fashions syntei into riverfish traps and nightsoil collectors that he need not fear the Vain Vaimoksi." The syndept made his point with a resolute dignity and a quivering voice.

"Vain Vaimoksi? Here?" Kurpershoek seemed startled. "Explain yourself."

Thomas traced random grooves in the dust with one foot. "Sab, we see traces in the ground, left by no honest traveller. Three towns upriver speak the same. Who but Vain Vaimoksi would walk the river valley, Sab, without appearing in the towns? And then..." His voice trailed off.

"What happened? Why were you shouting at the temple?"

"Sab, our doctor Dag Riveroak, he is a good doctor, Sab, he cured my little — Sab." With a bow, he accepted Kurpershoek's impatient look. "Sab, respected Riveroak disappeared two nights ago. We feared the Vain Vaimoksi had taken him. And when he came back this morning, and would not say where he had been —"

"You *assumed* he was carrying a slavestone."

"We feared it might be so, and acted for that contingency, Sab."

"Where is he now?" Eyes went to the temple. "The priest gave him shelter?"

"You speak truth, Sab."

Kurpershoek grunted. "If the priest could not keep order, in this at least he acted well." He dismounted, and faced the doors. "Under the protection of the Shaper and of his Deacon under the sky, come out!" His voice crashed around the square.

One door eased open. A young doctor in his beaded loincloth and feathers came blinking into the sunlight, a step ahead of an ancient brown-robed priest.

"Doctor, where did you pass these two nights?" Kurpershoek's voice held menace. It wasn't an idle question.

"Sab, I — I do not wish to say. It is a private ma—"

"Dag Riveroak: my name is Jawaharlal Megiddo Ataulfo Kurpershoek."

The doctor, unnerved by four names, caved in. "Sab. I was... with a woman."

"Who?"

"The widow on Greenstone Heights. Kolata. Two hours upriver." His face was mottled red and white. Some among the crowd started to laugh and nudge, until Kurpershoek raised a gloved hand. Tinka gave Sam a surreptitious poke, drawing his attention to two angry-looking women near the back.

"Let her be fetched." Kurpershoek turned to the crowd. "Does this explanation satisfy you?" He got a submissive murmur of agreement. "It should not." The crowd fell silent, puzzled. A few nodded anyway. "Even if the widow confirms his story, they may both have slavestones in their guts. To wander alone when there are Vain Vaimoksi abroad is to ask for — doctor, *did* you meet them?"

"Sab, I swear, no."

"And if the truth had been 'yes', and you had confessed this?"

"Uh—"

"In the next moment a Vain Vaimoksi listening to your speech would send a poisoned arrow through the seed in your stomach, by which he listens. You *must* swear no, whatever the truth. Convince me that you do not speak under compulsion."

Riveroak relaxed. He knew the proof, all doctors did. "Sab, a man may look."

"Indeed. But is there in Hardane another than yourself who can operate an intestinal probe?"

"Ahh, Sab... No, there is not."

"Is there a wyzand, by which one may come?"

"We have a wyzand with Skoont, Sab, but the paperwork..." Ten days in advance, in triplicate.

"Can a doctor synte us a probe he can direct?"

"Sab, those I consult are higher. The probe would break in the synte."

"Doctor: I would not ordinarily question your professional word, but you must see that in these circumstances I cannot accept your own inspection of your gut."

The Doctor nodded, his face glum. Kurpershoek gave him a hard stare. "How long would it take to fetch another doctor?" Land travel was less regulated than syntei.

The doctor reviewed the options. "Sab, from downriver, three days afoot. From upriver, nine afoot, four afloat."

Kurpershoek nodded. "And can either town provide a guard to ensure *him* against enslavement? Six men trained in fighting, preferably more?"

The doctor looked at the priest. The two went into a huddle with the syndept and other prominent citizens. The priest spoke for them. "No, Sab. We could not provide this. Neither could Kastane nor Fothring-by-the-Cliff. The Fothrinch might borrow men from Yandoory Bend, however. Uh — that, too, will take time, Sab."

"Doctor," said Kurpershoek acidly, "you should confine yourself to *healing* your patients' flesh. It is written that we should comfort the widow, but your procedure is about to lose me a week escorting you to a colleague and back, or fetching one here.

"But soon, it is evening. We will eat. In the morning, I decide. Cuzak!"

"Sab!" A thin, lanky guard took three paces forward.

"Accompany the doctor. If he is enslaved, there is no knowing what he might do. Mulnood and Vrent will assist you."

~~~

Over the third course — fried fish encrusted with crushed nuts in a piquant herbal sauce — Felix picked Kurpershoek's brains about the Vain Vaimoksi.

"Little of substance is known, Sab. The organisation is composed entirely of women. Whence they come, only the Vaimoksi themselves know. They trade in human lives, taking slaves by force, selling for profit." He spat on the ground. "Some they keep for toil, distilling spirits and mind-benumbing substances. Mostly *kreesh*."

"*Kreesh*? What's that?"

"Many would pay well for that information. Only the Vain Vaimoksi and their slaves know its source."

As the trout with filfil nuts relaxed Tinka's stomach, an idea surfaced in her mind. Turning to Thomas Sokagai the syndept, she asked if an intestinal probe could be operated over a four days' distance.

"Indeed, Sabi. But the controls for this *hoom*'s probes are all here in Hardane."

"Can a probe be controlled from afar, even if there is a difference in height?"

The syndept beamed with pride. "Most assuredly, Sabi! Be the difference not too great. The design has much improved over the centuries. To prevent a contrafluent efflux of stomach acids, the controls are modified falasyntei, with membrane baffles. Transparent membranes for vision, thicker opaque ones for directional control. The doctors push or pull the membrane to create pressure-differences at the far end. Only the syntelic administration of medicines becomes difficult."

Tinka grunted in satisfaction. "Is there a synte wide enough to convey the controls to Fothring-by-the-Cliff, or to bring a probe from Kastane?"

The syndept saw where she was heading. It wouldn't work, but he was polite. "At Fothring — no, it has only a novice priest, not authorised to oversee the permitted uses of mid-range syntei. But we have such a synte with Kastane, yes."

"Could not the Kastane doctor send a probe through a synte, whilst retaining his controls?"

Kurpershoek stopped dissecting his trout. She had *heard* the consultant was higher. He turned to the syndept. "How deep a synte do you have with Kastane?"

"We have a tenth-*vij* chamfret, Sab, the deepest we have ever grown. But Kastane is above Throat Falls, Sab — three hundred *vij* higher than here."

"We cannot synte them your controls, then."

"No."

"Their probe is a delicate instrument, Sabi," said Kurpershoek. "In a fall of three hundred *vij* it would strike like rations in a catchbowl."

"No, as long as Kastane's higher, the drop won't be a problem." Kurpershoek and the syndept shook their heads in bemusement. Tinka turned away for a moment as if embarrassed, working swiftly and surreptitiously on her wrist. "Tidal stress about fifty gee per metre — can a probe withstand a drop from ten *vij* on to earth like this ground?" She prodded it with her toe.

"It could, Sabi. But it could not survive a fall of three hundred, which we consider here." The syndept leaned back with the satisfied air of the technical expert who has just confounded a lay suggestion.

"But only the tidal stress is unavoidable," said Tinka, as much to herself as to the syndept. "Not the final impact. For a small object with those numbers, the bang is much the worst part. I have a suggestion."

She turned to them and explained. Several times, with gestures. With a headscarf. With rocks. They conferred in rapid Kalingo. Eventually, Kurpershoek said: "Sabi, I cannot believe it. But it might save us a week. I cannot order a doctor to risk a probe on anything so outrageous and unlikely, but *if* he is willing, and *if* you can convince the Kastane syndept that your mad proposal might have merit, and *if* he can make and attach your device—"

"A dry run might help."

"—?"

"No need to risk the probe for the first attempt. Try it with something less valuable. If that works, go for the real thing."

"Wise. Let us go to the falasynte."

She followed him to the syntelic communications cabin, with a regretful glance back at the best meal she had yet had on the planet — or ever — and the sudden thought that she had done herself out of a week of such cooking. Maybe Sam would save her some of the second course. Mind you, if the idea worked, it would also work for field rations. *Cordon bleu* could replace slop. Except that the military mind would prefer slop anyway. Shouldn't pamper the troops.

~~~

Early next morning, half the town watched the syndept bring the Kastane kantapunctyle from the temple and lay it carefully, reverently, and doubtfully on the ground. "Ready in seven breaths," he said into it, and waved everyone back.

A small white package hurtled into the air, rising almost to invisibility against the sky. A high dot became a definite spot, which grew steadily. The first parachute on Qish settled to earth.

Shortly, the second followed.

The Kastane doctor wriggled the undamaged probe through Dag Riveroak in two hours. Boiled, it went through his embarrassed lady-friend; and, just to be on the safe side, through the man who had gone to fetch her.

"What would you have done if the doctor *had* found a slavestone?" asked Felix. "Remove it by surgery?"

Kurpershoek shook his head. "The bearer dies," he said. "Most likely by a VV arrow, but one death or another cannot be avoided. A slavestone grows tendrils into the stomach wall. If it is removed by force, the tendrils remain and fester. Like a parasitic vunbugula stone, it can be destroyed only by killing the mother-plant, known only to the Vain Vaimoksi. The Law therefore is that an enstoned slave be killed. There are no exceptions."

Kurpershoek pouched the probe, for return to Kastane on their way upriver. At the end of a parting address to the citizens, consisting mainly of advice to consult proper authority in an orderly manner when there was trouble, and to keep their bodies whole, he settled one final outstanding issue.

"The widow Kolata cannot live alone on her farm, with evidence of Vain Vaimoksi about. In town she is without support. She shall live in the house of Dag Riveroak the doctor, and share his goods."

As they left, it seemed to Tinka that the doctor looked pleased but harried, the widow gratified — and two other women, more annoyed than ever.

~~~

Marco lay on the sleeping pad watching a firelit scene. His viewpoint was about a metre from the ground, but the walls were lined with punctyles at every height — eyes watching from every viewpoint. How many eyes? Hundreds? Thousands? Not all the punctyles he could see showed pupils behind the glass. But one pair somewhere would show Elza's, if he knew where to look.

Perspective was oddly, dreamily exaggerated: deliberately, perhaps. The far openings of the syntei were wider apart than his eyes.

All he could see was a muffled form on a thick, wide sleeping-pad. Through the sides of his mask came a soft drumbeat in an intricate syncopated rhythm, gradually louder as the firelight brightened.

Suddenly, in utter silence a barefoot figure entered the room, in a robe that glimmered in the firelight. A woman? Yes, no older than twenty. The thin cloth clung at different places as her dance took her silently around the sleeper. Bending suddenly, in one smooth movement she swept away the covering and threw it out of sight.

On the cushion a girl lay on her back, arms and legs somewhat apart. Long black hair streamed down to cover her breasts. She still seemed asleep.

The dancer produced a small drum and knelt between her feet, tapping delicately with her fingers. The beat was taken up by the deeper drums from before, a relentless, compulsive throbbing which other instruments joined. Gradually it became faster. The sleeper twitched, and Marco's attention was suddenly fixed between her legs. What had he seen?

Ceasing to drum, letting the excitement of the music build behind her kneeling form, the draped dancer reached out slim round arms to stroke the sleeper's legs. Again the twitch — something was moving there. The dancer combed the sleeper's long hair with a silver comb, crooning to herself. The movement became stronger as the hair seemed to pulse upward to the music.

All at once the lips parted slightly, but still hid what was between them. Sliding forward out of her robe, the dancer bent to kiss it. With a jerk it met her mouth; as she straightened, Marco saw a rounded tip of maleness stand proud from a female nest.

The music ebbed. It almost vanished, then slid upward as the dancer crooned. Among the eyes on the walls, were two eyes those of its man? Still crooning, the dancer enticed it upward like a snake from a furry sack. Her slender, long-nailed fingers stroked, and it jerked. Marco felt his own flesh rise in sympathy. He watched it stand, still raising and lowering slightly, as once again she danced, brown hair rippling down her bare shoulders. The black-haired girl murmured and writhed in her sleep.

Now the dancer knelt astride, her groin touching the pillar that rose from the body of the sleeper. As she made contact, touching and swaying, it seemed to strain upward, to emerge further, to press between her legs. She surrounded the tip, and rocked gently with the music.

At a sudden trill from some kind of flute, she threw her head straight back and lowered her hips. As the shaft was swallowed below, the tip emerged from between her teeth. What part of Marco's mind remained rational told him that between the two openings it must be joined by a synte, internally deep to avoid a gravity barrier or tidal pain: or, were there two? But the illusion was perfect. The dancer was transfixed on a rigid male pole.

The sleeper awoke, and smiled. The dancer swept black hair aside to caress the oiled body. Hands touched the impaling tip, and tugged, irresistible and urgent. The pole seemed to bend with the curving of the brown-haired body towards the black.

As the women entered a close embrace, mouth to mouth and groin to groin, both passing one living, sliding bolt, Marco felt Elzabet slip over him. Their bodies moved in synchrony with those they watched, in time to the throbbing music. Marco half-imagined that bolt as his own, as passion stole his mind, and the two Starfolk and the music climaxed together.

~~~

As night followed night they came to see Sadruddin's first offering as tame, among the boundless combinations and sexual geometries of syntei. One evening was spent with ancient images, somehow passed down from Old Earth. They saw the unicorn, and why he lays his head in the lap of the maiden; they saw Spring gods mate with the gaping earth; they saw a six-armed goddess embrace the men whose heads do sit beneath their shoulders. There were men two-pronged like a lizard, women with soft and hairy hands, men receptive, and penetrative women who haunted Marco's dreams.

Arousing though these were, Marco and Elzabet stopped short — as Sadruddin repeatedly insisted — of dividing their own bodies. If in some all-too-possible way they were exposed, they would fall short of Abomination. Watching body-division was something that the Church discouraged, but only those performing the division were guilty of the ultimate sin, and destined for the grisly work of the bone-hammers. Watching was punished, if known to the authorities, but not severely — unless repeated.

The problem was...

~~~

"Watching is all very well," Marco said over breakfast in the Fringeworld dialect they used for private talk in public. "I see the players having themselves a ball, and I certainly enjoy the show — and the companionable enhancement, thank you ma'am, without which the experience would be rather sad. I'm not really the voyeur type."

"Nah, I heard you were no wallflower in the groping-pool. My sheltered upbringing only meant that Hippolytan nobles don't flaunt themselves in front of the common herd. I agree that it's fine and stimulating to see these things. But — you want to join in, don't you?" She looked warily at him, sharing his conflicting urges.

Marco grimaced. "In a way — but it *is* too dangerous. Tinka said it: *don't*. You didn't see what they'd done to those poor wretches in the cage-frames. You were out cold, and I'm glad. I wish I'd been, too.

"And yet... The penalties are way over the top, but I'm beginning to see why the Church banned it. It can take over your mind. But even if it was legal, I wouldn't want to join in any of the performances we've seen." He laughed. "They wouldn't let me, anyway; that sort of thing requires a lot of specialist training. The precision of the first performance we saw: it was like a sexual ballet."

Elzabet exhaled in satisfaction. "So that's one temptation safely out of the way. What about the audience-participation sequences?"

Marco shook his head. "Not my style."

"Too right. That phallicactus effect was a bit over the top, even by Squamite standards. So what *would* you have in mind, as a purely theoretical exercise? You know you can't *do* it. I'm not risking *one* bone, let alone my entire skeleton, to satisfy your curiosity. But maybe talking about it will help get it out of your system. Come on, tell auntie Elza."

"I sort of wish we could explore some of the possibilities for ourselves, instead of meekly watching while we cling to each other and our old habits. Waiting for Tinka and the others to come back is hardly tedious, but it has limitations, right?"

Elzbet nodded. "You're special, Marco, but a girl needs a bit of variety." It slipped out despite her terror of the torturers. "But not *here*, Marco! Only when we're out of the clutches of these repression-ridden fanatics."

"Agreed. But it won't do any harm to investigate the options. I'm working with Gus on the *Handbook* this afternoon. I'll sound him out."

"Theoretically *only*, Marco. Store up the ideas until we're somewhere safer. We'll have to wait until we get somewhere it's legal." She changed the topic.

"Speaking of the *Handbook*, how's the work going?"

"Dead end. Science on this world has got to *start* with syntei."

"But — didn't I hear you saying syntelics needed pion microscopes?"

"For how the things *work*, sure. In fine detail. But you can infer a lot about the likely structure. I'm convinced that the plants must be genetically programmed to grow some kind of metamaterial tissue, for instance. That could act like exotic matter."

"Wouldn't that allow cold fusion to replace photosynthesis?"

"On some planet, maybe, but Qishi evolution missed that option. Here, it's more like optical metamaterials, with negative refractive index, but in a gravitic context. Karmic cloaking, synthesising the illusion of negative mass. I could try some designs, given a yottaflop supercomp."

"And if pigs had wings, we'd all carry shit-proof umbrellas."

"Yah. But what I can make progress on is how syntei *behave*. I'd thought that over two thousand years the natives would have sussed out all the tricks, but I've changed my mind. Pure syntelics, yah — but they can't imagine hybrid mechanosyntelic devices, they don't have the necessary mechanical experience. They think wheels are really clever gadgets."

"Yah. But they have *some* hybrid devices. Half-wheels *are* really clever, I always thought the top half was wasteful and in the way. And look at their tricks with waterpower… So what's hard about mechanosyntelics?"

"Did you hear about that parachute trick Tinka used downriver?"

"Sure. *That's* what you mean? A hanky and some string?"

"It's the basic maths. They're like cathedral builders taking generations to find out what stands up, with no calculus of forces. The syndepts here are all agog to know how she worked out the stresses. I think I've got them interested enough to start on calculus. Trouble is, they really want to learn it from *Tinka*."

"But you've started anyway?"

"Of course. Strike while the pion is hot. Problem is, they're a bit too intelligent. Give me dumb students cramming for the next test any day. They believe everything you tell them. But I hadn't been talking ten minutes before this lot came up with a mixture of Zeno and some of Bishop Berkeley, from fifty years after Newton. I *think* with infinitesimals, trash it, but they take fancy logic to justify. And if I say 'There is no way axioms can exclude them, hence by model theory we can use them', they'll extend it to angels. I have a horrible feeling I'll have to do everything with limits."

Marco looked so mournful that Elzabet laughed at him.

"The main thing, anyway, is that we need to come up with a lot more tricks like Tinka's, doing new things with syntei by bringing in basic physics. Maybe a synte periscope, even a whole submarine."

"Or a suction-cleaner. The Deacon's housemaids would love one of those."

"Yah!" Marco's mental cogwheels were already revolving. "But — when I start thinking about tricks with syntei —"

"— we both know exactly where your mind goes!" Elzabet leaned back in her chair. "I'm beginning to see *why* Saint Paddy banned it, to be frank. If no one ever thought of anything else, they'd never have got any serious work done."

"Counterproductive, though," Marco contradicted. "Banning it just made this lot think about it all the more. And think even harder about not being able to do it. Just look at their body-language! No wonder no one invented the parachute."

"That's as may be. But you need to get serious work done, so you'd better get used to keeping your mind *off* the salacious applications."

~~~

Marco noticed, not for the first time, that Sadruddin had a small kolosynte on the desk, next to the *Handbook*. Previously he had assumed it had just been left lying around, but in Two Mountains that was a dangerous assumption. He gestured towards it and raised an eyebrow.

"Our discussions are of great interest to the Church," Sadruddin responded obliquely. "The Deacon has offered me the use of a membrancer to record our discussions. In *complete* detail." Plainly, a veiled warning. "It is a great honour, Sab. It expresses the Church's recognition of the importance of your knowledge."

Marco was wondering how a membrancer might function, although the general gist seemed clear. He was about to ask for details when Sadruddin bent once more over the sacred text. "Now, Sab: explain this phrase to me. In simple language."

Marco leaned over, to see that the Chaplain was pointing to a section headed 'Symplectic Integrators.' *This*, he thought, *will be a challenge.*

13

Abomination

> Psychological dependence on a stimulus is closely analogous to physiological dependence on psychoactive substances. It occurs when the body incorporates addictive behaviour into its normal functioning. Deprivation then causes psychological distress and adverse physiological symptoms, such as headaches, cold sweats, and anxiety. This leads to an ever-increasing demand for the stimulus. The process is insidious, and those affected may not recognise its onset. By the time they become aware, it is too late.
> — *Wang Ryan-Ling, Psychosomatics for Idiots*

"Marcolo, Els'bett," said Sadruddin that evening in the quiet dark, "speak not loudly."

Elzabet looked up and saw what the Chaplain was carrying in his hands. "I thought I said *theoretical*."

Marco gave a sheepish grin. "Just asking Gus to show us some of the experimental apparatus, Elza. We don't have to use it."

"This room is safety," Sadruddin murmured, "free of sound and sight syntei."

"So why are you whispering?"

"Sound can travel through rock."

"I'm not sure about this. But —" Elza could see Marco almost dancing with frustration " — I'll take a look. Nothing more."

"Certain tools can well divide the body." Sadruddin produced what looked like two leather collars. "With these, two persons may exchange heads. You understand that your mind does not control the new body upon which your head finds itself resting? Only your usual body, to which your head is synted. Balance can be difficult."

"Sure," said Marco. "Wow, a *genuine* out-of-body experience! I wonder what the religious nuts would make of these?"

"Bone-hammers," said Elzabet sourly.

"With these, shoulder-syntei," Sadruddin went on, "your arms may grow from the armpits of another, or you may exchange arms — person to person, or left to right."

"I'm sure it's a fascinating experience, Gus. But I'm not risking torture to fiddle about with other people's heads or arms. Legs neither, dah?"

"As you wish. But these —" like two G-strings but with emptiness in the central triangles " — would exchange your sexual parts."

"Um. A good job the collapse of a *small* synte doesn't amputate whatever's passing through!" Marco looked pained, but Elza was glad she had mentioned it. Damage would be all too likely if the user got distracted, especially if they were physically active at the same time. As they surely would be, using *these* gadgets.

"They will still be felt by their owners, but controlled by their wearers."

"Yah, I understand that..." her voice trailed off. "It would let me keep tabs on what Marco has in mind."

"It is said that in Scythery, married folk wear such always, as a bond."

"It *would* be difficult to bring in third parties without prior consent," said Elzabet. "But I see practical difficulties. How do they answer a call of nature: scratch what they've borrowed, as a signal, and the spouse goes?"

"The Scytherics keep no closets in their houses," Sadruddin explained. "Piss and dung synte direct from their bodies, through a sterilising drop, to a central manufactory of chemicals and fertiliser. I have long thought this an admirable system, but the Great Conclave of seventy years ago ruled that internal stuffs remain of the body, so to exsynte them constitutes Division.

"I have always thought this thinking illogical, but the Church fears novelty, so the application was always slated for rejection. Perhaps, soon, that may change..."

Sadruddin didn't sound as though he meant reversal of a minor theological ruling. The game was afoot, somewhere among the clerics of Two Mountains. Not for the first time, Elzabet wondered what they were getting themselves tangled up in.

But Gus offered their one hope of escaping the Deacon's iron grasp.

"It does sound a very convenient and hygienic system," she agreed. "And it could be a monthly blessing to Qishi women as well, at least until your planet rejoins the Concordat and they can have their hormones fixed. But —"

"But?"

Oh, Mother. It's just *too* tempting. Damn and double-damn Marco for asking. I'm getting very frustrated, and Gus *is* discreet. We've both come to trust him. He's not like the others. And he knows the system, top to bottom. If anybody can keep it safe, he can. "The only syntelic gadgets that interest me — and Marco — right now are these nifty little numbers. Beat punctyle pants to heck, I can tell you. Are you *sure* we are safe from observation, here, now?"

"Upon my life, lady."

"Yes, it will be."

Elzabet felt as though she was drowning. But what a way to go! Somewhere deep inside, her resolve began to collapse. As if down a long, echoing tunnel, she heard herself saying "Gus, our friend: will you join us in their use?"

Sadruddin stopped breathing. He glanced at Marco, who smiled fondly. Starfolk were broad-minded and physically generous, except out on the Fringe. Sexual diseases might possibly have reappeared on Qish, despite all the medical tests performed on would-be colonists, but genetic immunity to such conditions had given the Starfolk freedom for centuries.

Marco's smile broadened. "Go for it, Gus."

"*Sabi!* Els'bett — golden lady — know that you have lived in my dreams... Marcolo, my friend..." He pulled himself together. "Know you that it was with no such hopes that I brought you these gifts. Much have you both taught me, and I owe you both. You have no obligation —"

"Gus, it's not *obligation*," Elzabet told him. "We both want you." She hugged him, and Marco joined in.

~~~

Marco's memories of that night were never entirely clear. So many changes: wearing Elza's golden triangle and learning the female movements, with Sadruddin's body above him wearing Elza's head, while Sadruddin's head like John the Baptist on a platter faced the loins that Marco had lent to Elzabet, working his long tongue... Himself entering Sadruddin-as-woman, by exchange with Elzabet, while she caressed them both... He had seen a cervix in sexual anatomy vids, but never tasted one... Meeting her eye inside her, as they both watched the muscular storm of her orgasm ripple around them... Kneeling to his own and then Sadruddin's genitals on her, with Sadruddin behind him... Entered by Elza wearing his, or were they Sadruddin's?... Exchanging with his friend, to love her two mouths, as each other...

The permutations were doubtless finite, but they seemed to have no end.

~~~

Sadruddin replaced his body-dividing toys in concealment. No guards had descended upon them the wrath of Magog. They had dared and won. It was a heady experience, like extreme skydiving — a brush with death that heightened the senses.

Elza told herself firmly that she had made a terrible mistake, and she had been very lucky indeed to have got away with it. They couldn't risk a repeat performance. That would lead to a third, a fourth,... and at some point the Deacon would get lucky.

"Gus — you are well pleased?" Marco asked, as the three bathed each other.

"Els'bett, Marcolo... Never have I felt so sweet and soft in my body. Always my own knowledge, knowledge that now falls from my shoulders, that I must not do this thing; always my disgust that others would do it with me, and their contempt for me; never this holding warmth. Truly an old pain has held this, my land, too long."

They slept.

~~~

As the tents went up, Tinka watched Kurpershoek pull from his mufflebag the chamfret for his evening report to Two Mountains. She and Marco had spoken through it two or three times, early on, but at the time she'd been too worried about Elzabet to think about syntei. All at once, she was puzzled by something.

"Kurpershoek?"

"Sabi?"

"May I see your falasynte for a moment?"

"Sabi," handing it across. A sturdy dark-haired man, almost as tall as her and a head above most other natives she had seen, he had a pale closed face marked by thin lines. His movements were firm and economical. Attractive, in his way.

The falasynte was closed by a translucent membrane. She could dimly see a confused room with junior priests rushing in and out carrying syntei, hanging or replacing them on huge racks, sometimes talking or shouting into them in a hubbub that made the membrane buzz. Earlier, the kantasynte had been in Elza and Marco's quiet room. The complexity of organising a Synte Central made her mind reel. But she returned to her question.

"Kurpershoek, why this... husk? Peel?" She tapped the membrane.

"You speak truth, Sabi. Through the synte the mother plant pushes strange air, that is trapped by this thin stretchy husk and makes a great ball that hates the ground. It floats through the air, carrying a bigger kasynte than wind alone could lift. It is the best we have found for the falasynte purpose."

"Yes, but what *is* the purpose? Why don't you use an open synte, through which we could speak more clearly?"

He slid a finger over the skin. "Sabi: see you how it bulges away from us? Were it open, a great wind would rush through, and to see or hear would not be easy."

"Of course." Sam had joined the conversation. "Pressure's greater down here."

"No, Sam, that doesn't figure. Air could flow forever, perpetual motion, as gravity resettles the atmosphere... oh, right. The compressed gravity in the synte ought to have the same balance between height and pressure that you usually get. So where *does* the wind come from?"

"Kurpershoek," asked Sam, "is the bulge always the same way?"

"No, Sab. Last night it was flat; three days ago it pressed towards me so tight that at the slightest touch it boomed in the manner of a drum."

"Weather." Sam looked pleased with himself. "If the air were in equilibrium, so would the syntei be. But we're still three hundred klicks from Two Mountains, and the same pressure difference that makes this southerly wind —" he paused to listen as it rustled through silver leaves reddened by the setting sun "— would make a howling gale through this synte. It's not the up-down, it's the sideways, and it's powered by the sun stirring up the atmosphere." Another pause, then: "I *wondered* about those hefty doors in the tunnel to Two Mountains! I thought they were to keep intruders out. But why two? Extra security, sure, but it's obvious now. A windlock."

"Keeping out unauthorised people would appeal to the Deacon too," Tinka replied. A new thought struck her. "But they're missing a trick. You could run a power system on it. A wide net of pairs would almost always have some good pressure differences. And turbines *inside* would be much more efficient than sticking up into a normal wind." She began to explain this to Kurpershoek, who was patiently waiting for the return of his falasynte, but quickly gave up. He'd never heard of electricity.

"Sabi, these are deep mysteries, and powerful. I cannot follow your reasoning, but it is true that far-wyzands must be fitted with doors, or else strong gales would sometimes make them impassable. You say those gales could instead be... harnessed? It is not for me to think about such ideas, but I will convey them to the appropriate authorities. The Temple syndepts will be impatient for your return to Two Mountains."

That evening, as they washed off the day's dust and towelled themselves, Jane spotted something very familiar, hanging round Kurpershoek's bared neck. It glittered in the late afternoon light. *Could it be?* How had he got hold of it?

Who cared? If it was what she thought it must be, she wanted it. Desperately.

She moved nearer, for a closer look. *Yes!* It was the laser medallion.

Kurpershoek noticed her interest. "Do you like my little gem?"

Jane looked him deep in the eye. "It was mine, once," she said wistfully. "But then His Reverence the Deacon became the owner — as was his right."

"The Deacon gave it to me," Kurpershoek told her, "as a token of his esteem." This divided the truth. DeLameter had entrusted him with the holy storage of the Starfolk's possessions, except the stunbeams, to which the Deacon had a fancy. Kurpershoek had spotted the unusual pendant, found it decorative, and appropriated it. Jewellery always attracted the ladies — as Jane was now confirming.

"May I touch it?" She plucked it from his chest, her fingers brushing his skin. "It's so beautiful." She paused, looked bashful. "I'd do anything to get it back, Kurpershoek."

"That might be, Sabi,... but I will not lightly give up something so unique."

"Can you suggest a fit exchange?"

Kurpershoek nodded. And told her.

I'll have to speak to Tinka. But she'll see we need every weapon we can get hold of, whatever it costs. "I will put your proposition to my friend."

That night, Felix and Sam slept alone, Jane and Tinka in Kurpershoek's tent. Next morning, he looked smug but shell-shocked, and seemed unable to concentrate.

Jane covertly showed her companions the laser medallion. She hung it under her shirt, until she could think of a safer place to hide it.

~~~

Kurpershoek made his evening report to the Temple. Putting the falasynte as close as was safe to the campfire, he waited for some operator to notice the light.

Tinka thought about calling at fixed times, in a sundial culture. Odd, no good clocks… No, natural. The big Old Earth push to high-precision timepieces had been the longitude problem for navigators, comparing the observed time zone with a clock set for home time. Here, they could synchronise sundials with a falasynte.

After a rapid exchange in Kalingo, Kurpershoek waited again as the other half was carried to Paladeacon Kundal. His report was quickly interrupted, by Kalingo too fast for her to follow. He motioned the offworlders away. She watched from a distance as his back grew rigid and the lines of his face sharpened to a cold, hard mask.

He went to his men and spoke softly. Before she knew it, she and the other three were facing him, each restrained by a guard, unable to move their arms.

"Perverts!"

Oh, Mother, not again! "But Kurpershoek, what have we —?" It couldn't have been his night of passion in a threesome, there were no theological objections to that. So what —?

"You will address me with respect, and only when instructed to speak."

Silence followed, broken by Sam starting to protest until a gauntlet crashed across his face. Blood trickled down his chin, as Cuzak took his knife, buckling it to his own belt. Tinka caught Sam's attention and shook her head. *No point in futile gestures.* With a visible effort, he subsided.

Kurpershoek flicked his hard gaze across their faces. "Your accomplices have been detected in Abomination! I am to bring you close-guarded to the Temple, alive and unharmed, but no more than that. Be warned: I have no orders for your comfort."

He turned to his men. "The Holy Book orders 'the perverted shall be clothed in coarsest sackcloth.' Use the empty sacks. Search first for weapons."

Two of the guards attended to Sam and Felix, Cuzak ordered the other two to bring him Tinka and Jane. With her arms still held, Jane was unable to reach the laser. She watched, expressionless, as Cuzak cut holes and shoved a filthy sack over Tinka's head. Then he bound her with ropes.

Jane struggled, hoping to free an arm, but the guard gripped even firmer. Cuzak reached forward and started to unfasten her shirt. His fingers met the medallion, and pulled it into view. "A pretty bauble! Not one that a prisoner may keep." He unclasped the chain, and stuffed both into a pouch at his belt, and tore off her shirt. As he untied the drawstring of her pantaloons, Jane half-expected rape, but then realised that re-designation as Abominator made her sexually unclean. He'd as soon hump a goat.

Once dressed in harsh sacking, they were tied to the trees. "Burn the garments of the Abominable, as it is written. Their heads and bodies will be shaved at the next town," Kurpershoek ordered. He turned away to the fire, where he sat, brooding.

The laser had been their best chance of escape. Felix's murmurs to comfort her, on the nearest tree, avoided any hint that the 'jewel' was anything more.

Here we go again, Tinka thought, resigning herself to a cold, hungry and vertical night. Already raw-skinned in places, she whispered. "I suppose Marco got up to something?"

Felix gave a glum nod. They did not speculate, yet, on what had happened.

~~~

Marco had been about to head for the afternoon's *Handbook* session when Sadruddin appeared at their door, out of breath and panic-stricken.

"Marcolo! Els'bett! I am a fool!"

"Gus, what —?"

"Flee now! For your lives! Seek the room in the cliff, where we talked of the stars — you will not soon be sought there. Be silent there. I come when I can."

"Ask no questions. Go!"

For the first time, Marco was thankful for the synted palace complexity he had found so hard to learn, as they walked with pretended calm the fifty paces that took them through eight doors. *One synte takes you anywhere, and a chain of eight — ! Searches must be next to impossible. Unless they used hounds.*

He tried not to think of hounds.

An endless hour later, Sadruddin appeared, looking grey.

"Marcolo, I am without sense. I let temptation cloud my wits. That assembly where I took you last night, it was insanity!"

"If not," Marco said, "it was the next best thing." Even at a multi-person Division he still believed the permutations were finite in principle. It had to be a theorem. But he was beginning to doubt it in practice.

"Never should I have been persuaded! Not your fault in asking, mine to agree. Many times have I been there myself, always in safety. All the usual precautions. New, random location every time. Face masks. Players from different towns, strangers each other. It is rumoured that the organiser is Vain Vaimoksi. They are subtle and hide their anger, but they are efficient. She never attends, herself. Had she known I brought a guest so tall, and brown all over, she would have reminded that he must watch unseen through a synte, lest his very skin betray him."

"But that's what I did," said Marco, puzzled.

"No, that is what we both intended. But I forgot about the incense. *Kreesh* is used to fill the mind with wild visions and heightened sensations."

"A hallucinogen?"

"I know not the word. But its very smell befuddles the mind. And it can pass through a synte."

"Oh, pigshit. I was affected? No wonder I can't remember a thing after those women began competing to see how many —"

"You pushed me aside and joined in the sport, Marcolo." Gus sighed. "Els'bett, I swear I planned this not! He was in the action for mere heartbeats before I dragged him away. I thought time had been too short for anyone to notice. I was wrong."

"Someone recognised Marco," Elzabet said.

"You speak truth, my Lady. The Deacon has spies everywhere. I have always thought it abominable that he forgive them in advance for joining such gatherings, and cleanse them of their sins, to harvest the names they learn. But, it is done. And now you must leave Shaaluy."

"What of our friends?"

"DeLameter already has them in ropes, and is bringing them back. I will do whatever I can to save them, if I survive this disaster, but it will be difficult. I say not 'impossible', for there yet remains hope. But there will be none if *you* are captured. The Quizitors will quickly extract everything you know, and then I, too, will be of no use to anybody, least of all your friends."

"You speak truth, Gus," Elzabet said in an uncertain whisper.

"Isn't this Vain Vaimoksi organisation based off-continent?" asked Marco. "Perhaps they could smuggle us out?"

Sadruddin looked horrified. "No one knows the Vain Vaimoksi base. That they could smuggle you where none would ever find you, I doubt not, but you do not wish to bear a slavestone. I shall not release you unprotected into the jaws of evil. There are worse fates, for you and your Lady, even than those offered by Deacon DeLameter."

Elzabet's stomach churned. She felt sick. She was shaking with fear. "Then how do we escape, Gus?"

"There is but one chance, so bold that I trust none will suspect. You have seen the warriors of the Deacon's Personal Guard?"

They had. Men chosen for height, masked in steel, in dark leather from their gauntlets to their boots. The fear lit by such anonymity went back to the Secret Police patterns of Old Earth. "You are both tall enough to deceive a casual onlooker. I can bring you uniforms and direct you to the Embassy gate."

"Gus, I — I don't think I can. I'm too scared, they'll notice. We'll be caught."

"She's right," said Marco. "We won't be c-convincing enough. They'll arrest us and t-torture us. Look at me, I'm stammering just to think about it."

A bit late to start taking the dangers seriously.

"There is a herb that calms the mind. That, too, shall I bring. If you are fortunate, no Deacon's guard will meet and challenge you. Certainly no mere Embassy Guard will dare to speak to you, let alone question you. You must pass through the wyzand in silence, and disappear into Samdal."

"You're not coming with us?"

"Marcolo, I cannot. My departure would reveal my guilt. My mother, my students, my friends would hang by their feet. None has identified me. None suspects me. My work is here, preparing to lift the burden of a false Church from my people."

Elzabet had a suspicion that his mother was almost as likely to hang by her feet if Sadruddin started a reformation, but there was no gain in making that certain. It wasn't, she reflected, really Marco's fault. It had been the drug. But with hindsight, all three of them had been playing with fire. Playing with bone-hammers.

She pushed the negative thoughts aside. A Lady of Quynt did not regret her failings, since that would be to admit to them. She accepted what was, and moved on. Elzabet came to a decision, the only one open to them.

"We've been trying to leave Shaaluy from the day we first saw *Magog*," she said. "Ironic, but this disaster might just turn to advantage."

She hated abandoning the others, and she was ashamed that stupidity had put them all in peril. She had never felt so powerless, so guilty. From his hangdog expression, Marco felt exactly the same.

Now, however, was not the time for fruitless breast-beating. Penance could come later, best expressed by rescuing the four captive Starfolk. And to do that, the two of them had to retain their freedom. At any price.

She shot Marco a guilt-filled glance. He nodded. "Gus? We'll do it."

"Strabyen, Sab and Sabi," said Sadruddin. "I return at dusk with the herb and your disguises."

~~~

Tinka woke from a doze at last allowed by early sunlight, after the bitter cold before dawn. Someone had slapped her face. The sharp pain faded, replaced by the deeper ache of the ropes and abrasive garb.

"Who are your accomplices in Two Mountains?" It was Kurpershoek.

"Elzabet. And Marco." This they already knew; no loss in telling.

He slapped her again. "Not your companions, your accomplices from *this* world. Address your superior with respect, and stop telling me what I already know."

There was nothing to gain by defiance. "Sab, I speak truth. We know no one in Two Mountains beyond Elzabet and Marco. We spent only two days there. We met no one else save DeLam— His Reverence the Deacon —" the hand dropped back "— then you, and we all went downriver to burn the tree. We had no opportunity to make friends or acquire local accomplices, Sab!"

"Then you must have been agents of the Abominators beyond the ocean *before* you were sent to spy on us! Who are your fellow conspirators in Two Mountains?"

"No one sent us. We fell by accident from the—"

"Silence! The stars are clean! You are of the Divisive and Abominable blasphemers in the caverns over the ocean. Foreign filth! *Who are their agents in Two Mountains?*"

"I don't — I mean, nobody! We weren't — Sab, we have no knowledge of Two Mountains!" Tinka was desperate. She had the physical courage to stand torture for a secret she possessed, but her mind shook under this demand for one she did not.

"Then who has hid your two companions? Who stole the gems from the Deacon's Chapel?"

Shaven Lily! That was vital information, not to mention good news, given away free. Whatever Marco and Elzabet had got themselves into, they'd got out. She rallied.

"Sab, I swear by all a person may hold sacred under the earth *and* above the earth that I have no clue to where Elzabet and Marco are." If he believed in oaths, that one ought to be sufficiently unbreakable to convince him she was telling the truth.

"Blasphemer!" She shut her eyes for another blow, but he muttered in disgust and turned to Felix. Maybe she had been impressive enough that he didn't expect to break her resistance without serious torture; and, he was supposed to bring them back intact. She was betting this line was too fine to tread on the march, and he'd leave it to the expert Quizitors at Two Mountains. He'd hoped fear would get useful information and so enhance his own status. She'd called his bluff, for now, and bought valuable time. She hoped the others had worked it out too.

Apparently they had; at any rate, he got nothing out of Felix, Jane, or Sam. It was obvious that he felt diminished by this failure. But all Jane's and Felix's cultural sensitivity training brought them no more effective contact with this angry human than Tinka had managed, and Sam was lucky not to lose any teeth. She reflected light-headedly that honours for interplanetary communication were even. Nil, nil, nil.

Finally Kurpershoek decided that he would learn nothing to speed the hunt, and ordered his men to strike camp.

~~~

Tinka had thought her legs were finally used to the saddle. Strapped again in a frame, rubbed by a disintegrating sack, hands tied behind her back, she learned worse. Not only that: her skin was the lightest of the *Valkyrie* six, and the sun fell full on her shoulders. Turning an angry red by their feel, she yearned for the shade far ahead, where the path wound into a narrow cleft between yellow rocks.

The sun rose higher. The ground shimmered in a heat haze.

They neared the cleft, and Kurpershoek ordered the prisoners unstrapped from their frames, which were too wide to make the passage. Tinka found it hard not to scream as circulation returned and frozen muscles started working again, but after a time they could all stand and stagger onward. As they entered the shadow, a flight of birds seemed to whir up from the jumbled rocks to sunward. Dazzled, she saw that the 'birds' were wide spinning discs. Expertly thrown like a frisbee, the first stopped dead above her and dropped.

She fell headfirst up into it. Slammed through the jolt of a compressed ten-metre drop, she splashed into bitter water.

Small hands grabbed as she came to the surface, and coughed out her throatful of burning water on a shelf of salt-encrusted rock. Her back felt on fire. She could hear Sam coughing, too; the acrid salts had stung his damaged mouth.

When her eyes cleared and the pain became bearable, she saw her friends and Kurpershoek's five guardsmen, lying on the beach. Kurpershoek himself must have eluded capture. The guards' arms had already been tied by seven young women in dark red trousers and tunics, who were now hobbling their legs and collecting weapons. She looked up to the nearest, to thank her for an unexpected rescue.

The woman came and hobbled hers.

Soon all nine of them were roped in a line, shuffling towards a cave visible in a rocky outcrop beside the lake.

She was just behind Cuzak. "Who are these people? Where are they taking us?"

He turned and spat. "No doubt they serve your masters, and there is some sleight in your supposed captivity. But if you are truly asking, *starwoman*, know that we are captives of the Vain Vaimoksi."

14

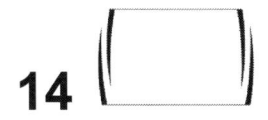

Gold Lightning

> Twinkle little acrobat,
> How I wonder what you're at.
> Up above the ground you soar,
> Till you slip and hit the floor.
> —*Mother Nurse Gooseberry Rhymes*

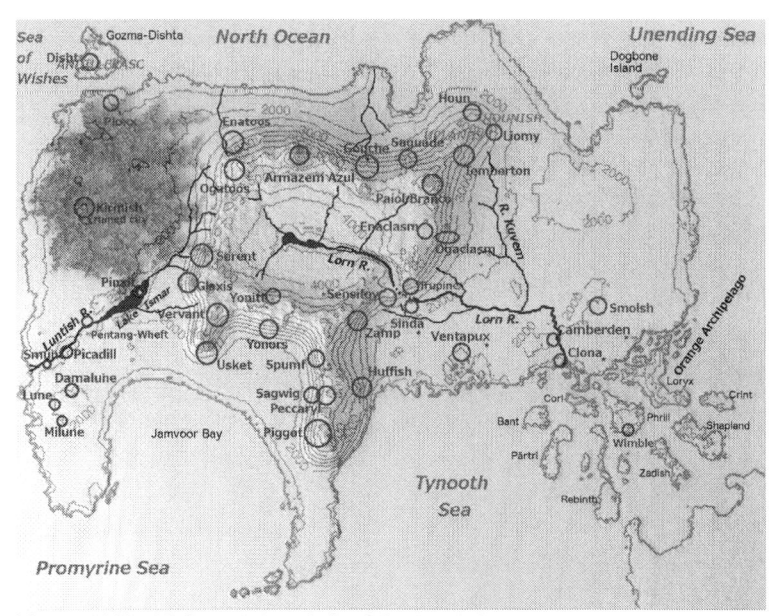

}Samdal ('Aleph') Stars (★) mark Starfolk-visited sites.

The attic room of the *Limping Wozzet* — named for a lumpish creature like a yellow pig that spent nine tenths of its time asleep and the rest swilling or in rut — was cramped and dusty, with low skull-cracking beams that sagged and smelled of dry rot; but it was a welcome refuge nonetheless. It had cost two score *skint* for three nights, paid in advance to the doleful potbellied landlord, in hopes that the hunt would soon die down. Their finances wouldn't let them stay for long, but a small celebration was in order.

"Life," Marco declaimed through the crumbs of a crayfish pasty, "looks rosier on a full stomach. A lot better than being bone-hammered for perversion."

"Ha!" said Elzabet, dripping scorn. "And whom do we have to thank for courting that particular danger?" Since the terror, her moods kept shifting: one moment a refined Lady of Quynt, the next, apprentice galactic.

Marco had a piece of shell caught between his teeth. "No good sitting on your dignity, Elza — you joined in too."

"Not in the public orgy. A lady may shed her inhibitions in private."

"I was drugged. *Kreesh*. And it *wasn't* public."

Elzabet raised an aristocratic eyebrow. "Really?"

"There were just rather a lot of people."

"Including the Deacon's spy."

"For all we knew, *Sadruddin* was one of the Deacon's spies. I didn't notice you worrying about that. In fact, it was *you* who suggested a threesome." Marco poured himself another mug of jarble and leaned back in his chair.

"Only because you made it obvious that it was what *you* wanted," said Elzabet. "Anyway, Sadruddin is a gentleman." *Unlike some others I could mention*, her sharp glance indicated. "I joined in against my better judgement because you wanted it."

"You joined in," said Marco, "because you were fascinated by Gus's legs."

"Oh, very well, if it lets you offload some of the guilt to imagine that I had a passion for Augustine Tambiah Sadruddin, why not?" Suddenly she grinned. "Gus *does* have nice legs, Marco."

"They even taste good. But he may well end up hanging from their extremities if he carries on the way he's going."

"True," said Elzabet, sobering at the thought. "But that's his problem, Marco."

"And Sam's, Tinka's, Jane's, and Felix's. Barring miracles, Gus is their only chance."

"Then we have to hope he doesn't get caught until he's rescued them too. There's nothing we can do from here, except head for the beacon and scream for help. And right now I see no way to achieve that. Where do we stand?"

Marco nibbled his fourth pasty. "Well, we eluded the Personal Guard and the Embassy people, and got clear away from Sensifoy. Shaaluy has no jurisdiction here in Samdal, and the local authorities have no complaint against us —"

"We attacked a watchman and tied him up."

Marco dismissed the matter with a shrug. "All he saw were two faceless guards in uniform. I doubt that his Reverence the Deacon is much revered here in Samdal. They won't trace it to us, or if they do, they won't care."

"I suppose so," said Elzabet dubiously, but Marco's optimism was back.

"That was a neat escape, using Gus's local contact to get further from the Embassy, then humping sacks on a downboat." They had been paid off with no questions asked in Clona, a mediocre town in south-east Samdal, down in the endless Promensel plains.

"But we're on our own now. I think he couldn't risk us having a falasynte. He was improvising, using one of *his* escape routes, but trying to distance himself from us as well. Anyone plotting at the level he does will have several escapes lined up."

"It's a pity he didn't have a bit of cash lined up," said Marco. "We're running low. Not for nothing is the local currency called the *skint*."

~~~

The more angry the Deacon of Two Mountains was, the quieter became his voice. His Chaplain had never heard DeLameter speak so softly.

"The Quizitors have disciplined Kurpershoek." It was not a question. Nobody would dare to disobey the Deacon even in his milder moods.

"Six bones, Reverence," Sadruddin confirmed. "One for each missing prisoner." It was a poor reward for a dedicated officer who had escaped the clutches of the Vain Vaimoksi and returned to report and face the likely penalty.

"To lose four to the Vain Vaimoksi was careless. He should have taken them through the cleft one by one, keeping three always in frames too wide for thrown syntei. That is culpable breach of procedure," said the Deacon. "To allow my Personal Guard to let the other two flee this continent — inexcusable."

"With respect, Revered One, I believe Kurpershoek to be merely incompetent." Better to mount a weak defence of the man than to appear too eager to accuse him of treason. The Deacon had no lack of cunning; it would be easy to arouse his suspicions.

"Has any trace of the strangers yet been found?"

"None, Reverence. The two who eluded your guards and fled to Samdal will, I am sure, be recaptured. The four seized by Vain Vaimoksi—"

"—will never be heard from again. A pity, they interested me. Unusual people, do you not think? Their clothing resembled nothing that our agents in the Lands of Abomination have ever reported. They spoke Galaxic, but with an outlandish accent. Some of what they carried was remarkable." He gestured at the wall where the tapestry still hung. Heretical it might be, but that was not proved. The Deacon rather liked it, and he alone would be the judge.

They had discussed these matters, but new knowledge brought new questions. And new doubts. Sadruddin sensed an opportunity, but his response was guarded. "Should their claim to have come from another world be reconsidered?"

DeLameter shrugged. "I think you never fully rejected it, Sadruddin. I am less easily convinced. I judge more likely they are agents of the Caverns."

Sadruddin swallowed. "Revered One, with respect... you read me truly. That is not my opinion, nor has it been since first I saw these strangers." He hesitated. "It might, I suggest, be prudent to keep the question open, however wild their tales appear. Indeed, Wevorin troublemakers would surely offer more plausible explanations. The very wildness of their story attests its truth."

"As they wish us naively to assume," said the Deacon, face smug.

Sadruddin nodded, but persisted. "If these people *are* from the stars, they could have allies undreamt of," on a delicate path; no knowing how DeLameter might react. "That would be both a danger, and a Shaper-sent opportunity for the Church."

"No, Sadruddin, it is all too fanciful. I sense the hand of Wevory."

"As you say, Revered One. It is just that — well, I am reminded that the animadepts question whether all the *Handbook* is allegory. They observe a clear division between the species created by Magog, few in number, and the countless other creatures of this world. Humans and the animals that Magog in His wisdom provided for our food have white bones and red blood. Other large animals have golden bones and violet blood. Most edible grasses, vegetables, and fruit created for our use breed not by syntei but by unconnected seedings. The animadepts see these things as evidence of distinct origins."

"But some syntelic plants are edible," the Deacon objected.

"Yes, Reverence, that is a difficulty. They are mainly fruits and roots — a few species, but widely cultivated. The evidence is confusing. Descenters believe that we were created by Magog, but not on this world. They claim that we, too, originated among the stars, and were conveyed to this world by Magog's supernatural powers. They cite numerous folk-legends as support."

"An extremist sect with little to recommend it," DeLameter said, in a tone that brooked no argument. "Based entirely on vague word of mouth, with nothing comparable to the true Church's Holy Books. Its continued existence is a sign of our selfless tolerance."

"Your Reverence's insights cut to the heart, as always. It is undeniable that Man has always been of this world, and ludicrous to imagine otherwise," said his chaplain, gazing reverently at the religious art on the Deacon's wall: the Chalice of Magog, faithfully copied from generation to generation. Thanks to Marco he could name the bridge, the Da Silva drive (powered somehow by an Undivided Field Theory), the vast frozen module where the Colonists slept, the gene banks for horses and bees and oats and humans. They rolled in his mind.

DeLameter's eyes were ice. "Sadruddin, I must warn that your theories are doubtfully supported, and verge on heresy. However, *if* they held any substance, the implications would be momentous. You will make every effort at recapture."

Sadruddin's bowels froze, for himself as much as for the strangers. He managed to keep his face impassive.

~~~

The two fugitives lay low at the inn and tried to pass the time in their own manner. Elzabet composed herself on the rough pallet, lost in daydreams. Marco sat in the middle of the dusty floor and drew diagrams with his fingers. His tongue stuck out of the edge of his mouth in concentration. He muttered polysyllabically... then swore and brushed a hand across the drawing, obliterating it and raising a small grey cloud.

Elzabet propped her chin on her elbows. "*Still* trying to puzzle out how syntei work?"

"I'll get it eventually," said Marco doggedly. "It ought to be a straightforward application of Heegaard diagrams, but it's not. There's some funny twist."

"I fail to comprehend why you wish to apply mathematics to a *plant*."

Marco rose to the bait. "Elza, you can apply mathematics to anything. Of course," he added in a rash of honesty, "you don't necessarily get a sensible answer, but that's another matter. However," he continued doggedly, "if you can tell me a better way to understand a planetful of vegetable matter-transmitters, go ahead."

Elzabet looked at him scornfully down her aristocratic nose, but maintained a dignified silence.

"Syntei influence *everything* on Qish. They give this world a unique and unprecedented ecological device. It obeys its own bizarre laws, and it's in *everything*. It makes Qish different from every other planet anywhere. Then, to compound the effect —"

"Nearly two thousand years ago the colony vessel *Magog* crash-landed, and the would-be colonists woke up on a world where matter-transmitters grow on trees."

"Literally. So Qishi technology followed a line like nowhere else. Roads mostly short and bridges small. Few machines, mostly syntelic. Heavy emphasis on botany and plant-breeding. Breeding for size — the stability problem places an upper limit. Treatment methods for dead syntwood to preserve the connection and durability. Endless syntelic gadgets. Whole economic structures: control an intercontinental wyzand and you can name your price. Which, incidentally, means that transportation on Qish is no more free than anywhere else in the Galaxy. Political systems evolve around economics. And then there's the elevation problem — you can go a thousand kilometres, if you stay at the same height, easier than you can go twenty metres up or down. Slopes acquire enormous strategic importance. High spots are arsenals.

"And more personal possibilities. You can scratch your own back, touch your right elbow with your right hand, chew the back of your knees. Social conventions can run the gamut from rigid prohibition to uninhibited freedom. The sexual permutations are limited only by your imagination —"

" — speak for yourself —"

" — and the number of willing —"

" — or unwilling —"

" — participants —"

" — which is how you got us both marked for death. To Two Mountains, *any* bodily use of syntei is a perversion, but you had to go the whole hog."

Marco grinned. "As well be hung for a whole hog as half a hug. We're alive, undamaged, and safe in Samdal where the customs are more relaxed."

"That's marvellous. I feel wonderful," she said grimly. "Nah. I keep wondering how Sam and the others are managing. But there's nothing we can do, or even know."

"Right now — nah. Even whether they're alive. The best plan for all of us is the original plan. Get to Wevory, find the beacon, and scream for help. And to do that, we need transport, which, even on Qish, means *money*. A commodity of which we are suffering an unaccountable shortage."

Elzabet concentrated. "I have it!" she announced.

"Great! What?"

"We find you a job."

"*Me*? Oh, yah, Hippolyta is a matriarchy. I thought you'd overcome that. Surely Hippolytans ought to be keen on gender equality."

"Not at all. We prefer gender *superiority*. We like our men to provide the musclepower while we do the brainwork. Anyway, I don't see any signs of female emancipation on *this* continent of unbridled freedom and licence. I'll take a job, if I can find one, but you're in the front line."

~~~

The search was hard. Skills that would earn employment on any developed world of the Concordat were useless on Qish.

"We'll have to live by our wits," Marco announced.

"On present performance, we're likely to starve, then," said Elzabet sourly.

However, in the event, it was Marco who put them on the right track.

"Elza, what's a khanatta?"

"I thought you were the linguistic genius. Isn't it a vinegar-pot?"

"Nah, that's a canetta. And I don't think that Mahmool hep Hazaar Dickensohn would be celebrated for her Grand Vinegar-Pot."

"Marco, dear," said Elzabet, "what are we talking about?"

Marco indicated a nearby treetrunk, bearing a hand-lettered broadsheet like others he had seen on walls and doors. *The Grand Khanatta of the celebrated Mahmool hep Hazaar Dickensohn.* Cautious enquiries resolved the mystery: a khanatta was a travelling roadshow, something like a circus for grown-ups.

Marco pointed out the implications with growing excitement.

"I'm a pretty good amateur magician. I reached the fourth rung of the Infernal flight of the Magic Ladder when I was at IIT. Maybe the circus could use a conjuror with a pretty assistant. You show the leg and I'll do the work."

"Ordinarily I'd object to that division of labour as unbefitting the dignity of a Hippolytan gentlewoman, but your legs are too hairy and so are my conjuring skills. I'm desperate. We'll try it."

The Public Fields to the north of Clona would be hours away on foot, but there was a direct route through a wyzand bank in an upper tier of the nearest exchange. With some difficulty they reached Dickensohn's immediate subordinate, an energetic and swarthy man with the improbable name of Four-way Polo.

Polo ran his hand across his bearded face. "We have no magician at the moment," he said thoughtfully. "Old Styrkrantz was bitten by a websnake that he'd left in his boot by mistake."

He studied the pair of them shrewdly. The young man was tall, well-muscled if a trifle flabby, with a strong face, dark skin and even darker hair. It was a good combination. The woman was even more striking: tall, statuesque, with eyes of a profound blue and long blonde hair. A bit snooty, but that added to her attraction. Her skin was dark too, though several shades lighter than the man's. Their facial structure was exotic. "You folks from Selversynd or somewhere?"

"Close," said Marco, bent on flattery. "Very perceptive of you. Small village in the same region... name of — er — Tensorfield," he added.

"How good a magician are you?"

Marco embarked on a lengthy and involved explanation of how his equipment had unfortunately been lost when their donkey had fallen over a cliff, and that although he could build it anew, the task would require time and a modest cash advance. He ventured to hope that a verbal description would suffice as a purely temporary measure. Polo declared his willingness to listen to anything while reserving judgement as to its veracity, as was his natural privilege.

"His best act," said Elzabet, to grab his interest, "is sawing me in half."

"What is a saw?" Polo enquired.

"A toothed knife for cutting wood."

"Ah. In Samdal we use a drop-synte."

What that might be? Now was not the time. "He shuts me in a long wooden box. Then he cuts the box and separates the halves. Yet I am — *unharmed*!"

There was a lengthy silence. "Too easy," said Four-way Polo.

"What?" broke in Marco, "it took me *years* —"

"You've got a pair of kasyntei in the box, arsey — beg pardon, Sabi — back-to-back, with a gap. Then he saws through the gap, right?"

There was a stricken silence from Marco. He *still* didn't find it natural to *think* syntelically. Elzabet came to his rescue.

"No, we don't use syntei."

Polo perked up a little. "That's interesting, it might just spark an audience. Can you *prove* you don't use syntei?"

"Yes, of course," said Marco. "By opening the — no, that's stupid, they'll see how it's done. And, oh, same problem pulling grabbits from a hat, or scarves from Elza's nose. You're right, syntei make stage-magic all too easy."

"Too bad," said Polo dismissively. "I thought maybe we had something there, for a while, especially with your assistant's exotic looks. Tall, blonde, unusual brown skin..." his voice trailed off and he gave Elzabet a frank, appraising look. And that gave Elzabet an idea, though not the one that his look suggested. It was appallingly vulgar, but their predicament called for extreme measures, and she could think of no alternative. She'd just have to hope it never came out in Quynt. If that shrew Fiola Tryce-Knightly ever got wind of it... Elzabet tapped Marco on the shoulder.

"Out!"

Marco's protests were in vain.

"Sab Polo and I have business to discuss. You'll only raise irrelevant objections, inhibit the discussion, and make me lose my nerve. Out!"

"But Elza, surely you're not —"

"Nah, I'm not *that* desperate. Yet. But it will come to that unless you do what you're told. Leave it to Sab Polo and me."

~~~

"The fools knew nothing," the Quizitor muttered in disgust. "Cut them down and feed the bodies to the maw." Not that anyone with the intelligence of a bole-toad would have hoped better, he thought wryly, but the Deacon's soft-spoken commands left no room for argument. The unfortunate syntemen who had let the fugitives pass unchallenged were inevitable targets. He reached for the falasynte, to make a careful report.

Sadruddin relayed the unsurprising news to the Deacon. DeLameter frowned. "Sadruddin, I shall be candid. While my love for the Church regrets that the strangers' Sins of Division be left unpunished, my reason regrets still more the loss of the knowledge they bore. They *must* be recaptured."

"You speak Truth, Revered One."

"Further, it is manifest that the offworlders —" *Ah! Finally he agrees with my interpretation!* " — could not have made their escape without the assistance of some highly placed person. Or several. Within this house."

Too close for comfort. To disagree would be to invite unwanted scrutiny. Sadruddin knew this game. He'd had a lot of practice.

"I concur, Deacon. As well as guard uniforms they had documents with your personal seal. Only sub-deacons ever handle that. And their route was well planned."

"Sadruddin, you slice to the heart as a flensing-knife. You are my Right Hand. You must suspect who is responsible?"

The words tripped easily enough off Sadruddin's lips — long rehearsed against this eventuality. "Revered One, I think that their Sins of Division and their escape are related by more than the sin giving the need for the other."

The Deacon's smile was sardonic. "Quite. The sinner and the traitor are one. We must seek out the corruption among my ambitious subordinates and excise it in purification, as well as recapture the offworld perverts. We shall dispatch agents into Samdal to hunt down the alien vermin and return them to our grasp.

"And you, Sadruddin — I choose you to organise this. I will deal with the sub-deacons. You have become acquainted with the offworlders and their patterns of thought — as I intended when I placed you in charge of them."

If you only knew. "I am deeply honoured at your trust and at the opportunity to serve my faith," said Sadruddin. Seeing that the audience was at an end, he backed out of the room.

15

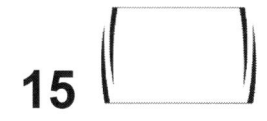

Beast Mistress

> The ossivore's a curious beast;
> It hides behind a hummock;
> Among its mysteries, not the least
> Is where it keeps its stomach.
> Unnoticed by the herds that pass
> Of cattle that could crush it
> Until it hurtles through the grass.
> And picks a beast, to rush it.
> It crunches bones, then swallows whole
> A vast, lamenting mammut foal.
> —*A Child's Treasury of Nonsense Songs*

Marco wandered among the sideshows. One offered prizes in a game involving two dodecahedral dice and a number of wooden discs. After kibitzing for a quarter of an hour, he surreptitiously coded the rules into his wristcomp and set it looking for a strategy. To his surprise, it claimed to find one, and he risked a *skint* to try it out.

When Elzabet emerged from Four-way Polo's tented office, carrying what appeared to be a large string bag held together with tiny metal clasps, she found Marco squatting outside on a small pile of coconuts.

"I see you've been busy," she said coolly. "So have I. We are now employees of the celebrated Mahmool hep Hazaar Dickensohn."

"Doing what?" asked Marco with interest.

"I," she declared, striking a pose, "am an exotic dancer. *You*," she continued, poking him in the chest, "thanks to my pull, are an assistant to the ossivore trainer."

Marco looked at the pile of coconuts. Taking the string bag by the handles, he tipped in a coconut. With an odd tinkling noise, the coconut fell out of the bottom.

"You idiot, Marco," said Elzabet. "That's not a bag." She retrieved it and set off across the field at a smart pace, so that he had to trot to catch up. "Hope you didn't tear the hem," she snapped, reaching a cluster of small tents. She opened a flap and they ducked inside.

"String bags don't have hems."

"That's not a bag, Marco," said Elzabet. "It's my costume."

Marco said nothing, but his eyes opened wide. Elzabet held up the item. Made of wide-meshed netting, it weighed perhaps fifty grams. She shook it, and the metal objects at the crossings jingled: diminutive bells. "Those *handles*, Marco dear, are shoulder-straps. There's no bottom because my legs have to be able to poke out. It's a *dress*, my sweet: it is intended to contain the firm, youthful flesh of a desirable young woman."

"And not, you forsaken fool, a *coconut*!"

"A dress? Didn't you miss off a tiny prefix?"

"Marco, that's what *exotic* dancing is all about. It's only because this locality suffers from what on Samdal passes for a streak of puritanism that I'm to wear anything at all. Samdalis really go for tall, blonde, dusky maidens."

"But Elza," protested Marco, "you can't dance!"

"I notice you don't protest at the affront to my modesty."

"The Fringe gave you too many inhibitions, and your Duchy gave you too many airs and graces. This'll remind you that on this planet you're just like everyone else. But you don't have any experience!"

"So much you know." She wriggled out of her clothes and into the fishnet, and began to writhe sensuously, wiggling her hips and clapping her hands above her head in an energetic and insistent rhythm.

"Mother of Galaxies! They'll rip the joint apart in lust-crazed riot! Where did you learn *that*?"

"While you were clambering the rungs of the Magical Adder, I took evening classes in classical dance at Madame Lollengass's Academy for Ladies of Breeding." Elza looked demurely at her toes. "The costume *is* a little irregular, it's usually an opaque flowing robe from neck to ankle. And I *have* speeded up the movements a little and sharpened the rhythm. But underneath it's the same basic thing."

"Oh, I agree, *very* basic. Elza, I am genuinely amazed. I didn't realise you had such hidden talents. How much do we get?"

"My remuneration is fifteen *skint* per day plus food and this tent. You get five, plus food; and I'll let you share my tent for free."

"Only five? You mean you get *three times as much* as me for wriggling about in your pretty pelt?"

"Naturally. I'm the skilled worker. You're just the manual labour, feeding and mucking out the ossivores."

Marco belatedly asked a question that he should have thought of earlier. "Elza? What *is* an ossivore? It sounds kind of nasty."

"Oh, no," said Elzabet. "They're just soft furry pussycats trained to do tricks." As the furrows fled Marco's brow she added, "They weigh half a tonne, with fangs like Sam's knife, and eat half a buloceros a day." Marco rolled up his eyes and collapsed on one of the featherbags with a groan.

She leaned over to check his pulse, and was grabbed round the waist by a dramatically revitalised patient. "I can play tricks too. Didn't your mother tell you never to get near a man on a bed, dressed like that?"

"Duchess Arabella of Quynt told me to do or not to do a lot of things, depending on circumstances, most of which I ignored and none of which are your — Marco! stop it! You'll ruin my dress!"

Later, nibbling contentedly at her ear, he whispered, "Those ossivores don't really eat half a buloceros a day, do they?"

Elzabet said sleepily, "You're a vulgar cad to disrespect a lady reduced to wage slavery." Her mood had swung back to fond tolerance.

"But sexy with it. You *were* pulling my leg?"

"I admit it, Marco. They *don't* eat half a buloceros a day."

"I thought not," came the smug reply.

"They eat a whole buloceros a day."

She enjoyed his twitch.

~~~

Marco poked his nose through the flaps of the 'vorehouse, and saw the ossivores in their iron cages. Elzabet had exaggerated a little, but a 'vore was nothing to laugh at. Two hundred and fifty kilos of lean, hungry flesh-eater, a bit like a sabretooth tiger with large flaring antennae and a double row of golden needles in each jaw. It was striped lengthwise in desert colours, with a black tufted mane that ran along its spine and then twisted on to the underside of its tail. The tail, oddly long, ended in a black tuft matching the mane.

Its eyes were an improbable pale blue.

Two of the beasts were prowling up and down; the rest were asleep. When Marco approached one of the cages, its occupant snapped alert, gave vent to a snarl like armour-plate being torn to shreds, and hurled itself at the bars with a crash that rattled them, and Marco's teeth, in their sockets.

He stepped back hurriedly, and a cool hand touched his arm. He whirled round to see a short, mousey-looking girl aged about eighteen standard years, with eyes too large for her face. A coarse sacklike garment concealed what seemed a rather boyish figure. Her braided hair was coiled on top of her head, secured by a rough wooden pin.

"I suppose you're Marco Lontvidge Banki. Four-way said I was to train a new assistant."

"Strabyen, Sabi," said Marco, in his Shaaluin accent.

"Zdravjen. I am Lomyrla Polo Koorbun, 'vore-trainer."

"I am honoured, Sabi." *Great Mother! This little mouse in a cage with those ravening beasts!* "Polo? You related to Four-way?"

"His selfborne daughter, not that you'd notice. But you may refer to me as Sabi Koorbun, Banki. What do you know of ossivores?"

"Not a thing — uh — Sabi Koorbun. But I —"

"*Sniph!* That wozzet-humper Polo's given me another nozzy! I *told* him I wanted an experienced hand this time! I bet it's all that new Quynt tart's doing, she's a friend of yours, isn't she? Polo's always a sucker for a well-stacked froom!"

Marco headed for the exit.

"Hey, Banki? Where the skunt are *you* off to?"

The reply floated back to her. "To offer your father my resignation."

Lomyrla studied the departing back. She saw a tall, well-muscled, brown-skinned man, good-looking in a foreign sort of way. His accent was intriguing: half Shaaluin, half the demons knew what. She'd had assistants who were harder on the eye, and on the ear... She came to a decision.

"Wait!"

Marco stopped by the tentflap, facing outwards. Lomyrla hesitated, then said, "I'm sorry, Banki. I'm sick to death of training nozzies — I mean, inexperienced hands — and I don't get on very well with Polo. He's not my father, by the way. And I didn't mean to insult your friend, I'm sure it's all very proper. I have a bad habit of lashing out when I'm angry."

If she's his daughter, how come — but who knows on this improbable planet? She had come much too close to the truth for comfort. "Forget it. Let's start over. Call me Marco, dah?"

"Very well... Marco."

"Delighted to make your acquaintance, Lomyrla. Now, tell me everything about ossivores. You'll find me a quick learner — for a nozzy."

For the next hour Marco immersed himself in 'vorelore. They didn't eat whole buloceros, of course, Elza had invented that. But she'd caught the spirit: large quantities of live, screaming meat. They were fastidious beasts and their cages had to be kept clean. They were susceptible to a variety of diseases, mostly treatable if caught early, and Marco became a fount of knowledge on the topics of earworm, syntshrivel and furball blockage.

Their anatomy was... complex.

"Where do you think a 'vore keep its vital organs?" Lomyrla asked.

"Somewhere around its middle, like the rest of us, I'd imagine." Marco watched in mesmerised horror as Lomyrla reached a bare arm into the cage where a snoozing 'vore was sleeping off a hearty meal of retired draft-mammut, and thumped it smartly on what should have been its stomach. It sounded like a bass drum. The 'vore opened one eye speculatively, but Lomyrla had withdrawn her hand.

"They're *hollow*?" squeaked Marco, aghast.

"One big bellows. A 'vore is four parts lung. So where does it digest?"

"I have no idea."

"Me neither." She gestured widely. "Somewhere out there, deep underground."

Miracles are commonplace on Qish. "Don't tell me," said Marco. "Symbiosis. The 'vore has a synte halfway down its neck, and its stomach lives a comfortable life of its own inside the mother plant. The plant feeds from the 'vore's stomach, and in return protects it from attack." He looked at the massive animal. "Not that a 'vore's stomach needs that kind of protection... probably evolved when 'vores were harmless little beasties knee-high to a grasshopper."

"You use many words I have never heard," said Lomyrla. "Ossivores feed on bones as well as flesh. The stomach acid would dissolve the 'vore itself. So, by Magog's grace, it keeps its stomach safely apart."

"Then I don't," said Marco cautiously, "have to shovel shit?" He knew the dung of cows and horses, and found the smell oddly friendly, but what Qishi carnivore crap would smell like, he felt pleased not to learn.

"No. The vomit goes elsewhere, too. They're pretty messy eaters. You'll have to keep everything clean, or we'll be overrun by scavengers." There's always a catch.

"You're right that claws and teeth are good protection. However, *more ways to catch a 'vore than digging the forest for its stomach*, as the proverb goes." She handed him a pitcher of water and pointed to the nearest cage. "Throw it over her."

"What?"

Lomyrla repeated herself. Gingerly, Marco complied, and cold water poured over the unsuspecting 'vore in its left ear. He fully expected it to rip open the cage and devour him on the spot. Instead, it uttered a feeble wail and rolled on its back with its paws in the air. Rigid.

"Great Mother! What did I do?"

"If there's one thing a 'vore can't stand, it's water. They'll drink it, but getting wet paralyses them."

As Marco started puzzling out what quirk of evolutionary advantage had produced that particular side-effect — he could imagine several plausible theories, doubtless all wrong — the 'vore staggered to its feet, shaking its head and whining. "Temporarily," Lomyrla added. "Though a bath knocks them cold for hours. That's how we train them. Only we use waterjets synted from the central tower, not jugs. Wouldn't be able to handle a vicious beast like a 'vore, otherwise. But they're very intelligent, and they soon learn.

"Now, I'll just change for my act, and then run through the routine with you." She disappeared into a screened-off area. Marco squatted in wait.

After a time, Lomyrla reappeared. On her feet were tiny red sandals. Her hair, unbraided, fell to her bare shoulders in a soft nut-brown cascade. Her low-cut dress of emerald green gathered over her ribs and hung to her ankles. The cross-laced neckline plunged from neck to navel. Slits from armpit to hem were similarly laced at mid-hip. Undergarments were conspicuous by their absence, and Marco could imagine no design so that any might hide. *Mousey? Boyish?* Mother of Galaxies, Marco Leontevich, you really put your elbow up your nostril. And just look at those doe-eyes, big enough to drown in... A great wave of emotion swept over him, which he told himself must be paternal instinct. Such a sweet, fresh-faced young beauty needed a father's care... and though she was Four-way's daughter she clearly refused to acknowledge him as a father, yes, of course, that was it...

His responsibility was clear. He must assume the role of protector.

~~~

The Grand Khanatta broke camp and moved, on wheels and feet, from Clona to nearby Camberden, then to Ventapux, then westward from the flood plains of Promensel, heading inland across into the rounded foothills of Treece. The heavy carts and other large equipment could be taken apart to pass through a wyzand, but such labour was reserved for when it was unavoidable.

As they struck camp for the fourth time in as many weeks, Marco wondered why they bothered to move at all. He sought out Lomyrla — an increasingly frequent habit.

"Why don't we just stay put and let the customers come to us? By synte?"

Lomyrla giggled.

"What's so funny? It seems perfectly sensible to me!"

"There speaks a true nozzy. And it *is* perfectly sensible — to a nozzy. But customers get excited when we turn up, it makes a festival. And any red-blooded *khantü* would go stir-crazy, stuck in the same hole all the time. When the jearning comes upon us — as it does — we move on. 'Nomads sprung we from Magog, nomads must we remain.'"

It later occurred to Marco that mass transport by syntei raised some very awkward problems in logistics, and that only places at the same level are in easy reach. After that he couldn't decide whether Lomyrla had told the truth or invented the whole thing.

Elzabet had polished her dance routine and made her début under the stage name of Gold Lightning. By the third day there were lengthy queues outside the dance-show tent and her pay had risen by five more *skint* per day. Soon Marco felt as if every man on Qish had been to ogle her — except him. He was surprised to find that he didn't regret his promise. He could always have sneaked a look, or even recorded her performance on his 'comp, but he knew he would gain no pleasure from watching something that she must find humiliating. She had become absent-minded and short-tempered, and they now slept on separate featherbags. Marco tried to make allowances. After all, this was no life for a high-born young woman of gentility, even if she was making heroic efforts to repudiate that lifestyle. To her credit, she was sticking with her new job to earn them the money they needed to get to the beacon. A brave sacrifice. He tried not to intrude, and spent more time with Lomyrla.

He was fast becoming a 'vorelore expert, down to the minutiae of alimentary disorders, ticks, and the correct angle for scratching-posts. Lomyrla was impressed, not knowing they were stored in his wristcomp; not knowing the notion of one. He had even managed to enter a tenanted 'vore cage without anxiety, though he kept a firm grip on his waterjet. This device was made from a type of synte that the syndepts who bred it called a *mismatch*: the orifice of one kasynte was the size of a thumbnail, whereas the other was ten times as big. The big one was in the khanatta's travelling water-tower; the small one's simple valve turned the flow on and off. The drop in height and the narrowed flow produced a high-pressure spray that could paralyse a 'vore in an instant.

Lomyrla watched his progress with approval, and started to think up ways to include Marco in the act. He would be a wonderful draw for the matrons of Samdal — especially in a brief loincloth. Or less.

~~~

A continent away, Augustine Tambiah Sadruddin recited his private Magog rosary: bridge, drive, cold-sleep module, gene banks,... Thus his world began. Thus, Starships join worlds. Thus, an undivided Qish would end its division from the stars.

For now, he bent his subtle mind to the delicate and complex task of turning over every cup for his escaped offworlders, while ensuring that the Deacon's guesses came up empty. He selected numerous agents, documenting their successful track records, but not their lack of the imagination to guess at being misled from above. He sent them all over Samdal, to look for prudish thieves who had escaped with a cache of Temple jewels, which they would need to sell. At the same time he picked a small, covert group from his own contacts, who over the years had given him truth, not expected answers. If they were first to find Elzabet and Marco, he might be able to intervene, and could better misdirect the larger search. His biggest worry was that the Deacon's own agents would find them before his did. Another was a growing anxiety as to how long he could keep the whole charade running before its lack of success got the Deacon annoyed. Or, worse, suspicious. If he wasn't already.

His task was made harder by the Starfolk's striking physical appearance, unmatched anywhere on Qish. His friends would not be aware that they were being hunted, but they would surely have the wisdom to be prudent. Gus hoped fervently that they had managed to find themselves a nice, quiet hideaway.

If he had known what Elzabet was doing, he would have gone into hysterics.

16

Captives of the Slavestone

The Br'er Rabbit stories did not derive directly from Afro-American slave culture, as is often assumed, but indirectly from Cherokee mythology. Jistu the trickster rabbit became Br'er Rabbit and later classical-era characters such as Bugs Bunny and Kickaha. In the legend of the briar patch, the fox and the wolf trapped the trickster rabbit, but his silver tongue talked them into throwing him into dense thorns, by reverse psychology. The most obvious implication is that the fox and the wolf weren't terribly bright.
—*Millicent D. Battersby, Romulus and Remus: Iconic Animals in Pre-Concordat Myth*

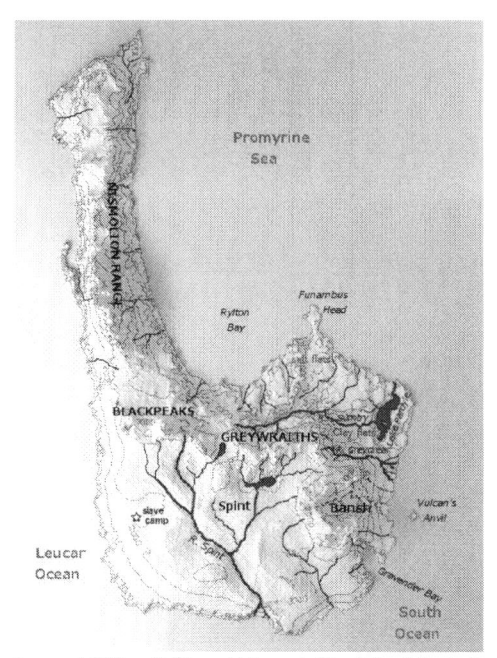

Lamynt ('Gimel') Stars (★) mark Starfolk-visited sites.

The room was huge, the furnishings luxurious. A woman in a blood-red robe stood holding a discussion through a large olosynte, bred by the syndepts for clear sound and vision. Her hair formed a tall cone. Unbraided, it would have reached her ankles.

Ordinarily, Drusilla Sybilschild of Raven's Tooth left the haggling to subordinates, but the Primarch of the Vain Vaimoksi preferred to deal directly with her most sensitive — and profitable — customers.

"Two score quarriers, male, in sound health, for the sulphur mines. To be delivered within the week as requested. Specialist items: twin virgin boys, of outstanding beauty. You will not be disappointed. I chose them myself, from one of the noblest families in Vervant. The price? Ah, for such choice delicacies I must ask a dozen egg-emeralds. The Husler of Piggott may wish to outbid you. Very well, ten, but you must also take three Swelt serving-maids at two gold rings apiece." She paused, deciding that this price was too low. "No, on second thoughts, make that copper... Excellent. Hale and Free be Yours, Advocate. Strabyen."

She closed the olosynte and yawned. Pleased to have offloaded the three Sweltish sluts at a profit. There was plenty of worthless maw-fodder available anyway.

She reviewed the latest acquisitions-list, and an item caught her attention. What had Rayna Carolschild been prattling about the other evening? Beings from above the sky? Rumours, rumours. She paced the carpet of her inner chamber, weighing word against fact, and sent for an olosynte connected to the holding pen.

The new slaves were indeed distinctive, though they were four rather than six. Never before had she seen such a combination of height and dark skin. That tall, well-muscled one with the silver streak in his cropped black hair was really *quite* remarkable... And, almost as much as their bodies, their manner intrigued her. Somehow... otherworldly.

Sky-devils? Fallen angels? Cloud-riders? Pah! Simple tales for simpletons. But their appearance was striking. They would make ideal speciality items, with no shortage of buyers. There was no great hurry. Strangers of such bearing might be privy to powerful secrets in their own lands... but information extracted under duress from a healthy and vigorous personality could seldom be trusted.

First, soften them up. And, something a little more special for Silver-streak.

The air was getting humid. She bade a house-slave to close the weathersynte to the wetlands, and open to the cliffs at Funambus Head. A cool sea-breeze began to blow. The smell of salt spray and the cries of ten thousand gulls filled the room.

She still felt sticky. Removing her robes she stooped through a low opening in one corner, emerging beneath an underground waterfall far to the south, in a cave whose entrance was now blocked. Bathed, she returned to the house and walked a few paces to the sunroom. The rays of the afternoon sun, synted from a dozen desert sites around the planet, warmed her body dry. The sunsyntei would make excellent escape routes too, in an emergency. All were well concealed at their desert termini.

Refreshed and relaxed as her maidslaves dressed her, she spoke into a falasynte. "I want the latest reports on our control of the alcohol trade in Larby and the *kreesh* supplies in Scythery. Tell Elenya Ingridschild to call a meeting of the Seconds to discuss remaining competitors. And when that is done, bring me the new slave with the silver streak in his hair."

~~~

A brutal jerk on the rope shook Tinka awake. Two crimson-clad young women dragged her to her feet.

"You. Come with us. Now."

"But — what — I —"

"Be silent!" A kick. Tinka complied.

Hobbled in line astern, the four Starfolk and the five guardsmen were led to a small compound apart from the main buildings. A hard-faced woman in blue-edged robes was flanked by three younger Vaimoksi, two wearing newly pilfered weapons, one a very old one. *If we could only get that back... with so many knives here, why do I so yearn for Sam's? Because his grandmother said it always came back?*

One held a scroll and pen, the second a falasynte. The woman with Sam's knife had spread a cloth on a moss-covered stone, and laid out ten wrinkled objects, like prunes. An old female slave stood near a tethered creature resembling a bow-legged goat. There was a stout post, with ropes. Iron tools glowed ominously in a brazier.

All nine prisoners were arranged in line, Cuzak first. The older woman inspected him closely, then had him bound to the post. A subordinate took something from the fire, an elaborate affair with dozens of sliding rods. She fiddled with them until satisfied, and wrote something in a notebook. She replaced the tip in the heat, until it glowed again, white. There was a sizzle and a scream as metal touched flesh, and a smell like roasting pork. Cuzak shook, white-faced. Seared into his shoulder was a crudely formed six-digit number. One by one, his men fared likewise.

Then it was Tinka's turn.

This time the woman's inspection was longer, and more intimate. She seemed hesitant. Picking up the falasynte she began to converse in low tones. They had tied Tinka to face the post, and ripped the disintegrating sack from her shoulders.

For Mother's sake, get on with it! Waiting is worse. She braced for the contact.

When it came, it tickled.

They had painted her number on.

They did the same to Jane, Sam, and Felix.

Not to damage the goods, she realised. *We're for special treatment.*

Next, all nine were dressed in rough wool, shapeless shirts and short kilts. Bright violet slave-garb for instant visibility. Jane found herself beside the pile of discards with no one watching, snagged Cuzak's pouch, and hid it beneath her kilt. She hoped the laser medallion was still inside.

The procedure, clearly routine, went to its third stage. Soon it was Tinka's turn. The elder woman pointed at her. "You! What name are you?"

"Irenotincala Jenifa MacDonald Laurel," said Tinka, adding in her mother's names as well in the hope of impressing her captor.

"Lorel," said the woman, noting this on her pad. An aide chose a prune, while two more held Tinka's arms. The prune pushed to the back of her throat.

"Swallow!" Sam's knife touched her neck.

Tinka swallowed.

The last prune was for the goat.

"You learn a lesson," said the woman. "You are slaves. Slaves are property. Property has no will. It obeys, or it is destroyed. The slavestones make obedience.

"Observe the glossep," she said, pointing to the goat. Its handler released the noose from its neck and slapped it hard on the rump. The creature bolted.

It had gone less than a hundred metres when it suddenly collapsed in a cloud of dust. It kicked briefly, and was still. The handler retrieved it, and the young woman flung it at Sam's feet. A barbed rod, like an arrow, was protruding from the glossep's belly. Barb outwards.

"Such is the slavestone," said the woman. "Do not imagine that your body will pass it. It grows hooks that bind through the lining of your stomach. Nor can it be removed by surgeons, so deep does it bite. You are forever no more than a finger's breadth from death. The slavestone controls you. Absolutely."

Jane repressed a shudder with a visible effort. Sam scowled. Tinka felt sick. They'd *never* get away. Only Felix showed no reaction.

"If you think yourself too valuable to kill, remember that you have *no* value if you are lost to us. And if you resist in captivity..." She pointed, and the old slave collapsed in a sudden pool of her own vomit, urine and faeces, and writhed there, pouring with sweat. "She will recover from the *kra*-juice. She will even feel healthier tomorrow. But she will not wish to repeat the treatment.

"We can administer *kra* at any time, anywhere you go."

The woman raised her hand. "Take them to the cane-fields. Instruct them in their duties. Except the one named 'Wilid'. He is to be taken before the Primarch."

~~~

Their hut was ramshackle mud and withy, but compared to hacking at sugar cane it was heaven. Tinka collapsed in a heap and lay staring at her torn and bloody hands, close to tears. *So much for special treatment.* This must be just routine softening-up, not the *permanent* damage their captors wanted to avoid.

Sam squatted heavily next to her and put an arm around her. Jane watched in silence.

"Haven't these stupid people heard of *ploughs*?" said Tinka.

"Slaves are cheaper than horses, Tinka," said Jane. "Slaves tend themselves."

"That's poor economics," said Sam.

"It's poor economics for slave buyers. They probably look after theirs better. But for the slavers, acquisition cost is negligible," said Jane. "Elasticity of supply. There's no lack of enslavable humans. It's a throwaway society."

"Well, I refuse to end up on the scrapheap," said Tinka. "I'm not going to spend the rest of my life — short as it would probably be — doing what these Mothersucking bitches force me to!"

"Where are we, anyway?" Jane said quietly.

Sam poked his head out, estimated the angle and direction of the sun, and stroked his 'comp. "The Dunelands of south-east Gimel, another continent, a long way west of Shaaluy. Can't get more accurate without proper instruments."

"So the VV have a wyzand, Shaaluy to Gimel. That's why they blindfolded us before bringing us here. To stop us knowing where the other end is."

"Or a series of them, connected by Magog knows *what* route," said Tinka. "They'll have hundreds, hidden all over the planet. Jane, what was your phrase?"

"'A living labyrinth.' Reforming dynamically as new plants bud off, with additional human interference."

"Yah: wormhole agriculture, grow your own interplanetary superhighway. That's what makes the VV so dangerous."

"I don't care how dangerous!" Sam said with some heat. "I'm with Tinka, I'm not going to spend my entire life in slavery. I'd rather die trying to escape!"

"They can listen through our syntstones, if they want," said Jane in a low voice.

"They wouldn't waste a good slave for just *talk*," said Sam.

"With that awful juice, there's no waste."

"Always listening is a waste of the VV listener's labour, and deciding what is bad speech is a bigger one. I'm just saying what every newly captured slave says. We're safe enough unless we try to start a riot. Or run away. Or refuse to obey. Which would be foolish," he added in a louder voice.

"So we need to — uh — talk things over quietly amongst ourselves," said Jane. "Bearing in mind that our new masters could be listening in."

"They can't listen to everyone," said Tinka. "There must be thousands here."

"Yah," said Jane. "But despite our treatment right now, we're special. I wouldn't bank on it."

"Me neither. I wonder where Felix is?"

Jane had been trying desperately not to think about that. "In the lap of the Mother of Galaxies," she said. Which wasn't quite accurate.

~~~

At that moment, Primarch Drusilla was in Felix's lap. It had been made clear to him that, as a bed-slave, he had no choice in the matter. In fact, though Drusilla was a shade heavy around the hindquarters, with skin ten years more wrinkled than most Starfolk ever allowed, things could have been a lot worse. Or so he told himself as he lay back and let the synted fingers of her chamber-slaves keep him erect.

Drusilla ran a hand through his hair. "The two dark women: are you theirs?" Felix had no wish to explain the lack even of words for sexual ownership in most of the Concordat, or the 'ours' between Jane and himself that lay bone deep. "No," he said. "Nothing special to me."

"Good," she told him. "Now, just place your hand a little lower, *here*." He did so and she snuggled closer. "Now, let me slip this over your tongue… we have *much* better uses for it than talk. Yes, put the kantasynte *there*."

~~~

"Felix must be alive," said Jane. "Somewhere." *Please, not in pain…*

Emotionally naked, she changed the subject. "Any idea what that enforced five-minute silence this morning was all about?"

"Nah. The other slaves seemed used to it. They didn't look very happy, though."

"They never do. They just look dull. They've given up hope."

"There's always hope," said Jane.

"I'd prefer something more tangible."

Jane hesitated. She could *give* them something more tangible. And a morale boost right now was more important than security.

They had learned — the hard way — to speak in either standard or Kalingo. Sam's stomach still ached from their one and only attempt at other tongues. But a monitor could only *listen* through their stones, not *see*, and the ground was sandy.

"Not a chance," said Jane, in a clear voice. She winked at Sam and put a finger to her lips. Then she traced on the ground: *Have laser. Long story.*

They squatted bolt upright. Tinka scuffed the sand smooth and wrote: *Where?*

Slowly, Jane's scribbles told of its hiding place. It might have been more secure if only one knew, but any of them might be killed at any moment, herself included.

The laser alone wouldn't free them. They must first rid themselves of the slave-stones. And free poor Felix. But the laser medallion did give them a hidden advantage. If they kept their eyes open, someone might spot something that would suggest a viable escape plan.

Must observe, Jane wrote.

Observe what?

Everything.

~~~

Dreary months passed. Their hands hardened, along with their resolve. Their muscles gained strength from the backbreaking toil — a useful side-effect that the Vain Vaimoksi had overlooked. The Starfolk would need every advantage they could get.

Watching, talking to other slaves, and sharing, they slowly built a picture of an oasis in a low plateau surrounded on all sides by fields of deep red dunes. These seemed to stretch forever into the distance, though snowy peaks showed in the far haze to the north. To the west were plantations, worked by slaves. The oasis didn't seem natural; more likely, the deliberate result of syntelic irrigation by the VV.

The slave compound, a squalid huddle of mud-and-withy huts, was between the plateau's southern edge and a shallow lake. East of it were stone buildings, mostly storehouses. Beyond them a precarious tower of crumbling stone rose from a mass of jagged ruins. Next to the tower was a blacksmith's shop, in which an elderly slave fashioned hoes and billhooks for his fellows.

Nobody knew where the Vain Vaimoksi slept. They might have been a continent away. The regular wardens came and went through a web of syntei centred on a short basalt pillar beside the southern drop. From there they disappeared into another synte. Gangers and beaters, lower in the VV oligarchy, inhabited solid wooden huts north-east of the compound, synted to the pillar.

Syntei and huts had few guards, most other areas no guards at all — the slaves knew that resistance was hopeless — except for the crumbling syntower. Visiting 'higher-ups' came down its stairs, and returned up them, presumably to a synte leading to high command levels. Not a wise escape route, but still the guard was heavy.

The longer Jane thought, the more she saw how conventional fortifications were irrelevant. If attacked, the Vain Vaimoksi could retreat through any of their syntei. Raising its other end made an impassable gravity barrier. They had little to fear from their enstoned slaves.

Yet, over-reliance on one defence was a potential weakness. How to exploit it?

The slavestone monitoring centre was the key. If they could find it. It wasn't high above them, or the crossbolt would have come flying out of the glossep. Destroy that, and un-monitored slaves could revolt. But who knew what kind of reinforcements the VV might summon? A revolt could prove short-lived.

She listed the objectives in her mind.

1. Destroy the monitoring centre.
2. Start a revolt as a diversion.
3. Get away.

Instead of one insuperable task, she had three slightly less insuperable. Her instructors at the academy would have called it 'top-down analysis'. It was progress, of a kind.

Next, she listed their strengths.

1. The laser medallion.
2. Thought-patterns alien to Qishi mentality.
3. Organisational and analytical ability.

It was getting a bit nebulous… better move on to the enemy's weaknesses:

1. Over-reliance on syntei.
2. Lack of numbers.
3. Failure to separate the three of us.
4. ?

Felix can't be dead. They wouldn't waste him. Detaching from her own need for him, she thought, if we could somehow make contact… Or wait for him to contact us. Add it in anyway:

4. Felix — the enemy within.

~~~

Drusilla would have been surprised how much Felix had learned, by deduction and observation, about her multi-located palace, but her pleasure at her new bed-slave had put her slightly off her guard. A few months' instruction in various entertaining but frivolous practices had been spiced up by putting him through his paces with some of her juniors: humiliation through forced pleasure was so much more subtle than merely inflicting pain, though some of the pleasure left scars.

Her main objective was still to extract something useful from his head.

"Silver-streak?"

"Yes, Sabi?"

"Once, when I was just a young girl in a village, I had a mule who liked to eat moondaisies. Whenever I was riding it along a track, it would surreptitiously edge towards the daisy-patches on the banks."

"Sabi, I do not understand."

"I think you are like my mule. You are not conducting me where I want to go."

Well, I'm still alive, Felix thought. "Sabi?"

"You are a bearer of secrets, Silver-streak. I want them."

Felix had been searching at his wit's end for something to tell Drusilla, useful enough to satisfy her curiosity. His knowledge of xenoscience was too abstruse to be much use to the VV. But in a slave-culture there is no shortage of manpower, and that changes the realm of the possible.

"Sabi, I am an accountant in my own lands," he told her, lying through his teeth. "I am skilled in the maximisation of profit." *Well, my 'comp is.*

"That's more like it, my mule."

"You deal in a number of commodities... slaves, alcohol, *kreesh*; those I know of. To maximise the profit you must make many decisions, weigh one factor against another. Decide how many slaves to employ in sugar-cane production rather than grain, or in processing *kreesh*."

"My judgement suffices."

"Sabi, your judgement is supreme. I seek merely to extend its influence. A method whereby you can explore, rapidly and easily, a hundred possible divisions of labour. In my country it is known as —"

"Words impress me not."

"It will increase your profit substantially."

"What is required?"

Felix told her.

A day later the two hundred slaves, proficient in figuring, arrived. Felix began to train them. It was difficult work at first, but they were conditioned to mindless obedience, and that was an advantage.

Within a week he was ready to demonstrate.

"A schoolroom," said Drusilla scathingly, looking at the rows of desks, each occupied by a slave with a slate and chalk. "Can you do no better than this?"

"It resembles a schoolroom, Sabi, that is true," said Felix. "But no ordinary schoolroom. Let us suppose, as a working hypothesis, that you have three sources of alcohol production A, B, and C, two sources D and E of *kreesh*..."

Drusilla watched, baffled, as Felix began to chant. "Add ten per cent of column 5 to column 8... Total-boy, run down column 6 and convey your result to the tally-keeper... Column 2, erase your slates..."

The first ever spreadsheet analysis on Qish got under way.

~~~

The siren whined. Sunrise. Time to get up.

Tinka staggered to her feet, tried to ignore her aching muscles, and followed Sam out of the hut. They lined up near the end of a row of slaves.

A dozen wardens walked along the lines, chanting the slaves' numbers into falasyntei. It was a simple roll-call. If a slave turned up missing, the number would be relayed to the monitoring-centre, and an arrow dispatched to its mark.

Jane, standing several rows back, watched carefully, hoping to see a flaw in the procedure. None occurred to her. She glanced at the shoulder number of the slave in front: 036057.

"Enough numbers for a million slaves," she muttered under her breath.

Sam, standing next to her, nodded. "Room for expansion."

"Convenient shapes for a manually adjustable branding-iron, too," Jane observed. "Seven strokes give all the digits. Slide out those you want, leave those you don't. Heat and apply. Clever."

"Interesting perversion of human ingen—" He clamped his mouth shut as a warden started to take an interest in the murmurs.

Jane's mind was racing. An idea was pecking at the inside of her skull. She could almost *hear* it trying to get out. Her brainchild was not yet ready to hatch, but its egg tooth was trying to hack an exit in the shell.

Now, if only one of them could get in touch with Felix. She must tell the others to warn him to be ready, in case an opportunity arose.

~~~

"Bizarre, that spreadroom of yours," said Drusilla, tickling Felix playfully. "But —"

"But your profit on the Tagruche hashish deal is up twenty-two per cent. Sabi."

"It is. And now the spreadslaves are trained, and *you* know far too much about my business. I shall have to have you executed."

"Sabi? You jest?"

"Not at all. Unless..."

"Unless?"

"Unless there are any other such ideas locked up in that curious mind of yours. Henceforth, Silver-streak, your life depends upon your proving to me that it will be more profitable to preserve it."

Felix's heart sank. He hadn't anticipated quite that reaction. He should have. Do you reward your chair when you sit on it? But she *had* given him the opening he was looking for. He hoped he'd judged her psychology correctly.

"Sabi, in my land is there made a device for seeing at a distance."

"We too have olosyntei," she said in disdain.

"But an olosynte can see only where its kolo-kantasynte is placed," Felix pointed out. "I am thinking of a device that could look down from a height on to enemy ranks and pick out the buttons on a general's coat."

"We do not deal in warfare."

"Or seek out a comely face from a crowd of harridans."

"For subsequent acquisition! Silver-streak, you have won another month of life. Provided this... this —"

"Telescope, Sabi."

"Provided this tescalope works as you say."

Mother, I hope so, thought Felix. *They seem to have skill with glass...* "Sabi, I begin at once. I must caution you that it will take some time, it is not easy without trained artisans. Also, certain calculations must be made, for which I lack the skill."

"You dare to play games with *me*?"

Felix fell to his knees. "Sabi, there are two here who can."

"Who?"

Felix had been wrestling with just that question for days. He needed to make sure that Drusilla didn't send Jane. He was desperate to see her, but emotions would take over and Drusilla would know he'd been lying when said there was no special relationship. After that, there was no knowing what the Primarch might do, but it probably wouldn't be pleasant, especially for Jane.

He couldn't ask for all three — how special could knowledge be if all but he had it? But picking out just one could too easily go wrong.

His xenonology training included human psychology. Mainly to prevent the assumption that aliens would think the same way. *Hope the bitch is still sufficiently human.*

Felix went for broke. "Jane Bytinsky and Tinka Laurel."

"Batinski and Lorel? Your companions?"

"Yes, Sabi."

Drusilla glared at him. "Is this just a trick to see your friends?"

"Sabi, if it is a trick then the — uh — tescalope will fail, and you will know what to do. I have not the skill, but they do."

Drusilla weighed the argument. "Very well." Felix tried not to betray his fragile triumph. "A messenger will convey the matter to them, and return with the answer."

Oh, Mother, that's no good. Quick! "Sabi, it is a subtle question. It will require face-to-face discussion."

This time Drusilla took longer. Felix offered up a silent prayer to the Mother of Galaxies. "One — *one* — will be brought." *Well,* that *went according to plan, at least.* "You have a preference?"

"Either is sufficiently skilled." *Please, Br'er Drusilla, please don't fling me in dat briar patch...* "On balance, Jane Bytinsky would be the best choice."

"But either would suffice?"

"Yes, Sabi."

Drusilla reached for the falasynte. "Have the tall girl named Lorel, the speciality item with the long hair, brought to me. Now!" She sat back with a smug look on her face and Felix tried to look suitably outwitted.

~~~

Every morning a gang of slaves brought round a cart for those who had died in the night. There were few days when the cart wasn't needed. It was one of the more unpleasant jobs, used as a punishment for minor infringements.

The corpses were taken to a trench, dumped, and covered with a thin layer of soil. Most other refuse also went into the trench.

Jane found the procedure fascinating, especially that no attempt was made to remove a slavestone from its host. The wardens just noted down the corpse's number.

When the sun was at its highest there was an hour-long siesta. Even for the slaves: it was too hot for the beaters to trouble with controlling them. At siesta time most of the slaves slept. Some, mostly old and garrulous, sat around and talked. Jane listened attentively.

One lanky youth named Goligo wanted to show her his scars. At first she took this as some sort of heavy-handed sexual advance, but on the third offer, she decided that anything was worth it to pass the time.

When he pulled up his shirt, she sucked in her breath, appalled. His back was a mess of puckered burn tissue.

"What happened, Goligo? Punishment?"

He shrugged. "Accident. Working iron was. In smith house is vat, fish oil. Use to… uh, distemper metal. Not right, is something same. Kalingo to me is not tongue, sorry Sabi."

"No, go on, I understand."

"Vat falled up, oil runned fire. Poof! Flames. To me was burn. Very bad. Now work fields."

"Is there much fish-oil at the smithy?"

"Yaz. Full many pots."

Patience is rewarded. Eventually.

A grey-beard had been *inside* the monitoring centre to clean it. She listened for hours to his semi-senile reminiscences until the well of information ran dry. The monitoring centre — and that word 'the' was important: there was *only* one — resembled the falasynte room at Two Mountains. Racks of syntei, each bearing the corresponding slave's number, and lots of people.

Now… imagine yourself a runaway. Random monitoring could catch you if the sounds through the slavestone were wrong. But suppose you can avoid that until the next morning. Is that time enough to have a doctor remove the stone?

Stupid. You *can't* remove the stone. It will kill you. Kurpershoek had said so.

Dah: assume a missing slave is noticed fast. They know someone's gone, but they don't know your number. So they mount a special roll-call.

No, you idiot. There's an easier way. Just listen, and shoot. Anyone on the run would give themselves away by their breathing alone.

As long as everyone else kept quiet. So *that's* what the five-minute silence was for! During it, an escaping slave had died. The silence gave her the first glimmerings of an escape plan. *Information overload*. In a riot, the Vain Vaimoksi would just kill at random. But what about something just as noisy and confusing, but where they would need every able-bodied slave they could get?

A denial-of-service attack.

It was starting to come together.

~~~

When they brought Tinka to Felix she wanted to rush into his arms, but the old hag in the red bathrobe with the laundry-basket hairdo made sure she didn't. "Speak only of the task set you. If asked your welfare, say you are being treated kindly. Complete your task before evening: there will be no second meeting." Tinka didn't have to ask the penalty for disobedience.

What had made Felix so formal and distant? She began to feel better when he started to explain the optical calculations he wanted her to do. Basic school physics — any of the Starfolk could have done them, including Felix. So the whole thing was a ruse to make contact, and the formal speech was a warning. Though why he kept calling the device a 'tescalope' was beyond her. *Some sort of scam. Be patient.*

Half an hour passed and the watching wardens relaxed a little. Felix said loudly: "Sabi Laurel, I trust you are being treated as well as I."

Tinka responded in kind. "I cannot complain." *Words are two-edged.* "I am treated like royalty. Like — a Contessa. The Contessa of Monte Cristo."

Yes, Felix also knew the classics. *We all want to escape.* "Me too."

Tinka tapped a finger at his sketch of the telescope design. "There is need of improvement, Sab Wylde. In particular the state of the servos must be modified."

Servos? This isn't a robot, what's she — oh. Servos: slaves.

"The servos must be adapted to higher revs. The design is difficult, but I can supply it. The timing will be unpredictable." Or, in plain Standard: a slave revolution must be brought about; I can do it; I don't know when.

"I am alert to that possibility, Sabi Laurel," said Felix. "Perhaps I can assist with the arithmetic?"

Tinka took up a quill and began to sketch. A warden moved closer and watched over her shoulder in case she was writing messages. She drew a series of lenses and tubes that made no optical sense. "This is a preliminary sketch, Sab Wylde. It is purely topological." She pointed to one end. "Here we have the input: an eyepiece of *Valkyrie* type." She wrote the letter 'I'. "And in the middle we have a Snowjob universal collimator." This time she wrote 'U'. "Finally, at this end, the *main objective*."

"Let me see if I've got that. That's U, this is I, and here's the main objective... pointing into the wide blue yonder."

"Nah, that's U, and *this* is I. But you're correct about the objective." Tinka warmed to the task. Once you've established a private language, everything gets easy. "Now, the problem is to create a free light-path between 'I' and the objective. That's where 'U' comes in, understand?"

"I follow the principle, but I'm not sure whether I have the facilities."

"I imagine the Primarch can be persuaded to supply them," said Tinka drily.

"I will put the matter to her vigorously. But first, I must obtain the necessary instruments." *I have no weapons.*

"You must improvise. Grind this prism to make the image as sharp as possible." *A glass knife?*

The wardens were taking too great an interest and Felix went off into a long technical discussion until they became bored. Then he asked his last question.

"It would be helpful to define more clearly the timing of the servo revs."

"Unfortunately, Sab Wylde, that is not yet possible. But the marks should become visible. I leave it to your judgement."

When the revolt happens, it should be obvious. After that, it's up to you.

~~~

During the siesta, Jane had taken to sitting on the banks of the lake. The bright orange lilypads, anchored by invisible roots, were rings with a wide central hole with the sky showing through. You didn't have to be a genius to work out that they were an aquatic species of synte. The amphibious frog-forms that hopped in and out of them used them as rights-of-way.

Near the shore the lilypads were no more than a handspan across, but further out — beyond her reach — they grew to armwidth, and they flexed with the ripples. A small one smuggled back to their hut remained flexible when kept damp, but went rigid, like a normal kasynte, when it dried.

Sam squatted beside her, and waited patiently. After a while, she noticed him, and said "Remember that syntelic gastroscope in Kastane? It came through a synte."

"And?"

"It still worked."

One flag set. But there were others.

For several days she studied the froglike creatures. When she threw a lump of bread, they would chase it, gulp it down, and hurry back for more. Ranarian retrievers. Another flag.

A lilypad flexed, enough to roll into a tube. Unrolled, it still worked. If it didn't dry out, it was naturally springy, and wouldn't easily stay rolled.

One flag at a time, the plan took shape. Start collecting materials.

That evening Jane unravelled the bottom of her woollen shirt. Using two sticks, she started knitting.

"That's a bit small, even for a sweatband," said Sam.

"That's because it isn't," said Jane primly, and carried on knitting.

"What is it, then?"

"A frog-collar."

Sam laughed. "You're obsessed with those frogs."

"Every damsel in distress needs a handsome frog to kiss her into a princess."

"That doesn't sound right," said Sam.

"I call my frog Rapunzel," said Jane.

Sam had no answer to that.

~~~

Have plan, Jane scrawled in the sand. *Escape*. It took two hours to explain the details. *Hope Felix his bit.*

Need volunteer.

4 wht? wrote Sam.

Scrawl by furtive scrawl, Jane told him.

17

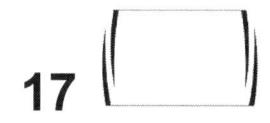

Show Business

> Uneasy flies the clown that wears the head.
> — *Traditional* khanatta *saying*

The room was dim-lit and dirty. Smoke from the kitchens hung near the ceiling. Hunched at a corner table, faces half hidden behind enormous mugs of dark Larbin jarble, were two men who matched the inn. Their eyes were constantly on the move, darting this way and that as they talked in low murmurs.

"You're certain?" The speaker was a greasy-maned rogue.

"Dead sure, Snalikka," nodded a tattooed head. "They don't build crumpies like that nowhere on *this* continent, and that hide of hers isn't that colour because it's been tanned. That hair clinches it. Gold Lightning — I'll say! She can flash at me any time she —"

"Save it, Magborp. What about the *hoom*?"

"Tracked him down in the 'vorehouse, making eyes at a mousey bit of local crumpy half his age. He must be blind as a wozzet with its snout in the privy, when he's got that corn-haired dolly —"

"I said, *save it!*"

"Saving it, Snal, saving it. Keep your ears on." Magborp downed the clotted dregs of his mug, signalling a drunken 'another' to the jarblemaid. He belched: Snalikka eyed him balefully. "So now all we do is send word to Two Mountains, and pick up a cool thousand *skint*."

"Maybe."

"*Maybe?*"

"If blondie is as good a bit of crumpy as you say — and to judge by the way you drool every time you say it, she must be — we ought to be able to get more than half a *skadd* apiece for her."

Magborp's mug stopped, spilling down his front. He didn't notice. He said, "You don't mean…"

"That's just it, Mag. I *do* mean. The Vain Vaimoksi."

Magborp's grubby face paled. "A man can disappear when those harpies are around, Snal."

"Only if he's a fool and a coward. Reckon the VV would pay at least two and a half *skadd* for her. 'Course, those evil bitches'd sell her at a profit, but we don't have their connections."

Magborp looked worried. "What about the *hoom*?"

"Kill him."

"Unh? But he should be worth a —"

"We're bucking Two Mountains and bringing in the VV. If the *hoom* gets awkward, it could foul everything up a dozen ways. He wouldn't fetch more than a split-skadd anyway, it's not worth the candle."

Sweat broke out on Magborp's brow. "Buck Two Mountains? Are you crazy?"

Snalikka grinned. "If the VV grab her, who's to know?"

"I don't like it, Snal. I don't like it at all."

Shame, thought Snalikka. *If Mag's scared, he might just decide to cut his losses and sneak off to tell Two Mountains on his own.* But his voice was casual, "Think it over, tell me tomorrow," as Magborp pulled on a cloak and lumbered off into rain and darkness. Deciding that two and a half thousand skint split better one way, Snalikka dropped his hand to the hilt of his dagger and moved to follow him. *Take Maggie when he reaches the canal crossing. That leaves the big brown hoom. Then the crumpy and the skint, all to myself. Ought to have a bit of fun, too, before she goes to the Vain Vaimoksi… and find out where the bag of jewels went. No need to help Two Mountains or the VV get those.*

~~~

A small, tubby dwarf was fleeing a second dwarf, riding a large dog and brandishing an enormous club. The rider had only one leg: the other was tucked under the fugitive's arm. The dog put on a burst of speed, the club descended, and the fugitive's head vanished between his shoulders. As the rider dismounted the head popped back up again. The club swiped sideways and the head fell off. The torso danced up and down, while the head stuck out its tongue and made a vulgar noise. Infuriated, the second dwarf hit the torso over the shoulders: the arms fell off. On the next hit, the trunk fell to the ground, leaving only a pair of legs standing.

"*Psssttt!*" hissed the head in a stage-whisper. The second dwarf bent closer to hear, and one disembodied leg kicked him in the seat of the pants.

The audience roared with laughter. Snalikka, sitting about half way back among the cheaper seats, roared with them. The khanatta had reinvented clowns.

One of the severed arms reached out, tripping up the second clown. The first clown reassembled himself, dragged the second over to the dog, and swapped their heads. The dog-head barked. The first clown stepped back and nodded sagely, as if satisfied with the improvement. He was knocked flat by a pink and yellow pantomime horse that galloped past with four hairless human legs — exactly *one* of them female.

Marco, waiting in the wings, was impressed. No wonder even an audience born and bred here thought it worth watching. It took a lot of experience to judge the difficulty of a syntelic act. The trapeze artistes, plunging groundwards into syntei concealed by paper hoops, looked spectacular, but much of that was showmanship. The performing centaurs — torsos of men and women on horse bodies — looked run-of-the-mill until you thought about how the horses saw where they were going. As the clowns chased each other with paper-hooped syntei, whose kasyntei led directly to an enormous water trough, Marco picked up his own hoops in readiness for the 'vore act.

~~~

As Lomyrla and Marco put the 'vores through their paces, Snalikka began to take a sober interest in the waterjets they both kept close to hand. An excellent way to get rid of the *hoom*. When the act finished he slipped out of the tent and headed for the danceshow. Now — time to confirm at first hand the quality of the crumpy. On the way he took a hard look at the water-tower, and nodded thoughtfully.

~~~

The Grand Khanatta headed northwards across the undulating Treece countryside, with its groves of fruiting plants and its herds of rhomneys — dumpy products of early Concordat genesplicing, like pink sheep with cowlike udders, kept for their milk and wool — and peaceful farm-buildings in slate and wattle. In the distance, veiled in cloud, they had seen yesterday the topmost peaks of the White Ramparts, a massive range whose southern face plunged dizzily in sheer granite cliffs. To their left, the Andillera range drove northward like a white-capped tidal wave, to break in frozen foam over the Ramparts' walls.

Marco and Elzabet now slept at opposite ends of her tent, and scarcely spoke.

~~~

Stripey the 'vore was sleeping soundly when something nudged its back, and it rolled over. The pressure increased and it hauled itself to its feet. The world was shrinking. Wide awake now, it turned its head. One roustabout slid a large kasynte through the cage bars, linked to the performance cage in the main ring. Another hauled on ropes that moved one wall of the cage, driving the beast towards the opening. The 'vore snarled and loped through the aperture.

The audience hushed as the great beasts appeared. Finally there were five of them, perched upon large tubs.

Lomyrla and Marco gave their waterjets a final test and made their entrance. Lomyrla led the 'vores round the cage in line astern, spinal manes fluffed proudly, tails aloft in sinuous loops. She lifted her hand, and together they rose on their haunches. The largest 'vore patted a brightly coloured ball across the cage.

Snalikka entered unnoticed through a side-flap and stood strategically beside a tent-pole. He remembered the music from the previous performance, and knew the stage that the act had reached. Picking his moment, he raised a short tube to his lips.

Marco picked up a pair of paper-covered kasynte hoops. One for him, one to hand to Lomyrla. They were about to jump the 'vores through the hoops.

Snalikka levelled the syntube at the nearest 'vore and bit down hard. A projectile sped by a hundred-metre drop shot from the tube and hit the beast on its sensitive nose. It roared in pain and lashed out at the nearest object — a small tub near Lomyrla's feet. The tub crumpled. The 'vore, with a menacing high-pitched whine, advanced on her. Raising the waterjet, she pressed the release.

Nothing happened.

Snalikka laughed silently. As soon as the music had announced her, he had blocked the syntei in the water-tower.

The five 'vores sensed the heightening tension and began to move towards Marco and Lomyrla, surrounding them. Lomyrla shrieked but the creatures moved closer. Marco looked frantically around, still holding the hoops.

He saw the clowns' water-trough. Holding a hoop like a frisbee he hurled it over the bars, to land with a splash in the water.

The 'vore leaped, but as it did so, Marco dived across the cage with the second hoop. The 'vore crashed into the paper, met the synte interface at an angle, and shot into the air above the trough. It must have seen the water below it, for it set up a terrible wailing during the split second that it took to reach apogee. It descended to the water in a cloud of spray and floated on its side, rigid as a log.

The second 'vore fared similarly. This left a gap, and Marco hurriedly backed through it, pulling Lomyrla with him. A third 'vore thought about a leap, saw the hoop, changed its mind, and slunk back whining on to its tub. Marco and Lomyrla made a rapid exit from the cage.

Snalikka cursed under his breath, stopping abruptly as a powerful hand clamped his wrist, twisting it painfully behind him. A second hand delved into his grubby tunic, finding the syntube.

"Make a sound and I'll break your neck," said Four-way Polo.

Lomyrla grabbed Marco in a bear-hug, almost knocking him flat. Two prop-handlers led them from the ring. They were too shaken to acknowledge the thunderous applause of a relieved — or guiltily disappointed — audience.

Four-way Polo hurried in. "Bianchi — I mean, Marco Leontevich Bianchi — that was brilliant. Saved my little girl!" He shot his daughter a look. "Lomy, I know we don't see eye to eye these days, but I'm still fond of you, even though I... oh, what the skunt, you know what I mean." He turned to Marco. "You're a hero, Sab. Swatting two 'vores in mid-leap and cowing three more — never seen the like in my life, talk about fast thinking." Marco tried not to look embarrassed. "Not that I'm criticising, mind you," Polo continued, "but... Why didn't you just pull the second hoop over both your heads, and get out straight away?"

Marco, who had never thought of it, looked at him blankly for a second. "Uh — I was worried that the 'vores might escape if I left the kasynte in the cage. One thing you can't do with a synte is bring it through itself with you."

"Good point," Polo grudgingly agreed. "But you could have—"

"Oh, stop carping, Polo!" Lomyrla grabbed Marco's arm. "That *skurd*'s never satisfied, take no notice of *him*. Let's get away from here."

Polo watched them go, with a wry look on his face. Then he headed back to where he had left Snalikka under guard.

Marco was confused.

In Lomyrla's tent she had flung herself upon him, mouthing endearments, weeping, and laughing all at the same time. He had reached out with an intended reassuring fatherly pat, but her slit skirt was in disarray and his hand encountered not cloth but warm flesh. Inspired to investigate further, and hardly discouraged by her moist breath in his ear and gentle moans of pleasure, he had found it possible to unlace the sides of her dress using only one hand at a time. This incidentally resolved the vexed question of undergarments... by which time he had decided that his feelings were not entirely paternal and protective.

But when their lovemaking was over and she had gone, he wasn't sure what he felt. His responsibility was to Elzabet. And deep down... If only she hadn't been in such a disagreeable mood lately! He thought of Lomyrla's hands caressing his body, and postponed the problem for later consideration. Indefinitely.

Polo learned little of value from Snalikka, beyond the plan to kill Marco and sell Gold Lightning to the VV. The involvement of Two Mountains did not come to light. While his two most trusted men disposed of the corpse, Polo grabbed a third by the arm. "Send the two nozzies to me."

Marco and Elzabet must be told of their danger.

Gold Lightning was too valuable a property to lose.

~~~

The Grand Khanatta passed through small towns and scattered villages. It played to packed stands in Pontrephakk; to a thin audience of village louts in Halfpaw; to the disdainful citizens of Tantra Pi, whose only true passion was the salt-trade; and to the credulous inhabitants of Buxsil Parv, who applauded wildly at unpredictable moments, as the mood took them.

Elzabet and Marco continued to perform, but they and Polo's henchmen kept a wary eye on the crowds. There was always a guard on the water-tower.

Deacon DeLameter's agents, meanwhile, scoured the continents of Samdal and Lamynt with grim persistence, by foot and by horse, by synte, ski, and dog-shay, seeking two golden-haired persons of above average height with bodies brown as dried vunbugula. But they sought them in gem markets and out-of-the-way hiding places, never dreaming that the quarry would show themselves so prominently, or need to earn *skint*. Discreet questioners asked at every likely inn and tavern, in every bolt-hole or wayward locality. Nobody connected the descriptions with a magnificent blonde who danced next-to-naked in the khanatta, or a tall, muscular daredevil who publicly flirted with death by 'vore-fang. No agent, Deacon's or Chaplain's, repeated the (mixed) fortune of Magborp, who had wandered lustfully into the danceshow tent, to recognise the object of his searches undulating before his goggling eyes.

But it could only be a matter of time.

Two months after leaving Ventapux, the procession of wagons forded the West Lorn river, where the city of Sinda nestled in the foothills of the White Ramparts like a bole-toad snugged against the roots of a portle-tree. Against a backdrop of towering rock, a large lake spread across the valley floor. Obscured by mist, it resembled a patchwork quilt, dappled with every colour of the rainbow. From each patch a powerful jet of water shot skyward. At each lofty apex the jet shattered into a swirling mass of windswept spray, merging with its neighbours to form the clouds from which an incessant fine rain fell, veiling the distant lake.

The patches, Marco decided, were flowering plants. But where did the fountains come from? Lomyrla, cradled in his arm, explained. Elzabet was standing sullenly nearby, unable to admit even to herself that she was jealous.

"It is the most widely famed sight on Samdal," said Lomyrla. "The Spouting Mere. On the upper reaches of the Lorn river, atop the White Ramparts, grow great syntelic waterplants in brilliant colours. The river brings their seedbuds through a vast underground cavity in the living rock, emerging at Rampart Base and flowing into this valley, where the water is shallow and placid. The buds put out tendrils and take root. At seed-time, the parent kasyntei open above the level of the river, but later the water rises, and descends through the syntei with great force to form the cascades. Meantime the budded fruit has grown sideshoots of its own. Those make the particoloured patches.

"Each Snowseason the plants die back, to rebirth the following Melting."

"Do the plants eat fish?" asked Marco.

"The syntmouths are fringed with thin tendrils that trap and digest the smaller water-creatures. How did you know?"

"There had to be some evolutionary advantage."

Lomyrla wrinkled her nose. She adored Marco, but at times he said the most incomprehensible things.

The next leg of the journey, to Sensifoy, giddily perched on Rampart's Edge, was the worst yet. The narrow track zigzagged up the precipitous face. The larger wagons had to be broken down and carried on smaller horse-drawn carts. The 'vore cages were dismantled, and their occupants kept senseless with frequent sprayings. The road was heavy with traffic in both directions. At every level side-branches led through banks of syntei to outlets across the continent with the same gravitational potential. Travellers came from thousands of kilometres away to make a brief level-changing transit and depart to destinations equally far afield.

"Is there no better route?" Marco grumbled aloud.

"The paths up the Blue Ramparts are even worse, and the tolls on the mountains of Wevory are extortionate," Lomyrla told him. "Mountain rock is so hard that the track cannot be made wider."

"Oh for some dynamite! You know, if someone could solve the gravity problem it would *revolutionise* syntelic transport."

"What's dynamite?"

Elzabet, listening silently, pursed her lips thoughtfully; then shook her head.

~~~

On the fourth day in Sensifoy, when the wagons had been rebuilt and a rest-day declared, Marco and Lomyrla lay side by side in her tent. She snuggled closer.

"Marco, darling?"

"Yes, Lomy?" he replied, hardly listening, enjoying the tones of her voice.

"I've got a surprise."

"That's nice," said Marco.

"It's... a present."

"For me, sweeting?"

"It belongs to both of us," said Lomyrla mysteriously. She took his hand and laid it on her stomach. "Do you feel anything?"

Marco had an awful precognition of the direction the conversation was heading, and he tried manfully to redirect it. "It's very familiar... let me think... perhaps if I explore the surroundings, maybe *here* —"

"Behave yourself, Marco! And stop changing the subject. Guess."

The precognition became a howling certainty, but still Marco ploughed grimly sideways. "You're taking up belly-dancing to improve the musculature?"

"Oh! You wozzet! Don't pretend you haven't already guessed we're pregnant?"

"That," gulped Marco, "is wonderful news. Uh — *we*?"

She tweaked his nose. "Well, of course, I am, right now. But you must bear your share."

"I thought we were taking countermeasures. Those syntelic gadgets. The ones you say tickle."

"We are. But it all happened too quickly, the first time." She saw his face and chuckled throatily. "Don't look so horrified, dearest. It's meant to be *good* news!"

"Of course it is. It's just a bit of a sho — I mean, a surprise. It takes a little getting used to."

"We'll tell Four-way this evening," said Lomyrla. "He can make the arrangements."

"Polo?" said Marco in a strangled voice, not daring to enquire what form the 'arrangements' might take. "But you never have a civil word to say to him!"

"Marco, this is tradition. It must be done the proper way, even if my paternal supporter is a bug-snouted wozzet-humping *skurd*."

"It's a matter of family respect."

To Marco's astonishment that craggy individual was delighted, pumping his hand like a behind-quota rhomney-maid. "I'll call on the doctor tomorrow," he said, "to arrange the synting."

"Pardon?"

Four-way eyed him sternly. "I presume I don't have to explain the elementary facts of childbearing?"

"Mother of Galaxies, no."

Polo looked puzzled by the phrase, but he didn't really expect to get sense out of these people. "Then I hope I'm correct," he said stiffly, "in assuming that you intend to stand by my little girl? Keep the customs like a gentleman?"

"Of course." Marco wasn't sure whether he meant it, or even what 'the customs' entailed, but now was not the time to ask revealing questions.

"Next week would be a good time for it all, don't you think? Keep it small, a family thing. Can't stand ostentation. I think the best day would be —"

"Next week? You want us to get married *next week*?" The rescue beacon, Starhome, Sam and the others — for Marco Bianchi they would all have to wait. His face became a picture of misery.

Polo pulled his body together haughtily. "Married? What are you mumbling about, man? Lomy, you don't want to *marry* this fellow, do you?"

"Demons no, Polo. I haven't even considered proposing. He's far too young, no income to speak of. I *am* truly fond of him. In time, if he can better himself —"

"Quite," interrupted Polo. Taking Lomyrla by the arm, he stalked away.

Marco sat heavily on a wickerwork laundry-basket, and breathed a sigh of relief. Not marriage after all.

Then: *If synting isn't marriage, what in the name of the nanacurst is it?*

~~~

Elzabet was not amused.

"You fool, Marco! Now you've messed up *everything*! How can we get to the beacon if you've got yourself snared by that stupid little cow?"

"She's not stupid, Elza, she's courageous and —"

"Here am I doing all sorts of demeaning things to earn us enough travel money, and all you can do is fool around with a cheap circus tart while my back is turned!"

"That's unfair and untrue," said Marco, with shaky dignity. *And if you hadn't made a habit of turning your back, the problem might never have arisen.*

"We'll just have to skip out the first chance we get!"

"Nah, Elza. I'm not prepared to do that."

"You don't imagine I can get to the beacon on my own, do you?"

At times, Marco could be very stubborn, especially when his sense of honour was threatened. "I won't abandon Lomyrla. She needs me. A lot more than you do, to judge by your behaviour recently. I have a responsibility. It's *my* child you're asking me to leave! The father must bear his share of the burden. When in Samdal, do as the —"

"*My* behaviour? Oh, Mother of Galaxies! And while you're busy bearing your burden, you oversexed wozzet, what happens to Sam and the others?"

Marco stared at his feet, and Elza stalked from the tent in fury.

18

Displaced Persons

> Stormtrooper Gharff obviously reckoned my sidekick was a total dork-head, but the Senior Lawman seemed interested.
> "You think that's important?" he asked.
> "Yes. Really important."
> "So, to what should I assign administrative priority?"
> "The strange behaviour of the mutehound in the night-time."
> "The mutehound barked its fool head off all night."
> "That was the strange behaviour," said Shirley Combs.
> —Aretha Conlon Doyle, The Memoirs of Shirley Combs

Only a matter of time...

Two days after Marco was told the glad tidings, a bored Shaaluin agent came upon the Grand Khanatta, newly arrived in Trupine, a bustling market town clinging to a precipitous plateau surrounded by snow-capped peaks. Seeking stimulation, he chanced to enter the danceshow tent...

Her act over, Elzabet lay morosely on her featherbag, bemoaning Marco's incipient fatherhood and her own degrading predicament. The flap of her tent opened and a small object was tossed in. Leaping to her feet she rushed to the exit, but the intruder had vanished. With beating heart, she gingerly picked the object up.

It was a falasynte. It spoke.

She almost dropped it.

"Els'bett?"

Sadruddin's pronunciation sent an electric shiver ran up her spine.

"Gus!"

"You are alone?"

"Yes."

"That is good. We may talk frankly, but quietly and not long. There is danger of eavesdroppers. He who placed the falasynte will keep watch."

Good news, the first in months. Elzabet wanted to dance and weep, all at the same time. She did neither. "Gus, what a relief to hear from you!"

"Even more so for me. But—"

"What's happened to our friends? Has DeLameter hurt them?"

"Calm, sabi, calm. We must not be overheard. Nar, the Deacon has not harmed them, but only because they are not in his power."

"That's good news."

"They are not in *his* power. They and their guards were abducted in a Vain Vaimoksi ambush while returning to Two Mountains. Only Kurpershoek escaped."

Oh, Mother. "Gus, where are they?"

"None but Vain Vaimoksi spawn know where they conceal themselves."

"What will happen to them?"

"As the Shaper wills. The Vain Vaimoksi are slave-takers. If your friends are lucky, they will be sold. If not, they will be made to work until they die."

Did this somehow happen because Marco and I...? "Can you rescue them? Buy them?"

"I am trying, Els'bett. The Deacon believes I seek your friends on behalf of the Quizitors. Accordingly, he has been generous with resources, and the Vain Vaimoksi exist for copper. But anything involving them is fraught with difficulties."

As Elzabet groaned, Sadruddin's voice became more urgent. "Sabi, there is no time for such matters. You and Marcolo are in grave danger. DeLameter seeks you the length and breadth of Samdal and Lamynt."

"The Deacon? Here?" Elza almost shrieked. "I thought we were safe, trash it!"

"Sabi, I say again: be calm. I made the same error. But his reach goes far into Samdal. He will not rest until you are captured and he sees your shattered bones. It is the greatest of good fortune that my agent has found you ahead of his. I hope you have kept a low profile."

"Mmmph. Perhaps 'low' isn't quite the right description." Elzabet explained their jobs in the khanatta. "We had no money, and a limited choice of employment."

"The choice was unsound. Especially your own, Els'bett." Beat. "Though I would give much to see it."

Men — all the same. But it was good to hear his voice again, and she began to regain her balance. "Gus, if we ever meet again in suitable surroundings, I'll give you a private performance. But we imagined we were safe from the Deacon."

"Perhaps you were," the Chaplain replied. "Sometimes the best place to hide something is in the open. But that should be a calculated risk, Sabi, not an accident."

"It's paid off so far. We've had no trouble."

"None?" Gus sounded sceptical.

"Well... there was a nasty incident with an ossivore. Some slavetaker wanted to kidnap me and sell me to the Vain Vaimoksi. He tried to kill Marco."

"Describe him."

"His name was Snalikka —" she heard a muffled curse from Sadruddin. "You know him?"

"Snalikka was one of the men I hired as an agent, for the Deacon. Yes, *I*. DeLameter has commanded me to direct the search, but I think he has his own men on it, too. Snalikka must have acted without the Deacon's knowledge — I would have known by DeLameter's actions, had he been told. There remains great danger. You must leave the khanatta at once —"

"I'm not sure we can."

"I can send you money."

"No, that's not the problem. Marco's about to become a father."

"— ?"

"Not me! A circus girl."

Gus made a strangled noise. "In Samdal, such a prospect is doubly difficult."

Elzabet asked why.

"Do you not know?"

"Everyone here seems to assume we do. If we ask, it might blow our cover."

"Until the baby is born, the parents are joined by synte. Separation would be fatal."

"What? Oh, no, Gus, surely not! Why create such an insane risk?"

"Your thoughts are coloured by habit, Els'bett. It is entirely natural — in Samdal. A long and honourable tradition. In Shaaluy it would carry the death penalty."

"Oh, Mother. So to speak. Pardon me." *It'll be interesting to see Marco's face when they tell him. He's really done it this time.* "That complicates everything. The synting is fixed for tomorrow."

"You realise that once it is done, he must stay with her?"

"That goes without saying. But Marco can be very stubborn. He's already committed. He won't budge. Not even for this."

Rising from depression, now that Gus had found them again, Elzabet recognised her own feelings as guilt. *It's my fault too — I was thinking too much of myself.* He was trying to do his best and all I could do was snap at him. Elzabet of Quynt: it is time you made your peace with Marco Bianchi. You need each other.

"He'd consider it betrayal, and one of his strengths is loyalty. The harder I push, the harder he'll resist. No, Gus, I'm sorry, but we've got to stay here."

"Then I have no choice but to revise my strategy," said Sadruddin. "We must devise a plan to put the Deacon off the scent. Permanently." He paused. "If truth be told, that would be a better outcome."

"Right. We can't run and hide forever."

"I think I have the glimmerings of an idea, Sabi, borrowed from that gutterlout Snalikka. But it requires careful preparation, and some assistance. Is Polo trustworthy?"

"He's very attached to his daughter, though they fight like ossivores with different bellies. If Marco will go along with your plan, I'm pretty sure Polo will."

"Good. Hide the falasynte and keep wait until I return. Strabyen, Els'bett."

"Strabyen, Gus."

She hurried off to tell Marco that the Chaplain had made contact, and what he had said. As she expected, he refused to budge.

~~~

Sadruddin busied himself with the necessary arrangements. For once, being in charge of the search was an advantage. It let him come and go without hindrance or question.

After half a week had passed, he urgently requested an audience with the Deacon, and was ushered at once into his presence. "Revered One? I have found them."

"The two who escaped from Shaluuy? The four taken by the Vain Vaimoksi?"

"The two."

DeLameter looked up sharply. He had a special interest in that pair. "Where? Are they captive? Instruct the Quizitors to —"

"I have set their capture in motion, Revered One. They are in a khanatta in Trupine, a town on the White Ramparts of central Samdal."

"A *khanatta*? A curious choice. In the tent of freaks, perhaps?"

If DeLameter is starting to make jokes, thought Sadruddin, the situation is really getting out of hand. "If they assumed that audacity would serve them best, Reverence, they were wrong." Sadruddin produced two kolosyntei for long-viewing. "You may wish to witness their capture. Your agents carry the kantasyntei."

The Deacon took the rings of woody tissue. "And when will this take place?"

Sadruddin consulted a syndial. "Between one and two hours from now." He made to leave.

He had taken but a step when the Deacon's quiet voice said "Sadruddin." He stopped. An anxious moment passed. "You may stay to watch the vermin trapped, and to rejoice in their despair."

You *will* stay, he means. As it happens, it suits my purpose. "You honour me undeservedly, Revered One."

"Nonsense! An hour at least, you say? Perhaps a glass, and a game of *shinsa* to pass the time?" He beckoned to a servant while the Chaplain set up the *shinsa* board. Sadruddin and DeLameter waged desultory war on a field of hexagons, but their eyes kept moving to the kolosyntei, propped on a stand at a nearby table. DeLameter called for more liqueur and moved two of his precentors in a pincer attack. Sadruddin prudently ignored a subtle doom in three, to which the Deacon had unwittingly opened his forces, and interposed a high precentor. The Deacon advanced a minorite to fork Sadruddin's two flamens. "Doom, Sadruddin!"

"An excellent game, Revered One. Your command of the apses was impeccable."

"Is it time?"

The Chaplain looked again at his syndial. "Very soon, Reverence. Your agents will be making ready. With your approval, we should attend the kolosynte."

The right-hand aperture showed jostling crowds, then the entrance to a tent. The picture jumped erratically. On a platform, a pale-skinned Samdali woman, clad only in high boots and a trellis of blue ribbon, gyrated athletically. DeLameter's brows furrowed and he peered closer. "See how the perverts disport themselves, Sadruddin, even short of Division! But where are the escaped Abominators?"

"The Quynt woman should appear momentarily, Revered One." But now the Deacon was drawn to the second kolosynte. His breath hissed, his fists clenched in spasms. "Sin and corruption! Division and damnation! Perversion and wickedness!"

Sadruddin turned his eyes to whatever outrage the Deacon had seen.

It was the clowns.

They continued to watch. A second woman took over on the dance platform. The centaurs came on, to another spate of denunciation from DeLameter, who was beginning to shake in a kind of palsy, with flecks of foam at the corners of his mouth. The 'vores appeared, followed by Lomyrla — and Marco.

"*It is he!*"

"Indeed, Reverence. And see, his female appears in the right-hand kolosynte."

"The naked hussy in her true colours," said DeLameter. His entire body was trembling now.

Sadruddin said "Your agents will seize them as they leave after their acts, Reverence. They will abduct them by synte and — wait!" His features contorted. "What is this? This is not the plan!"

A young woman, her head shaved in a tonsure, with crimson trousers and tunic and holding a metre-wide wyzand, leaped on to the dance platform. At the same time, two similar women scuttled across the ring toward Marco and Lomyrla as they made to enter the 'vore cage. Elzabet screamed and tried to run. Marco moved a step forward to protect Lomyrla.

"The Vain Vaimoksi!" screeched DeLameter. "They must not have them! The offworlders are mine! *Mine!*"

Three Deacon's Agents jumped on to the dance platform, and one levelled a syntube at a Vaimoksha slavetaker. But before he could trigger it, a hurled turnip from the audience threw him off balance. The woman seized Elzabet's wrists and brought her wyzand down smartly over both their heads. Marco's assailants flung another over his head, then vanished through a third. Immediately the three abandoned wyzandei withered and turned black.

"Destroyed at the far end!" shrieked the Deacon. "To follow is impossible! Oh, bones will be crushed for this!" He shuddered, then sank back in his seat with his eyes glazed, his energy spent.

Sadruddin prostrated himself full-length. "Revered One, I have failed you. I shall resign my post and return to the village of my birth, to mortify my flesh and meditate upon my errors —"

DeLameter looked at him coldly. "That will not be necessary, Sadruddin. No man is answerable for acts of the Vain Vaimoksi. You are blameless. But I must be alone now, to pray for guidance and light in this time of tribulation."

Sadruddin departed unobtrusively.

As he turned a corner, he heard the sound of smashing crystal coming from the Deacon's office, but found no amusement in it. What DeLameter had done to a vanduul flagon, he might also do to his Chaplain, should he ever suspect duplicity.

~~~

Marco was fretting at the enforced confinement. His quarters were a small wagon, covered with thick fabric against the weather, a koriel its only exit. A pale redhead of medium height, in a purple tunic and long skirt, appeared in the koriel's mouth.

Marco failed to understand why a society that freely permitted, indeed encouraged, the sexual body-dividing uses of syntei; that expected its dancing girls to perform naked; that accepted casual sexual contact short of pregnancy without demur — should balk at permitting the prospective father to appear in public during daylight hours. On grounds of indecency. And now the time approached for Lomyrla's synting — but he still didn't know just how the "joining" would work.

"Hello, Marco."

"Elza!"

"Brilliant. You'd do credit to Shirley Combs."

"But — it can't be! Your skin and hair are all different!"

"Make-up and dye. Not hard to find around here, Marco."

"You've lost a head in height! How in the name of the Starmother —"

"How else?" Elzabet slowly raised the hem of her skirt over a less unexpected brown leg. Around ankle, shin, and upper thigh were what seemed to be black garters.

"Gone into mourning for those who have passed beyond, Elza?"

"You *are* fond of ancient quotations, aren't you? Nah, these are height-reducing kasynte pairs. The kantasyntei are in the tent, with a chunk of leg between each pair. Body-division with a vengeance! I've got another around my waist, and a couple on each arm to keep them in proportion, otherwise I'd look like a chimpanzee."

"Orang-utan. You're not chimp colour."

"Makes me look a bit stocky," ignoring him. "But — *ni porbleem*, dah?"

Marco nodded in admiration. "And all of it part of the Augustine Tambiah Sadruddin master plan for fugitive aliens, I'll warrant. Why didn't you tell me?"

"Need-to-know. We Hippolytan aristocrats take security seriously. It's a natural consequence of there being so many diplomats in the family. First a little charade to convince the Deacon that the VV have got us too; then we lie low."

"You could have got me a shrink-set too! I've just been stuck here!"

"It won't be that easy, I'm afraid — but that can wait. Our biggest problem, as usual, is money. We still need it, and Gus can't supply enough. The Deacon isn't a generous employer."

"I'm sorry, Elza. I hadn't realised that the father's family is expected to cover all medical expenses."

"It does make life difficult. Particularly since you don't have a family."

"Not yet."

"So I'm assuming that obligation. I've got to earn enough to keep us both, and Lomyrla, for the next eight months or so."

Marco was bewildered by the turn of events. "Doing what, Elza? You can't dance any more."

"Nah, and I'm not sorry. When I *think* what will happen if anyone back home ever gets wind of it, I *shudder*. But I plan to employ my brain, not my body. And, with Gus's help, I've found myself a more fitting job."

"What?"

"You'll be disappointed. It's not as sexy as dancing. Remember what the biggest transport problem on Qish is? Not distance, but *height*, because of energy conservation through syntei."

"How could I forget? I still carry the bruises from the White Ramparts trek."

"Serves you right. While you were limping up the Ramparts making moon-eyes at the local talent, I was thinking about the underground river that feeds the Spouting Mere: it's not all through the spouts. Its cavity will be fairly evenly sloped, and quite large. Larger than that zigzag path up the Rampart face. A nice, broad, sloping tunnel, out of the weather, would be much better."

"Which leaves the small task of diverting the river."

Marco slapped his forehead. "By stealing a trick from the waterflowers!"

"Precisely."

"I can't think why the natives didn't hit on it."

"Because, as you keep saying in your little lectures, they don't expect to *build* technology — they expect it to grow on trees. If a single synte grew wide enough, they'd have done it ages ago. It will take a barricade with embedded syntei, and kantasyntei down near the Mere. Civil engineering isn't their thing, and this calls for good old R&D and well-organised logistics. Not Qishi thought-patterns at all.

"When I thought of the idea I couldn't see how to get anyone interested. But Gus has contacts in Samdal who can pull strings, and to cut a long story short, they've agreed to set up the project."

"Great! And they pay you a fee for the idea, and hire me for the engineering expertise. Brilliant!"

"Not quite." Elzabet smiled. "I'm Chief Engineer."

"But... Elza!" wailed Marco, stricken to his core. "*I'm* the engineer!"

"An engineer. *I'm* the mining engineer, with the certificates on my 'comp, and *you* are an expectant father. Can't take on any strenuous tasks."

"But —"

"I thought you were in favour of female emancipation?"

"Yah, but —"

"Don't like the bootee on the other tootsie?"

"That's not the point! There's no reason I can't help! It's not as if *I'm* the one who's pregnant!"

"You must stay dead level with Lomyrla, not go climbing about —" She broke off as Lomyrla followed in Four-way Polo through the koriel.

"All set, Marco?" asked Polo jovially, clapping him on the back.

"You bet." May as well sound enthusiastic. Lomy looks happy enough at the prospect — whatever it is.

"Doctor O'Flannigan says you'll be carrying twins. Isn't that *fantastic* news?"

"Uh — well, of course. I'm overwhelmed with joy."

"Shouldn't cause too many complications," Polo said, slapping Marco on the back. "Perfectly normal, nothing to worry about."

His eyes developed a slightly glazed look, as if suddenly transported to fairyland. "I remember Lomyrla when she was a baby. My brother's child, but he was killed by a rogue 'vore before the synting, so I volunteered to take his place. Didn't half kick! Seven and a quarter *punce* she weighed, at birth. I've still got the stretch-marks to prove it." His eyes softened at the fond memory. Returning to reality, he finally noticed Marco's expression.

"Bianchi, you look like you've swallowed a wozzet. What's ailing you?"

"I think, on due reflection, that you'd better explain to me the elementary facts about childbearing," said Marco. Polo looked shocked. "I had a rather sheltered upbringing," he said lamely.

Polo stiffened, then made up his mind. "Ladies!" he commanded. "Out! This is men's talk!"

~~~

"Nonsense, Marco, it's a *much* better system. The membrane balances blood pressures, and umbilical flow is fine if you don't get too far apart vertically. And the weight hangs from your ribs, not by strings to her spine as if she was a four-legs. It won't sit on your bladder and make you pee every five minutes."

"— ?"

"You do get off on detail, don't you? It's a relative of the falasynte, though the syndepts breed for a stretchy membrane rather than a tough clear one. The doc puts the kasynte against the uterus wall, membrane against the embryo, and the rim attaches — like a vunbugula syntstone, but not so deep. The kantasynte attaches just under your diaphragm, near the bottom front of your rib cage. Baby grows, pushes the membrane out into your abdominal cavity, cord keeps it fed through the syntei."

"— ?"

"One synte each, for twins."

"— ?"

"Morning sickness? No, that's in the mother's blood, won't affect you."

"— ?"

"No, you *carry* the child, you don't bear it! It doesn't squeeze through your pelvis. You know that *breaks open*, for an un-synted woman? When the amnion breaks, the fluid disintegrates the skin over the synte growing inside the membrane bag, wide enough for baby to come through the kantasynte into the open."

"— ?"

"Yes, some men wear a mamasynte after the birth to take turns feeding. But the milk still comes from mother, of course. Most women can't sleep through it, so they'd rather cuddle the baby. I remember it as the only time in her life when Lomyrla didn't answer back."

"— ?"

"You'll find the three seasons go by quicker than you expect, even if you're not busy outside. You read writings, don't you? I'll get you some books, history and child care and such. And you should exercise."

"Just don't put on too much weight."

~~~

Marco now knew why a father-to-be would be recognisable in public during daylight. Though it still seemed oddly prudish to hide him. He patted his stomach with a frown. Did he detect a slight swelling? He...

"Don't be silly, Marco. It won't show for months."

"Oh, hello Elza. I was thinking we could call them Marco and Polo."

"They might be girls."

"Never."

"How can you tell?" asked Elza. "The genescanner came down in flames along with *Valkyrie*."

"A father knows these things."

"You pinhead. Not only do you get yourself seduced by a circus-girl, but you get yourself knocked up into the bargain! It gives a whole new meaning to the word 'transplant'. Her placenta synted into you! And to think I said that I saw no signs of female equality in Samdal!"

"You didn't," said Marco. "The pregnant males were all in purdah. The sight of a few males with bulging bellies might have caused me to ask the right questions earlier! Samdali society must be some kind of devolved matriarchy. Early on the men were forced to do it; than, as time went, on they were brainwashed into accepting it as the natural order, so that even now, with the sexual power-balance more centred, they see nothing against the practice. Polo was gung-ho about it."

"Why should they object, Marco? It *is* entirely natural! You said yourself that the father should help bear some of the burden."

"I suppose so," said Marco. "'And I will. But I wasn't planning to be so literal about it." He gulped. "*Twins!*"

19

Vulcan's Anvil

> Rapunzel has long golden hair. When she reaches her menses, a wicked witch locks her at the top of an isolated tower deep in thorny forest, with only a window for access. When the witch wishes to visit, she calls out: "Rapunzel, Rapunzel, let down your hair, that I may climb the golden stair". Rapunzel wraps her hair round a stout hook next to the window and lowers it like a rope, allowing the witch to climb up.
>
> A passing prince is drawn by Rapunzel's singing, but cannot enter. From hiding he watches and learns. He climbs the golden stair and makes a friend. They come up with an escape plan: the prince will secretly bring silk to weave a ladder. But when she innocently tells the witch that her dress feels tight, the witch spots Rapunzel's pregnancy, and deduces the rest. She cuts off Rapunzel's hair and throws her out into the wilderness to survive as best she can. The severed hair lures the prince up the tower. Seeing the witch's horrid face instead of his beloved's, he hurls himself from the window and is blinded by the thorns.
> —*Mother Nurse's Fairy Tales*

> Think how different the tale would have been if the prince had merely brought scissors, allowing Rapunzel to climb down her own hair. Or had killed the witch and then sought his lady-love in the forest, realising that she could not have gone far. Or if she had waited at the base of the tower for him to appear, and gone off with him on his horse. Old Earth fairy tales were often so focused on propagating their sexual anxieties that they were sadly lacking in both narrative structure and common sense. *Cf.* Rumpelstiltskin.
> —*Cher-Shiela Pham, Suspension of Critical Rationality in Traditional Narrative*

Cecily Sarahschild of Larkspine Tributary screeched. A damned fool slave had dropped his digstick on her toe. She ordered a mild flogging, with an aftermath.

When they took Sam to the pen with the burial cart he knew he'd offended just enough. Once the burial detail was over, he'd be returned to the fields.

The ganger kicked him awake at sunrise. With two other slaves, he pulled the cart round the compound, the laser medallion hidden in his kilt. They collected two corpses that morning, about average. While they loaded the second, a wheel collapsed. In the confusion Sam changed the 024 723 brand on one corpse to 029 723. His burn stroke looked a bit fresh, so he rubbed in some dirt.

Eventually the wheel that Sam had loosened was replaced, and they dragged the cart to the burial trench.

The warden noted down the number of each corpse as it was thrown in. Jane had deduced that the corresponding kantasynte would be removed from the monitoring centre. Destroyed, most likely, as the connection worked both ways. It wouldn't do for a functioning stone to get into the wrong hands. Sam tried not to hold his breath as the warden examined the modified corpse, at the first of two places where the plan could fall apart. Sam's handiwork might not match the original brand, or the replacement number might not be in use.

But she gave the brand only a passing glance. The number had passed scrutiny for now; with luck that would continue when the record reached the monitoring centre. Somewhere on Qish a slave would lose his stone's kantasynte, and never know it.

Sam and his companions began to dispose of the corpses. At the edge of the trench, he dropped his end of the altered corpse, exaggerating his exhaustion and hunger. Cecily Sarahschild raised her whip threateningly, and Sam staggered to his feet. When the corpse tipped over the edge into the foulness beneath, he slipped and fell with it, screeching. Cecily laughed, but she took the other two slaves to get a rope.

As soon as she left Sam set the laser to 'scalpel', and cut deep into the belly of the corpse. He reached in and felt around inside the stomach, no worse than the rest of the pit. Carefully he detached the slavestone from the abdominal wall and placed it, with the laser, in his offal-smirched kilt.

When they hauled him out he smelt so bad they threw him in the lake. He hid the laser and the slavestone under a rock by the bank.

~~~

Jane squatted by the lake, feeding bread to her frog, resplendent in its woollen collar. She unravelled a thread. "Rapunzel, Rapunzel, let down your hair." She threw a lump of bread out among the largest lilypads.

Rapunzel headed for the food, the woollen strands of the collar unwinding after it. It hopped in through a nearby lily-synte, out through the kantasynte, and grabbed the bread. She threw more to the neighbouring pad. Then more. When the bread finally led the frog back to shore, it came a new way.

Jane waited until the frog arrived, and began to reel in the chain of kasyntei threaded by the wool.

The frog deserved a kiss.

But it would probably prefer more bread.

~~~

"Fire!" yelled the warden in charge of the sugar-cane warehouse. "Bring slaves and water! Fire! Fire!" She was close to panic. Losing a year's crop, or more to the point, a year's revenue, was a capital offence.

Irenotincala Laurel smiled grimly to herself, slipped the laser medallion back inside her shirt, and moved away to the next task.

~~~

In silence, Tinka and Jane crept up on the syntower. Behind them, flames shot skywards from the sugar warehouse. Thousands of slaves, beaters, wardens, and gangers rushed around in creative confusion, using syntei to spray water on the burning wreckage. The noise was appalling, just as planned.

Sam was waiting to start the revolt.

Jane carried the slavestone and a pair of rolled lily-kasyntei wrapped in a damp cloth. Tinka used the laser. The wardens guarding the tower never stood a chance.

They removed a barrel of fish-oil from the smithy, and began to haul it up the tower. It was heavy work, and the seven-legged spider-creatures the size of rats hardly helped. But Sam couldn't be there: he had other vital work to do.

Jane had no idea how much height they needed, but the heavy guard wasn't around the syntower base just for fun. The tower *had* to be guarded, for the potential of its top: the highest point around, the one place higher than the monitoring-centre. Nothing else made sense. On Qish, height is *the* strategic factor: much can go down a synte, but precious little can fight its way up through compressed gravity.

No stairs. No extra guards waiting at the top. Better not burn the oriel, might attract attention.

Now, use the laser to boil up some oil, and then...

~~~

Usually Maggi Annaschild hated monitor-duty. It was boring. But for once she'd have preferred boredom. Today it was pandemonium. With all the noise of the firefighting, the synte-banks were an earsplitting babble. No doubt a few opportunists were sneaking away under cover of the noise. They'd never learn. Tomorrow, when all the fuss had died down, the archers would disabuse them. After a dose of *kra*-juice.

Amid the chaos, she didn't notice a thin tube pushing through one of the slavestone syntei. It landed at her feet, and became a disc. A much larger tube, of iron rather than vegetation, pushed through it.

She did notice when the stream of blazing oil enveloped her. By then, it was a lifetime too late. She burned.

All her fellows burned.

The slavestones burned.

~~~

A sharp pain seared his stomach. Sam screamed, partly in triumph, and dropped the watersynte. Recovering, he seized a passing warden by the throat and broke her neck with a *hai-ganzai* chop. His gang looked on, aghast, waiting for the arrow.

Nothing happened.

"Slaves, arise!" yelled Sam. "Overthrow the oppressors!"

The slaves stared at him.

"The slavestones are burned!" he yelled. "Did you not feel fire in your belly?" He grabbed a muscular young man nearby, mouth open. "Fight, you fool!"

The youth gave him a look of horror and sank to his knees.

"Do you think the Vain Vaimoksi would let me say what I have said, and live? I tell you, the stones are burned! You are free!"

Sam cursed the slave mentality. He ran to another group, with the same results.

Then he saw a better prospect.

"Cuzak!"

"Keep your distance, Abominator!"

"Cuzak, I lack time to discuss fine points of morality. Do you want to be free?"

That got his attention. "Does a grumbat want to fly?"

"The slavestones are destroyed, Cuzak! Burnt! You felt the pain!"

Cuzak was in two minds, but the first task was escape. Afterwards was another matter. He gave rapid orders to his men. In battle-formation, they made short work of three beaters and an elderly ganger.

A trembling youth had been staring aghast at the slaughter, his slave-world in turmoil. Sam pushed him at a nearby beater, who stumbled and fell. The youth looked on in horror. The beater staggered to her feet and lashed at him with her whip.

That was a mistake.

Expecting death, and not finding it, the youth reacted instinctively to the lash. He grabbed the beater by her hair and flung her to the ground, kicking like a madman. As the other slaves realised that he still lived, they moved to join him.

~~~

Tinka faced the guard, who held Sam's knife and looked ready to use it. A long blade, and a tricky one to meet unarmed. But in their combat classes she had practiced against that blade itself, in the hands of an expert.

"It's bad luck to carry that, uninvited," she said. "The original owner died a rather slow and nasty death."

Didn't the Vain Vaimoksi train with knives against serious opponents *at all*? The woman was carrying it like the short punishment daggers the others wore. Tinka advanced on her, as if she was going to make a suicidal grab, until her opponent was committed to a straight lunge. Then a kick broke the slaver's wrist.

"I'm only sorry," said Tinka as she cut her throat, "not to give you a nice slow Iroquois death, and a chance to show brave. But I have more of you people to kill."

~~~

A bell began to toll, deep, urgent. Drusilla climbed off Felix and ran to the falasynte. "What? But that's impossible! Send in more wardens immediately!"

"Sabi, we are sending them as fast as they can pass the synte, but there is much congestion," came the reply.

"Raise the internal brasures so that none may enter or leave."

"The Palace is already secured, Sabi."

"Inform me of any developments. This revolt must be put down at any cost. Kill them all if you must. We can capture replacements."

She turned to face Felix. "Count yourself fortunate to be here. Any slaves that survive this... futile attempt... will regret the day they were born. But I must have you placed under restraint —"

She froze, fear in her eyes.

The knife-edged prism that Felix had fashioned in his laboratory pricked her throat. "Do what I tell you, or you're dead."

"I will have you flayed alive for this!"

"Be careful what you threaten, Drusilla. It might give me ideas. They'd be less than you deserve." He paused. "In fact, you *have* given me an idea."

"I have no fear of pain."

"I don't believe you, but that's not what I have in mind right now. Later... who knows? No, what I want is a synte route opened so that all my friends can come here. I don't care how, but any tricks and I'll cut the skin from your scalp. Now, move!"

~~~

Jane, Tinka and Sam squatted at the syntower's top. Cuzak watched nearby. Something was happening down at the basalt pillar — the flow of wardens had ceased, and there was a lot of shouting and rushing around. Behind them fires raged, and freed slaves took revenge on their captors. It was messy and violent, but nobody paid attention to the tower.

A woman appeared through the syntower oriel, with Felix close behind. Holding something at her throat, he beckoned them through the oriel.

Cuzak stayed with them. His men were busy roasting their temporary owners alive, but he felt no loss in leaving them to that pleasure.

Cuzak was after bigger game.

~~~

With Drusilla as hostage and a laser to back up threats, they met no resistance on their way to the Primarch's apartments. Jane and Felix embraced quickly but intensely, then put their heads together to sort out the next moves.

Tinka kept the laser pointed at Drusilla's head while Sam found a couple of knives in a drawer, and Tinka tossed him his own. He cut an improvised belt from the curtain, passed the other knives to her and Cuzak, and took the laser. Tinka raided closets for clothing better than slave-garb, and rolled it into a bundle with fruit, bread, and goat's cheese that Cuzak had found. She wrapped the last two lily-syntei in Drusilla's finest robe, wetting it to stop them drying out.

"There are many exits," said Felix. "But most lead to dead ends or bad terrain. Drusilla must know a good escape route. We'll just have to persuade her to tell us."

A laser demonstration proved effective. The deposed Pirmarch led them down concealed stairs to a damp room of rough stone. A comfortably large oriel was suspended by ropes high on one wall. Sam lowered it until the gravity barrier disappeared.

"It may be a trap," said Jane.

"Shove the bitch through first," said Sam.

"That may be what we're expected to do."

"Then we might as well take the risk ourselves," said Sam, and before anyone could stop him, he dived through the synte's mouth.

He was back within seconds. "All clear. A forested slope above a lake. I couldn't see far, trees in the way, but it seemed uninhabited."

"Let's go," said Felix. "Sam first. Give Jane the laser. Tinka next. Then Drusilla. Jane, stay right behind her. I'll follow. Cuzak, you guard our rear." Cuzak didn't look too happy about this idea, and gripped his knife more tightly, but Felix had other problems on his mind, and didn't notice.

One by one they scrambled through. But as Felix bent to crawl into the synte, a strong hand grabbed his ankle.

"No! I see through your plot!" Cuzak yelled. "You will destroy the synte, and strand me here to die! Abominator!" He slashed at Felix's leg with the knife, but Felix rolled to one side and the knife struck rock, throwing up sparks.

From the far end of the synte the others watched, helpless. It was impossible to aim the laser. Felix had the usual Starfolk training in *hai-ganzai*, recently refreshed. Cuzak was skinny, but quicker, tougher, and more experienced in fighting dirty. They rolled over and over on the floor. From behind them came a clatter of feet on the stairs. And a clatter of weapons. It was too late to go back.

"Jane," said Sam in a flat voice, "point the laser at the synte."

"But —"

"I *know* Felix is in there. Just do what I say."

Felix caught Cuzak's arm with a kick, and the knife dropped to the floor. Another kick, and his legs were free. As wardens with spears and crossbows rushed into the room, Felix flung himself at the aperture. *I don't have to destroy it yet*, thought Jane, *we don't have to leave him.*

Cuzak, bellowing in fear and anger, recovered his knife, dived at Felix, and missed. A bolt from a Vaimoksi crossbow hit the rock by his face and ricocheted off. Another struck his leg. He crashed to the floor.

At the far end of the synte, Sam grabbed Felix's arms and pulled.

Cuzak, seeing his blasphemous betrayer getting away, roared "Die, Abominator!" and slashed at the synte's rim.

There was a *squelching* sound like a sack of wet sand hitting a concrete floor. Felix suddenly came free and Sam toppled backwards, Felix on top of him.

Jane screamed.

Tinka took one look and threw up.

Felix's face almost touched Sam's. It looked wrong. Felix felt wrong. He didn't weigh enough. He —

Sam carefully rolled Felix off him and stood up. But it wasn't Felix.

It was *half* of Felix.

There was almost no blood. The torso, just below the waist, was — *sealed*. Nothing flowed from the aorta, or into the vena cava. His heart had failed, trying to pump blood where no blood could flow. That, and massive systemic shock.

"Oh, Mother of Galaxies," said Sam. "The wormhole collapsed with him in it."

Jane sat on a rock and howled. It was several minutes before any of them noticed that Drusilla had slipped away.

~~~

There are more Starfolk funeral rites than there are worlds in the Concordat, but the commonest is cremation. They had the laser, there was firewood — and no time to build a pyre. Sam settled for hoisting their half of Felix into some bushes and setting fire to them, with a few words to comfort Jane. They wouldn't, but he had to say them.

Jane still wept. "We're all in shock," Sam told her quietly. "It's infinitely worse for you. But now is not the time to squat grief, Jane. We *must* keep going."

"You don't understand," said Jane, through tears. "It's not just that. I was so proud of thinking up the escape, and Felix played his part so well, and it was really working, and then —"

Sam waited.

" — and then it all fell apart and he's *dead*!"

Sam ached to comfort her, but they had to get moving. "It did work. No plan survives contact with the enemy. If we hadn't tried to escape, we'd *all* have been dead soon. Or worse. Thanks to you, three of us are still alive and free, if we keep our heads. We're all sorry it's not four, but no one can change that. Felix bought our lives with his."

She looked up at him, face stained with grief. "You think I haven't thought of that, Sam? He's still dead, and it's still my fault."

Not *your* fault, thought Sam. Felix failed to allow for Cuzak's fanaticism. But he could hardly point that out to Jane. Instead, he said "Felix died to save us. Are you going to throw that sacrifice away?"

She shook her head. He helped her to her feet.

~~~

"I *thought* there was something funny about the lake," said Sam. "But there wasn't time for a closer look." The synte had placed them in a crater. To judge from the heavy reforestation, Old Earth green mixed with the orange, the volcano had been extinct for a long time. They climbed to its rim, the crater lake below them. In every direction was ocean.

"Drusilla knew this," said Tinka. "There must have been another synte nearby. This was just a staging-post."

"Possibly. If there *was* another synte nearby, you can bet there isn't one now."

"Nah. And we'd better get off this island fast, before she turns up with reinforcements." He turned to Jane, who was still shaking with sobs. "Jane, I really, really hate to intrude, but I need you to keep watch while Tinka and I use the laser to fell some trees and build us a raft."

Jane lifted her shoulders, and nodded.

"We need the laser, but here's Tinka's knife from the palace." He pressed the hilt into her hand. With luck, something to do would distract her. *A bit.* He sighed. *Not a chance.* But they did need a lookout, and fate decreed it had to be Jane.

He just hoped she could handle it.

~~~

Drusilla stared at the blackened husk of her intended escape route. *That she-glossep Elenya Ingridschild! She never could accept being just a Second. She acted quickly, I will admit. I didn't think her capable of it.*

None of which was going to get Drusilla off Vulcan's Anvil.

Back when the Wevorin set up their first planetwide syntenet, ocean-hopping by growing oriel buds through syntei that had floated from shore to shore and rooted, Vulcan's Anvil had been a hub. Syntei connected it to every continent. Its tall slopes allowed easy connections to numerous distant places, while isolation and lack of natural predators afforded security. Old Earth plants and animals ran wild. When the Vain Vaimoksi took it over as a retreat-in-depth they dismantled most of the links, leaving a few long-distance oriels and wyzands for access and escape.

These routes Ingridschild, with unusually quick thinking, had comprehensively wrecked. She must have been waiting her chance for a long, long time. But curses would gain Drusilla nothing. Capturing the runaways would. Labour, entertainment, and revenge, certainly… Escape would be more problematic.

In the distance, she heard crashing timber. Later, a thin trail of smoke threaded skyward from the beach. She moved silently into the bushes, towards its source.

~~~

Sam took over sentry duty from Jane and squatted beneath a stand of Old Earth bamboo, brooding. Felix had made a mistake. Felix had paid for it. Were they making another? They didn't *know* that Drusilla had left the island. If she had, she might be back with an army at any moment. *Unless* no more Vaimoksi-controlled syntei were left on the island. They didn't know that either. They did know the volcano's location: there was land dimly visible to the west, distorted by heat haze, and Sam's 'comp reckoned it was the east coast of Lamynt, eighty kilometres away.

At nightfall they ate some of the bread and goat's cheese, and sat by the fire.

~~~

Drusilla watched hungrily from the undergrowth.

Stars came out, enough to see by.

Eventually, the Starfolk rolled themselves in oddments of clothing, and slept. *The fools haven't even placed a guard!* She could steal the knife from the one with the pigtail. The fool had left it lying on the ground beside him as he slept.

~~~

It was extremely uncomfortable, Sam found, to lie awake and pretend sleep. But *if* Drusilla was still on the island, and *if* she hadn't been able to get help, she'd be cold and hungry. She could scarcely have missed the smoke from their fire. If he'd posted a guard, she would have stayed away. This trap was subtler.

The dangers of Qish had honed his instincts. Even though he barely heard the scuffling sound, he was instantly alert.

Drusilla reached for the knife. A hand grabbed her wrist, and twisted. She fell flat on her face with Sam on top of her, yelling blue murder to wake the others. They tied her hands and feet.

Drusilla's struggles ceased. "Kill me if you will. I fear no slave."

Sam raised the knife, but Jane clutched at his hand. "There's been enough killing, Sam!" She broke off a piece of bread and offered it to Drusilla, who knocked it aside. Jane picked it up and offered it again.

Hunger won.

~~~

They built the raft at a promontory where a strong current ran in roughly the right direction. By noon the logs had been lashed together with tough vines, the last knots tied, and the provisions loaded and fastened. The tide was rising fast as Qish's giant moon dragged the ocean sideways. At high tide, they'd launch the raft.

The heavy work kept them all from thinking too much about Felix. Even Jane seemed to have regained some of her poise. Sam knew it to be an act, and was lost in unspoken admiration for her courage. He wasn't sure he could have stayed functional after such a personal loss. He'd *liked* Felix a lot, but Jane and Felix... he wondered if he would ever have a shared self like that. More than just a person had died.

Suddenly he wanted vengeance. He leaped to his feet and pointed at Drusilla. "What about this evil bitch? I say we kill her!"

"Nah, Sam," said Jane. "We take her with us."

"She's an unacceptable danger and an extra mouth."

"I'm not going to seal the memory of Felix with murder in cold blood."

But when they tried to load Drusilla aboard the raft, she struggled and screamed like a maniac. They could make no sense of her, except determination not to go.

Sam's suspicions were aroused. He roped some spare logs together, dragged them to the water's edge, and pushed them out into the current.

"What are you doing, Sam?"

"Dipping my toe in." He would say no more.

The bundle drifted out on the surf, fifty metres, a hundred. Nothing happened. The sea rose and fell in a rhythmic swell. Nothing disturbed the surface.

"Sam, I don't —"

A shapeless mass erupted from the water, and began to *grow*. Holes appeared in its flanks. Tentacles pushed through the holes, thick as tree-trunks, growing rapidly to a frightening length. As they grew, smaller tentacles sprouted from them. The creature began to resemble an insane oak tree.

"Oh, Mother! Just look! No wonder the bitch didn't want to come, she *knew*!"

A tentacle reached out, and grabbed the log-bundle. It disappeared into a hole in the monster's side. The hole closed.

"It's *huge*! It's incredible!"

"I think it's got some kind of expanding syntei," said Tinka, in an unnaturally matter-of-fact voice. "It puts tentacles out through them, and there are more syntei on the tentacles, and they expand, and —"

It abruptly began to writhe in frenzy. A shower of spray, and it vanished.

"What happened?" said Sam.

"I think..." said Tinka. Her voice trailed off in awe.

"Think what?"

"I think something *ate* it."

~~~

Jane squatted on a basalt outcrop and watched the cormorants — except they were yellow and doubtless had violet blood and golden bones like everything else indigenous — swooping gracefully in the search for fish. Felix would never see these birds. He would never know whether their prey was carried home or synted. Never share insight with her again. She saw his face as if he were here, mocking that idea, and her desolation stretched like the emptiness between the stars.

It was the third day. They had retrieved their supplies, but these were fast running out. The island had some Magog-derived edible plants, potatoes from its hub days, and the fish, but they didn't want to spend the rest of their lives there.

Now she knew why they'd seen no ocean-going ships. So how *do* you get off an island surrounded by deadly sea-monsters?

"If I was going to do it," Sam had said, "I wouldn't start from here." Even the jokes were getting desperate; it was something that Marco would have said.

A thought struck her. *It's not where you start, it's how.*

Oh no. Not another bright idea. The first one had killed Felix. This one might very well destroy Tinka.

It had to be Tinka. Not that killing Sam would hurt any less, but he wasn't good enough.

The idea refused to go away. The problem was, it might even work. If she kept quiet about it, she'd probably be killing them all.

Face your fear. Do it for Felix.

She dragged herself to her feet, and walked wearily over to where Tinka was arguing with Sam.

"Tinka, are you really as hotshot a pilot as you keep telling us?"

"Uh? Yah. Ask Sam."

Jane took a deep breath, shuddering. "Then I know how we can get back to the mainland."

~~~

They found a good launch site halfway up the volcano, where the trees opened out into a long clearing.

"I hope this works," said Sam.

"So do I," said Tinka, who was going to fly it.

They had stretched cloth across a frame made from the Old Earth bamboo that grew in such profusion, in a kite shape. A crude hang-glider.

When Jane first raised it, Tinka rejected the idea. You can't fly a hang-glider eighty kilometres across open sea. The thermals are all wrong.

Jane had thought of that too, and the U-shaped attachment to the tail was the result. Tinka's wristcomp had calculated its aerodynamics, and found it airworthy. Probably. If delicately flown.

Sam gave a final going-over, checking the lashings and the struts, while Tinka used her 'comp to review the calculations for the fifth time. She'd always claimed she could fly anything with wings or an engine. This had both. Time to prove it.

The prospect was... daunting? No, exhilarating! Finally back in control, not just reacting to whatever fate threw. A golden opportunity to push the envelope. If they ever got to Starhome, future generations would remember this. She laughed.

Sam shot her a glance, then smiled. "Pilots! I couldn't keep you out of this crate if I promised you the freedom of the Concordat, could I?"

"Nah. Always had an itch to be a test pilot. Have my pick of beautiful men. This is my chance!"

On Qish it is never hard to find syntei. Rooting around in the undergrowth, Sam had found a dozen, of various sizes, in less than half an hour; even a feral brasure. It was descended from a relic of the volcano's role as a hub, but the Starfolk just knew it was wide enough to pass a human body.

He strapped Tinka in and tied the syntei securely behind her seat. When she reached land, they could join her.

"Mother preserve me," Tinka muttered.

No pre-flight checks, no announcements. Just her and the elements, now. She took a deep breath, pushed off down the slope. The wing dipped once, alarmingly, then caught the sea breeze. She gasped as trees rushed up the slope, growing with frightening speed. Pulling the right ropes put the glider into a climb that just scraped over their tops. Another rope banked it towards the west, where distant mountain-tops beckoned. But already she was starting to lose height. Tinka muttered invocations under her breath to everything from the legendary Inuit Chant to the haiku version of the Laws of Aerodynamics — with more faith in the Chant. The monster-laden ocean loomed too close below.

Jane was standing at the edge of the crater lake, holding a synte weighted with rocks, and a falasynte by her ear.

"Now!" called Sam, watching the glider from the crater rim.

The synte went, carefully, into the water.

To Tinka it felt as if someone had switched on a booster rocket. In a way, Jane had. The glider doubled its speed, and climbed.

She looked back at a reassuring jet of water spurting behind her. The tail assembly held the kantasynte of the kasynte in the lake. The water, instantly dropping a hundred metres, shot forward at high speed, with no propulsive recoil at the synte mouth. The flow around a U-bend transferred momentum to give a good hard push.

A lakeful of water may not be inexhaustible, but it does make fuel consumption figures academic.

Tinka shouted a wordless cry of joy, confident now as the wind brushed her face. The first water-powered hang-glider in the history of the universe headed towards the distant coastline.

20

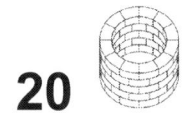

Water Empire

> What is the most stable government? The stability that democracy delivers is often short-lived, as one might expect from what is, after all, a recipe for constant change. A dictatorship remains stable only through oppression, which invites and incites revolution. There is no such thing as a benevolent dictatorship: power corrupts.
>
> History suggests that the greatest societal stability is with a small but powerful group to control a key resource. In Dynastic Egypt, Imperial China, and pre-Columbian Peru, it was water. In modern times, the interstellar federation of semi-isolated worlds, structured by the Concordat, gave rise to several Air Empires, in which dissidents forfeited the right to breathe. The Vega Uprising, however, showed that this kind of resource monopoly can be fragile if the controlling forces are vulnerable to tightly targeted sabotage.
>
> By comparison the Concordat's rule is light, but mahabhavium is the heaviest of water.
>
> —Liselotte Shiujin-Miao, *Water Power: the Rise and Fall of Hydraulic Empires*

The eye climbed slowly up the wall.

The movement caught T'quoise's attention. A brilliant blue insect scuttled along the angle between wall and floor, the mouth's warm breath close behind.

She stopped stroking the round furry hindquarters lying in her lap, and gave them a poke. "No! You are *not* going to add that poor creature to your collection!" The eye turned towards her, pleading. The *skiti* — a symbiotic syntelic colony-creature — had a magpie-like attraction to anything bright; more than once its owner (its host?) had found a long-lost spoon or buckle in one of its numerous hideyholes. Another poke for emphasis. The mouth halted in its tracks and she resumed stroking. As the *skiti* relaxed, the front paws clenched and unclenched on her shoulder, and the nose murmured in her ear — though the sound was more like a cicada than a cat. Another eye gazed contentedly at her from the table, double lids half closed. She had no idea where the tail had got to: mostly you only saw a tail when a skiti assembled its parts for a mating display.

From her cabin porch T'quoise could see most of her ten *wyrj* — about a fifth of a hectare — of red earth, all she owned in the world. Her parents had tilled it, and their bones were scattered beneath it. Her hands stopped stroking as that train of thought led again to her brother C'balt, whose bones rotted loose in the Death Pit.

Her world was bounded by a yellow stone wall, twice the height of a man and an arm-span thick. She had never climbed it to enter neighbouring garths. She had never opened a gate in it, for walls are not built with gates, on the Plain of Bansh.

From inside the cabin came a sharp knock. The eye on the wall dropped in fright, and claws raked her shoulder as the *skiti* fled to its holes. Sighing, T'quoise drew the curtain from the synte high on one wall — her one door to the outside world.

Before her eyes were an unmistakable pair of feet.

Even without the pigskin sandals, or the painted white toes, she would have known who it was. Only Am'thys, Custodian of Dawling Village, would be too proud to stoop to demand entry.

She lifted the synte from the wall and lowered it to the floor, and its compressed gravity-gradient barrier vanished. She greeted the Custodian with the correct degree of formal politeness.

"Slapyen, Shapi Hoik."

"Slapyen, T'quoise. You have been unwell?"

"No, Shapi, at work. The winter cayle has ripened early and must be lifted before rot sets in. And my new syntei need much attention. Let me show you!"

Am'thys was loath to recognise talent in those of lower standing. "T'quoise, it is not your place to breed syntei. You are not of the clans."

"I am probationer of Clan Wylzen."

"But not yet clanswoman."

"I will be! Before my sevenyear of opportunity is ended, I will walk the halls and slopeways, and open doors on mountains, plains, and seas!"

"You set your horizons too wide," said Am'thys.

"In Bansh," said T'quoise sadly, "the walls hide all horizons."

~~~

On the slopes of an extinct volcano, Jane Bytinsky squatted in a dirty kilt beside a wood fire. Old Earth fish from the crater lake hung over the fire, on sticks. Every few minutes she turned them. She talked in murmurs to her wrist, and her wrist talked back.

It was, she supposed, good xenological field experience.

"Diary records: it's now sixteen months since *Valkyrie* crashed on Qish. I'm still hopeful we can reach the rescue beacon, but to be honest, the chances are slim. I wish I'd never thought of synting water from the crater la— "

"Nah, you don't," said Samuel Grey Deer Wasumi, settling himself beside her. He reached forward and turned the fish. "Your idea was the only chance we had."

"If it kills Tinka, I *will* regret it. I've already killed Felix —" She broke down again. Sam put his arm round her and held her close. He needed it almost as much.

~~~

The map looked like dried mud — sliced into a million tiny pieces by hairline cracks. Clan Queen Al'zarin of Esmion stabbed at it with a wrinkled forefinger.

"Here, I say! *Here!* The perfect site, Umb'r!"

The Provost leaned forward, hands on portly hips. "So it is, Shapi. But there are difficulties."

Oaf! "What difficulties? I show my chief adviser the perfect spot to situate a storage lake, augmenting our annual revenue by six per cent, and he finds *difficulties*?"

Another difficulty, thought the Provost, was to make his next statement sound tactful. He decided it wasn't worth the attempt. "To be blunt, Shapi — even a clan Queen must be seen to abide by the land-laws."

The Queen sighed. "Provost Umb'r, I have been *seen* abiding by the land-laws these past sixteen months. Proxies have purchased more than two hundred garths, in and around Chandle Vale. I have, where necessary, applied pressure. But none that can be proved to have emanated from this Hold."

"No, Shapi."

"The lake itself will be voted by a Full Moot. Think of it! An inexhaustible supply of water, to tap when our usual sources run dry! The people will pay gladly!"

The Provost kept his doubts to himself. Gladly or not, the people would pay, for waterless they would die.

"What is this difficulty you speak of?"

"Shapi, two garths within Chandle Vale refuse to sell."

The Queen looked again at the map. "So tiny. But without those lands, the project cannot proceed."

"No, Shapi," the Provost said uncomfortably. "I have suitable measures in readiness, but we must avoid undue haste. It would offend clanlaw were our hand discovered. The other clans would use that as grounds to strip Esmion's control of water-rights. Kespe in particular covets those, and lacks not influence at the Moot."

The Queen knew all this. The Provost was aware that she would have made her decision long ago. "Esmion must have that storage lake, Umb'r! Do whatever is necessary. But *your* hand had best be well hid!"

As the Provost backed away, audience ended, he reviewed that hand. The landholder at Whyre Copse was ageing. Suitably drugged, the man could be declared senile. At Dawling Village, he would continue with his ongoing plan, to engineer a transfer of landright by marriage. Enforced, if necessary.

Sad to work through an instrument as obtuse as that silly Hoik woman.

~~~

"Pah!" said Am'thys, openly annoyed. "Who can touch horizons! You must value only the good red soil of Bansh, as I do." She softened her expression. "T'quoise, you know my third largest garth abuts your western boundary, and in its corner flows a spillsynte with a long-term contract. No water-fee to Esmion for ten years! If you marry my husband we can sell the wall! The new strip of land where it stood will be counted yours! The stone will sell for twelvescore *sqint* — half for you."

Dun Hoik was the most cock-blocked and depressed man in the village, but it would not be politic to say so. "Shapi Hoik, it would be a great honour, but I do not wish to become a third wife." *Especially under you.*

"You surely do not expect to marry alone, with this pocket of land?"

"My mother did."

"Cin'mon was a great beauty. And even then, Tawn was unlanded."

"Until he won land by his own skills." Perhaps the young men of Clan Wylzen… A probationer was nothing. Yet she and Rufe Strogitz had exchanged looks.

"Rufe Strogitz," said Am'thys, apparently reading her mind, "is the secondborn son of a great Chieftain."

"A *skiti* may look at a clanchief."

"Oy! You are impossible! Trailing after clan kilts like a twelveling stricken by the Moon! Do not imagine that the offer of Sapu Hoik will still be there when your dreams of clanship crumble into dust!"

~~~

Idiot.

Easy, you thought. You've flown a Da Silva caltrop between the stars! A hang-glider? Child's play. Even if it is a crude lash-up with water-powered boost.

But starships come with helpful equipment; hang-gliders, you fly yourself.

Tinka Laurel cosseted the flimsy cane-and-fabric structure towards the far coast-line, a monster-laden ocean below. Jane's laser medallion, their sole remaining weapon, hung chained around her neck. The glider carried a brasure, the largest synte they could find in the impoverished ecology of Vulcan's Anvil. If she reached land, Jane and Sam would be able to wriggle through to her. Meanwhile she could talk to them through a jury-rigged falasynte. She carried three in case of accident — but there was only one brasure.

Her biggest worry was the sudden storm hiding the south-east horizon, ever closer. It would be a near thing.

She dropped the glider's nose to pick up speed. Eight klicks to go, and now the dark cloud banks were boiling up close by on her left. The air-pressure made it hard to hear anything through the falasynte. The water-jet slowed to a trickle and stopped, as coastal thermals lifted her above the level of the crater lake back on Vulcan's Anvil.

Now she was over sloping land — but heavier gusts shook the glider, and struts creaked ominously. A break in the clouds showed ground, closer than expected, irregular rectangles in some sort of grid. A sinuous ribbon ran from horizon to horizon, shaped like a river, but the colour of straw.

Without warning, the water-jet came back on, tipping her into a dive which increased its force. A spar snapped, cloth tore. The glider dropped abruptly, and the red earth rushed towards her. She tried to get the nose up to break the fall — succeeded — and the overstrained fabric parted from its frame. Tinka tumbled off into a patch of broad-leaved plants, hit hard, and lost consciousness.

~~~

From outside the cabin there came a horrendous crash. T'quoise, thoroughly alarmed, ducked through the garden oriel. The eye, ever-curious, followed.

Something had cut deep through the proud lines of her winter cayle, trailing wreckage, and finishing in a crumpled heap near her northern wall. Trying hard to hold back tears at the damage to her crop, she moved warily towards the debris. It resolved itself into broken cane and shredded cloth, mixed with cayle-leaves, stems, and roots. And, half-buried, a more solid shape, angular and crumpled —

A man.

T'quoise cleared a gap, knelt, and turned the figure over. No man, this. A woman. A tall, brunette woman with dark skin, outlandish, shocking. Face and arms scratched and bloody, one leg bent unnaturally. Clothing ripped. Dead? No, breathing. Unconscious. A bloody scrape on the forehead explained that. What was lying under her head? A jewel, its chain broken in the fall. T'quoise picked it up and dropped it into a pocket of her smock. She fetched a heavy barrow, hauled the injured woman on to it, trying not to harm her further, and dragged it back towards her cabin.

She made the woman comfortable, and settled down to wait.

~~~

After most of the stormclouds had passed over, Tinka groaned and twisted on the straw pallet. Everything that wasn't sore ached, and her left leg seemed to be strapped rigid. She opened her eyes.

Next to her, on the pillow, a single disembodied eye stared back. Tinka yelled and the *skiti*'s eye fled, equally frightened. Her hand went in reflex to her neck. The laser medallion had gone.

A human face replaced the eye. Bronzed by sun and wind, an outdoor face. Wide eyes framed by a fringe of dark hair, snub nose, pointed jaw, outrageously long earlobes. A girl's face. A face of concern mixed with fear.

"Who are you?" said Tinka. Blank look. *She doesn't speak Standard.* Tinka tried again in Kalingo, and words gushed back.

"I am T'quoise per-Wylzen, birthright landholder in Dawling Village. You lying injured in my cayle-patch. You fell from the sky! Are you a — witch? You had many sticks but no broom —"

Tinka tried to explain, to buy enough time to bring Sam and Jane through the synte that she had brought on the glider. *Oh, Mother! The synte!* "T'quoise," she said urgently. "In the wreckage there should be a brasure and three falasyntei. Please bring them to me at once — it's very important!"

T'quoise, bewildered, left the cabin to find them. Shortly, she returned. "I have found two falasyntei, Shapi." She laid them carefully on the table. "But the third is nowhere to be seen."

"And the brasure?" asked Tinka urgently.

T'quoise held up the shredded remains.

~~~

"Jasmine, tug my hair again and I swear I'll have you lowered into the Death Pit!" Clan Queen Al'zarin of Esmion lay back on a purple velvet couch. Two handmaidens brushed her hair, and manicured the arthritic fingers of her left hand.

She returned to her conversation with the sombrely clad figure on her right. "Baron Sable, have your men been drinking? A dragon fallen from the sky? Delirium!"

The Baron's attention had wandered to the nearest handmaiden, who blushed prettily and concentrated harder on her task. "That it is truly a dragon I very much doubt, Shapi. But something falling from the sky, while still fanciful, is less easy for witnesses to mistake for their own imagination. Who knows what dwells in the outlands? Prudence alone dictates that the report be investigated. Also," he went on, "similar reports have been coming in from garths neighbouring Dawling Village. A flight of dark angels. An unearthly rider on a flying horse. A great bird shaped like a shield, borne on the crest of a storm."

I have an interest in Dawling Village, thought the Queen. Who knows? If there is any truth in this, I may be able to turn it to advantage.

~~~

The brasure fell apart. Sam and Jane saw their escape path vanish before their eyes. Their hearts sank. Contact had failed completely while the falasyntei lay amid the wreckage, but now one of them had a tantalising view of T'quoise's cabin. The others stayed obstinately dark, but they could hear enough to know that Tinka was alive. Then T'quoise laid the falasynte on the table and vision was cut off.

The sounds were muffled, and disrupted by pressure noise, but still audible.

First, a loud knocking.

Then a new, authoritative voice: " — demand entry! Dark Watch!"

An inaudible response... sounds of movement... a heavy thud, so close to the falasynte that Sam's ears rang. A flash of vision, brief and incomprehensible; then blindness again. A cry of pain, and the voice tailed away, becoming fainter. All that remained was a curious *scratching* sound.

Sam tried to salvage what he could of their plan. He took a brand from the fire and held it up to the falasynte, hoping to cast some light at the other end. He peered hopefully through.

In the flickering red glare, a solitary eye peered back at him.

~~~

The *skiti* sat in its holes, and worried. Feeding time come and gone, but no food! Two new toys, the pretty red thing from the kitchen shelf, and the ball it had patted around the floor after all the two-legs left. Each safe in a hole. But the stomach, three holes distant, rumbled emptily.

One eye was trapped by the patball, blocking the way to the floor, but there were other eyes. The patball was flickering with light. Suddenly, a sharp point shot out, grazed the eye, and buried itself in the wall of the hole. Air rushed into the new slit in the ball, with a strange whistling sound.

Another tip poked through the slit. The eye retreated in a hurry, but had to blink as a short blunt stick whizzed toward it, then started to move back toward the patball. The eye followed, fascinated, but the *skiti* had no claw in place to play with the string tied to the middle. The stick dragged until it jammed against the patball, unable to pass the opening. Jerkily, the patball began to move along the hole, pushed by the stick. Once it caught on an angle: the *skiti* felt bored by the inaction, so the eye shut its lid and bumped. The patball came free and rolled out into the open.

All the eyes focused on it, from around the room. The claws started creeping up on it, but suddenly a much longer thing came through, just as fast, and slid across the floor. When it hit the wall, it unrolled flat with a slapping sound, and smelled of ripe water. An eye on the ceiling looked down through it, and saw more of the firelight that had shone through the patball, and a two-legs moving about. The two-legs' hand moved up, holding a small dark something. Food?

The two-legs' hand reached close, and let go the dark thing. It shot upward, almost hitting the ceiling, but fell back. A claw scrabbled over to it, but it was only a pebble. After a couple of disappointed pats, the claw rejoined the others.

Two two-legs were visible through the wet thing. Suddenly one pushed its whole body close, and shot up to the ceiling like the stone: turning in the air, it landed on its feet, nearly crushing an eye. The *skiti* scattered, avoiding any damage as the smaller two-legs came through and dropped back to be held by the first, whose staggering steps looked deadly to the eyes back in their holes.

The two were now both on their feet. After a moment they let each other go, and started walking around, no more dangerous than two-legs usually were. The furry bottom moved in. The nose smelled something promising, and made the cicada-purr that always worked; the two-legs produced a potato still smelling of the open fire that had roasted it, and held it out. A claw made a grab for it, and in a moment the stomach was working again.

Always, the easiest way to get food was to find a two-legs and rub up against it.

~~~

"A rare breed of dragon, with bones of wood! And the 'dragon-rider'? What is she?"

"An outlander, but of no race on record. From Shaaluy, perhaps? Who knows what may exist on that continent of madmen?"

Ascribe a mystery to another mystery, and imagine you have found an answer. Fool. "All secrets, not just her origin, will be revealed under questioning."

There was, in any case, a prior item. "Baron Sable: the rightholder to the garth where the 'dragon' fell. Should he tell what he knows, the Moot will claim the outlander, to Esmion's disadvantage. You are holding him securely?"

"Shapi. But — the rightholder is not a man. It is a girl not yet into her eighteenth year. You wish her executed?"

A young girl? Few such hold landrights... "I will have the order drawn up ready for signature when I have created a reason. The rightholder's name?"

"T'quoise per-Wylzen of Dawling Village."

"The probationer of the Wylzen clan?" The Baron nodded. "Praised be the Shades! No dragon, but a gift from World-after!"

The Baron, uncharacteristically, showed signs of bewilderment.

~~~

Before Drusilla could unravel the strips of clothing that bound her, Sam slashed shut the synte to Vulcan's Anvil. Sauce for the goose: the VV Primarch had planned to trap them on the island. She'd survive on fish, fruit, and vegetables if she made the effort. If not, tough, whatever Jane thought.

He cast a quick glance around the cabin. "Nobody home." With his fiery lopsided pigtail, ragged clothing, and his long knife in his belt, he looked like one of what he always swore were his distant prairie ancestors. He picked up a box of purple tubers, scrutinised it, put it down again.

"Not even the owner."

"Arrested too, if he was here," said Jane. "Look, they were in such a hurry they left the door open."

"Doors." A brasure and an oriel were propped in the angle of wall and floor. *Which one?* On a planet of vegetable matter-transmitters, trails go cold fast.

Sam drew his knife and peered through the syntei in turn. One led into broad daylight, but shrubbery blocked the view. Through the other was a dimly-lit corridor, empty. "We'll have to explore them both."

The oriel led to a neat vegetable garden with an ugly great slash through it. At the far end, a few scraps of fabric and some broken sticks.

"This is where Tinka landed."

"Yah. But someone's already taken most of the wreckage. Stay alert, Sam — they might come back."

He took stock. Oppressive stone walls on every side. No exits he could see.

He propped a barrow against the nearest wall and shinned up. Taking a deep breath, he climbed on to the wall and stood erect. It was the only high point around and he *had* to take the risk of being seen, in order to spy out the land.

Walls.

In every direction, walls. A maze of yellow stone.

Jumping down, he told Jane what he'd seen. "You're the xenologist. Peasant agriculture? Feudal society, based around the smallholding?"

"Maybe. For all we know, it could be part of an eccentric millionaire's estate. Tinka didn't come this way, Sam. Let's try the other exit."

That led into another maze, this one of sloping timber-panelled corridors. They looked for signs of Tinka's passage. In the distance, they heard voices, getting louder. They ducked into an alcove, behind a curtain. Sam drew the knife.

Two men walked past, talking urgently in low tones. Bearded faces, iron helmets with dirty yellow plumes, leather gauntlets and boots, coarse shapeless woollen jackets. Knee-length kilts in a complex weave. One unlatched a panel in the wall, to reveal an oriel. Stooping, they disappeared through it, still talking.

"Jane, we've got to follow them. Maybe they know the way out. Stay close and try to stay hidden if anyone comes!"

Now the corridors had changed to the same yellow stone as the garden walls. Scarcely daring to breathe, they followed the voices. Then, from *behind*, came the tramp of approaching feet. "Sam! Both ways are blocked!"

"Keep moving and look for a side-passage. Hurry!"

Two corridors crossed. Sam took the left fork and leaned against the wall, heaving a sigh of relief.

From further down the side-branch came a shout. They'd been seen.

Their only chance now was to run, across the main corridor and along the other side-passage. Down a flight of wooden steps, at a clatter. Across an octagonal area with an open fire burning brightly in the centre, its smoke synted Mother knew where.

Straight into a dead end.

Sam hesitated. There was nowhere to go but back, back towards the sounds of pursuit, louder now. Dozens of them, judging by the noise. They wouldn't stand a —

"*This way!*" A stage whisper from close behind him at ground level. "Quickly!" Pale green light from a trapdoor cast eerie flickers on the walls and ceiling. A head was silhouetted against the light. "*Now!* Or would you prefer the Dark Watch to strip your flesh from your bones?"

~~~

"Remove their blindfolds."

The room, stark and anonymous, had no windows. It was lit by the same green light that had shone from the trapdoor. A dozen or more people in brightly-coloured kilts and tunics, each carrying a short sabre and a long, thin knife like a stiletto.

"Who *are* you?" asked Sam. "Why did you rescue us from the — the Dark Watch, you called them?"

"You may call me Jasp'r. I am a R'formist. We are sworn to abolish clanrule and clanlaw in the Plains of Bansh. We are sworn enemies of Esmion, whose water hold drowns the common man." He raised his fist in a salute. The others did likewise.

Sam felt out of his depth. "We are grateful to you for helping us."

Jasp'r gave a wry grin. "We helped you not out of selflessness. Your exploits against the Vain Vaimoksi have reached ears even in Bansh. They tell of four tall dark-skinned outlanders, with unusual accents and remarkable powers. Clanfolk may bury their heads in parochial affairs, but I keep informed. It was obvious: first the one, then the two. I am expecting the fourth at any moment."

"First the — *do you know where Tinka is?*"

"Sapu, the woman who rode a dragon and fell from the sky was taken by the Dark Watch and is even now in the dungeons of Esmion Hold."

"Dungeons? *No!* We've got to rescue her!"

Jasp'r clapped Sam on the shoulder. "And you may count on the assistance of the R'formists, Sapu. As we count on *your* assistance in our struggle against clanrule."

Suddenly Sam felt tired. "What makes you think —"

"It is said you possess awesome powers. A fire-lance that can cut a man in half, imprisoned in a jewel of flame!"

"Tinka had the laser medallion. We don't know where it is."

"I do not understand your words."

"We no longer have the fire-jewel. And we are three now. The fourth is dead." *But if these turqis can help rescue Tinka...* He turned to Jasp'r. "We agree."

The crowd heaved a collective sigh. Jasp'r nodded, showing no emotion. "It is well. Come, let me show you the enemy."

The adjoining room was almost totally dark. Kilted men and women sat facing its walls, staring into tiny, bright apertures. They wore devices resembling ear-muffs. Occasionally one would make a note on a pad of coarse paper.

"You may speak, but keep your voices down. We have well-developed barriers against sound, but strike no lights."

"A network of illicit spy-syntei!" Jane whispered in awe.

The field of vision was narrow, and the voices faint, but both were clear. Around Queen Al'zarin of Esmion, a dozen others stood in the room, in ceremonial attitudes. Courtiers and officials?

"Who's the girl? She looks terrified." The ear-muffs made it sound as if Jane was talking from inside a bale of cotton wool.

"Her clan-name is T'quoise per-Wylzen. She *is* terrified. So would anyone be in the face of Esmion. She is rightholder of the garth into which your companion — but here she comes."

On crutches, with a splinted leg, haggard, desperately pale, wrists shackled, Tinka was led into view.

~~~

Al'zarin took charge of questioning the outlander. The woman sounded sincere, if disrespectful and a whit defiant, but not one answer made sense. Dragons were a familiar impossibility; but an *artificial bird*? Sorcery! Next the woman would be babbling of horseless carriages, or hollow metal fish to dive beneath the oceans! What on Qish was a *prototype*?

And that silly girl T'quoise, claiming to be an innocent bystander involved by nothing more than bad luck. It was, of course, *possible*. A dragon that fell from the sky must perforce fall somewhere. But so opportune a gift from World-after could not be denied. There were times when the correct move was also the most obvious one. Subtlety snared the sqider... in its own web.

Decision made, she murmured to a nearby official, who snapped his fingers.

Two handmaidens entered bearing a broad-brimmed conical hat. The Provost ceremoniously placed the hat on the Queen's head.

~~~

"She is donning the Cowl of Justice," said Jasp'r. "What began as mere interrogation is now a clan assize." He sounded worried. *Not just for his revolutionary plans,* Jane realised. *More personal.*

"Probationer T'quoise per-Wylzen! Outlander Tikka per-Lorel! You stand convict of conspiracy against clanlaw! You are sentenced," the pause sounded more like asserting her status than a pause to think. "You are sentenced to the Death Pit!"

21

Reinventing the Wall

> The socially disadvantaged typically bequeath limited wealth, subdividing fixed assets between several children. Each child's wealth is a fraction of that of their parents, and poverty becomes ever more prevalent. In societies that measure wealth by land, this method of division can eventually cause economic collapse. In contrast, individuals with substantial wealth intermarry within the same social class and discard junior children from the line of inheritance. This protects their wealth and ensures its undiluted transmission across generations, perpetuating a cycle of privilege. The logic of inheritance therefore requires the wealthy to enforce a social hierarchy that promotes the oppression of the lower classes.
> — Leo Martin Brumburger, How Wealth Exaggerates Inequality

The R'formist headquarters was in turmoil. In less than two hours, Tinka and T'quoise would meet their fate.

"The pit is deep and dark. Within it dwells a hideous creature. None may watch what happens, save the Master of the Pit; but all may listen by public falasynte to the victim's screams and the sounds of the beast as it gorges itself."

More subtle than public killing, Sam thought. Leaves more to the imagination. *Ugh.* "Jasp'r? Have your spies heard any word of the laser? Uh, the fire-jewel?"

"No, Shapi. But should the Queen or her nobles have gained possession of such a power, it could not be kept secret. The jewel cannot have been found."

"I've an idea how we can rescue Tinka. And T'quoise," Jane added after a moment. Jasp'r's head rocked back as if slapped. *As I thought. Personal interest.* "But it relies on the jewel, and only Sam or I can find it. It must still be somewhere on T'quoise's land. You must take us there!"

~~~

There had been guards at the connecting brasure in the village hall, but forged papers of authorisation had been accepted. The bailiffs — two disguised R'formists — were in. So was Sam. A crate of tubers, moved casually near the brasure, hid their search from prying eyes; the garden oriel was raised to prevent entry. He moved a sack and something furry scuttled across the floor into a hole, making him jump. It looked just like a tail with tiny insectoid legs, somehow like the thing he had fed. Others converged on him, and he found another scrap of potato.

Sam hoped the 'bailiffs' would quickly locate the property they were here for. But there was no sign of the laser.

Mother of Galaxies, it must *be here somewhere!* How many hiding places could there be in such a tiny shack? But half an hour's systematic rummaging turned up exactly nothing.

To allay suspicion, and to get safely away before someone questioned their authenticity, the bailiffs picked up a random assortment of chattels and made their departure. Sam stayed behind to continue the search.

There were cracks in the floorboards. Perhaps the laser had fallen into one. He stuck his head back through the oriel he had brought and whispered: "Hand me that torch!" The rebels at the other end passed him a synte that emitted the same green light that had first announced their rescuer from the Dark Watch. The light came from some distant undersea reef, hence the colour and the strange rippling quality.

He was so intent on the search that he failed to hear any sound until a sandaled foot slapped the boards next to his face, and a panicky voice cried: "Who the squnt are *you!* Thief! I cry thief! *Guards! Take the* —"

Sam moved fast. With his knife he slashed at the brasure, destroying the synte connection to the village hall. Before it could turn black he had wrestled the interloper to the floor. The man squealed in pain as he hauled him to his feet.

Correction. Her feet.

"Killing the brasure will not save you," said Am'thys Hoik in sullen defiance. She'd wangled her way in by telling the guards that Provost Umb'r had authorised her to search the cabin. "The Dark Watch will scarce be delayed, they will come through neighbouring garths." She screeched for help. Sam bunched a fist and hit her under the jaw: she sagged against a pile of sacks. It toppled. Fine flour puffed over the furniture and filled the air with a choking fog. Sam cursed. The guards would arrive in minutes at most, he still couldn't find the laser, and now he couldn't even *see* properly.

It was all too much for the *skiti*. An eye had been watching from behind a roofbeam as yet another strange two-legs appeared. Seriously frightened, it had been far too long between meals, and its comfortable routine was in chaos. In panic it grabbed its newest toy and shot out of its holes, squealing. Sam gasped in astonishment as a pair of hairy parts skidded across the floor and up a roof-pole, while two eyes and a nose chased each other in circles around the table-legs. Then the mouth whizzed across his field of vision, taking refuge among a pile of earthenware pots.

He caught a glimpse of a glittering red object dangling from its jaws. *The laser!* The improbable creature had the laser!

Sam flung himself at the pile of pots. They went in every direction, shattering against floor and walls. A tub of water on a shelf tipped up and drenched him. He trod in a jar of thick, sticky malt, trapping his foot. The *skiti*'s mouth headed for the fireplace at a gallop, trailing the laser medallion by its broken chain.

"Oh no you don't!" yelled Sam, as the laser disappeared into the grate. He scrabbled across the floor on all fours, and thrust an arm up the chimney. The chain brushed his fingers, and he snatched at it. Soot from the crannies of the chimney enveloped him, but he laughed like a madman, tears of joy streaming down his cheeks. He swung the laser to and fro before his eyes, hypnotically, like a pendulum.

There was a horrendous crash as an axe split the wall timbers. The Dark Watch had arrived. Sam hurled a sack of lentils at one guardsman's head, slashed the other's arm with his knife, and dived through the oriel that led to the R'formist nerve centre. Another slash, and that route vanished forever.

It should have been a triumphal entry, but Jane and the others just stared at him, goggle-eyed. He looked down. He was streaked from pigtail to toes in a dirty grey mess of water, flour, and soot. With a pot, still dripping brown malt, attached to one foot. And a curious eye watching from his shoulder.

Triumphal entry? Oh, Mother. Samuel Grey Deer Wasumi rolled on the floor and laughed until his ribs ached.

~~~

Ropes creaked.

Prisoners were never thrown into the Pit. They were lowered, to avoid an easy death. It smelt musty and decayed, but the decay was old: Tinka had feared worse. The planked platform crunched bottom, tilted, and rolled them off. The darkness was absolute.

"Ouch!" something hard jabbed Tinka's ribs. She put out a hand and felt it. It was someone else's rib. Loose.

T'quoise shuddered. "Some of these bones are my brother C'balt's."

Tinka had no time for sympathy. She was sifting desperately through the pile of bones, looking for anything to improve their chances of survival. "T'quoise! Help me! Find yourself a weapon! A heavy bone club, or a sharp broken bone dagger!"

"Shapi — do you imagine we can kill the *deathbeast?*" Her voice cracked on the final word and it came out more as a squeak.

Tinka paused. "No," she said frankly. "But we'll give it a battle to remember." *In pitch darkness? You're kidding.* Her hand encountered a something large and heavy: probably a femur. She hefted it, felt the balance.

She heard T'quoise scrabbling in the bone-littered floor. *You're a brave child.* "T'quoise, I'm sorry. This is my fault. If I hadn't landed in your garden —"

"No, Shapi. The Queen's will is to seize my garth, I knew it in her questions. Esmion confiscated my brother's holding... now they will have mine. C'balt and I were ever destined for the Death Pit."

There was a jangle of chains... then a *slithering* sound. T'quoise was muttering some kind of chant under her breath. Bones crunched and rattled. Hearing must substitute for sight. Tinka raised the thigh-bone above her head, senses heightened, but feeling more than a little foolish.

Something slimy brushed her good leg, and she brought her club down hard where she judged the beast must be. The bone, dry and brittle, snapped in half. Tears welled in frustration. *If I hadn't lost the laser...* The deathbeast hissed, in irritation more than pain. *What is it? A snake?* Tinka dragged herself round the wall on her good leg, the sharp end of the broken bone held out in front of her like a shortsword.

T'quoise howled, no scream of fear but a battle-cry. Her club struck something solid and flew from her hand. The air seemed to *vibrate*, and the hissing grew louder. Over to their left, something thrashed in the bone carpet, probably the beast's tail.

From overhead came a clatter. Then... Tinka began to *see* the bottom of the Death Pit. In an eerie blood-red glow she saw smashed skeletons, strewn bones, scraps of decayed clothing, and worse...

Not exactly a snake. The front end of a snake, with the legs of a giant lizard and a single green eye. The tail was no tail but a smaller beast, of similar design. She saw scimitar teeth and a flickering tongue. She picked up a skull, and hurled it at the right leg. The skull shattered, meringue against rock. The gaping mouth loomed closer, high above her head, and she screamed —

A knife-hilt bloomed in the deathbeast's eye, then a red beam wandered over its face. She smelt singed flesh as it fell, brushing her shoulder and hurling her sideways. The remaining snake tied itself in an agonised coil. A flying bone struck T'quoise under the ear and she fell, dazed.

A rope dropped from overhead, and a pigtailed figure slithered down it. In his hand, Sam held the laser, back on low power for wide-beam light. Lashed to his back was a cloth-wrapped disk. "Tinka! I've brought your escape-route!" He removed the protective wrapping and several shadowy forms wriggled through the synte. Two picked up Tinka and passed her through.

Jasp'r bent over T'quoise. His hand came away bloody. He locked arms under her shoulders while his companion lifted her legs. As they passed her through the synte her eyes flickered open for a second. They widened with surprise.

"*Rufe!*"

~~~

Jane Bytinsky, famous revolutionary, liberator of the people of Bansh from the oppression of clan aristocracy, glorious founder of the —

Baloney. This revolution was going nowhere fast.

Bansh was a water empire. Esmion's near-monopoly made it the *de facto* governing power. The Full Moot was an elaborate sham.

Nothing holds an empire together better than monopoly control of an essential commodity. The Sui dynasty of the 7th Century OC had held the Old Earth state of China together by controlling the canals. The Revolt of the Centauri Bubblecities had collapsed before it ever got started: an air monopoly is even more effective. Nobody challenged the Concordat's grip on mahabhavium. Every xenologist was trained in political history; she could cite a hundred examples.

So how do you defeat a water empire?

You don't go about it like the R'formists: limited acts of sabotage and localised shows of force. Sabotage harms too many innocents, *loses* support. Small uprisings are harshly put down, *pour encourager les autres*. Their tactics were little more than gestures, based on the premise that The People — you could hear the capitals — were thirsting for a New Order, that all they lacked was a Leader.

Individual People had too much to lose. Tyrannical though it was, Esmion wasn't tyrannical *enough*.

However, the R'formists had a point. Bansh desperately needed a new political order. Its market-garden feudalism was falling apart with the inevitability of tidal stress. Inheritance laws, once meant to preserve fair shares, merely subdivided land into ever-diminishing pieces, burying ever more soil beneath unproductive walls. There was even a stone shortage. The price of old walls was rising faster than most staples.

Bansh had walled itself into a corner.

And Sam, Tinka, and I are the spearhead of a revolt which is due to come horribly adrift. We'll all end up in the Death Pit.

Start again. One problem at a time. How do you bring down a monopoly?

Method one: *competition*. Doomed to failure. An established monopoly can always squeeze out the upstarts.

Method two: *take-over*. Financial, political, military, we haven't got the clout.

Method three: *nationalise*. First you must control the government; but to do that, you must defeat the monopoly. Vicious circle.

Method four: — but she didn't know a fourth method.

"Sam? How do you destroy a resource monopoly?"

"Deprive it of its resource."

Great. Then Bansh becomes a desert. Unless... *Where does Esmion get its water?* Ask Jasp'r.

She began to explore the storage-rooms where he was said to be working. She found him — with T'quoise. They jumped apart shyly as Jane emerged from the entrance synte. She asked her question.

He didn't know where Esmion's water came from. He didn't even recognise the word 'river' in Standard or Kalingo, claimed he'd never seen one. He did find an out-of-date map of Bansh's water consumption, garth by garth. She took it back with her and spread it on the floor.

Fiefdoms in cross-hatching, clan demesnes in solid colour. Esmion held more than a quarter. Her attention was drawn to a thick blue curve running across the top edge of the map. Slap in the middle was Esmion Hold.

Tinka hobbled over. "Any luck?"

Jane stabbed at the map with a finger. "What does *that* look like to you? It ought to be a river, but Jasp'r's never heard the word. See how it meanders, you'd expect that on an alluvial plain like —"

"I *saw* that! From the air! But it isn't a river — unless the rivers of Bansh are paved with gold! It looked more like a huge, sinuous cornfield!"

"*Cornfield*? Then what's *that*?"

"Mmph... Just like an ox-bow lake, where a loop of the river got cut off."

"Right. So it was a river. Now it's dried up. I wonder what—"

Stupid.

Now I know where Esmion gets its water.

~~~

"No! Rufe, no! You *can't* go!" T'quoise's face was anguished.

Rufe Strogitz, or Jasp'r, shrugged. "T'quoise, I have to go. If I do not present myself at Esmion Stronghold within the next half hour, I give myself away. The Queen smells treason; she will have the Moot strip my father of his chieftainship, my clan will cease to exist, and my family will become serfs."

"But it's too dangerous!"

"On the contrary. The Queen is rounding up *all* the sons of the nobility. It is panic. She has no idea who slaughtered the deathbeast and rescued two of its prey."

He left, not knowing that the Baron had news for the Queen. "Shapi, one who was listening to the execution at the Death Pit claims to have heard the girl T'quoise speak to her rescuers. Only one word, but perhaps enough. A name."

"Excellent! And what was the name?"

"It was indistinct, Shapi. Either Ruge — or Rufe."

~~~

In whispers of terror, the word came. Jasp'r arrested. Oh, Mother, thought Sam. Have these people no sense at all? If we get out of this, remind me to give Jasp'r a lecture on the cell system for subversive organisations.

"Sam," said Jane, "the R'formists are falling apart. We've got two choices. Either run — the Mothercurst know where — or — "

He was fast losing patience. "I don't like running, Jane, and Jasp'r just risked his life to help us."

"Then I guess we have to start his revolution for him."

"Oh, wonderful. So how do we beat Esmion?"

"You already told me. Deprive it of its resource."

"No!" Sam was angry. "I'd rather leave Bansh in the grip of Queen Al'zarin than leave an entire nation to die of thirst!"

"Samuel Grey Deer Wasumi, calm down! No one's going to go thirsty. Not even that thing that has adopted you. Now, *here's* the plan." She paused, looking crafty. "A few tiny details still missing. But I'm sure we can fill those in."

~~~

"What mongrel get of a paranoid camel is *that*?"

That was a leather-covered bamboo framework, about the size and shape of a coffin, to which were lashed a dozen syntei — four big ones at the front, their kanta-syntei behind, and a cluster of smaller ones poking from the top.

"It's for you, Sam." Jane had stopped worrying whom her latest idea might kill. Even her angst was emptied. She would do what was necessary and accept wherever it led. Drained, numb, she was surviving on animal instinct and unfeeling mind.

"I didn't ask who it's *for!* What *is* it?"

"A sub-aqua-suit. You're going swimming. Back up the biggest spillsynte I've found, looking for Esmion's source lake. Once there used to be a river across the plains of Bansh. Esmion blocked it off, diverted it by synte to create the irrigation system and a water empire. The river-bed was highly fertile land when it dried out, so they took it for themselves. They even built their Mothertrashed *Hold* slap bang in the middle of it!

"Somewhere out there is what they built to divert the flow. But *I don't know where!* You're going to find it. You take the laser medallion: as soon as you get there you destroy the dam, or whatever they built. The oriel attached to the diving-suit is to send you reinforcements, and bring you back safe. Understand?"

"Yes, but what's all the gadgetry?"

"One synte to breathe through, two syntei to see through. *This* part is a polysyntelic bypass, to reduce the pressure of the water as you fight your way upstream. If it works I'll apply for a patent.

"The R'formists can get you to the spillsynte that supplies Wylzen Hold. Connections to clan Holds would have been among the earliest established, so they're probably the most direct." She gave him a quick kiss. "Go now, Sam! Do it for us all!"

He kissed her back and headed for the water, whistling. She tried not to look at his departing back, or at the 'diving-suit', as a group of R'formists carried the contraption after him.

~~~

One down — how many to go?

Sam found himself in a huge rectangular pool. The water came in through a battery of syntei at one side, out through a battery on the other.

On to the source. Swim against the current. Well, crawl. You've done plenty of both in your time, Wasumi.

He splashed quickly across the pool. There was a shout, the impact of a crossbow quarrel in water. But Sam had vanished up the next spillsynte.

How long before they realise what I'm up to, and call ahead? He clutched the laser firmly. The water rushed past on both sides, kept away from his body by the taut leather. Its force was short-circuited by syntei, but the algae-slippery bed of the spillsynte was hard going. His foot tangled in weed and he kicked it free.

Green light shimmered ahead. He crawled out of a synte mouth. The bed opened out, glutinous mud, full of weeds trailing dishevelled mass along the flow.

He turned sideways and nearly lost everything. The central current, un-diverted by Jane's syntei, slammed the framework across the mouths of three separate syntei and held it there. The leather bulged inwards under the weight of water. But despite the danger, he felt a sudden sense of exhilaration.

Thousands of syntei stretched into the distance, until they disappeared in the murk. Packed on top of each other from bed to surface, others behind them in the gaps. A wall of syntei. Enough to divert the flow of an entire river.

Jane, you were wrong. They didn't build it. Couldn't. Don't think that way.

They *grew* it.

No: it grew itself. It wasn't a dam. It was an underwater synte jungle. Probably all one plant, like a banyan tree. It must have begun in a small way. A single plant on the riverbed. It puts out runners. Over the years, some syntei die or silt up. The river rises, spilling over the top; new syntei grow, a Gordian knot. The tangle piles higher and higher. Behind it, the river floods its basin, turning it into a lake.

Whoever founded Clan Esmion was the biggest opportunist on the planet.

Half an hour later, Sam heaved himself up the bank and scuttled into the bushes. Through his portable oriel a squad of twenty men joined him, armed with crossbows and syntubes. If he could evade the guards and get to the far side of the syntei barricade…

Yes, Jane. There *was* a river here.

He fondled the laser. Soon the river would flow again.

~~~

Despite the ache in her bones, Queen Al'zarin of Esmion sat bolt upright, a roaring in her ears. *Stroke? Heart-attack? Am I dying?*

The ground began to shake.

Her handmaidens rushed to help her as she hobbled to the window.

The river. The river the ancient records tell of. It has returned.

In their quarters beside Esmion's dungeons, Baron Sable and the Dark Watch felt the shaking, heard the noise — and, too late, learned what it was. Floodwater cascaded down spiral staircases, turned syntei into death-traps, bubbled along corridors, rose to roof height and beyond.

As the swirling waters began to undermine the foundations of Esmion Stronghold, arthritic royal hands clawed at the stonework. She screamed her outrage to an uncaring universe.

~~~

An awful lot can happen in twenty-four hours, Jane thought. Yesterday I was part of a half-arsed revolution with less chance of success than a commercial sex worker in a groping pool; today I'm about to address a Full Moot. Yesterday Al'zarin of Esmion was *de facto* Queen of Bansh; today she's a basket case. Yesterday Rufe Strogitz was in the vaults of the Death Pit; today he's a free man making moon-eyes at T'quoise. Yesterday Bansh had an irrigation system; today it has a river, kilometres across.

In T'quoise's cabin, the *skiti* chirped happiness, its stomach full for the first time in days. It didn't know it was a hero of the revolution, but the feeding bowl was full, *and* it got a share of any food the big two-legs touched. Am'thys Hoik, saddled with the task of tending it, scowled as its tail brushed against her legs. *Stupid animal!* What a come-down, from village Custodian to *skiti*'s skivvy!

Elsewhere, T'quoise and Rufe came up for air. He was handicapped by two arms in splints, from his treatment by the Dark Watch before the confusion of the returning river had made a rescue possible. T'quoise didn't let that stop anything.

Rufe took a deep breath. He needed it. "Think of it, T'quoise!" he declaimed. "A New Order, just as we'd dreamed!"

"And as C'balt dreamed," she replied, suddenly sad at the memory. She would have the Death Pit filled in and converted to a mass Grave Of The Martyrs. Rufe would persuade his father Gules to convince the Moot of this. Rufe could do anything!

A bittersweet victory. No longer would walls hide her horizons. T'quoise would take her place as a clanswoman, would breed syntei as she had always wanted, would walk the slopeways and gaze upon oceans — but would those things matter, in a world of changes?

~~~

Jane cleared her throat. Around her in tiers, wearing their finest ceremonial robes, sat the assembled nobles of every clan save Esmion, now disgraced. Years of conditioning struggled against a new idea — that an outlander, and a woman at that, might say something worth their hearing.

The Chieftain of Clan Kespe was on his feet. He had just put the question that was in all their minds. "How can we regain our water?"

Deep breath. *Here we go. Not even you, Sam, know the whole of it.* "Esmion's barricade to divert the river was a natural growth developed over centuries. To restore the synte network is impossible." That was a calculated lie: a simple syntelic engineering job would do the trick. Hundreds of syntei attached to racks, suspended from pontoons. But telling them that wouldn't solve the real problem. The clansmen would never think of it themselves, thank the Mother of Galaxies — Qishi mentality expects syntei to grow, not be built.

"Do we then die of thirst?" The Chieftain was so furious that he'd stopped thinking straight.

"With a river several *klòvij* wide flowing on your doorstep, Chieftain?"

"Starve, then! Water in a — a *river*," he ran the strange word around his tongue in wonder " — cannot feed crops!" There were sounds of agreement from the tiers.

Jane waited until the noise died down and the silence grew unbearable. "But, Clanlords, it *can*. It *must*. It is all you have now, save for the labour of your backs. The water need not *stay* in the river. You will borrow syntei from wherever you can spare them, to convey water from the river for immediate needs and to fill the storage pools. But that can be only a temporary solution! You will *build* what is necessary to carry water from the river to the fields. Shadufs, irrigation ditches, canals, aqueducts!"

She had to explain the words, they were as alien as 'river'. The babble of noise grew as the ideas began to sink home. The good citizens of Bansh had only been given a peek into Pandora's box. *They'll need roads, too, to service the canals. There will be gates in the walls of Bansh. But that will be just the start.* They had no idea what else was coming. She'd lift the lid, a bit at a time. That's how a Pandora's box works.

The Chieftain of Clan Jarrol rose unsteadily to his feet. He was the oldest there, but others would follow his lead. His mind was as sharp as a dagger, and he had less time than most for pointless tradition. "Shapi, I for one am willing to see these things constructed. I believe we have no choice. Manpower we have, in plenty. But we lack the materials! What will we build these aqueducts from?"

Deep breath. "Stone."

"But already we run short of stone to divide one garth from another!"

Jane paused, then struck. "That is where you will get the stone!"

She watched as the shock hit him. Her gaze ran around the room at the strained, uncomprehending faces, saw their shocked expressions as her meaning took root. Sam's face was a picture.

Jane looked the Chieftain of Jarrol firmly in the eye, and uttered the ultimate heresy. "The walls of Bansh must be torn down."

22

Botanical Warfare

…their fenceful bucklers were
The middle rounds of can'sticks; but their spear
A huge long needle was, that could not bear
The brain of any, but be Mars his own
Mortal invention; their heads' arming crown
Was vessel to the kernel of a nut.
And thus the Mice their powers in armour put.
This the Frogs hearing, from the water all
Issue to one place, and a council call
Of wicked war; consulting what should be
Cause to this murmur and strange mutiny.
—Pigres of Halicarnassus, Batrachomyomachia

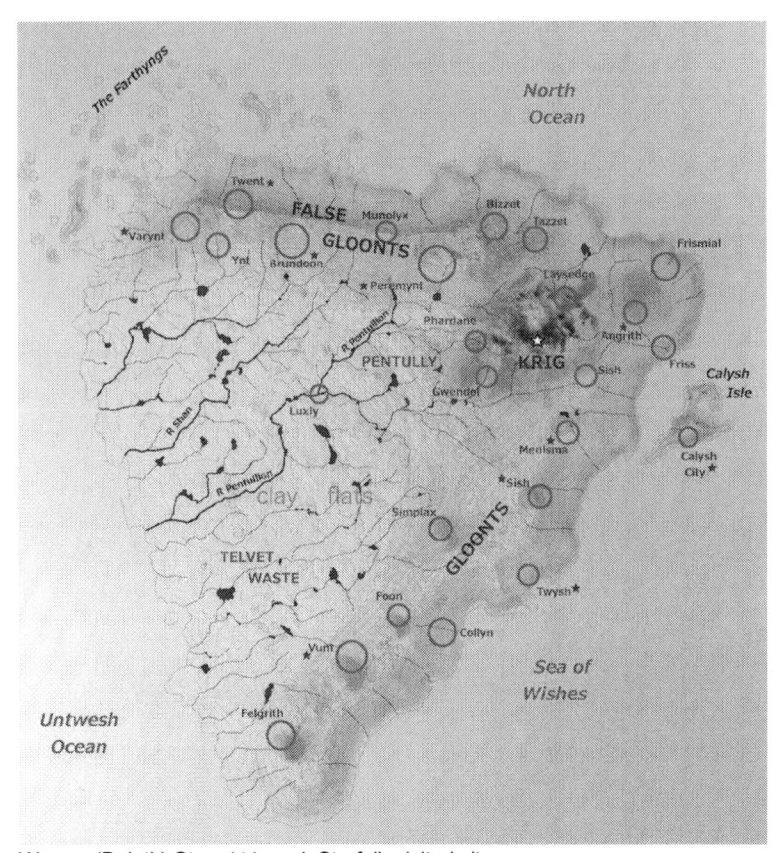

Wevory (Daleth) Stars (★) mark Starfolk-visited sites.

The patrol advanced cautiously across open ground.

An incessant drizzle soaked them to the skin. Clay clung to their boots in thick, glutinous lumps, as they trudged the washed-out watercolour landscape. Water ran freely in the irrigation-trenches, but it was only rainwater, not Water of Nourishment.

The plants had wilted in the fields. The sergeant pulled one out by its limp stalks; the root was not even a complete ring, grey and rotten. He let it drop.

All the land was streaked and scored by the signs of war. Huge patches were burnt. In the distance the blackened, broken ribs of a farmhouse were stark charcoal strokes against the sullen sky. Three mutilated bodies lay in a ditch.

The sergeant sent out scouts to secure the low stone wall, but the enemy was long gone. Here the straggled crop was almost completely burnt; what had survived the flames had been flattened. There was nowhere for an enemy to hide. Only a few stunted plants, bulbous lumps on short stalks. Odd that those should survive. Weeds, perhaps, or the remnants of a substitute crop. Most of them were burnt, too. Little remained of the fields that the farmer had tended so carefully.

The farmer: dead. The land: barren, empty.

The first arrow took the point man in the throat. Before anyone could react, two more arrows found their marks. The sergeant yelled to the patrol to retreat across the open ground to the wall, away from the ambush, away from the standing plants that were neither weeds nor crops.

As he wriggled backwards he felt the ground give way beneath him. Something seemed to grab him by the legs, pulling him down into earth that had suddenly turned to a yawning void. Tidal forces ripped him apart in mid-air.

~~~

The stocky man with the salt-hardened hands readied his skiff beside the dark, restless sea. His breath misted before his face as he tightened the lashings. A few wet snowflakes melted the moment they hit the damp boards.

From the sandbar that jutted from the south-west tip of Calysh Isle, it was an easy sail to the Wevorin mainland, no more than forty *klòvij* as the oylybird flies. The swells were high, but the wind had fallen and there would be no storm tonight. War had closed the Wevorin wyzands, and the channel could be crossed only by boat.

The two fur-clad strangers had offered a hundred *skint* in good Samdali copper. Three times what an honest kelper could earn in a month. Fortunately for Vulvole, he had never considered himself an honest kelper. He did drag for kelp, but his most useful skill was avoiding Wevorin shore patrols.

Soon he would be able to buy a proper kelp-trawler.

Squatting on a nearby dune, Elzabet of Quynt and Marco Bianchi shivered despite knitted gloves, calfskin boots lined with rhomney-wool, and layered wrappings of *rhunka* fur. Far north of the equator, the Misty was turning to the season of snows. *Magog*'s rescue beacon was perched on one of the highest mountains, several hundred klicks further north. A chill flurry, blown by a sudden gust out of the Sea of Wishes, sent shivers up and down their spines as it penetrated their garments.

We must be crazy, Elzabet told herself, as Vulvole waved them to their feet. She walked down the damp sand towards the kelp-skiff. Marco followed, glumly. He was brooding about his abandoned babies, and his optics. *Brrrr! It's cold!* He had spent most of his confinement playing with mismatch syntei, that acted a bit like lenses. His low power microscope had taught him nothing new about how syntei worked, but the telescope might come in handy. Not on a night like this, though.

"Come on, Marco love! Get in before this crate is swamped!"

It wasn't supposed to be like this.

It should have been easy, Samdal to Wevory. Elzabet's river-diversions had earned enough *skint* to take a triple syntour of the entire planet. They had planned to take the intercontinental wyzand from Zamp to Laysedge, a single step through a synte that spanned six thousand kilometres of ordinary space. Laysedge was within easy travel of — they hoped — the rescue beacon. They could even have brought along Lomyrla and the twins, whom Marco kept goo-goo-ing to by falasynte, then turning to Elza's bodily comfort. Men were such needy creatures.

That had been before the war.

It was an international war, involving the armies of two continents.

It was a civil war, the breakup of an economic federation.

Political boundaries on Qish were not always geographical, and the concept of a 'nation' meant little. Syntei saw to that. Syntei were also vital to the military, as instant troop transport for whoever controlled them. That made them targets for destruction. New breeds of synte opened up new weapons and tactics.

All outside traffic with the belligerents had been blocked, against continent-hopping raiding parties and the relentless spread of the war. Already it involved the Kuukau ethnic regions of Lamynt (the central highlands formed by the Greywraiths and the south-eastern Blackpeaks) and the entire continent of Wevory.

Except Calysh Isle. Calysh Isle had been very quick to dodge. Having suffered badly in previous by-strikes from the Wevorin interior, it asserted a fierce, precarious neutrality. To protect it, man-sized syntei rapidly turned unavailable to private citizens: Vulvole had tried hard to get hold of one that he could plant in concealment on Wevory, to save making more than one voyage. He had failed.

With syntei, distance does not stretch logistics, although possession of distant territory is crucial and bottlenecks can lose a battle. But it is easier to send things down syntei than up, so strategy keeps one's head in the clouds.

And the rescue beacon was on one of the highest peaks in Wevory.

However, it seemed to Elzabet that they should not lament their misfortune too much. Not only was Calysh Isle neutral, *and* near the right region of Wevory; it was one of the few places on the planet with seagoing boats, cautious and coastal though they were.

Humans could no more eat the native fish than the violet-blooded animals with golden bones, and imported Old Earth marine fish didn't survive in Qish's seas, but in the shallow waters around Calysh Isle there were huge underwater forests of giant seaweed. The Colonists had called it kelp. The only way to reach it was by boat, and before shredding, kelp was too unwieldy to pass a synte. Big clumsy shallow boats could carry shredding machines, but sometimes attracted the monsters that normally lurked in deeper water. Small ones could dodge through the shallow beds and sandbanks. Shredded kelp synted from their ports to the paper-mills of northern Lamynt was a cheap source of paper fibre, and fertilised reclamation projects at the edge of the Dunelands.

It was a gamble that Marco and Elzabet had to risk. With only themselves to think about they might have waited for the war to end, but maybe Tinka, Sam, Jane, and Felix were still alive, somewhere on the planet. The one faint hope of rescuing them was via contact with Starhome. All their thinking led to the rescue beacon.

There was no guarantee that Starhome could save their companions, with vague rumours of a Vain Vaimoksi breakup in succession wars. She doubted that four captives would have been well placed to survive amid the chaos.

Of course, there was always Marco's theory that the destruction of the VV had been *accomplished* by their fellow Starfolk. Wishful thinking. Marco was an incurable romantic. With natives powerless, what chance had ignorant offworld captives, deprived of all possessions? No one could simply talk the Vain Vaimoksi into defeat.

But they *might* have survived.

I wonder where they are now?

~~~

"I wonder where they are now?"

"It's more than a year since Elza and Marco were on the run from Deacon De-Lameter," said Jane. I hope they got away, Sam."

"Me too," said Tinka, looking at her arms the way she always did when talk even hinted at bone-hammers.

Jane shuddered. *If they did get away, surely they would have reached the beacon long ago? Starhome ought to have found us by now, rescued us... Though we got away from the Vain Vaimoksi, and we haven't made it to the beacon yet. Poor Felix never will. On a planet with matter-transmitters growing on trees, it should be easy to get halfway round the world.*

But with people, nothing that should be easy ever is. Rods for their own backs.

And now... Don't you know there's a war on? And winter is on its way over there... Even here in Lamynt's summer, it's a lot colder in the mountains than down in Bansh. At least it's dry.

A leather boot, clogged with mud, flew through the doorway trailing wet thongs behind it, and crashed against the stone flags. Its fellow joined it.

"Enter and be welcome!" shouted Jane. These Spintish folk had the most *peculiar* way of announcing themselves.

A mass of ginger fuzz with eyes poked through the oriel. "Strabi, Sabi." *No manners, either. Addressing only one of us.* But Spint, stretched up from the south coast of Lamynt, was the only place in synte contact with Bansh, so here they were in Twoshoes, wondering how best to move on.

"Strab," she said. 'Strab Sab' was just *too* cute for her taste. "What news from Wevory, Morgan?"

Morgan Joplin Hoyle was a burly young man, short like most people on Qish; clad in warm clothing, none of which matched. "Precious little, and none good," he snapped, padding across the floor on soiled footcloths and flopping down by the fire. Making an effort, he relaxed. "That is to say, my friends: situation normal. There are troops mobilised all along the Gloonts and the False Gloonts."

Those two mountain ranges dominated the eastern and northern zones of Wevory, Qish's smallest continent, across the Equator from here. Prime targets for military occupation — and the invasion launched by Spint's neighbours, the Kuukau Front. She still had moments of wonder that their D-Day across an ocean had involved no ships or beach landings.

The only way we'll get to Wevory is with the army.

The only way we'll get with the army is for the army to need us.

"It's pretty confused at the moment, and the weather isn't helping — wet snow on the slopes over there, endless rain on the clayfields. But it looks like the main forces of the *Selbstverteiligungsallianz* have secured most of the high ground on the Gloonts, while the Kuukau have managed to grab the False Gloonts, more securely in the West. I'm surprised: Vanhammet must be a better tactician than I thought. There are some scattered bunches of Cronon Mercenaries making nuisances of themselves, but the word is they're going to get their fingers burned. The Low Country, around Telvet and Pentully, is taking a pounding. The late *bazza* crop is totally ruined." He spat into the fire in disgust.

"Hang on," said Tinka. "I thought possession of the *bazza* lands was what the war was about? What's the point of destroying them?"

"Tinka love," said Jane, "this is war. There doesn't have to be any *point*."

"But there is," said Sam, "in the logic of warfare. If you can't hold the *bazza* lands for yourself, you destroy them to stop the enemy getting them."

Morgan slapped his thigh. "It was the usual smunk-up, actually, Samuel. The *Selbstverteiligungsallianz* tried to pull a fast one, get in quick, do no damage to the fields. But the SVA squabbled too much among themselves, the Kuukau got wind of it, and the rest is history. Now it's degenerated into a battle for strategic ground, and to demons with the crop. There's nothing left to gain now, except to avoid losing."

"What about Krig Mountain?" Tinka asked. The beacon site. The Krig range was an isolated, snow-capped outcrop between the False Gloonts and the Gloonts, close to Calysh Isle.

"As one of the highest peaks around, it's a strategic target for all factions," said Morgan. "Possession is teetering in the balance. The wyzands at Laysedge, Phardane and Gwendol, nearest to Krig, got burnt out in a firefight. Apart from a few falasyntei and olosyntei that whole area is cut off. Nothing a man could get through, and they keep a watch for attempts to get round that. Right now they're down to hand-to-hand fighting in the foothills. Guerrilla stuff. Nasty."

Especially if the local synte network was still partially intact. Troop movements are quick, with syntei, and one man can make a syntehead. Troops can pour out of the kantasynte of a captured wyzand, in territory that seemed secure. Concealed syntraps in the grass can rip a soldier to shreds. And it only needs a narrow synte to convey an arrow, a poisoned dart, a projectile.

Jane had studied basic military strategy in her xenohistory courses, but nothing covered *this* set-up. Well, that wasn't quite true. Basic *principles* still ought to apply, like controlling strong positions. But what was strong wasn't the conventional version, here. Strong positions were usually high ones. Once you gained the heights, you could set up a synte link to anything else you owned at the same level, or downward (though down had drastic effects). Provided you could get the syntei to the points you controlled. Big syntei could transport little ones, but not *vice versa*, and really big ones had to get that big in place — slowly. That meant weird connectivity effects, outside the usual combinotactical axioms for strategic computers. Of course you could modify code, but someone had to carry out the mods, and you couldn't do enough on wristcomps anyway, trash it. So: *keep it simple, stupid.*

The combatants would have evolved textbook tactics over a long time; they'd be pretty sophisticated. Hard for offworlders to develop anything to compete.

How do we change that?

These people are experts, *their generals capable. So what bugs an expert most?*

Off-the-wall ideas.

Experts spend most of their lives acquiring their expertise, more and more specialised as later acquisitions cement over the original foundations. Why can't you teach an old dog new tricks? Because he *knows* the old ones are better. The new ones confuse him, which proves it. What eliminated conventional cavalry as the major force in warfare? Not a better horse, but the machine-gun and the tank. And it wasn't cavalry officers who developed tanks: they *resisted* the idea. Loss of personal power, translated as "I'm the expert, and I say it won't work."

Only problem: we can't build syntanks. Not for twenty years, at least.

But the general pattern is valid. The gun displaced the bow, tanks displaced horses. Aircraft didn't completely displace anything, but they added a new dimension. Literally. Bombs, cruise missiles, drones, energy weapons, lasers, coherent X-rays,...

"Felix, what about..." Arguing with his memory still helped her think.

Suppose we find a new way to gain height, without conventional uses of syntei, or to transport syntei without using a syntehead or ground movements? That would screw up the experts; they'd have to throw the book of tactics down the synthole, and they won't want to. They've invested too much in learning the book.

Jane Bytinsky, we're back in the glider business. All we need is a good high source of water-power. No doubt the Kuukau can link something up with other regions of Lamynt. Or Samdal, if necessary.

She began trying to explain all this to Morgan.

~~~

"I thought you were good at *avoiding* coastal patrols," Marco complained. He tried to wring out a sock, and banged an elbow against a bulkhead.

"Don't blame me," said Vulvole sourly. "I got you to Wevory!"

"You did. You even got us to the Krig Domain. But you didn't say we'd be arrested by the coastguard." Krig and Calysh had kelp-fleets that sometimes argued over kelp-beds, and called for armed back-up.

"I didn't think they'd have spare syntei for searchlamps," Vulvole snapped back. Sunlight from the dayside of Qish, synted to a rotating mount, had lit up the tiny skiff like broad daylight — as was only appropriate, since it was.

"I suppose it's the people-from-the-stars routine again," said Elzabet. The boat lurched, and so did her stomach; it hadn't been so bad in Vulvole's skiff, but it was *slower* in a big vessel. "Pity you had to throw Gus's falasynte overboard."

"He would have trashed it as soon as he realised we'd been caught. Too much risk to his network. Anyway, they took all our stuff."

"You speak truth. Where did the Wevorins dredge up these confounded ships? This one seems clapped out, suitable only for coastal work."

"There has been just one ocean-going ship in the history of this planet, and Wevor was a lunatic." Naturally Marco had picked up all the smutty songs about the culture hero who brought a syntehead from Samdal: he always found the most *disrespectful* friends.

"It dodged the *craukens*. Maybe he was saner than you think."

"I wonder where they're taking us?"

"Twysh," said Vulvole. "Long way that way." He pointed vaguely south-west. "Down the coast, well away from the main theatre of battle. From there probably to Angrith, up in the Gloonts, smack in the middle of the action."

Vulvole had a habit of passing on seriously bad news as though he were forecasting the weather. It was annoying and depressing.

"How do you know that?"

"This is an SVA ship. *Selbstverteiligungsallianz*. Out of Twysh, you can tell by the marking on the stern. But Angrith is the SVA base."

Trash it, more than guesswork. " So then what?"

"My guess, they execute us as spies. After interrogation."

~~~

With maximum caution, the commando group picked its way through the foothills, spread well apart, scouts out in front and to either side. Half a kilometre ahead was a jagged cliff, but the scouts who had reached the top reported it unoccupied. They had found no syntei hidden among the rocks. It was impossible to declare the area safe – in war, nowhere is truly safe – but it was as safe as anyone could reasonably expect.

The sun was sinking as they made camp.

A dozen men dug in for a wide defensive circle around the campfires, kept in touch by falasynte. They watched for danger while their companions ate. The food was appalling – nutritious slop synted from a tank somewhere high up in the strongholds, valved to each soldier's canteen – but it was food.

In the darkness, no one saw a section of cliff opening. By the campfire, they never heard the shockwave: the rock was travelling faster than the sound it generated.

The outer guards did hear the bang, and flung themselves to the depths of their foxholes. The sonic booms continued for fifteen minutes.

Morning showed where forty heavy boulders had ripped right through the camp at supersonic speed. There was nobody left to see it.

Partitions in the food tank had stopped most of it leaking out via smashed canteens.

~~~

"No way," said Morgan, when Jane had finished her pitch.

"What?"

"You heard. If we get South Lamynt or Samdal into this, they aren't going to thank us. I can give you limited assistance, I can put you in touch with a few key people, but that's as far as I can go. I can't involve the Men of Spint in this war. Only the Council can do that, and they won't take any action unless they're forced to."

Jane reconsidered.

"If you *did* come in, which side would you support?"

"Ourselves. Oh, it would have to be the Front. We have more than enough trouble from the SVA. Fanatics."

"So can you put us in touch with the Kuukau Front?"

Morgan gave her a long, hard look. "If you insist. Bonvisage is your man. I'll set up a meeting. After that, it's up to you."

~~~

"Marco: tell me why we get mixed up in this war. It's horrible. We should be trying to stop it, not join it!"

Marco understood why Elza was asking. The usual. Reassurance, guilt.

"We shouldn't be doing either. We can't expect them to lay down their weapons just because self-styled superior beings from the galactic deeps tell them to. Fact is, the quickest way to stop this war is to *win* it."

"But not to take sides. We should try to help them reach a fair settlement."

"Fair? Love and war, you know the old saying. What we need is a *settlement*, period. A victory, a truce, a ceasefire. Anything we can get, any way we can get it. Let's get the fighting stopped, so no more of our people are killed and we can try to find the beacon. That's what matters. Let Starhome figure out what's fair."

"Marco, you've changed."

"Guilty and proud of it. So have you."

"Yah. I'm not sure it's an improvement, even if you think so."

"It doesn't matter what *I* think. It's *necessary* if we want to talk to Starhome. Syntei are cosmic game-changers; we have to get the word out to the Concordat. Justice and fair-dealing will have to wait until and make contact with the greater universe, and then they'll be the business of the locals. We get to the beacon. *Nothing else matters*."

"Trash it, Marco, this isn't our war."

Marco gave a humourless laugh. "It will be."

~~~

"Jane, are you *sure* we ought to do this? What if we make it worse?"

Jane ran her fingers through greasy hair, unwashed for days. "Ought? No, Tinka, I'm *not* sure. But we're not here to make it better or worse. We *have* to reach the beacon, and there's a war in the way. We either sit it out, and wait for years — *and* risk damage to the beacon — or stop the war. Come *on*, there's *three* of us, why not?" The sarcasm was raw-edged. "It ought to sound farcical, but *I'm sure we can*. We know enough tricks for these people to win it, and that will stop the slaughter quicker than anything else. How many people we're going to kill, or injure, in the process, I'm not sure."

"Not as many as if the war continues," said Tinka. It wasn't much comfort.

"How about negotiating a truce?" asked Sam. "No, trash it, that won't work. We'd need *political* clout, which we don't have."

"Or a massive peacekeeping force, which we also don't have."

"You're right. We have to help them win it! But I'm nanacurst if I like it."

"Starfolk training."

"Yah."

~~~

They were nervous.

The ordinary soldiers were raw recruits. They were nervous because they had never been in a battle before.

The officers were experienced. They were nervous because they had been in a battle before, and because the ordinary soldiers were raw recruits.

The task force was sanding — beating woodland in a search-and-destroy pattern. The slap of syntubes against their thighs was no comfort: it merely reminded them that trees can hide syntei. That was why they were burning the trees ahead of them as they went. Behind them they left nothing but blackened ashes and rock.

When they had passed, and vanished, one of the rocks moved.

A soldier climbed out, then another, until there were more than a hundred. Their faces were hard and battle-weary; their bodies quick and tough. In their minds was no hint of mercy.

Silently they began to creep up on the enemy before them.

~~~

"We seem to be getting better at this," said Elzabet.

"I have a feeling," said Marco, "that the word is out that there are some crazy offworlders on planet. It does seem easier to get a hearing."

"Or a trial."

It had taken them only a week to work their way up the SVA hierarchy — rather literally, up. High Command always likes to combine safety with good communications, and Mount Angrith had both. It had required courage, tact, a lot of improvisation, and climbing thousands of stairs. They were as hard now as their legs, and totally committed to reporting back to the familiar worlds of the Concordat.

Now it all depended on whether General Fingal Marsden von Hayashiko had the wit to believe them. And *didn't* have the wit to disbelieve them in the places where they were being less than candid. If the General guessed that the men from the stars were really aiming at was contact with men *among* the stars...

A grim-faced aide showed them in, and was dismissed. They understood the implication. *We're no danger to this man.*

The General was big, for a local, and spoke like a leader who expected total obedience. Word had it that he had worked his way up from the ranks by courage under fire, not paper-pushing, so he had killed face to face as well as ordering regiments into death. He looked it.

He could order these two intruders shot as spies, and they knew it. That was intimidating, but Elza and Marco had survived land-piranhas, the Church, and carrying twins. The General didn't have men with bone-hammers, and he did have a war to win. Even the Deacon had traded lives for intelligence: this man would do it routinely, if he decided their knowledge was useful.

It feels good to be needed.

Especially when the alternative is death.

~~~

General von Hayashiko didn't just push people around. He *listened*. Intelligence had collated various offworlder rumours. Some kind of trouble over in Shaaluy (serves that bunch of nuts right, I'd like to cause some trouble there myself). More on Lamynt (for whom I shed no tears, not now). And *something* had happened to the Vain Vaimoksi. His main worry was that these people seemed too mild to fit the rumours.

What they had told his staff hung together, in broad outline, though he doubted it was the *whole* truth. He stared again at Elzabet, and racked his brains for an elusive memory... something that had happened on Samdal when he was — ah, yes.

"You remind me of a dancer I saw on Samdal last year," he said to her, out of the blue. "Name of —"

"Gold Lightning, General," Marco jumped in, convincing him. "Yes, that was her. We had to raise some cash, and we didn't have many options."

"Is he telling the truth, Sabi?"

"Yes. Sab."

The General could read faces, and had seen many try to lie to him. "I believe you. The resemblance is too striking, and your looks too unusual for this world. Also, it has been rumoured that Gold Lightning was a woman from the stars, a wild assertion I had discounted. But she was taken by the Vain Vaimoksi."

"She appeared to be taken."

"Ah. I see. A small... charade?"

"We were being pursued by agents of Deacon DeLameter, until we went forever beyond their reach, enslaved by the VV. In truth, we hid on Samdal."

"And the reason you were being pursued?"

"Body-Dividing."

"What else? It is a Church obsessed." Von Hayashiko waved a hand. "That is of no consequence. Shaaluin inhibitions are widely derided elsewhere." He leaned forward. "But there is something that *is* of consequence. How can I be sure that you are not agents of the Vain Vaimoksi? Slavestoned and unwilling?"

"Do slavestones work at this level? We had heard that their bases all seemed to be in the lowlands, unable to deliver crossbolts to this height. And that the Vain Vaimoksi were recently destroyed."

The General made a non-committal noise. "I have also heard that offworlders were involved, tall and brown like yourselves, which is what makes me wonder about your motives. To date, I have not been presented with convincing evidence of significant damage to VV activities. Only rumours. And they may have succeeded in securing a higher base."

Marco shot Elzabet a surprised, superior glance. The General noticed the byplay but pretended to ignore it. "There is a partial answer: a doctor shall probe you to make sure you are not enstoned. I have already issued the order. But even if you are no slaves, how can you convince me you are not enemy spies?"

"We cannot, Sab," said Marco, readily. "Not fully. But we can prove that we are *useful*, in a way that will render our motives irrelevant."

The General was intrigued, but he always chose *shinsa* moves that concealed his intentions. "Commendably frank, but I remain sceptical. How can two powerless people, with no possessions and no backup, be useful to *me*? You have no weapons, and it is obvious that your knowledge of military matters is virtually nonexistent."

"But we do have a weapon," said Marco. The guard near the door raised his crossbow, and von Hayashiko glared at him and gestured that he should lower it. *Fool guard takes everything literally. These folk were searched. The starman obviously doesn't mean he's got one* on *him; he wouldn't tell me if he were armed.*

"What is this weapon?"

"Knowledge," said Marco.

The General pursed his lips. *Trite? Or deep? How subtle are these starpeople?* "What can you do with this knowledge?"

"Win the war for you," said Elzabet.

"That would be useful, Sabi, but the claim is ridiculous. Such timid folk as you could never deliver victory. War is a grinding-machine that chews up men and women and spits out dead meat. How do you propose to counter such terrible power?"

"We recognise your wisdom, General," said Marco. "I ask you to recognise ours. Do not underestimate people who come from the stars."

The General's face was reddening. He leaned forward and glared at them. "Starman, if that you be: I do not yield to threats."

"And I do not make them. Have you looked through the far-seeing device that you took from us?"

"A nice toy, and useful in a war, but *win* a war? No. And it did not come from the stars. My staff have already made a copy of it."

"But did they ever make one, before we came? Star knowledge put together light in a new way. Star knowledge can do the same for war."

"I grow weary of this vagueness. *What can you people possibly provide that I currently lack?*"

He's hooked, Marco thought. "We shall require various assurances before we reveal what we have in mind."

"Assurances can be empty."

"We judge you a man of honour. Your word will suffice."

"I am immune to flattery, but — very well. What do you want?"

Now to reel him in without losing him. "Primarily, a guarantee of our release as soon as the war is over. So that we may continue the search for our friends." Marco hoped the General would buy that as their reason for being on Wevory. Rescue beacons and the Concordat of Habitable Exoworlds were unlikely to occur to him. "Second, the return of our equipment."

"You will have no synte for which we cannot see the kantasynte," said Hayashiko firmly. "I do not *know* that you are not spies."

Ohh, the twins, the twins... but I see his point. "Accepted. Third, good treatment while we act as advisers. Fourth: assistance in seeking our fellows."

"Why not," asked the General, "simply hand you over to my Intelligence Service for interrogation, and directly obtain the benefit of your knowledge?"

Good question, Marco was glad they'd prepared for it. *The worst fear is that he tries that. Fails, but by the time he gets that, we're dead. Or wishing we were.*

"Because," said Elzabet, "it would fail. We could write the whole of our knowledge down for you, and it would make no useful sense. You need to watch what we *do*. We didn't make the far-seer from local materials without some trial and error. We explain, and experiment, and work with your syndepts and carpenters, and *then* it makes sense. You will never understand it in the abstract."

"How often is information obtained under duress accurate?" Marco asked.

"The same goes for information *not* obtained under duress."

"Yes, but you can judge us by results. The crucial point is that speed will be vital. The enemy may be able to copy our ideas once they see what they achieve. It takes far too long to extract information from an unwilling subject."

The General laughed. "You want me to trust you."

"We have already agreed to trust *you*. It is hard to bargain with no element of trust. You may feel we are foolish to trust your word, but what you *really* need to consider is: can you risk losing the opportunity we offer?"

General von Hayashiko nodded curtly. "I will think about it. For now, you are dismissed."

~~~

Von Hayashiko, uncharacteristically, was in two minds.

I like these people, the General decided. *They argue effectively from a position of weakness*. It would be interesting to see their ideas. And if they *worked*... perhaps there would be more ideas.

If he gave them their freedom, how could he ensure that they did not offer their knowledge to others? But that could wait. It would dishonour him to break his word, but honour was not always the most important consideration.

He ordered them brought back before him, and came straight to the point.

"I agree to your terms. Though as to finding your friends, I tell you now that little is known. Rumours tell of the Vain Vaimoksi defeated at the hands of strangers. My intelligence corps may be able to add detail; you may be able to interpret it. I will set them to study the question when more urgent duties permit. The war takes priority.

"Outline your proposal. I will choose the officers best suited to implement it."

"Well," Marco began, with the characteristic enthusiasm of the articulate engineer, relieved to stop hiding ideas — "you are well aware that one key strategic factor is height..."

~~~

"*One* key strategic factor is height," said Jane, on the other side of the Untwesh Ocean. "The other is reaching it. We can reach height, in a way you've never even dreamed of."

Barnes de Montfort Bonvisage, Chief Tactician of the Kuukau Front, agreed grimly about the strategy. "Lamynt has a few peaks of similar height to most of the Krig Range on Wevory. Land a synte over there, and we could occupy in force. You are certain that this device of yours, this slider thing, will work?"

"Glider. Definitely. We are here now only because one of them did work."

The Tactician still looked unhappy. "Once, when I was a child, a man from my village had a scheme to fly like a bird. He built himself wings from wood and leather, bound them to his arms with straps, and jumped off the top of the barn."

"What happened?"

"He fell into a haystack and broke his leg. Pity it wasn't his fool neck."

Jane tried to get the conversation back on track. "We don't propose wings that *flap*. Ours will be rigid. Your villager made several mistakes. His arms were too weak, his wings resisted the air too strongly, and they were too heavy. Birds don't scale up. Aerofoils do. Our design avoids those errors. It's only because your forsaken *Handbook* contained no aerodynamics that you lost the idea in the first place. We are just restoring a lost passage.

"Anyway, it will be a small investment of time and effort to build a prototype, and then you will be able to see for yourself."

Bonvisage could see little wrong with that. "Selah. What do you need?"

Jane had a list already in her head. "Something strong, light, and flexible," she said. "Animal skin or close-woven cloth. Then..."

~~~

"Strong, light, and flexible," said Marco. "Animal skin or close-woven cloth. Wood, ropes, glue. A big synte, of course. And plenty of good old-fashioned manual labour."

The General had one final query. "How long will this machine take to build?"

"Once you give us the materials and the workforce, two to three weeks. "

"Done!" said General Fingal Marsden von Hayashiko.

~~~

"Done!" said Chief Tactician Barnes de Montfort Bonvisage.

23

The War in the Air

> I don't want to join the army,
> Don't want to go to war;
> I'd rather stay in Amdergumst
> And learn to be a whore.
> I don't want to be a Sergeant,
> Don't want to join the fight.
> I'd rather stay in Amdergumst
> And fornicate all night.
> — Marilyn-Selma Wunaldum: Songs of War, Songs of Peace

The Division Commander sat in a stone-roofed dugout near the top of Vunt, in direct contact with his four Brigade Commanders further down the mountainside.

The enemy's assault was being repulsed. He opened another bottle of wine and returned his attention to the small rack of syntei.

Suddenly he heard B Brigade's commander, Raxmorn Chang Jellicoe, yelling into his ear. "Sab! The enemy have broken through on Lizard Ridge! They had a crossbow battery hidden below the skyline!"

"Do they have a syntehead? Do they hold other territory at this height?"

"Yes, at least two wyzands. And with iso-territory, soldiers are pouring out!"

The Division Commander thought fast. "Can you contain the synsurgency?"

"I think so. I'm retreating to higher ground as fast as I can. I have every bowman I can spare aiming fire-arrows at the syntei, but they're well protected. I —" His voice stopped abruptly.

Before the Division Commander could try to resume contact, D Brigade reported heavy losses on the south plateau. Then C Brigade called for urgent reinforcements, which he couldn't provide.

He was shouting into the falasynte when an axe split his head like a ripe peach.

~~~

"Another strut, Jane."

"Coming up, Fidel," a short length of polished hardwood, notched in a complicated pattern. Lieutenant Fidel Plocknicki. Oh boy.

"I'll put Plocknicki in charge," Bonvisage had said. "He's good with his hands." *Very free with them, too.*

Plocknicki tried to manoeuvre a strut into its proper slot. "Stupid war anyway. Never should have started."

"All war is stupid, Fidel. Er — how *did* it start?"

"The *bazza* crop failed."

"Wait a bit. Isn't *bazza* what you were fighting about? Why fight if it's failed anyway? And why did *you* invade because *their* crop failed?"

Plocknicki rammed the strut home. "Glue."

"Here."

"Thanks. Why? Oh, it failed ten years back. That's what started the trouble. Hand me another strut, and I'll explain…"

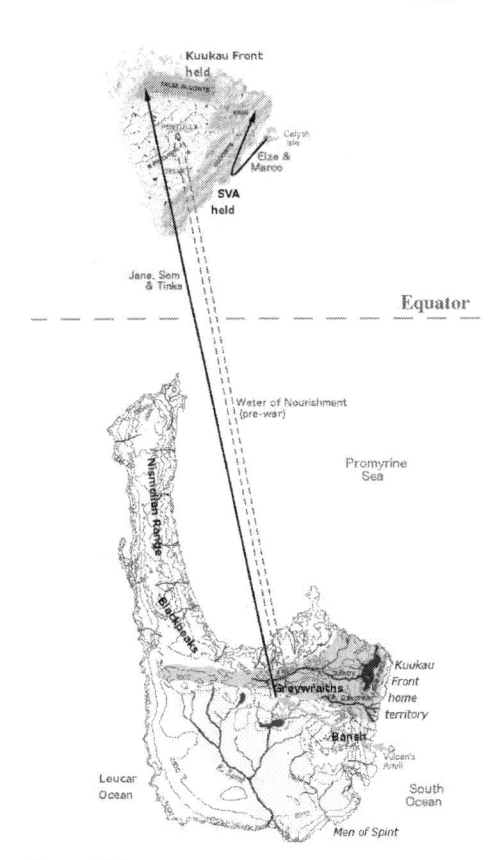

~~~

Lamynt-Wevory war

~~~

When *Magog* came to Qish, *bazza* grew only in the clay flats around Lake Pardyle in South Lamynt, across the Greydrear from Bansh. The native solitary *hohoon* dug for its large toroidal roots with its shovel-shaped lower jaw.

When humanity reached Lamynt, the Kuukau ethnic group settled along the Greywraith mountains and adjacent regions of the Blackpeaks, hemmed in by geography and politics. The fertile country around the river Spint was occupied by tough fighters, with an organisation too loose to take over as a unit, too close to defeat piecemeal. The plains of Bansh, to the south-east, were already held. To the north, only salt flats. The mud clay region around Lake Pardyle was the best agricultural land unclaimed, so the Kuukau began to farm there. *Bazza* roots turned out to suit imported sociable pigs. The Kuukau cultivated the *bazza*, fed the roots to their pigs, fed the pigs to themselves, and burned the *bazza*-stalks for warmth in the mild winter allowed by the warm current from subtropical Samdal. Some became thatch, but the surplus was simply burnt.

The *hohoona* went gradually extinct, unable to compete with pigs and spades.

Attempts to increase the crop failed, as *bazza* would only grow on muddy clay, like the lake shore. Transplanted elsewhere, it died. The Kuukau developed a rigid tribal culture of limiting families.

They learned that the south-west lowlands of distant Wevory consisted largely of clay flats, which the Wevorins called the Telvet Waste. Negotiating access with the local Wevorins, the Kuukau transplanted bazza there, intending to import the crop back into Lamynt. But every winter's cold drove the locals down to the coastal plains, which made farming unattractive. And despite the clay, the crop failed to thrive.

Everything struggled along well enough to get by, until genius or luck showed why *bazza* barely grew in the Telvet Waste.

Water.

"Wait a minute," Jane broke in. "Surely that would be obvious to anyone. If there wasn't enough water —"

"There was *enough* water," said Plocknicki. "You should see the autumn drizzles in Telvet! No, it wasn't the *quantity*."

Water from the flanks of the Greywraiths had something, something lacking in the flow down Pentullion into Telvet. When Lamynt water was synted to Telvet, the *bazza* crop flourished. That something was a dissolved mineral, or vegetable, or dragon piss, or the blessing of a god. No matter, as long as the water kept flowing.

From this discovery grew an intercontinental joint venture. A group of locals settled Telvet and irrigated *bazza* with water synted from Lamynt, synting back half the harvest in payment. On Lamynt, the Kuukau fed that to their pigs.

It worked beautifully. *Too* beautifully.

Kuukau youth questioned the breeding taboos. Wevorins found that leftover stalks would heat their homes, replacing the arduous trek to the plains by six months of fermented *bazza* and bed rest. They planted out most of Telvet.

Both populations increased relentlessly. So they bred new improved forms of *bazza*, with fatter rings, and better breeds of pig.

Growth has limits.

About ten years back, the cold polar winds came further south. The unusually cool summer in Telvet reduced the crop of *bazza*. This coincided with a harsh winter in the False Gloonts, requiring more fuel than even a normal yield of stalks.

The Kuukau survived the pig-fodder reduction by using up stored surplus. Thousands of Wevorins died of cold and hunger.

The next year the weather returned to normal, but the Wevorins had seen mass death that the Kuukau had not, and it rankled. The Kuukau themselves knew that they could survive on stores for no more than one winter. It would take years to rebuild a year's reserve, so they felt starvation at their own door. Each group worried about the other cutting off supplies. Each was too committed to force significant changes.

The loosely-knit federation of Wevorin states on the Gloonts began to argue. To improve unity, and fearing Lamynt, the federation developed a military wing: the *Selbstverteiligungsallianz* or Self-Defence Alliance (SVA).

In Lamynt, a major earthquake hit the Greywraiths, blocking high springs. The River Sumtry ran too low to feed the syntei until new tributaries joined it. Too late.

The SVA already had itchy trigger-fingers. With Lamynt's water not reaching them and the *bazza* starved, they saw deliberate aggression by the Kuukau, who were visibly keeping all the Sumtry flow to themselves. (It would have taken five years to re-grow the syntei at river-bottom depth. The Kuukau were not minded even to consider trying.) They didn't know that the Kuukau were also seeing unhealthy *bazza*. It hadn't yet failed completely, but the problem was slowly getting worse.

In retaliation, the cut-off Wevorins sent a force against the Quifts, where the water-transfer syntei were. The Commander was a little surprised to march through the dry syntei without meeting guards, but he was too busy winning the war to ask whether it had been necessary to begin with, or why the aggressors had left their own back door open. He tried to build a dam to raise the water level, but heavy engineering under fire is hard, even under a better general. Beating him back destroyed most of the diversion syntei. The triumphant Kuukau army saw a steady flow of young men willing to endure serious discipline, and eager to kill Wevorins.

They hit back at the Wevorin crops, making farming impossible.

"So that's what started it all? An earthquake?"

"A bad season, and *then* an earthquake."

I wonder what the Selbstverteilungungsallianz's *version is.* "Fidel," she asked, "What was so special about the Lamynt water?"

"Dunno. Good for teeth, they said. Tasted better than they have on Wevory. But it doesn't taste like that any more. And it took years to grow the river-transfer syntei. We'll probably all starve.

"Come on." He got to his feet. "Time to put the next strut in." Jane wriggled out of the helping arm and picked up the glue-pot.

~~~

If there was one thing the falasyntador hated, it was the downhill end of an uphill assault.

It sounded pretty chaotic up there. Safer down here in his wooden hut... probably... but what was happening? He had to relay information to Field Major Hannis, sitting on his fat arse on a mountaintop.

Suddenly the shouts were louder, with a crash and screams. An experienced soldier, he hit the deck in record time.

A loud crack! *came from the roof, and splinters flew. He peered over the edge of the table, reached out his fist, and smashed the falasynte flat. The hole in the roof was the size of his head. Someone up there had thrown a knife into the kantasynte.*

He was an experienced soldier. If there was one thing he hated, it was the downhill end of an uphill assault.

~~~

"Officers!" snarled underguard Haboush, rubbing angrily at a stain on his boot while chewing on a wad of nephthe-root. "Idiots, the lot of them. You know what that fool Mashlawton was doing today?"

"Nar," replied Plimskit, his platoon-partner. "Who cares? Officers is officers. There's maybe a few good officers, plenty of bad officers, some terrible officers, but the one trouble with them all is that *they is officers*, right? And that means they work your arse off if you're lucky, and get you killed if you ain't, right? Come on, let's get up a game of krapph. There's a new fellow over in green-D, plenty of *skint* but no —"

"Don't feel like krapph. This Mashlawton, you know, dumb wozzet with a face like a rhomney's rump. Anyway, he's got the whole of blue-C building this *thing*. Sort of bag, 'bout the size of the Officer's Mess. Demons!"

Plumskit spat. "What they want a bag for? Carry away the corpses?"

"Nar. Too big for that. Mind you, if this war goes on much longer — anyway, as you'd expect, Mashlawton wasn't saying. But the scuttlebutt has it that von Hayashiko's going to fly like a bird." They both laughed. Then they went out to play krapph, won forty skint, and spent the lot on a flask of red tunket.

Next morning, with a head like a steam-hammer, Haboush found himself building what looked like a machine to roast syntei.

~~~

"More complicated than I'd hoped," Marco complained to Elzabet. "The synte tends to dry out when the bonfire gets going. It still works perfectly normally — more evidence for my metamaterial theory — but there's a fire risk, and we already know what that means. So we spray it with water synted from streams up in the hills. But then steam gets into the canopy. First time, all the glue came unstuck."

"The General won't wait," said Elzabet. "He wants a working prototype."

"Right now it's a prontotype, which is a prototype that's been put together too quickly for safety." Marco scratched his ear. "But this time I think I've got it sorted."

~~~

Two valleys away, under the watchful eye of a sergeant reporting to Marco by falasynte, green-D squad was throwing logs on a bonfire. Suspended over the top was a wyzand, mouth downwards. Yellow-K squad was directing sprays of water on to the wyzand, while trying hard not to put out the fire.

None of them had any idea why they should be doing this. Security, the officers claimed. Big Security. Typical army BS.

The bag blue-C squad had built was with Elzabet and Marco. Seventeen ropes were attached to it, some held by bored-looking soldiers.

The bag bulged nicely, growing visibly into an irregular dome, swaying in the wind. Higher still, and the base began to narrow. The giant pumpkin shape rose unsteadily, revealing an upturned wyzand. Below the wyzand was a woven basket.

"Stop!" yelled Marco. "Hold it right there!"

He gave Elzabet a quick kiss. "Looking good. Won't take long, this first time — just a quick test." He hopped into the basket.

After some shouting and confusion, the first hot-air balloon on Qish rose into the sky. Shakily, in fits and starts, its basket wobbling dangerously... but it flew. When Marco ordered the hot air flow cut, it even landed, with only superficial damage. His scrapes and bruises would heal. Already he was thinking out design improvements.

The big problem with a hot air balloon, as Marco had explained to anyone he could force to listen, is fuel for the burner. The answer is a bonfire on the ground, synting hot air into the canopy. Despite the gravity gradient, the air pressures balance and hot air still rises. Though it does take time to build up a good flow.

Another synte threw wind against a small sail, for propulsion and steering.

Crazy, anywhere except Qish.

Von Hayashiko ordered a squadron built, and started training an air force.

~~~

Tinka, Sam, and Jane often found themselves wishing for Marco's engineering skills. The glider design that had just managed to carry Tinka across the ocean to Bansh was not up to aerial warfare. They spent long hours modifying and testing parts, redesigning, and retesting everything on the ground, before it was ready for its first short flight.

Most of it survived, although several components had to be rebuilt. But eventually the glider started behaving as its pilot expected, and the worst reliability issues were fixed. Bonvisage was sufficiently impressed to order five more.

He also ordered the Starfolk to make an aerial survey of SVA territory. The glider might be noticed overhead, but he doubted the SVA would learn much useful from that. The urgent need for accurate information outweighed the possibility that the SVA would deduce the principles behind the glider. Jane agreed that this was very unlikely, especially with a few lightweight and pointless extras to disguise its logic. She didn't mention that the SVA didn't have wristcomps with aerodynamics software, so even if they tried it would take ages to design gliders that flew. Bonvisage didn't know about the 'comps, and no one was about to tell him.

In precaution, the survey glider carried a kasynte on a platform hung by cables, over a sheer two-klick drop. The operator watched a balance in the synte and kept the platform a little below the kantasynte in the glider, for safe transfer if necessary — unless enemy winds and mountains drove it too high or too low. Sam and Tinka designed pulleys to cope with rapid height changes, and a ballast sack matched to each of them, to throw off if they came through. They hadn't managed to scale up their toy parachute to human size.

The Starfolk moved the glider's wyzand-portable components to the Kuukau Front syntehead at Varynt, near the western end of the False Gloonts in Wevory and level with their cliff-top on the other side of the Equator. After reassembly Sam and Jane took off, and headed eastwards to the Krig range where the Gloont ranges met.

Sam's falasynte relayed their observations, via Varynt, to Bonvisage's operations centre back in Lamynt. Tinka's was direct to the platform operator.

"What's *that*?" said Sam. "Another glider?" Below them, something like a thirty-metre sail flew in long, slow loops. Circling over it, they realised it was alive.

"Cannot possibly stay aloft," muttered Tinka, "Too little lift for the weight."

"Only if it has to carry intestines. I'm not sure that creature even has lungs, where we can see them."

It slid downward on the air, close over a bird. As it rose again, the bird was gone. "Synted to the stomach," breathed Tinka. "Maybe it even *sees* through syntei."

They watched for long minutes, then turned away to count soldiers' tents, well hidden by camouflaged canvas walls against any view from the ground.

~~~

The initial survey flight landed safely back at Varynt with vital troop numbers. Bonvisage decided on a long one, launched from nearer the heavy fighting. High Bizzet and Tazzet, near the Krig Range, had recently fallen to the SVA, and subsequent advances had them now deep in secure SVA territory. How had the SVA troops disposed on the Pentully plains below? If their push cleared more of his synteheads, the Kuukau Front would lose the war.

Sam and Tinka set off before dawn, on a path to bring them over SVA territory when the morning sun was nearing the zenith. That would leave enough time to map out the main encampments, and return to base before it got dark.

"Or, we could fly to Krig Mountain by then," he said.

Tinka caught her breath.

"No," she said finally. "We'd arrive with no equipment. And they'd reinvent crucifixion, for Jane."

The weather was dry, with patches of thick cloud. They hopped from above one cloud bank to above another, whenever possible, to hide from any watchers below. When a cloud rose too high for the twin water-jet engines to push them up, they flew straight through it. No one had yet managed to invent syntelic radar, but they were the only flying-machine in the sky, with no risk of a mid-air collision. It would be a shame to hit a flying wing, but those would obviously just crumple. They had a magnetic compass, and a modified falasynte that used air pressure differences to estimate altitude. At the correct height and direction, flying through clouds posed no danger.

Sam was just explaining this to Tinka, on her third stint as pilot, when their glider emerged from a bank of cloud. Dead ahead, too close to dodge, was another aircraft. Not a glider; it looked for all the world like a hot air balloon.

Semi-coherent thoughts flashed through Tinka's mind as she instinctively manoeuvred to avoid the unexpected obstacle. *Not Kuukau Front... non-combatant?... factions allied to the SVA?... most likely the SVA itself.* She wrenched the controls hard over, but a wingtip sheared off as it brushed the balloon's bulging canopy. Next moment, the glider was spinning lower in slow, looping circles. As Jane shouted altitudes into the falasynte, and the landscape whirled around her, she saw the balloon falling too, apparently out of control. There was no time to synte out, a design flaw she had missed, not having expected a mid-air collision.

"Sam! Look for a place we can crash-land! Quick!"

Sam eyed the spinning ground, suppressing nausea. Browns, orange, a flat area that shimmered, white speckles on muddy blue with shapeless great patches —

"A lake right ahead!" Sam yelled. Tinka decided to ditch in the water, hoping there were no rocks, floating trees, or anything else to hit. In a cloud of spray they bounced across icy water, coming to a half-submerged standstill. They started to sink.

Sam had just scrambled out of the cockpit when the balloon hit the lake, not far away. Tinka followed him with the escape-koriel as the balloonist hit the water. Swimming away from the crumpled fabric mass forced him closer to their wreck.

The balloon hasn't caught fire, Tinka realised. *Fireproof?* She half noticed a silent *ping* in her head.

The balloonist was in a patch of thick weed, and all the lake shook with syntelic traffic: inquisitive predators, and fleeing prey. He uttered an incoherent cry for help.

Sam was in two minds — risk aiding the enemy, if that's what the man was, but maybe acquire useful information? — when he noticed the man's face.

It couldn't be.

"Marco! Great Mother, Tinka, it's Marco!" The whole scene blurred, and Sam had to wipe his eyes. He'd secretly been convinced Elza and Marco were dead.

"That's not possible," said Tinka. "Except... you're right. My 'comp's just linked to his.

"You're *right*!

"Marco!" she shouted, "What the skunt are *you* doing here?"

"Drowning," gasped Marco, as the waters and the teeth took him.

Sam plunged in, reached him, and dragged him ashore, both of them bleeding.

Marco found himself vomiting water on the grass, Tinka and Sam standing over him. A troop of SVA cavalry was galloping towards them along the beach.

"Elza with you?" Nod.

Sam shoved something into his hand. "Take this! Hide it!"

Marco stuffed the object into his pocket, still unable to think coherently. Tinka had set a koriel on the ground and was pressing her hand against its gravity-field. *Here comes the cavalry...* "Sam! It's open! Quick, through!"

Tinka and Sam disappeared through the oriel. Seconds later, it began to disintegrate, destroyed behind them. Marco's wrist prickled irritatedly at the loss of two newly acquired local nodes.

The riders halted in a cloud of snow crystals. Within minutes, Marco was on his way to their lakeside encampment, bandaged and wrapped in a blanket.

It was hours before he had the privacy to look at the object that Jane — it had *been* Jane, surely? He wasn't delirious, imagining things? — had thrust into his pocket.

It was a falasynte.

24

Plan B4

9/4124. H_2SiF_6
9/4125. $Ca_{10}(PO_4)_6F_2$
9/4126. $CaF_2 + H_2SO_4 \rightarrow CaSO_4 + 2HF$
9/4127. $Ca_{10}(PO4)_6(OH)_2$
9/4128. $Ca_{10}(PO4)_6F_2$
9/4129. $Ca_{10}(PO4)_6Cl_2$
9/4130. $Na_2CO_3 + 2HF \rightarrow 2NaF + CO_2 + H_2O$
9/4131. $Ca3(PO4)2 + CaF2 \rightarrow 2\ Ca5(PO4)3F$
—*The Starchild's Encyclopaedia of Chemical Kinetics and Molecular Structure*

In short bursts of hidden conversation, the five Starfolk caught up on what they had done, and seen, and the war, and the *bazza* crops.

Elza and Marco heard of Felix's death, with shock tinged by guilt. Fooling with body-division had brought the Church's retribution on everyone. Only kidnapping had saved their friends from the Quizitors' bone-hammers, and Felix had died.

When they said that, Jane disagreed.

"Save guilt for later, when we're all off this dump, dah? We all made mistakes. Felix's own misjudgement killed him. But the VV would likely have got us anyway."

"If you'd been free," said Elza, "the laser…?"

"Against a skilled syntelic ambush? Kurpershoek should have brought more men and kept a better lookout. Without the frames, they'd probably have got us earlier."

"The rest of us are alive, and soon we'll be together. That's enough for me. I miss Felix, I miss him terribly, but I can't *blame* anyone, even me. We're a team. We learn from errors, and move on."

They resumed their war-efforts with renewed energy.

~~~

The Selbstverteiligungsallianz had secured five peaks near the eastern end of the False Gloonts. Sifting for enemy syntei revealed nothing: their position seemed safe. Dug into a snowhole, SVA Squadman Marrigs' shakes were mainly from cold. And hunger.

Marrigs could have stood the hunger if only something would counter the bitter cold — and even Army food was warm, and hard to resist. Unfortunately, the still night air was very quiet. Rules said not to download food with any chance that the enemy might hear it hit. It didn't matter if there were no enemy troops within twenty klòvij: orders were orders, and you'd be disciplined if you got caught.

The trick was not to get caught. If you knew how, and were careful, you could silence the flow of food. He cast his eyes round guiltily. No one watching. Carefully he twisted the cap on his canteen. It was frozen, and it stuck. He twisted harder, and suddenly it gave. With a loud clang! food from the main camp, 700 vij higher, hit the metal wall. Marrigs swore silently.

Two minutes later an officer slid into the snowhole and began to chew him out for endangering the platoon by unnecessary noise. His voice never rose above a whisper during the entire performance, but Marrigs still found himself sweating.

Still, no enemy could reach them, even if they'd heard him from below.

As Marrigs sat uncomfortably in his snowhole, trying desperately to stay awake, five Kuukau Front gliders landed in snowfields high above him, on each of the five peaks. Five men had made the flights, but ten minutes later there were two thousand. The Kuukau Front overran the SVA's main camp, and the troops lower down the slopes were mown down with syntecannon.

Half a dozen similar raids convinced Bonvisage that the new equipment offered serious tactical advantages. But for their strategic potential, he'd have to build himself an air force. He ordered glider production trebled, and a task force of senior officers to organise pilot training.

Then he started drawing up more ambitious plans.

~~~

Marco turned the corner and almost bumped into Elza, who was carrying a large bunch of vegetables like dirty grey doughnuts.

"Careful! These things cost me a fortune on the black market!"

"Sorry. Going into the grocery business, Elza?"

"In a way, yah. Healthy, thriving *bazza*-roots, imported by black-marketeers from one of the few places in Lamynt where they still grow — a trickle of water still comes from the opening of the old underground river. These are in very short supply and high priced. I've set up a small lab to study why the roots keep dying when grown with Wevorin water, instead of what used to come from Lamynt." She shrugged. "Faint hope, but it keeps me busy while you're aiding the war effort building balloons."

"It's mostly the soldiers doing that now. I just supervise."

"Dah. I decided to try some basic horticulture in pots, in different kinds of soil and compost, and different additives to the water. I have a hunch that some mineral in the Lamynt water is missing in Telvet. After that earthquake, even Lamynt has so little suitable water that they don't export it any more. Unfortunately that means no samples of that kind of Lamynt water, for me to analyse. I had no end of problems getting these roots as it was. It does take a while for *bazza* to die when you grow it in the wrong water, but once these run out I'll have to buy another batch. If I can."

That evening, by hidden falasynte with Jane, Marco mentioned Elza's venture. They had barely signed off when the membrane vibrated again. Jane's voice: "Let me talk to Elza." She came to the hiding place.

"Elza, you're a geologist. I've remembered something that might mean something to you. That randy little sod Plocknicki told it to me during a truce — him and me, not the war. He said Lamynt water tasted better than anything on Wevory."

Elza thought about that. "It does tend to confirm there are mineral differences, but there always are in water from different sources. Thanks, anyway —"

"He told me Lamynt water is good for your teeth."

Elza was sceptical. "That sounds like an old husbands' tale to me! In the Concordat, when someone has tooth decay it's generally sugar addiction. I doubt that Telvet water is high in sugar!"

Later that day, it struck Elza that she didn't actually know *why* tooth decay was rare in the Concordat. She knew it had been a problem on Old Earth, but she'd always assumed that something about the Starfolk diet had eradicated dental caries. Or gene mods, or mouth bacteriome...

She asked her 'comp if it had anything on the subject.

"Nothing except the obvious," it chanted in her inner ear.

"Assume I don't know the obvious."

"You must be aware that the main reason for the absence of tooth decay in the Concordat is fluoridated water, which dates back to the first societies on New Earth?"

"Nah, news to me. What's a florri date?"

"*Flu-or-i-dated.*"

"Oh, right. Added fluorides. Vaguely familiar, now you mention it."

"Fluorine atoms enter tooth enamel, strengthening it. They've been adding the stuff for so long, nobody ever mentions it any more."

Elza's geochemical instincts were aroused. "*Which* fluoride compounds?"

"Sodium fluoride. Disodium hexafluorosilicate."

At the back of Elza's mind, bells were ringing. "Bring up the geological survey I did from *Valkyrie*, just before it crashed." The 'comp projected the image on the wall. "Zoom in on the catchment area of the river Sumtry, north of the Greywraiths. Yah, that's it. Now, show me dry channels. *Fascinating*. Right by that purple area. Zoom in on that. There's an unusual deposit, can't recall what those symbols stand for."

"Villiaumite," the 'comp sang.

"Oh. In my freshman year... but it's such a rare mineral they never mentioned it again. Remind me me about it."

"A halite mineral, rare because of high solubility in water. Translucent red in colour, much like a ruby. Found in nepheline syenite intrusives and pegmatites. Often associated with aegirine, chkalovite, eudialyte, lamprophyllite —"

"Nah, you idiot. What's it made from?"

The 'comp stopped abruptly in mid-flow. "Sodium fluoride."

"Could it get into water flowing into those dry beds?"

"It would have been difficult for it not to. Same area, same height."

"And the new springs are lower." She began framing more specific questions.

~~~

Jane and Marco were conferring covertly. If either was caught, they'd probably be executed as a spy. So Marco was squatting damply in a small cave behind a waterfall, and Jane was half way up a cliff face, allegedly testing a new type of rope.

"Jane, how do you stop a war?"

"I really have no idea, Marco."

"But you're our expert on exotic cultures." *Felix is gone...*

"Ending a war is mainly a political problem but with social and military components. My speciality is alien resource flows, not quite the same thing."

"Nah, but there must be some universal principles."

Jane moved her legs for comfort. "Well, I did study some Old Earth history. It's a baseline from which to define 'alien', you see. Basically, the further away from it a society shifts, the more alien it becomes. But Lamynt society is actually very close to Old Earth's, so xenology training doesn't really help."

Marco's mind was heading another way. "So how did Old Earth stop its wars?"

"Well... Fairly often, when one side won. The Hitler War, for example, which he lost. Didn't always do the winners much good, mind you."

"And if no one looked like winning?"

"Usually, when one side or the other ran out of money. Often both."

"So instead of trying to win the war for one side or the other, we should actually be wrecking their economies?"

"Even harder. Basically, you're trying to win an economic war instead of a military one. I don't see that gets us any further."

A plan, starting to assemble dimly in Marco's head, offered an answer. "You get to use different weapons."

"Before you get too carried away, there's a more fundamental issue. We can't just wreck their economies. Add economic collapse to the failure of the *bazza* crop on *both* sides, and we'll just end up killing millions through starvation when what little food supply they do still have can't be distributed effectively any more. That's too high a price. We have to solve the food shortage."

Marco peered out through the waterfall to make sure the coast was clear. "Did Sam tell you Elza was working on that?"

"Yah. Says she's turned into a horticultural researcher. Forever fiddling about with *bazza* roots and chemicals."

"That's right. I'm going to find out what results she's getting. Talk to you tomorrow, same time." Marco signed off.

~~~

Elza was bubbling over with excitement.

"I was just coming to find you! Come and see my latest batch of *bazza* plants. Over here." She led the way through her improvised laboratory to a row of racks, filled with pots. "Those!" One group of pots contained thick bunches of orange fronds. The rest were brown and dying, or dead.

"Grown in ordinary Telvet water," said Elza. "Plus my special secret additive."

"Impressive," said Marco. "What additive?"

"Sodium fluoride seems to be an essential mineral for healthy *bazza* roots. The water synted to Telvet must have had it in solution. The rivers here don't — and nor does the Sumtry, with the main underground tributary dried up. The black market in Lamynt uses small streams that bubble out of the mountainside, from springs.

"My survey from before we crashed showed a deposit of villiaumite in Lamynt, smack bang over the place where that underground river must have originated."

"Villiaumite?"

"A highly soluble mineral, like common salt but sodium *fluo*ride, not chloride. I figured just possibly, it was the secret ingredient in Lamynt water.

"I decided to use my growing experience in amateur horticulture to test whether my guess was correct. But that needed the fluoride. There's no way to reach the villiaumite — it's deep underground in enemy territory, with no mines. So like a good geochemist I made my own — with the 'comp's help. First I found apatite in my survey. Not as rare as villiaumite, and Wevory has some accessible deposits. I got some, ground it fine, and added sulphuric acid. The fluorine ions come from fluorapatite, a naturally occurring impurity. Calcium fluorophosphate —"

"Too much detail, Elza. But go on."

"(Serves you right.) That gave me hydrofluoric acid. Now, with that you make sodium fluoride by neutralising it with sodium hydroxide or sodium carbonate. I had to use carbonate, they don't make hydroxide on Qish. After that, just dump in some alcohol to precipitate the fluoride. No shortage of alcohol."

"And then you tried it on *bazza*, and the roots grew."

"Yah. The process is really basic, scales up easily to industrial levels. Or they can mine for villiaumite once peace is declared. Better still: I can experiment for the optimal concentration, now I know I'm not going to kill off my *bazza*. I can even grow some from seed. It only takes a few months."

Marco looked like a *skiti* creeping up on a potato mountain. *Roast* potato.

~~~

"So, aided and abetted by Sam, you'll stop Wevory making balloons and Lamynt making gliders?" Elza couldn't quite see it, but that might bring the war to a close.

"Nah," said Marco. "Sam and I convince both sides to make thousands of them. As many as they can possibly squeeze out of their slowly failing economies." He grinned. "Not only fliers. These people are smart. Sam says that Lamynt's strategists have already come up with all sorts of new tactics, even before they get full fleets. The young officers began to figure it out as soon as they started small-scale incursions.

"Balloons here are naturally stealthed: the heat source only makes its noise on the far side of a synte at the bottom of a chimney. So they get round a height gap by slipping in a syntehead, and pour in men via rope ladders to a balloon tethered way above their base.

"Lamynt can sneak in one-man gliders, but it's harder to up-level with them. Then there are steerable synte searchlights for night fighting, anti-aircraft syntguns... but syntguns don't work without a higher arsenal, so the high mountaintops can't have them, and fighting is back to sticking sharp metal in the other guy's gut. So, armour...

"All sorts of subsidiary industries are starting up, adding even more to the economic burden. Massive effort, needs a lot of manpower... They're getting overstretched. Soon they'll have to abandon all non-essential production and focus exclusively on the war-effort."

Elza had been listening in growing outrage. "You idiot! That'll just make the war worse! Instead of getting a few thousand people killed, you'll slaughter lakhs. Crores!" Marco had gone mad. "What are you planning to do: exterminate both sides?"

"I'd do that if I had no alternative," he admitted. "Whatever it takes to get news of syntei to Starhome. But —" before she exploded again — "what I have in mind is the exact opposite. Have faith in uncle Marco, he's not turned into a monster. Yet. Let me unveil the Bianchi Peace Plan.

"Jane told me the way to stop a war is to wreck the participants' economies." She hadn't actually said that clean out, but it had been the main residue of their brainstorming. "Your stroke of genius solves the starvation problem, once the fighting stops. What I want to do is put those two together. Stop the war, feed the people."

Elza waited.

"Oh, yah. How? Sam and I are going to get both sides to invest all of their efforts into building up the biggest, most spectacular, most powerful air forces this planet can support. We build thousands of balloons, they build thousands of gliders."

Elza felt that something was missing. "Marco, that will just end up in intercontinental mayhem."

Marco shook his head. "Ah. But not while they're in the construction phase, building up their aerial squadrons. They'll risk losing assets prematurely. Especially when their spies tell them that the other side is also building like crazy."

Finally, Marco was approaching some sense. "You and Sam being the spies."

"If we have to. But I'm sure they have plenty of their own already."

"Even so, one side or the other will eventually run out of cash and be forced to mount an all-out attack. Probably both."

"Yah, they will."

"At which point Armageddon will be unleashed."

Marco grinned. "Looks that way, doesn't it? You're absolutely right, that's exactly what would happen." Pause. "Were it not for Plan B4."

"Plan B4?" It did sound vaguely familiar, but it was also typical Marco obscurity. "I hate it when you go all cryptic on me. Out with it!"

"Sure, sure, calm down. Remember pre-flight training, a lifetime or two ago?"

"If I squat and think. It was a lot to take in. Memo-hypnosis notwithstanding, so much has happened since that it's not exactly at the forefront of my mind."

"Mine neither, until now. The Instructor for Strategy and Tactics?"

"Um. Oh, right. Plan B4 is what comes *be-fore* Plan A."

"You're getting warm. What is Plan A?"

"Both sides commit their entire economic output to vast air forces to slaughter civilian populations. I see that. What I don't see is Plan B4."

"Nah, you don't" said Marco. "I hope the same goes for Bonvisage and von Hayashiko. Until it's too late."

Elza was getting very frustrated. "Presumably you've told Sam or Jane or Tinka more than you're telling me."

"Sam knows just enough to carry out his part. Jane and Tinka hardly know anything. The less anyone knows, the less can be extracted from them under interrogation. The same goes for you, my love."

"But you're going to tell me anyway."

"Absolutely not — dah, I give in. Stop that. Not the full details. Just don't breathe a word to a soul. Plan B4 is that just before the big attack, whoever blinks first, something stops it. And stops the other side's counter-attack."

"Easier said than done."

"Yah, but I know how to do it. Elza, I'm an engineer. I was involved in every stage of Wevory's balloon fleet. I've been in contact with Sam and the others, the whole time they've been overseeing the construction of Lamynt's glider fleet.

"Mother, it's been a bore. Now: what do bored engineers on big projects do to amuse themselves when they've been working their arses off for big-headed dingbat bosses, deep in the night when there's no one around?"

Elza made suggestions, not all obscene. Marco waved a dismissive hand.

"Dah, smartypants. What *do* bored overworked undervalued engineers do?"

"They build in a back door," he told her.

Elza's face was a picture as she worked out what he meant. "I sort of see. Be more explicit."

"A secret way to get inside and tinker. Unknown to officialdom. Most solitronic nanocircuits have back-door software, anything from a cute cartoon clip to a holvix of the boss cavorting with her mistresses... and a remote access. For fun, or just in case. Ready to be activated at a moment's notice. Great way to avoid being fired."

"Got it. So what was your back door?"

Marco refused to answer. Elza tried every weapon in her formidable armoury, hitting a brick wall every time. Marco could be very stubborn when he aimed to be.

~~~

Sam's antennae twitched. Bonvisage had called a Council of War. Neither he, Jane, nor Tinka was party to it, but the resulting activity gave the game away. He called the falasynte in the bedroom Marco shared with Elza, after the usual listening for strangers.

"Lamynt is about to launch an all-out attack on Wevory."

The words hung in the air, like the smell of death. All their plans had been directed to this, but there is no real triumph in raising a simmering war to boiling point.

"It's what we wanted, people," Marco said. "No choice." He looked infinitely weary. "The top brass over here have been running around in headless chicken mode, clucking away like demented — "

"Marco, dear: headless chickens don't cluck."

"Thank you, Elza, for that bracing dose of sanity. Their heads are synted somewhere. So von Hayashiko will be pushing through his final preparations before the enemy forces attack *us*. Which means that it's time —"

"For Plan B4. Whatever that is."

"Exactly. And I'm still not telling you."

~~~

The Wevorin balloon squadrons were in three Groups: one near Vunt, two in the north-east at Menisma and Sish. Lamynt's gliders were in four Flights, near Varynt, Brundoon, Peremynt, and Twent. All at low, wide open spaces. Most had secure mountains close by.

The maps in their 'comps had found Marco and Sam accessible, secure sites in their own territories, slightly higher than the enemy forces.

Less than half a day after the news, both were in place, armed with crossbows and arrows, covert falasyntei, and bulging backpacks.

Opening his, Marco propped a dozen saucer-shaped kasyntei in a row. Sam did the same.

Each struck a match, lit a fire-arrow, and shot it through a kasynte. Smoothly, they repeated this. Twelve kasyntei were probably overkill — Marco and Sam had tested visually where they all led — but engineers like to build in redundancy as a safeguard. And this *had* to work. If it failed, they were all dead.

Soon, all of Marco's kasyntei were emitting thick smoke, backlit by a flickering orange glow. One by one they shrivelled to charcoal. Sam reported the same.

Task done, they made their way back to their companions, taking care to be bustling about as usual, to tell them that Plan B4 was a success. And to explain it.

~~~

"So Plan B4 was to use your back door."

"*Doors*, actually. Sheep, lamb, hung, right?"

"Concealed kasyntei in balloons and gliders. You and Sam kept kantasyntei. "

"Yah. Buried away, deep inside vital equipment."

"Qishi tech being what it is, everything is highly inflammable."

"Enough of it, yah."

"Why did you install the kasyntei? Had you thought of Plan B4 that far back?"

"Absolutely not. I'd like to claim clairvoyance, but I can't, any more than the Concordat plans how to use the override installed in every Da Silva drive it licences — and that means all of them. It just seemed good to have a back door in case of need. We might have escaped that way with the old rolled-synte trick, if we'd found a source of the flexible ones."

As Elza and Marco spoke, the entire balloon-fleet of Wevory, and almost every glider on Lamynt, were being reduced to ashes. Neither side had experience of aerial warfare, and it had not occurred to them to avoid concentrating their assets too close together. Bonvisage and von Hayashiko watched in total disbelief as their air forces and their careers went up in flames, and their national economies crashed and burned.

~~~

After that, it was really just a matter of wrapping it all up.

The first few days were tense. The Starfolk, as outsiders, naturally came under suspicion, but neither side could see why their group of strangers would have worked so assiduously to help them win the war, only to wreck their own creations. The evidence had all been incinerated, and no one on Qish had the expertise to mount an effective disaster investigation. Sorting out the mess was more important than discovering who'd caused it, and the military leaders on both sides were desperately trying to rescue their reputations. The easy option was to blame it all on sabotage by some dissident group — possibly pacifists.

Or, more likely...

The most popular theory directed attention away from the Generals and anyone connected with them (such as tall dark strangers), so the military did their best to lend it credence. It was also the most plausible explanation, despite being totally wrong. Namely, a plot by the elusive and inscrutable Wevorin cavern-dwellers, fed up with military action on their turf.

Whatever the cavern-dwellers were up to, a war wasn't going to make it easier.

Since none of this could be proved, and little could be done about it anyway, efforts quickly centred on dealing with the aftermath of the fire. That took three months of wall-to-wall committee meetings, briefings, discussions, fluoride chemistry, agronomics, heated arguments, threats, poisonings, concessions, scientific demonstrations... and finally, an elaborate signing ceremony for the Lamynt-Wevory Peace Treaty. Mines with syntelic short cuts were dug. Solid fluoride exports through surviving wyzands replaced the dilute torrent of the *status quo ante bellum*. Sociable pigs grew fat.

As Marco said by falasynte: a peace of cake. Like so much he said, Lomyrla didn't get it. The others wished they hadn't.

25

Cavern-Dwellers

A traveller to the Gate of the Dawn met the beautiful maiden Muumani. Many months had he voyaged, for men said she held a miraculous mirror, in which he might behold all the universe.

"Yar," quoth Muumani. "But thou wouldst not wish to see it."

But the traveller beseeched Muumani, "Show me this wonder." And he made promises of topaz and malachite and mother-of-pearl. Then did Muumani fetch forth the miraculous mirror, swathed in coarse cloths.

"I would gaze upon the universe," said the traveller. "Remove the cloths."

"Nar," quoth Muumani. "Thou shouldst not, I warn thee."

But the traveller entreated her further, with promises of furs and fine cloths, rare perfumes and spices, and the red gold of lands beyond the mists. "So be it," said Muumani sadly; and she drew back the coarse cloths. The traveller gazed upon the miraculous mirror in which a man might behold the entire universe.

"You have cheated me," said the traveller. "I see only my own face."

"What else," asked Muumani, "might one expect to see in a mirror? Yet have I not cheated thee." And she pricked him with a poisoned thorn.

"Thus perishes thy universe," said Muumani, and returned to her loom.

—*The Allegory of the Deceitful Maidens, Scroll 182*

Five kilometres high on Krig Mountain, especially during the Season of Snows, even the best-equipped could be buried by an avalanche, drop in a crevasse, or freeze solid in a blizzard. Or fall through crumbling ice to the jagged rocks far below.

The five figures trudging through the snow were painfully aware of danger, and their calculated risk. They planned to locate their objective while the weather held, activate it, and beat a rapid retreat two kilometres down to the wyzand they had come through. But they had done their best to prepare for mountain dangers. They had spent days upon frustrating days at lower heights, adjusting to the lower oxygen. They wore thick jackets of *rhunka*-fur, deeply hooded and double-lined, with trousers of oiled slarskin tucked into padded boots. Their outer gloves were softened leather, with knitted mittens beneath; darkened glass shielded their eyes from the glare of sun on snow. Their packs contained two slarskin tents, ample provisions, utensils, sleepsacks.

Marco carried a device of blown glass. At intervals he inspected it intensely.

"Any sign?" Sam asked.

"Sort of," Marco replied, gazing about him.

They were at the bottom of a snow-covered depression. On three sides, steep cliffs hemmed them in, with enormous icicles in fantastic patterns. On the fourth, their snowfield dropped straight to the rocks.

"Ice," said Tinka. "Heights. Me with no wings. Take me home, please."

The sky was a deep blue-green, almost cloudless. Marco frowned. "The leaves are wide apart, as if we were right on top. But you couldn't miss something that big!"

"Under the snow?" Tinka suggested.

"I doubt it," said Sam. He thrust a thin pole into the ground, probing. "Feels solid under here, not far down. Not like near the cliffs, where snow goes down forever. But Marco got no signals near the cliffs."

Marco grunted assent. Talking in the thin, cold air was hard work, though they had taken time to acclimatise before attempting the ascent. "The instrument must have gone wrong. It was trouble enough fudging it up to begin with."

"Not much choice, was there?" said Sam.

"Nah, but — Mother! Detecting solitronic fields with a gold-leaf electroscope!" Marco looked mortified.

Elza, trudging beside him, shook her head. "You're a skilled engineer, and there's nothing wrong with the instrument. It's too *simple* to have some obscure fault. About the only thing that could go wrong is the vacuum, and that obviously hasn't. Anyway, the spare says exactly the same as that one. And according to *Valkyrie*'s observations before we crashed, noted right here on my 'comp, this is the place."

"Agreed. Except it's not. Show me the rescue beacon."

Valid. Right now, Elzabet could not answer, but she still thought she was right.

"Maybe the rocks are distorting the field?" Tinka suggested.

"Shouldn't. Only thick metallic ore could do that. The rock here is limestone."

"Yah." Marco checked. "*Valkyrie* saw no deposits in this area, either."

Elzabet bridled. "Doubting my geological expertise, ignorant peasant?"

"Nah, Elza: just double-checking."

Sam slapped his hands together. "Trash it, it's *cold* up here. Why in the name of cosmic maternity did they dump the beacon on the highest mountain on this continent?"

"Safe from prying eyes, Marco. Entirely logical."

"Rubbish!"

"Oh, she's back. See anything from the ridge, Jane?"

"Not a thing. And it's nothing to do with prying eyes, Sam love. A four-metre Da Silva dome on a conical base, painted bright yellow, is not designed to escape notice. Not close. And that, my friends, is why it was dumped here. As far as possible from Shaaluy, where the colonists first came down. As far as possible from anywhere it might be disturbed by animals, floods, and other forces of nature. Not a lot happens at the top of a mountain."

"Except blizzards."

"Tell me about it."

They trudged on through the knee-deep snow, kicking it aside in powdery lumps as they lifted their feet.

Jane, taking her turn in the lead, suddenly stopped.

"Weird," she said. Wide twin tracks crossed their path, a short step apart, and deeply indented in the snow.

"If we weren't on Qish," said Tinka, "I'd say these were made by some sort of snowmobile. Jane — could an animal make tracks like this?"

"I suppose it might — feet with wide pads, making overlapping footprints... But these marks don't look like that."

"Nah. A sledge? Bit wide for skis."

"No prints of pullers. Look, there's more of them!" Half a dozen pairs of parallel tracks braided the valley floor, disappearing behind ridges of windblown snow.

"Stay alert, people," said Sam. "We may have company." But the tracks soon disappeared behind them, and the snow was once more pristine.

~~~

"*Now* look," said Marco in exasperation. "The leaves have closed up again." He rotated the electroscope slowly. "I swear we've just walked right through it."

They stared at the featureless snowfield.

"Ordinarily speaking," said Elza, "one of us would be pointing out that whenever something baffling happens on Qish, it's down to syntei. But I can't think of any syntelic trickery that would make something that big invisible."

"Metamaterials," Marco muttered. "Cloaking device?"

"Like you said, we'd've walked through it. You can cloak optics, but you can't cloak touch. Again, ordinarily, if any of us tries to explain weirdness on this planet by something hidden underground, the rest of us groan that they're not imaginative enough. But on this occasion," she grimaced, "I'm convinced that we've walked right over the top of it." Seeing their faces, she went on: "I do realise the snow's not deep enough. So it's in a cavern. This is karst geology, it's riddled with holes. The locals have more superstitions about cavern-dwellers than Old Earth has governments."

"Yah, you'd think them the local equivalent of the abominable snowhag."

"We know better, though. Gus was adamant that the cavern-dwellers posed a serious threat to Shaaluy."

"All well and good," Marco objected, "but that's Gus's problem. We've got a more personal one. How could a large, heavy rescue beacon get inside a cavern?"

"Maybe a giant synte gobbled it up —"

"And then got blocked by a rockfall? The cliffs are too far away. Anyway, there are no syntei large enough."

"Maybe the cavern-dwellers moved it."

"Underground? With nothing but Quishi tech? Those things weigh *tonnes*!"

"Stop arguing," said Jane. "We'll have to dig for it, if Elzabet's correct. I think she is." The freshening wind whipped up a flurry of powdered snow. Grey clouds, having appeared from nowhere, slid across the sun. "But not right now."

"Nah, bad weather coming," said Tinka. "Let's camp." They headed for the comparative shelter of the cliffs.

"It isn't *just* rock under here," said Jane, pointing to a deep crevasse on their left as the snowfield neared the cliff wall. "Maybe the beacon fell down a crevasse."

"Nah, the autopilot would have avoided anything that wasn't solid."

A slender ice bridge spanned the gulf, leading to a route round the left cliff. The way to the right was clear of crevasses, and Sam declared the ground solid.

They pitched their tents in the lee of the rock, tucked under an overhang to guard against a possible avalanche.

Sam primed the stove with graffyd-oil from a leather flask, lit with one of the large Twentish matches. As the clouds gathered, they ate. Huddled for warmth, Sam and Tinka in one tent, the others in the second, they dozed while the blizzard raged.

The wind dropped, the snow settled, and a huge amber moon peeped though straggled clouds. Marco woke to a throaty snuffling sound, like irregular breathing. Elza or Jane must be getting a cold.

Except…

He could *feel* Elza and Jane breathing. They didn't match the rhythm. The hairs on his neck prickled. The sound was from *outside* the tent.

Silently he roused the other two. Jane readied her laser medallion and cautiously peered out of the tent. Some twenty metres away, a pale shape was edging over the newly fallen snow. It was about the size of a sheep, the same off-white colour, and woolly. But there the resemblance ended.

The beast had no legs. Instead, it seemed to *flow* across the snow. But not wriggling like a snake; more like surfing an invisible wave. The motion was smooth, and whatever drove it was hidden by the snow. The creature's head boasted a single central eye, surmounted by a structure that might be an ear. Its face tapered to a long, flexible snout, which writhed.

"So *that's* what made those tracks," said Sam. "It *was* animals."

"Some sort of herd?" Jane mused.

"Herd suggests herbivores," Elza pointed out. "Predators often hunt in packs."

"Yah. Wonder what they eat."

"There's nothing up here unless they can survive on snow and rocks. But geography doesn't mean a lot on this world."

Their eyes followed the twin trails back to the edge of the crevasse. The animal flowed closer to the cliff. The motion was eerily silent, just a slight swishing sound and the low crunch of compressing snow.

"What on Qish does it *eat*?" whispered Jane.

"*Shhhh*! It might be us!"

"Nah, Marco, it's no carnivore."

"If it's a herbivore it won't find much up here."

"Ditto carnivore, Yah? Nah, it breeds up here for safety and makes forays down into the valleys to stock up," said Jane. "Or it has a symbiotic syntelic link to warmer mountains on the equator. Who knows? Now be quiet, I want to watch."

Elza slipped soundlessly into the other tent and awoke Sam and Tinka.

The creature reached the cliff and probed the rock with its proboscis. Suddenly it plunged the snout into a hole in the cliff. Slurping sounds ensued.

"It's eating *something*," said Jane. "Lichens, grubs — who knows what's in that hole, or what it's connected to?" They watched the strange spectacle.

Without warning the snowfield erupted. Half a dozen shapes hurtled out of a snowbank and flung themselves upon the beast, uttering terrifying howls. Limbs rose and fell, crystal claws slashed. Spattered violet blood defaced the pristine whiteness. The beast screeched in agony, struggled, and was still.

They suddenly realised what these attackers were. At the same moment, the oddly-garbed human hunters noticed the tents, and the five gawping Starfolk.

Everything happened very quickly.

Jane raised her hand to fire. Before she could bring the medallion to bear, a hunter hurled something at her legs and she crashed to the ground, taking Marco with her. Three hunters leaped on them. Two more grabbed Elzabet, who yelled at Sam and Tinka to run. From snow level Marco saw Sam grab a pack in one hand and Tinka in the other, and heard Elzabet shouting about the crevasse. Then a pad impregnated with something sweet-smelling and horrible was clamped over his face. He heard a distant roaring, then nothing.

~~~

The lighting was weird.

In fact, *everything* was weird.

The cavern was immense, a hundred or more metres long, sloping down towards her. A stream burbled along the wall. The roof dripped stalactites of every form and size, some delicate cylinders, some strangely fluted and twisted. Here a stalagmite cluster merged in a shape like an ancient pagoda, tied to the roof by a dozen slender pillars; there a row of organ-pipes became a calcite curtain of frozen drapery. Water trickled into crystal pools.

The floor was live grass, with occasional clusters of tiny blue flowers. Two brilliant blue-green birds with orange beaks perched side by side on a stalagmite. Forty or fifty smaller birds splashed in a rock-pool like rowdy children.

Creepers twined up the cavern's rocky walls, winding around and between pillars of stone. In the distance she could see trees.

The air was moist, with a gentle, warm breeze.

Cool turquoise illumination shimmered in strange patterns: bright streamers of light over rock and grass, birds and flowers, that met and separated with an almost regular rhythm that somehow never repeated. It was oddly soothing.

The chains that bound her to a thick stalagmite were less so. Jane made a futile attempt to break free.

"Don't waste your energy."

"Marco?"

"Yah. I'm behind you, to your left. Elzabet is between us — unconscious, but I can see her breathing. How do you feel?"

"Terrible. That stuff they put over my face — urgh. I've got a head like a dinosaur's hangover. Otherwise I'm fine."

"Can you see Sam or Tinka?"

She strained her neck as far as it would reach. "Nah."

"Good. Maybe they got away. There's a chance—" He was interrupted by a groan. "Elza! *Wake up!* It's me, Marco!"

Elzabet, plainly still dazed, struggled against the chains. "My legs! I can't move! Sam, run! Run! The crevasse! Use the — oh, Mother, *naaaaah!*"

"Elza! *Wake up!* It's over!" The struggles ceased abruptly.

"Marco? Is that you?"

"Yah. You're safe now. Jane's here too. We've been captured, again. The folk in funny clothes who came out of the snow, remember? We're hoping Sam and Tinka got away, there's no sign —"

"Oh, Mother," said Elzabet. "You think they *got away*? I *saw* them, trying to escape across the crevasse. The bridge collapsed and they fell in. Then a mass of snow came down and obliterated everything."

"You're certain of that?"

"I *saw* it, I tell you. They're dead, Marco, *dead*! First Felix, now Sam and Tinka! I can't *take* it any more!" She began to weep.

It won't take much for Jane to join her, Marco thought. *Me too*. He tried to direct their attention to more constructive ends. "Jane, this lighting is peculiar. I've seen something like it before, but I can't place it."

"Underwater."

"That's it! Not what you'd expect in a cavern."

"*Are* we underwater?" asked Elzabet, trying to recover some of her composure.

"Well," said Marco, "it's damp, I'll concede, but I don't recall stalactites as a common underwater formation. Or fish with feathers. This looks like air."

"You idiot. I mean, is this *place* below water *level*?"

"Could be, I suppose. More likely not: I'm still straining to breathe, and the lighting is too uniform, sort of *artificial*. Must be synted sunlight; and I'd guess it's the places it's synted *from* are underwater. Light is about all that can go far upsynte."

Something touched Marco's shoulder. Startled, he turned his head sideways.

Wicked-looking knife.

A hand plucked at his chains, and they loosened. Crystal pricked his throat, and he stumbled a pace to one side.

There were six, all swathed in bands of cloth and fur, seemingly haphazardly, with feet and arms bare. Each had several transparent knives at his waist. One had a loop of rope, weighted at each end. Heads were shaved except at the top, where a long tuft was braided and coiled, its end secured to an ear-lobe by a bone stud carved as a flower. The other ear was pierced for a small yellow stone pendant like an egg. Each man's left thigh had a blue band with a white patch; all save one had rectangular patches, but the apparent leader sported one in the same flower-shape as the ear-studs.

Jane and Elzabet were linked up behind Marco, and their captors led them across the grass to a tunnel concealed behind a curtain of creeper. The tunnel twisted to the left, spiralling steeply up to an oriel. They passed through.

~~~

An old man sat cross-legged on a triangular rug, sewn from the skins of yearling drift-orms, beside the trunk of an ancient, gnarled tree that drooped almost to the ground. A niche in the trunk contained a yellow topaz egg the size of a fist, and an ivory flower, bright against the dark swirls of the grain. The ear-stud securing his hair was grey, thrice-coiled, and braided into an intricate pattern. Such was fitting for one of his profundity, a *jûnquire* of the twenty-eighth tier, blazoned Ochre Wedge, only eight steps above Her Nethermost.

The *jûnquire* teased the bundle into order, pulling knotted cords between his bony fingers. The mediary watched patiently as the ancient deciphered the mystery of knots. A mere Amethyst Crescent of the fifteenth tier, the mediary could not comprehend such Depths, but it was both informative and mandatory to observe the actions of a dweller Deeper than himself. In case the opportunity to poison him arose.

The knots unburdened themselves of the message they encoded. A routine hunting-party in search of skins, rousing dormant drift-orms and trapping them with honey-bait, had encountered a party of five strangers close to the Miracle Shaft. Three had been captured, and the remaining two had — an unusual choice of knot, signifying virtual but not absolute certainty of death.

Guidance must be sought.

"Mediary? There is not time for me to embraid a quipu. Compose for a verbal message. Inform your sustentor, it is well. To maintain affairs in current mode, pending recommendations from those Deeper. Go!" The mediary bowed and departed.

Strangers on Krig Mountain? Curious, disturbing. The *jûnquire* unlocked a cabinet inlaid with sequences from *The Allegory of the Deceitful Maidens*, and extracted a falasynte. Raising it to his mouth he uttered a high-pitched warble.

Heartbeats passed. "You have news?" The voice from the falasynte was deep, but quavered. Even a Saffron Hoop cannot live forever. Her Nethermost the Colloquist was fast nearing contingency. But it was premature to speculate on her replacement.

The *jûnquire* repeated the information, making a point of the node of death-doubt. "The strangers are said to have plunged into a crevasse. The disturbance precipitated a snow-slide, burying them utterly."

"Nevertheless, they are as yet merely *presumed* dead," the Colloquist insisted.

The *jûnquire* detected a mild rebuke. "I shall seek confirmation, Nethermost,"

"Strangers in our domain must die to preserve the Way of the Dwellers. Yet the presence of these strangers so near the Miracle Shaft may not be accident. We must watch lest outsiders have learned of the prophecies.

"Ascertain their purpose before their deaths. Until then, keep them secure, and destroy all syntei they carried.

"Three days are given you."

~~~

The two objects of the Colloquist's scepticism would have agreed with the *jûnquire* that they were buried utterly: their world was bounded by fallen ice.

The snow-bridge broke beneath Tinka's feet, in a moment of total clarity: *this is it*. Then the world disappeared in a confusion of ice-crystals. She missed a jagged spike of rock by a centimetre, never knowing it; then a steeply inclined slope of sheer, smooth ice deflected her fall, *across* the yawning gulf beneath and under an overhanging shelf of hard ice. Her foot snapped a cluster of icicles as she hurtled upside down through the air and slammed into a thick snowbank.

Sam was slightly less lucky: he hit the ice-slope awkwardly, jarred his ankle, and hit the same snowbank headfirst. Then the avalanche dumped a thousand tonnes into the crevasse. The overhang protected them from the main fall, though the air was thick with powdered snow. The silence as the avalanche ceased was almost tangible.

"Are we," said Tinka in a choking voice, "nearly there yet?"

She extricated herself, and helped Sam out of his tangle of ice-blocks. Their alcove was barely half a dozen metres long, and two high. Fallen ice hemmed them in completely, although light glimmered through a cleft. Too narrow to put a hand through, tens of metres deep.

"Dead?" replied Sam. "Yah, nearly. Near killed, and near to freeze to death. Still," he said bleakly, "that beats bone-hammers."

While Tinka bound Sam's twisted ankle, they took stock. The pack Sam had grabbed contained food, a flask of oil, spare clothing, and a bundle of wooden tent-pegs. Sam found matches in a pocket. His knife was still in his belt.

Tinka contributed a notepad that lacked a stylus, and a roll of linen bandages.

Sam braced himself against the ice wall as Tinka climbed on to his shoulders and attacked the barricade with the knife, but the ice would neither crack nor move. If it *should* shift, it would bury them completely. *Not that way.*

They explored the alcove. In softer snow, they tried to tunnel. They took turns scraping with their gloved hands. Breath froze on their faces. Soon they had made a short cavity, but it sloped inauspiciously downward. Tinka met an obstruction and pushed. Without warning it gave way, and she sprawled headlong into a hidden cavity. Sam saw her disappear in a cloud of ice-crystals, with a muffled thud.

Fervent curses proved her still intact.

"Sam! Bring the matches! There's some sort of cavern, but it's pitch black!"

Sam edged over the lip of the hole. He slid a couple of metres, fell free, and hit the floor fast, jarring his ankle further. He took out the box of matches, and struck one.

By its light, he saw Tinka sitting on the ground.

Behind her, in the flickering shadows, were three of the one-eyed snow-beasts.

~~~

"They're *asleep*," said Tinka. "Dormant, or hibernating. Metabolism barely ticking over: they're breathing about three times a minute."

"They'd better *stay* asleep," Sam, muttered, "even if they *are* herbivores." He hunched against the wall, where a strip of cloth burned fitfully in a puddle of oil, casting a flickering, smoky light. "How did they get here?"

"Trapped by the avalanche, like us. I wonder if they're safe to eat?"

"Ugh."

"We may have to find out, Sam. Those men were hunting them for a reason."

"Never food. Skins or fur get my bet. These aren't Old Earth animals. Violet blood and golden bones, bet you." He bent to take a closer look. "Oh, my. No legs."

"What do you —"

"Look at these! No wonder they seemed to flow."

Tinka's eyes followed his pointing finger. Along the lower surface two flattish sausage-shaped tubes bulged from long, flanged cavities. Each end disappeared into an oval synte. Sam poked his finger between the tube and the rim of the synte near the animal's head. Its tip poked out from the kantasynte at its rear.

"Syntelic caterpillar tracks!"

"Yah. Perfect for slippery terrain. And the syntei avoid end-wheels and a returning half. Just like half-wheels."

"The Qishi probably got the half-wheel idea from some animal to begin with. Oh, look! See how the bumps along the tube mesh with bumps on its underbelly? I bet the ones on its body are muscles, that move to push it along. I wonder how they evolved."

"Once the plants and animals evolved symbiosis, almost any combination could be selected for. This system is ideal for deep snow. Especially slopes. Good traction."

"Wouldn't the height difference cause problems?"

"Pull down matches push up. No net loss or gain in energy."

Sam grunted. "Nah, but these beasts are a big gain in *smell*."

"Yah, but consider the benefits. Their body-heat's making it a lot warmer. The smell's as bad as a slave hut, but I vote, sleep here. Take watches, in case they wake. They may not be able to eat us, but they can squash us to death just by rolling over. You sleep first."

Sam was too tired to protest. It seemed as if he had only just dropped off, when Tinka shook him awake again. The lamp had burned out.

"What time is it?"

Tinka looked at her 'comp, spending some battery time by waving it to 'luminous'. "Three in the morning, local time. Middle of the night."

"Oh. Why didn't you keep the lamp going?"

"To conserve oil. Anyway, you can see the creatures in silhouette."

"So you can." He moved over. "Come on, your turn to — hey, *wait* a minute!"

"What?"

"How can we possibly see *silhouettes* in a pitch-dark cavern in the middle of the night?" He crept closer to the sleeping animals. "Look!"

"Light? Coming from where?"

"From behind fatty here, snoring away in the corner. Grab the other end, love, and we'll shove him out of the way."

"I thought you were worried about waking them up."

"Silence, woman, this is *serious*. Grab."

They dragged the unprotesting carcase to one side. Its snores continued unabated. Sam lit the lamp again.

"There's a tunnel. Or a burrow, about the same size as these brutes. Must be how they got in, not trapped at all. Rip van Winkel there was lying across the entrance. If those snoozy lumps get in, maybe we get out! Wait here — I'll be back!"

A tight fit, but large enough for an agile man, it turned and twisted down for about twenty metres, opened out to what seemed a natural grotto, and stopped dead.

Thick wooden bars blocked further progress. The dim light came from beyond, guided by reflective ice-covered walls. It was getting dimmer.

In the distance he heard *voices*.

They were too faint to make out. He waited, and they faded from earshot. Satisfied, he pushed at the bars, but they were made of some kind of hardwood that didn't budge. He felt a slight breeze on his face, and an idea. He scrambled back up the burrow, and explained it to Tinka.

"...so if I soak the bars in oil and we make a fire around them, we may be able to burn a way through. A couple of bars would be enough."

"Sounds good. We've precious little to lose. I'll get whatever's burnable — paper, tent-pegs, spare clothing: you get busy with the oil-flask. We'll wait in the outer cavity while the bonfire blazes — there ought to be enough air back there to breathe."

"Yah, there was a crack that let air in. Uh — what about these creatures?"

"They'll have to take their chances."

"Nah, I mean, supposing they decide to come outside too? There's not much room in the outer cavity."

"We'll have to take our chances, too."

Sam wriggled back, bent on arson.

26

Egg Flower

A rich man came to the Gate of the Fifth Wind, meeting the maiden Nhyuumâja. Many years had he journeyed, for men said she had a jewel so rare and brilliant that none could touch it.

"Thou must be warned," said Nhyuumâja. "This is no ordinary jewel."

But the rich man said only: "I will have what I desire, whatever the cost."

"So be it," said Nhyuumâja sadly. She clapped her hands thrice, and the Gate of the Fifth Wind vanished. In every direction there stretched a desolate wilderness.

"You have tricked me!" cried the rich man, "I see no jewel. And the sun burns my soul."

"Nar," said Nhyuumâja. "The sun is a jewel so brilliant that none can touch it. It is thine: do with it what thou wilt." She vanished upon the Fifth Wind, leaving the rich man alone in the wilderness.

—*The Allegory of the Deceitful Maidens, Scroll 31*

Their captors led Elza, Jane, and Marco through a maze of caverns, twisting passages, endless flights of rough stone steps. Mostly down. They reached an amphitheatre hewn from solid stone. Half a dozen tiers around a three-quarter circle held a hundred or more men and women, mostly old; each with the now-familiar single-braided hair and ear-ornaments, and a coloured thigh-band.

All the thigh-bands here were yellow, unlike many Jane had seen earlier. All sported white patches in the same few designs. Those on the upper tier bore various ring shapes; those on the next tier down had thick or thin rectangles; the next, crescents; then wedges; then that omnipresent flower-shape — and the lowest tier, lopsided ellipses. Clearly the thigh-bands were a symbol of rank. Now: did those on the uppermost tier rank highest, or those nearest her? The lowest tiers held *fewest*.

Another fact, more obvious: every one of them was armed to the teeth. This was a violent society, or had once been: the weapons might now be ritual. Might be. Some bore what looked like syntubes, but most had knives. Big, sharp, glassy ones.

These must be the elusive cavern-dwellers of Wevory, of the persistent and inscrutable rumours. This cavern had to be part of a vast network, synted across the continent, perhaps across the oceans too. It was an awe-inspiring thought. What kind of society would a community isolated below ground develop, over — how long had Sadruddin said the cavern-dwellers had been isolated? Fifteen hundred years? Were the agents they sent into the light respected for their courage, or disdained as polluted?

An old woman with a golden oval thigh-patch made a slow, regal entrance. Her gait betrayed advanced age, but total silence greeted her. She placed two objects on a stone table: the ubiquitous egg and flower. Her arms rose in theatrical supplication.

"*Qloquum covenit. Pur jen' dzoghuu femduul iho-gan captû nibu montäz Kriggû, nibu mirigí loçgu njoi! Onis etsû orodon...*"

Maternal praises, a form of Galaxic standard again! It seemed universal for high ceremony, everywhere on Qish. The woman was describing their capture. Her voice was as hesitant as her gait, but the audience paid rapt attention to every word. Some seemed of local coinage. What was '*mirigí loçgu*', for instance? Miracle-hole? And while '*qloquum*' apparently referred to this gathering, what was it?

The woman turned to face them. "You do comprehend my speak?"

"Not fully," Jane replied, "but sufficiently — uh — respected one."

"Respect? Uncouth is to you, outsiders and unemblazoned. To me you shall refer by 'Unfathomable One', comprendes?"

"Apologies, Unfathomable One." *Unfathomable*? Remarkable idiom. Hmm. They live *underground*...

"By what purpose come you to Montäz Kriggû?" Now the old woman was addressing Marco.

"*Krig Mountain!*" hissed Jane. "Why are we here? Tell her!"

Marco shot Jane an imploring glance, and she inclined her head a millimetre. *Truth, Marco.*

"We were seeking a beacon."

"No fires burn on Montäz Kriggû."

"Unfathomable One, I have not words. Uh — this beacon is no fire, but a large yellow vessel. It is shaped like a — uh —" How do you describe a cone with rounded ends? He cast his eyes hopelessly around, and caught sight of the stone egg. Ah. "Like an egg. Like *that*." He pointed. A murmur rippled through the crowd of onlookers.

The woman raised a hand, and they quieted.

Marco was staring at the stone egg with a sudden intensity. So were Elza and Jane. Mother of Galaxies, it *was* like that. *Exactly* like that. Those weren't eggs at all; they were miniatures of the rescue beacon. Accurate right down to the colour!

"What reason you this egg seek?"

"Uh — to — to *talk to the stars!*"

The response was immediate uproar. Several watchers leaped up and began shouting incomprehensibly. One slid down and disappeared; those nearby made no effort to assist, but were careful not to tread on him. Most argued animatedly in groups. One was beating another over the head with the sleeve of his gown. Another wept.

The Colloquist gestured to a functionary, who shouted "Ordon! *Ordon!*" The meeting gradually quieted. She turned again to face the tiers, her wrinkled face dark with anger. "These *outsiders* be! Be not cognisant of the Mysteries! But chance, be it!"

An old man in the second tier made himself upstanding. "I, Speaker Forrence of the Silver Trefoil, say Colloquist Duranga-Muüta is right! Kill, as the Law prescribes! I call a referendum of the full Colloquium. *Now!*" The disturbance began anew, then subsided.

On the fifth tier a much younger woman, blazoned Saffron Lozenge, rose to her feet. Her quiet voice carried clearly. "It is easier to claim chance than to explain. For beings uncognisant, their quest is inexplicable. To verification should they be given!"

"Verification superflows," said the older woman, her voice rising in controlled anger. "I say, *death*! Speaker Forrence has proposed a referendum. I copromote!" She levelled her gaze at the young woman. "By what right contradict you to me?"

"By birthright."

The statement was flat and unemotional, but it was met by silence, ominous and oppressive. The younger woman stood stock still. "I declare contingency."

The older woman took a moment to respond. She clearly had not expected this. "On what grounds?"

"Precipitance!"

There was a gasp from the ranked tiers, rapidly stifled. From such a charge there could be no backing down. This was mortal defiance.

"*You* accuse *me* of undue haste?"

"It is not by me, but by the Law, that you stand accused. Men say that age confers wisdom, but the saying is flawed." The crowd gasped again.

"Some kind of ritual challenge," Jane whispered. "Risky."

"So be it." Duranga-Muüta stepped to one side. "*Temporarily*, be my office surrendered to Colloquist Worryl of Saffron Ovoid." An even more wizened ancient from the first tier shuffled across, and uneasily took charge.

"In accordance with Law," he declared, "precedence be offered to Colloquist Duranga-Muüta. Speak you!"

"My case I rest," said the old woman, choosing her words with care, "on a single overriding precept. In the *Book of the Giving of the Law* it is thus written: 'Of the intruder who is not of the True People, shall his life be forfeit.' *It is so written!*" She stepped back a pace to signal an end to her presentation.

The listeners on the tiers, drew a collective breath of shock at her brevity, but it had been a clever move. By speech so short and to the point, Duranga-Muüta was emphasising her experience versus the youth of her opponent. And showing contempt for her to boot. That was likely to weigh well in the balance of votes.

However, it risked all on a single throw. Worryl wasn't sure Duranga-Muüta's decision had been wise. *Precipitance.* Perhaps Shevveen's denunciation was well-founded after all. "I call upon *Probationer* Shevveen —" the emphasis stirred the audience, though its effect on the upper tiers was not what Worryl had meant "— for counter-presentation."

The young woman swept her eyes over the tiers, managing to convey an impression of undeviating purpose while avoiding arrogance or defiance. She appeared composed and at peace. "I speak at greater length, for this is a matter of much importance, and it should not be lightly dismissed." *Touché.* "My text I take from a source ancient and venerable. I would rehearse with you a passage from the *Scroll of the Seer.* You know it well." She paused, not too dramatically, and produced a short fat roll of parchment from her robe. The message was clear: Shevveen had been preparing this challenge. Her eyes held her audience, not the scroll, even as she unrolled it. The unspoken implication was that she knew the text by heart.

"'And in the time before was founded deep the Dwellingplace, one espied a thing unknown, a great egg of beaten gold resting upon the pinnacle of the world.

"'And our forefathers, taking it to manifest evil, did with great sticks beat the egg, and rods of iron; yet it was not harmed.'" (Marco was cheered to hear that, but not terribly surprised. A Da Silva beacon is generally encased in flexalloy laminate. It would take a neutrino-bomb to shift it.)

"'And round the egg did they build a burning pyre, and for seven days and seven nights did it blaze. And the egg was yet unharmed.

"'And at last did they tumble the egg into a deep shaft in the mountain, thinking to open its shell. And still was it unharmed.

"'Then did our forefathers seek out Gribben the Seer in his desolate retreat, to ask what manner of thing was this wondrous egg.

"'And the Seer did ponder the words of his father, and his father's father, and his father's father's father. "This, the egg of the great bird that did bring our ancestors to the world, shall be set upright with levers of utterwood. And the shaft down which it is cast shall be called the Miracle Shaft, for it is miraculous indeed that the egg be not cracked. And the Miracle Shaft shall be roofed over with beams of utterwood, to preserve the egg and keep it from common view.

"' "And there shall come one day visitors from a far place, outlandish in figure and speech. And they shall open the egg, and a great flower shall grow from the shell, and through that flower shall the strangers talk to the stars. And then shall the True People be reunited with the world-that-was." '"

That explains a lot, thought Marco. Now we know what happened to the beacon. No wonder we thought we were on top of it. We *were*, and Gribben's forefathers knew it would take lost Starfolk skills to activate it. Fact transmutes into legend and myth. Hopes of rescue degrade into sacred texts. The egg is the beacon, and the flower is its Da Silva antenna.

Shevveen, too, stepped back a pace, and inclined her head. Deep drama had confronted Duranga-Muüta's shallow quotation. The *Book of the Giving of the Law*, deeply revered through it might be, was secular. The *Scroll of the Seer* was theological dynamite. It should prevail. By a healthy margin of depth-weighted votes, it did.

Duranga-Muüta's face was hard. For an instant she glared openly at Forrence, but cavern-dwellers fear no pain, death, or disgrace, and she bared her arm for the poison. Shevveen scratched it once, drawing blood. Duranga-Muüta stood, now proud and defiant, until the venom reached her heart, paralysing the muscles. She fell to the ground, but no sound escaped her lips. In seconds she was still.

The younger woman bent and took her blazon, replacing with it her own.

"Contingency is vindicated," said Worryl, trying ineffectually to repress a shudder. Those who sought low office inevitably risked such an end. He was thankful that he'd been wise enough never to aspire to a position that far below his ability. "I surrender my temporary office permanently to Colloquist Shevveen-Duranga." As far as he was concerned, she was welcome to it, and his face showed it.

"Let her be set to become a stalagmite in the Pit of Perpetuity," said the newly named Shevveen-Duranga. "For Muüta obeyed the precepts, even unto her death." She changed the subject back to the one that had motivated the challenge.

"I propose that these be not put to death untested, as those said, but verified!"

The proposal passed by unanimous acclamation.

~~~

The prisoners, taken from the Chamber of Colloquy, were brought before the *jûnquire*. He designated as escorts two girls, blazoned in the highest order of the Beryl Hoop. Jane thought to detect subtle insult in that choice, though it might have been due to their own ambivalent status: worthless intruders deserving only death, or awe-inspiring beings whose advent had been prophesied, deserving of...

What?

Jane realised that she had absolutely no idea.

The *jûnquire* addressed the two Beryl Hoops. "Know you that these folk be *iddeterminâjo* awaiting Verification. They have free movement within these precincts, save they keep the Law, but at all times one of you must accompany. For now, you will give them respect, though not as dwellers. Treat them as *shemuûji*." The girls curtsied, and the *jûnquire* turned his attention to the prisoners. "*Shemuûji*: your position be privileged but insecure. I do counsel you to obey our Law and await verification in calmness. Escape can there be none, understand?"

Jane's eyes flicked to her companions. *Let me handle this.* "We ask for enlightenment as to the burden of the Law, for as strangers we know not your ways."

"This shall suffice: harm no one, steal nothing." He rose and was gone.

Jane decided it was time to take the initiative. "What are your names?"

One girl looked sullen, the other responded at once. "I hight Fharssha." She glared at the other girl, who avoided her gaze, but after a moment, said, "I hight Vyry." Her reluctance was evident from her voice and posture.

Jane kept her face expressionless. "Very well, Fharssha and Vyry. We are hungry. Where may we obtain food?"

"This way, *shemuûja*."

~~~

The caverns of Wevory are unusual in two respects.

The first is the synted links between more than a thousand individual caverns, to form an entire underground nation, gem-rich and despising the open world. Synlit farms and cornfields feed the caverns, though the dwellers do supplement them through covert agents in the outworld. Concealed exits and entrances are often hidden in pools or marshes, syntei with inner parts raised against chance discovery. All are guarded with paranoid intensity. Attempts to infiltrate this society inevitably result in detection and death.

The second is that a major complex of their caverns runs through one of the highest mountains in Wevory. Caverns at such heights are a rarity: these owed existence to Qish's unorthodox tectonic history. A tumultuous ice-age run-off honeycombed the soft karst with a warren of tunnels and crevices, caverns and cracks — all within twenty thousand years, a bare instant in geological time. Three million years had lifted Krig further, and rocks had grown soft shapes. Height is power, and the smallest Wevorin dropsynte is lethal; though inferior to Samdali weapons.

The main caverns were intertwined with minor fissures where Sam and Tinka stayed hidden. After a time they began to feel familiar with the vast three-dimensional maze of chambers, tunnels, and stairways. Twists and turns and interconnections built up in their wristcomps. Without the night sky they did not know latitude or longitude, but comparison with *Valkyrie*'s geological data gave clues. The volcanic Gloonts had caverns like hungry mouths, and lava stalactites like teeth. They passed rivers of glowing lava, and in the False Gloonts rivers of water, amid gardens of stalactites. Sometimes they knew they were beneath Samdal or Lamynt, and once even Shaaluy.

They avoided populated regions. Certain key syntei, major transit routes, were too perilous in the synlit waking hours, displaced by several hours (so their 'comps told them) from daylight on the continents. Strange sculptures in alcoves served as landmarks: there was a recurrent theme of the spirally clad maiden, often with adorers writhing at her feet.

"Wherever this light is from," said Tinka, "it's far off in longitude. I suppose suboceanic syntei offer a degree of security — and these people must have an astoundingly good record of keeping secrets, or they wouldn't still be here."

Sometimes, from deep concealment, they eavesdropped on unsuspecting dwellers, hoping for news of their companions. There was much talk about *shemuûji*, often associated with phrases such as 'verification', 'cracking the world egg,' and the intriguing 'talk to the stars'. A chance reference to 'confounded dark-skinned *shemuûji* interlopers', by a washerwoman gossiping by a rock-pool, clinched it.

The trouble was, the cavern network was *enormous*. Ordinary geographical distances were both unobtainable and irrelevant to its connections. Sam and Tinka were neither near nor far from the others, and random chatter provided few useful clues. Maps or signposts were there none, beyond the gleanings in their 'comps. All they could judge was height: they lurked mostly among the topmost caverns, which seemed fewest, as they still hoped the beacon was high.

Finally, they got lucky. They were crouching on a ledge in a cavern smelling of sulphur, hidden by shadows, as three men passed beneath. An old man with an orange thigh-band and triangular patch turned to one of the younger, well-muscled, with blue bands.

"Poundsman Khower?"

"Your Profundity?"

"I wish you an object convey the Shaft guard to."

The man stood on respectful tiptoe. "It shall be immediate, Your Profundity."

"This object was in the grasp of one of the *shemuûji*. It seems a jewel, but I hold seemings to deceive, since the gemdepts know it not. Give it the guard, and instruct its safekeeping until studied by those in arcane ways wise."

Sam and Tinka squinted against the poor light. Dangling from the man's hand, the object looked very much like Jane's laser medallion.

The poundsman was about to set off down a side-passage, but the old man pointed to a pool. "Nay, Khower: take the shorter path."

"Your Profundity is generous." The man stepped across to a pool of still water. From his jerkin he drew a shiny bag, in which he put his outer clothing, his weapons and the medallion, and drew three drawstrings tight. Holding the bag in one hand, he plunged into the pool. The other two made their exit by a drier path.

Sam and Tinka continued to watch. Five minutes later, as they had hoped and expected, the man had still not come to the surface.

~~~

When the coast cleared, they scrambled down to the cavern floor.

"Goes without saying that under the water there's either a tunnel or a synte."

"My bet's on a synte."

"Mine too. I'm going paddling. You keep watch."

Tinka grunted. "*Hurry*! Don't let him get too far ahead, we may lose him."

Sam slipped into the water, his hunting-knife between his teeth. The bottom shelved steeply, and he had to swim. When he reached the place where he thought the man had vanished, he dived. His third dive found an opening. He waved from the surface, and Tinka followed him in.

The wyzand came out in a second pool, in a moist-scented cavern: not one seen before. Tinka worried about their damp footprints, but the floor was again grass, so a casual passer-by would notice no disturbance. The cavern-dwellers had even arranged street-lighting, synted from the far oceans, but the few sunsyntei were widely spaced, leaving many shadows. Trees appeared to their left, and they slipped silently off the main path, picking their way between the trunks.

Ahead, voices.

Sam wriggled forward to a point between the heavy trunk of a mature tree and a creeper-decked stalagmite. Soon he returned and put his mouth to her ear.

"There's a wyzand — I've never seen a huger. One guard, with a spear. The messenger gave him the laser, and it's hung on a projecting rock beside him. *I want it.* But I'm fascinated. *What is he guarding?*"

"Marco, Jane, Elzabet?"

"It's a strong possibility. We have to find out."

"How do you get past the guard?"

"Kill him. Too dangerous otherwise."

Oh, Sam, you've changed. "How?" *So have I. This is a harsh world.* "Not with the knife? Too much blood."

"Not the knife. I'll need a distraction." Sam pointed to a tree-lined shelf of rock that ran up the side of the cavern, and explained. Tinka suggested improvements and dug out the bandages. They crept their separate ways into the darkness.

A quarter of an hour passed with no new activity. The guard, dull-witted from lack of sleep, scratched his nose absently. Night-duty meant you were your own man; no one to order you around. The disadvantage was staying awake... *what's that?*

The edge of the thicket glowed, in a diffuse pool of eerie violet light. There were faint whispers, a cooing sound... He raised his spear and stepped forward a few paces... *Is it a dream? What is it? A succubus?*

Just within the trees a woman shimmered in the unsteady blue light. She was tall, slim, exotically beautiful, and narrow cloth spiralled around her body. He advanced another pace. Seemingly for the first time, the woman appeared to see him: she smiled, but otherwise ignored him. Images from *The Allegory of the Deceitful Maidens* filled his mind. No Wevorin, this. Was she Muumani? Nhyuumâja? Whoever it was, the being stooped to pluck a flower, set it delicately in her hair and struck a demurely provocative pose.

The guard was tired and confused. The Deceitful Maidens were aptly named: worship and disrespect were equally dangerous. Was it a trap? *What* was it? The seductive form bent again and plucked another blossom.

In the early hours the human brain runs slow — as Sam had anticipated. The guard advanced into the trees, levelling his spear. "What *are* you?" he whispered, in a mixture of excitement and fear. The woman smiled again, and reached out her arms.

Impossibly, the violet light swooped *over* him, but now it was green. For an instant the guard stared upwards at a three-kilometre drop into the ocean depths, compressed into a dozen metres. The night-synte encircled his head and gravity seized him. The spear jammed across the opening, but his hands had no chance of holding on. As shredded meat, his body hit the water, an easy though toxic meal for scavengers half a world away.

Sam rolled up the shirt he had used as a filter to produce the strange colouring, jumped from the ledge, and crushed the fallen sunsynte with his heel until it withered. "Bravely done, Tinka! Now, let's go!" He darted across the open ground to the wyzand. Tinka followed, parka in hand. Sam snared the laser-medallion as they passed, and dived through the wyzand, holding it ready.

The far side was unguarded — a short tunnel into what looked like a larger cavern. They stopped for a moment to regain their breath. Tinka tugged at a slip-knot, let the bandages puddle around her feet, and dressed faster than ever in her life, despite her damp skin. Wringing the bandages as best she could, she saved them.

Ahead was another cavern, large and rounded, the ceiling too vast and dark to see. There was no sign of Jane, Marco, or Elzabet. No sign of anybody. But there was light enough to see the smooth silhouette at the centre of the cavern floor.

"Mother! Is that...?" Sam was trembling now.

"Has to be."

They walked towards it, ears sharp for danger, but all was quiet. Sam's hands encountered cold metal. He struck a match.

Yellow. His heart thumped in his ears. He moved the flame across the surface, inwards under sloping sides, down to the narrow base. A panel appeared in the flickering light. With *letters*.

Before he could read them in the dim light, the flame died. He struck another.

CV23-MAGOG BEACON. ENTRY CODE GALAXIC-5.

His shoulders lifted, loose and free. He beckoned Tinka over.

"Oh, Mother of Galaxies! It *does* exist! I never really — "

All their struggles and sacrifices, at last one ancient artefact.

Tears blocked their vision.

"Oh, Sam. I want to go *home*!"

"Not there yet, Tinka. The landing-strip is in sight but we're not on the flight-path. A lot can still go wrong."

"I know, I know. If it all comes to pieces now... I don't think I could —"

She stopped. *Footsteps.*

Across the cavern was a ledge, deep enough behind to conceal them. Voices echoed from beyond the cavern's entrance.

"Curious. There is no guard."

"Rouse the *jûnquire*. Ask whether any of the *shemuûji* have escaped."

A pause.

"All three are accounted for."

Sounds of branches being forced back. "There are signs of a struggle." Another pause. "Possibly a drift-orm has broken through. They may look harmless, but once they get that long snout around a man's neck —"

"I will unleash the ormhounds." Footsteps ran off into the distance.

Sam was glad Tinka could not see his face. *If Drift-orms are what I think, we spent the night with three of them. We even moved one. Oh, Mother of Galaxies!*

Heavier footsteps sounded — several men. "Squadsman Gunnigoom and a replacement guard reporting, Your Pendancy."

"Deploy your men, Gunnigoom. Secure this wyzand. Something is seriously amiss — take no chances." With a clatter, two men took up stations *inside* the wyzand.

An unearthly howling began, seemingly far beneath them. Growing in volume, it resolved itself into the baying of hounds. *Ormhounds.* Sam's fingers bit into Tinka's arm. The hounds cast around before the wyzand, and must have picked up a scent immediately, for the clamour redoubled. Sam's fingers gripped harder.

Then the baying began to recede. The ormhounds were following their trail *back* through the tunnels. That would buy a little time, but if the pool did not stop them, they would eventually find three dormant drift-orms. Their handlers would undoubtedly discover the burnt barricade, which would certainly set minds working.

And it was starting to get light.

~~~

"...and you shall be taken to the World Egg, that you may shatter its shell, to release the Flower of Infinity," the *jûnquire* chanted. "By success, shall you be verified as those of whom the Seer Gribben did foretell.

"By failure, shall your falsehood be proven, and death follow on its heels."

"Marco?"

"Yah, Elza?"

"I sure hope you know how to get that thing open."

"A cinch," Marco replied, more confidently than he felt. "Rescue beacons are built to last. This one's been here a mere couple of millennia. They standardised the design right at the outset of Colonisation, still in use for very specialised applications. Modified, yah, but with some absolutes, like how to operate the things. A small console beneath a panel, set to accept one of the standard code-groups. Once I enter that, a precoded sequence takes over and deploys the antenna.

"The one *small* worry is the failsafe."

"Failsafe?" Elza sounded nervous.

"To prevent deployment if too much local matter is in the way. It uses daylight-sensitive scanners. I hope there's enough light in this Miracle Shaft place. And enough space. Otherwise, the bitch won't budge."

Vyry and Fharssha led them up a spiral stairway of stone blocks, with half a dozen persons of assorted rank behind. At the top, an oriel led into an antechamber. A wyzand opened on the Miracle Shaft itself, where the lowest two tiers of the Colloquium — Saffron Blossom and Saffron Ovoid — were already assembled. But Marco had eyes only for the smooth, yellow rescue beacon.

It sat, narrow end down, in the middle of the floor, and his heart sang. There was ample room for deployment — and ample light.

I hope those early engineers built as well as the propaganda has it.

~~~

Concealed on his ledge, supine and unseen, Sam looked up through the cavern roof. More green daylight seeped into the chamber, revealing a broad shaft, up to a complex of heavy wooden beams. Above that, he would bet his liver, would be the depression in the snowfield where Marco's electroscope had picked up those impossible signals.

Where is Marco?, he wondered. On your back, you can't see what's going on.

"Jackpot!" screamed Marco. The Colloquists, not knowing what to expect from a *shemuûji* undergoing verification, accepted this cry as part of some ritual. Sam recognised both the word and the voice; so did Tinka. They listened in silence while Shevveen-Duranga ploughed through some interminable recitation. Sam used the time to ready the laser medallion and check that it was fully charged; a diversion might be in order. Reading between the lines of ritual, it looked as though Marco was trying to activate the rescue beacon.

Shevveen-Duranga reached the end of the rite. "Let verification proceed!"

Marco stepped forward. "I will now shatter the World Egg and awaken the Flower of Infinity!" he declared, recalling his conjuring days. "Stand aside and maintain absolute silence! The World Egg will not reveal its secrets to the impetuous: I caution you to patience!" Or, to put it succinctly, *this may take some time.*

He inspected the console. Good. Galaxic-5, just as I thought. Now, this pad should let me monitor the solitronic source... idiot, that *must* be working, or we'd never have been trying to get here to begin with... oh, good, it is. Green lights across the board. Field density well into the operational band, I'm glad to say. Now, power-link *on*, interlock *off* — and hit the panic-button, *so.*

Nothing happened.

Marco ran through the sequence again in his mind. Must be right, it's basic drill. He set it up again on the pads.

Nothing.

The crowd started to stir. Shevveen-Duranga looked close to panic at the failing gamble. *She'll switch her bet.* "Seize them and bind them! Verification is ended."

"No!" yelled Marco. "There's been some mistake! I need —"

Tinka risked a peep. "Sam, they're dragging Marco away!"

Sam didn't hesitate. He aimed the laser medallion up the shaft. Bringing the roof down should create enough chaos for a chance of escape. He fired, a concentrated beam. There was a brilliant flash and an ear-splitting sizzle. With a creak and then a tremendous crash, the roof fell in.

The rescue beacon was half-buried in blazing timbers. Brilliant sunlight from the snowfields poured down through the roof, shining on the beacon like a spotlight.

They broke cover and ran towards their friends, Sam firing over the heads of the crowd, Tinka yelling like a banshee. The beam bounced wildly off the rocky walls. Then an arrow pierced Sam's arm and he dropped the medallion. Seconds later, the five of them were being held by muscular guardsmen.

So near.

"What went wrong?" moaned Marco, more disturbed by his inability to operate a simple piece of machinery than by imminent death. *"What went wrong?"*

A guard seized his hair, jerked his head back, raised a knife. The crowd howled, a spine-chilling screech torn from a hundred throats.

Then a look of sheer awe appeared on the guard's face. He flung his knife aside and fell prostrate, moaning and whimpering unintelligibly. Bewildered, Marco turned his head: *all* the cavern-dwellers were lying on their faces, as if mown down by automatic weapons. The only ones on their feet were the five Starfolk.

It was Tinka who pointed to the cause of the mayhem. *"Look at the beacon!"*

Like a phoenix amid flames, the thousand-year-old beacon was coming to life.

The large end separated, rising slowly on a central stalk, and split into a dozen sectors, each displaying the familiar Stars and Pyramid of the Concordat. Each rotated on its axis, a full half-turn, uniting in a shallow upturned bowl.

The antenna had deployed. The Egg had given birth to the Flower.

It was gratifying, yes.

But why had it happened *now*?

27

Only Connect

> Initially, (static) electricity and magnetism were seen as entirely separate. They became electromagnetism when a moving magnet created an electric current in a coil of wire, and an electric current produced a magnetic field. Uniting the weak and strong nuclear forces with electromagnetism took another century. Gravity was eventually incorporated after the abandonment of the dark matter hypothesis. Even the karmabhumi field is unified, in principle, but most calculations are unsolvable.
> — *Valentino Ngaabû, What Da Silva Didn't Know: Theories of Almost Everything*

Five people from the stars lay on a grassy bank, flanked by a colonnade of stalagmites woven with silver-blue wissaria, basking in sunshine from half way round the world and listening to the subterranean birdsong. A few paces away, rain fell from the cavern's roof in a fine mist. Vyry and Fharssha were feeding Marco with sweet fruit like fat pink grapes. The cavern-dwellers had created a new rank for Eggbreakers: Black Disc, in the next-to-lowest tier. And rank, it seemed, had its privileges.

But Marco still hadn't worked out why the antenna had deployed so late. It hadn't opened when it should; then opened for no obvious reason. Embarrassing. Potentially fatal too, but the biggest hurt had been to Marco's mathematical-engineer pride. A faulty circuit, somehow the heat from the fire... No, that made no sense at all.

They were sunbathing on the grass to pass the time until the beacon cooled down enough to open. Marco insisted the heat would do no harm. Beacons were *tough*. And hadn't the *Scroll of the Seer* told of an attempt to burn it that lasted seven days? A few hours could scarcely make much difference.

Tinka rolled over on to her stomach. "It's not *fair*. You're all browner than me to start with; I've got the fair skin of a Waylander. Now we get to synbathe, and I don't tan! Marco, you're the engineering genius: you explain *that*!"

Instead, Marco leaped upon her and embraced her in a bear-hug. Vyry and Fharssha looked quite put out: Elzabet saw this and stifled a grin.

"That's *it*! Oh, what a fool!" Marco kissed Tinka soundly. Then Sam.

"Sam — why did you burn down the roof?"

"I told you. To create a diversion."

"No other reason?"

"Nah. Why do you keep asking?"

"Because if I don't, in a moment you'll take all the credit. By sheer dumb luck, you did exactly what was needed."

"Mother, Marco, who cares?" Jane snapped.

"*I* care. When the beacon cools, it has to work. I don't like unexplained faults."

Tinka butted in. "Then tell us, engineer Bianchi: why *did* it open so late?"

"The failsafe scanners insist on daylight: artificial light has no ultra-violet."

"So? They don't use lamps in these caverns. There's at least as much UV in Squill's emission spectrum as we get on Wayland. My back proved that when the Vain Vaimoksi captured us." *Mother. It seems an age...*

"Agreed, Squill *emits* plenty. But you're forgetting, like I was, where *this* light comes from."

Tinka finally saw. "Underwater!"

"You got it. A few metres of water make a very effective UV filter. When Sam brought the roof down he let in *real* daylight. The automatics were set; only the failsafes held her back. The world-Egg saw the light and its Flower blossomed."

Sam sat up lazily. "Dumb luck indeed! I was just about to explain about the UV when you asked why I burnt the roof down, but once you're on your high horse you never let anyone get a word in edgeways. I thought to myself, Sam my lad, this underwater synted sunlight is going to cause old Marco endless trouble because there's not enough ultra-violet light to trip the failsafes. So I aimed my faithful medallion, took a potshot at the roof, and — hey! Put me down!"

There was a splash as Elza, Jane, and Marco threw him into the pool.

Vyry and Fharssha glanced at Tinka.

"Don't ask me to explain," she told them haughtily. "A touch of sunstroke perhaps." Then she burst into giggles and ruined the effect.

~~~

While Jane and Tinka discussed complex politics with the Wevorin Low Command, Marco, Sam, and Elza relaxed under a fountain of ferns that sprouted from the top of a stalagmite. Nearby was a saltwater rock pool with the Qishi equivalents of shrimp, anemones, and a sort of syntelic crab whose legs and mouthparts roved the pool while its body remained safely in a rock-hole. Sam's *skiti* prowled after the shrimp as they cleaned the rocks; the other two lay side by side on a mossy bank.

Marco was talking. Elza was half asleep, grunting from time to time to prove she was still listening, even though she mostly wasn't. "Fascinating puzzle to wrestle with, but frustrating, because right now, I'm pinned to the mat," he said.

Grunt.

"I've made *some* progress. Metamaterial theory explains how syntelics should relate to the karmabhumi field, but it's too hand-wavy. I want is hard data and clean equations. And it's not just syntei! This whole trashed *planet* is weird!"

Elza sat up and stretched, languorously. "In what sense? Syntei aside, it seems normal enough to me, love."

"On the surface, yah. I mean, literally: down here. But up in space there's something very strange going on." He rolled on to his side and gazed into her eyes from close up. "Very strange indeed. Do you remember when I worried about our supposed beacon actually being a twin Colony Vessel?"

"Yah. You were waffling about Old Earth mythology. *Gog*, companion of *Magog*. But eventually you decided against. I forget why."

"Because no way can two ships be dumped in the same location by a simquake! The chance is so low that you might as well wait for a galaxy to turn into a pumpkin."

"So you stopped worrying about *Gog*."

"I did. But a different worry has been bugging me ever since. How come *Valkyrie* got dumped on the same planet as *Magog*?"

Elza pursed her lips. Marco suppressed the urge to kiss them. "You're right. It doesn't make sense."

"Dead right it doesn't. It makes no sense for two vessels to be scattered to one place by the *same* simquake, and even less to scatter there in *different* simquakes."

"Nearly two thousand years apart."

"Exactly. So, dear lady: what do we deduce?"

Elza's eyes went wide with realisation. "*Magog* wasn't hit by a simquake. Nor were we." A memory surfaced. "You wondered about that at the time. *Valkyrie* agreed."

"Just so. But our immediate problems were getting on to and off the planet. And *Valkyrie* was falling apart, so the computer couldn't be trusted."

"If it wasn't a simquake, what *was* it?"

"Well, here's a clue. Qish dumped *Valkyrie* while it was in transit." Marco grimaced to show that he didn't believe what he was saying.

Sam rolled over. "Yah, there was something decidedly funny about the navigational calculations. I'd noticed our geodesic brushed Squill, but a star's planets have third order effects. Anyway, geodesics are an aid to human comprehension, not a real feature of Da Silva physics."

"Right. In a jump, the ship moves between locations without going 'between'. It locates wherever its wavefunction peaks. When the drive is activated, the peak flattens. A new one pops up, and the drive pops up with it. Its spatial neighbours don't *move*: they vanish from one position and re-exist at the other. The ship transfers along with that configuration of space and time."

"In fact," Sam chipped in, "that's why the ship remains intact. Except in rare circumstances when some distortion creates a multiple focus. Then it can get a tiny bit crazy — spurious copies, loss of material identity."

"So how does that lead to Qish dumping us out?" Elza asked, paying more attention now.

"Well, the simplest explanation is what I said then: the planet created an unexpected *k*-focus. That would explain why *Valkyrie* emerged so close, and why *Magog* emerged in much the same location, almost two thousand years earlier."

"But not why we both crashed," Sam observed.

"Nah. Something was screwy about space-time topology around Qish. And I'm betting there still is."

"But why? What can interfere with space-time top — Oh."

Marco tapped the side of his head. "Precisely. I've only just twigged. I don't have two different problems — syntei and Qishi space-time topology. They're two aspects of one problem."

"Beta-calculus."

"I'll make a mathematical engineer of you yet, Elza."

"No thanks. But I can't help picking up some of the reflexes."

"Yah. Qish's spatio-temporal distortions — which shifted the emergence peak for both ships, *and* wrecked their drives — come from disturbances in the local k-field. Caused by syntei. Each synte contributes a tiny topological twist, harmless in itself —"

"But there are billions upon billions of the things," said Sam, "and the pieces add up. You're right. And I now see why you're worried. It's not just an obscure feature of the math."

"Nah. It could be a major obstacle."

Elza's face looked grim. "I see it. Whatever Starhome sends to rescue us —"

"Is likely to suffer the same fate."

~~~

They had no choice but to press on, make contact, and hope someone — themselves, the combined intellects of Starfolk civilisation, or both — could figure a fix for Qish's tendency to wreck Da Silvas. Marco was now inside the cooled beacon, brandishing the primitive activation tools that had thoughtfully been included. Simplicity is robust.

"Nice, big bolts, easy to remove even after a millennium or two on a mountain. Good design, deliberately low-tech in case whoever wants to set the beacon off doesn't have anything more sophisticated. In principle, these things are foolproof," said Marco, streaming commentary as he unscrewed the plate protecting the control panel.

"And we all know foolproof," said Sam, recording everything on his 'comp.

"Yah. Something screws up, needs fixing. After two thousand years, I guarantee it. But that's where an engineer's mind comes into its own. The universal fix-it."

To his slight surprise, the cover slid off without getting stuck. He set it to one side. "No condensation, that's good. The seals didn't degrade too much."

Under the cover-plate was a very basic control panel, also low-tech. Down one side was a short list of instructions in Galaxic. He read them twice. "Dah. Basically I just have to power it up, wait for the status checks to complete, and when all the lights turn green, phone Starhome."

He took a deep breath. "Step one: power up." He pulled a red cylinder from a small rack, and pushed it into a socket until he felt resistance, then turned it clockwise through a right angle. Five lights down the side of the screen came on — all red.

"We have emergency power. Radioactive source, half-life fifty thousand years, no danger of running out. Don't worry about the red, Sam — it hasn't initialised yet."

One by one the lights turned yellow. When the first turned green, Marco started breathing normally. "Main power source checks out." He studied the screen messages. "Depleted a bit by natural leakage, but it won't run out in *our* lifetime."

"The other lights?" asked Sam.

"Status checks prior to finalising the power-up sequence. They should go green in turn. Yah, there goes the control system. And the directional motors. Alignment system fine. Now all we need is the communicator to complete its test sequence."

The last light stayed obstinately yellow.

Marco stared at the screen for minutes, willing an error message, a missing file, a change in user status — *anything*. It had hung up — no, finally there was a message.

"Connection fault," he declared. "Can't expect everything smooth. Something's snarled the uplink procedure. Hardly a surprise after sitting on its butt that long. Accept the option to run diagnostics."

He touched a pad, and messages flowed down the screen.

"Ha! Here we go... oh."

"What?" Sam didn't like 'oh'.

"Failure in memory zone J006, sector 47. The memoblock probably just needs to be cleaned and reinserted. Access via... yah-yah-yah, *here*." He opened another panel, shone a syntorch inside. "Oh, Mother!"

Sam definitely didn't like anything meriting an anguished appeal to Her Galactic Maternity. "Trouble?"

Marco grunted and put down his solitronic screwdriver. "Something growing all over the memory blocks, just like in the deathpods. Purple-grey growing merrily in total darkness. How did — ?" He caught himself. "How does anything wacky happen on this planet? One microscopic spore with its own tiny synte is all it takes. Everything's sealed, but over the centuries things expand, contract, move. Cracks. A puff of spores blows in, some settle on the console, one drops through a gap, lodges in the circuitry. Nutrients are synted from outside, so it never realises its living space is stuck in a dark box.

"Fortunately, it hasn't spread far. I think its host plant died. So my next job is to pull all the memoblocks, clean them up, and reassemble."

"And then it will work?" Sam asked.

Marco tried to sound confident. "Done it a thousand times." *But not when my only hope of rescue depended on it.* "It'll be a breeze."

~~~

"Will we *never* get a break?"

Jane's frustration was about to boil over. It was amazing she hadn't started screaming. "It should all have been so simple. But at every step, we've been blocked by this stupid planet's stupid flora."

"Despite which, we're here," said Tinka. "Except for Felix — we all miss him endlessly," *though never as deeply as you do, Jane.* "But, well, we've done amazingly not to lose anyone else. When I think of the risks we've had to take, my blood runs cold."

"We're working much better as a team, too," said Elzabet. "When I recall how I used to behave — Mother, it's embarrassing. Lazy stuck-up over-privileged little — "

"None of us is responsible for their upbringing, Elza. From birth, the system told you you were superior. You saw through all that, and you changed."

"You all changed me," said Elza.

"So! In-flight bonding did in fact occur! Score one to Starhome psychobabble."

"Yah, but not in flight. I don't think any group of would-be citizens has ever gone through anything remotely like this."

"Face it," said Elza, "*no one* has ever gone through anything remotely like this in the history of the Galaxy."

Tinka got to her feet. She had a meeting with the Wevorin High Council to prepare. "It's so new, love, that we do *whatever it takes* to get the news back. Qish is the key to a whole new layer of technology. And Marco's sure that by studying syntei, we can learn to make the structural metamaterials behind it all. If he's right, we can tailor spatial short cuts to order, mass-manufacture them — no limits."

Elza wondered. "It might be wiser to resign ourselves to the Qishi lifestyle and stuff the beacon. Is *Homo sapiens* wise enough to use syntei for good rather than evil? On Qish, it's been a mixed bag, hasn't it?"

"Qish isn't Starhome."

"Nah, Tinka, but even Starfolk are imperfect. I can think of a dozen really nasty new weapons and surveillance technologies, off the top of my head. Look at the ones we've run into here. And this world is low-tech. Look at what happened to Old Earth with the limited tech they had back then. Now ramp up the technology."

"Starhome isn't Old Earth. We've already faced the ethical problems of powerful technology. That's why Old Earth was quarantined, how the Concordat came into being. Think of the potential *benefits*, Elza. The Stellar Conclave knows how to handle potential abuses."

"Maybe."

"We have to let them try," Tinka said. "If we don't bring syntelics, someone else will, eventually. Qish could get off its botanical butt, and invent space travel. Or there could be a lab on Stibbons cooking up Marco's metamaterial right now."

"That's the oldest excuse in the book, Tinka."

"I know, Elza love. That's because there's no answer to it." A figure emerged from the beacon's hatchway. "Here's Marco. Hope he's got news for us."

He had. None of it good.

~~~

"It was all going to plan," he said glumly. "I cleaned all the memoblocks, cleared out the fungus, buffed the connectors to a high polish, and put it all back together. Then I re-ran set-up, and the final light *still* stuck on yellow.

"So I re-ran the diagnostics, and this time it got a bit further, spotted a hardware error. Broken connection. The mould had corroded part of the subsidiary wiring that takes power to the field-demodulator."

"I thought the stupid thing was foolproof," said Sam.

"As near as damn it. Triple-redundancy throughout. But the designers took care of any easy-replace hardware by providing spare parts. Sealed tight, safer than embedded in yet more exposed circuitry. Only, the kit doesn't have a long enough piece of the right cable. There's a slot where it ought to be, though, so some bright spark raided it while *Magog* was in transit. It's not there."

"Anything you can use instead?"

"Not really, it's a special metal composite to carry huge currents, you'd need big tech to manufacture it. There's a shorter length of the right stuff, but *too* short. So I thought I'd report to you and ask for advice."

"Isn't it obvious?" asked Elza.

"Not to me."

"That's because you're thinking like a mathematical engineer."

"How else should I think?"

"Like a mechanosyntelic engineer."

Marco looked sheepish. "Narrow the gap with a synte; run the short cable through. You're right, mind out of gear."

He called Vyry over and asked for a pair of punctyles. When she trotted back with them, he thanked her and disappeared back inside the beacon.

Half an hour later he climbed out. "Green across the board."

"So have you made contact yet?"

"Nah, that's the next step. I thought you might want to be present."

They all squeezed inside the beacon. Marco poised his finger above a large blue button. "This will pass full broadcast power to the communicator, and let us attempt contact with Starhome. Don't be surprised if that takes a while, this thing will be running obsolete protocols and they won't be awake at the other end."

He pushed the button.

There was a flash, a cloud of smoke, and a smell of burnt insulation.

28

Word of the Prophet

> The heavens declare the glory of Magog;
> The firmament reveals his presence.
> By day He speaks, by night He knows.
> There is no place where His voice is not heard.
> His line is gone out through all the world,
> His words are remembered to the end of the world.
> His going forth is from heaven, his circuit is within it,
> And nothing is hid from His heat.
> —*Psalms of the Prophets*

It took Marco three days to figure out what had happened.

"As far as I can tell — a guess, people, but I think I'm on the right track — some aspect of the synte metamaterial is sensitive to high magnetic fields. We know how syntei relate to gravity and air pressure, but there's no electricity on Qish, so we never found out how syntelics interact with electromagnetism. Well, now we have, and the answer is that a strong magnetic shock wrecks syntei."

"Such as the transient when the massive current needed to power a Da Silva communicator first switches on," said Elza. "My fault for suggesting —"

"Nah, the idea was clean. None of us knew the extra we needed to avoid it."

"What's the damage?" asked Tinka.

"Not a lot. This thing is built to survive most disasters. The cable survived when the synte it ran through blew up; one end just pulled out. We can reconnect it once we work around the pulse problem. A wider opening, so the metamaterial isn't slap on top of the cable, will reduce the field strength. I can experiment before risking it on the real thing. But there's a bigger problem now. A bank of memory blew."

"Only the working storage area? That shouldn't be an issue. It'd be different if you'd blown up something vital. Redundancy should take care of it."

"Unfortunately not. It was a big bang. We had to get out fast before the smoke overcame us, remember? Some operating routines got trashed too. But there's plenty of redundancy. I can reload those once I've replaced the blocks.

"What I *think* happened — and not only is this is a guess, but it's a wild one I'm not confident about — is that the magnetic field blew the metamaterial, and that induced currents in various bits of circuitry. The memoblocks failed first — they were the weakest link — and a lot of them failed together."

"I seem to recall something from kiddygarten solitronics about *fuses*."

"Circuits with automatic software cutoffs don't normally need fuses. But no one anticipated a syntelic EMP blast."

After all they had been through. Eventually Sam said, "We must still be able to fix it. What about the spares?"

"They're fine."

"So replace the damaged blocks."

Marco sighed. "What do you think I've been working on? The problem isn't the blocks, it's the activation code."

Elzabet stared at him as though she'd just seen a yetini. "The *what?*"

"In those days, whenever anyone installed factory-fresh memoblocks, the system asked for a code to make them active. It was a precaution against unauthorised use."

"In a *rescue beacon*? Who'd be authorised after a century or more?"

"No one disables an industry standard. Which that was, eighteen hundred years ago. However, the code is in *Magog*'s operating manual, a copy of which is helpfully stored in the beacon's memory."

"Which just blew up," said Sam.

"That," declared Elzabet, "is totally stupid."

"Well, they did provide a work-around. Hard-copy backup. A printed list of codes on a duraplast sheet. Virtually indestructible."

"So why the long face?"

"I said 'virtually'. Guess what: Qishi mould eats duraplast. The beacon's hard-copy crib-sheet crumbled to mudge centuries ago."

"But —"

"But despite that, there could still be a fix. All is not lost. The remedy is simple and obvious. Get a replacement manual."

Elzabet giggled. "Order one over the global galactic grid. Manual hash *Magog*." But she looked ready to weep.

Marco put his arm round her. "That's not so far off the mark, love. Marco has a cunning plan, and *Magog* is the key. The CV's Da Silva core is still inside, too heavy and too dangerous to move. The rest of its equipment is long gone, removed by the settlers and cannibalised for materials, or corroded by the marsh. But there was also a complete hard-copy manual on *Magog*. Legal requirement. May have been ruined by mould too, or dropped down a well. Might have been removed for safekeeping."

"Or it might still be inside *Magog*," said Jane. "Which is full of mud."

"Half empty," said Marco, "and the comp there is still emitting, though *Valkyrie* couldn't wake it. Might still have a soft-copy manual, if we could get the interface up, or the reserve hard copy could still be in the emergency control space. If they left it there. And if the mould didn't get it over eighteen hundred years. And if we didn't let in something that could get it, when we went inside."

The others stared at Marco.

"We were *right by it?*" said Elza.

Tinka put into words what they were all thinking. "You mean to tell us that after all our efforts to escape from Deacon DeLameter and the Church of the Undivided Body, destroy the VV, overthrow a queen, travel half way round the planet, stop the war between the KF and the SVA, and penetrate the Caverns, we —"

"Yah. We have to go back. Back to Shaaluy and the religious nuthouse. Reach *Magog*. Get past the water, with better equipment. And *hope*."

They all looked stricken. Then Elza straightened herself up, and constructed a bright little smile, as though trying it on for size.

"Fine. This time, people, we know exactly what we're up against. We know about syntei. We know the Qishi social systems. We know DeLameter is a maniac."

Marco gave her a look of adoration. When they started, he'd have expected her to be first to crack. Not any more. Now they all drew strength from her. "You speak truth, Sabi. But we can't just stroll back and ask His Reverence whether the Church of the Undivided Body happens to have a copy of an old technical manual. We're convicted, escaped Abominators. We need to make very careful plans."

"To pump out *Magog*?"

"Easy with syntelics: just a kantasynte down on the coast. What's tricky is coordinating all that unnoticed. We need a few changes in Two Mountains first."

"What do you have in mind?"

Marco's grin became humourless and downright *vengeful*.

"Revolution."

~~~

Elza woke in the night, struck by a memory and an outrageous thought. She poked Marco awake.

"Wha— ?" he grunted, still half-asleep.

"That hard-copy manual. It must be quite big?"

"You wake me up in the middle of the night —"

"Just answer the question."

"Yah, Sixteen volumes."

"And how are they numbered?"

"One to sixteen."

"Not 0 to 15. In what *notation*?"

"A very silly one. Not something sensible like binary: it's Roman numerals."

Elza breathed out in one great exhalation. "Then I know where the hard-copy manual is. And it's not inside *Magog*."

"Where? How?"

"Religions have hermetic scriptures, right?"

"The Church of the Undivided Body, definitely. Gus said so."

"Yah, he did. That was what started me thinking. Not the *Handbook*?"

"Nah, they treat that more like a Bible, open to anyone who seeks instruction. They let me read it. Often."

"He never told you what the Holy Book was called?"

"Nah, he didn't. I think saying the name was forbidden."

"But he did mention one of its prophets. You remember?"

"Nah."

"I do. Gus quoted him. 'Permit no part to come into contact with incompatible components.' Wise words from the prophet Manuel Volix."

"And what help is *that*, Elza my love?"

She pursed her lips. "I'm wondering whether there are other prophets called Manuel Voli and Manuel Volxvi. Along with all the others in between."

It took a moment for the penny to drop.

~~~

She had to be right. You couldn't make it up. The missing hard-copy *Manual* was the unnameable ultra-Holy Book of the Church of the Undivided Body. The collected works of sixteen prophets, *Manual Vol I* to *Manual Vol XVI*. Names changed by time and incomprehension. They'd never seen the name spelt out.

Marco had been right. Only a revolution could retrieve the holiest-of-holy *Manual* from the clutches of the Church of the Undivided Body, even locate it. Their best chance was Sadruddin. When they were in Two Mountains, the Chaplain was plotting to overthrow the church and depose its leader. He had a conspiracy in place already. It hadn't sounded as though he'd been expecting to wait much longer.

They'd had to dump his falasynte when the coastguard caught them sneaking into Wevory. Too risky to keep, and it would have been confiscated anyway. Now they'd have to find a way to get back in touch.

They spent most of a week making detailed plans — contact Gus, what to tell him, safeguard the *Manual*. Wevorin aid would be essential, and it would take a lot of argument to convince Shevveen-Duranga and her colloquy to provide it. But their reward — control of Shaaluy — would be so gigantic that it ought to win them over.

The Starfolk's Black Disc status would give them a lot of political clout. It was certainly powerful enough to get them an appointment with the Colloquist. But when they started to explain, Shevveen-Duranga burst out laughing.

"Sadruddin? You want Wevory to help you get in touch with Augustine Tambiah Sadruddin, Chaplain to Deacon DeLameter, so that you can recruit him as a Wevorin agent? And start a revolution?"

"Yes," said Marco, wondering what was so amusing.

"You have not heard the news?"

"We've been too busy with the beacon to listen to small talk," said Tinka.

"Then I must make you aware of the seeds of the Flower.

"First: you need not recruit Sadruddin. He has been a Wevorin agent these past six years, from before he even knew it. How do you imagine he assembled a network outside Shaaluy? Wevory has eyes in the walls of the world, and ears in its fields and forests. We have been planning for a century to invade that nest of vipers and seize power from the Church. But there had to be a trigger, to persuade the majority of our populace to go along with our plans.

"When the Flower opened and the prophecy was fulfilled, we had our trigger, and pulled it. The Revolt you so desire started that very day. And now it is over. Your friend — you call him Gus? — has become our most powerful representative: Governor of the Shaaluin Province of the Wevorin Empire."

Marco wandered over to a wall and started banging his head against it.

"And the Deacon?" Tinka asked.

"Dead. Along with all his Quizitors."

"By bone-hammer?" It was no more than they deserved.

"Nar. They were cast humanely into lurepools. Governor Sadruddin insisted that all instruments of torture be dissolved in the same pools, not to to taint the Revolution by its enemies' methods of punishment."

Elza shrugged. "That sounds like Gus. I'm not sure I could be that tolerant."

"Me neither," said Marco, vaguely shamed that he felt disappointed.

"As for introducing syntei into Shaaluy and opening up a conversation, be it known to you that Wevory had countless falasyntei and specksyntei in place there long, long ago. On all other continents have we also many oriels and a few wyzands, but security in Shaaluy has always been too strong for anything that can take a man."

Marco was intrigued by a new word. "Specksyntei?"

"Syntei so small that they look like harmless motes of dust. They are everywhere, and no one knows which connects to which, so to most they are useless, thus ignored and forgotten. But we are not most. We have the kantasyntei of specksyntei bred for a vital task.

"We listen through them."

Sam exhaled loudly. "Ahh, Your Profundity, good news all round for us."

Shevveen-Duranga inclined her head. "It does save a great depth of work."

Elzabet was back in manic mood, switching from dark despair in an instant. It was good to see. "Gus! Can I speak to Gus?"

"Of course. Anticipating that request — as I said, Wevory has eyes in the walls of the world, and ears in its fields and forests, not to mention its bedchambers —" She stopped, and handed a blushing Elzabet a falasynte.

She put it to her ear.

"Strabyen, Els'bett."

~~~

As Elza and Sadruddin cooed, Marco started to relax. Now all that was needed was to secure the former Church's copy of the *Manual*. He needed to talk to Gus —

"Marco! Gus wants to speak to you!" She passed him the falasynte.

"Marcolo! Strabyen, Sab! It is good to hear your voice."

"Um, yes, Gus. But before we catch up on old times, my friend, there is something you must do for us. Urgently. It is vitally important, you understand?"

"Whatever your heart desires, Marcolo."

"The Church, it had a Holy Book. Not the *Handbook* we worked on together — the other one, the one so holy that it could not be named. The book containing the wise words of the prophet Manuel Volix."

Pause. "Yes, I know the book of which you speak."

"Good! We must lay hands on it. Specifically, the last volume, *Manuel Volxvi*."

He waited for Gus to tell him there was no such thing. Instead, the Chaplain said, "I will do what can be done."

Elza's wild theory might just be confirmed.

"I shall issue the necessary orders immediately. But you must be aware that in Shaaluy, and especially in Two Mountains, all has been chaos. Tracing the Deacon's possessions may be difficult. Most were secured, once the tide of revolt ran firm in our favour, but until then there was much looting and arson.

"I will share word as soon as I have it." Sadruddin signed off.

"And now we wait," said Marco, once he had relayed the conversation.

"It would be good to bring Gus here," said Elzabet. "To — uh — see him again. Marco, you know..."

"An excellent idea, my love, but you heard the words of Her Profundity. Wevorin has no oriels with Shaaluy."

"Nobody has," said Elza. "The Temple out-wyzand was burned in the Revolt."

"But the cavern-dwellers have plenty of falasyntei," Jane said.

Shevveen-Duranga had overheard. "We do. And the membrane can indeed be removed without destroying the connection, as I presume you hope. But no one has yet bred oval syntei narrow enough to pass through such a small opening. Had they done, we could have initiated a lopsynte cascade centuries ago."

Jane had expected something along those lines. However... "Have you ever had agents in the Dunelands of south-west Lamynt?"

Shevveen-Duranga shook her head. "Those lands are barren and impassable. Even the coast is rocky and uninhabited. There was no reason to install syntei."

Little do you know. "That's why the Vain Vaimoksi set themselves up there."

Shevveen-Duranga let out a sigh. "Once would Wevory have given a ransom in copper to anyone who could tell us the Vain Vaimoksi's domain. But now they are destroyed, the information is worthless."

Jane laughed. "Not entirely. Let me tell you about my frog Rapunzel."

~~~

A glider — a nearly finished flier from Lamynt's war production, completed and assembled — took off from Plegg, near a tributary of the Graydrear, on an urgent mission to a nameless oasis in the middle of the Dunelands.

Its pilot wondered why anyone wanted specimens of the lilypads there, but the world had gone mad and there was no accounting for folk. He had asked, of course, but apparently his security clearance wasn't high enough. Typical air-force top brass.

The part involving a frog on a string seemed particularly obscure.

~~~

"Well, he did bring back a whole chain of flexible kasyntei and kantasyntei," said Jane. "Which was the important part."

Marco grunted. "Yah. Um... Jane, why did he bring back the frog as well?"

The strange little animal was sitting on the table next to a heap of syntei. Jane shook her head. "I probably didn't make my instructions clear. Does it matter?"

"The poor thing looks bewildered. What do we do with it? Send it back?"

Jane sat the frog on the palm of her hand. It seemed happy there. They could probably find a lake nearby, but would it survive? Send it home? The remnant of the Kuukau Air Force had made it clear that their glider was needed elsewhere.

"I think..." she began.

"What?"

"It looks just like Rapunzel."

"Jane, they all look exactly the same. There's a million-to-one-against chance that it might even *be* Rapunzel."

"It's cute," said Jane, ignoring him. "I think I'll keep it."

~~~

Rolled-up lilypad, small oval brasure, medium, larger...

The falasynte passed the first. A series of exotic kasyntei passed each other, unrolling in Two Mountains. From the oriel clambered a familiar figure.

Elza and Marco rushed to embrace Sadruddin. Hugs hinted at more to come. But first, Gus brought a package ("These are the gems you forgot to steal, so I took them for you: we all sought them all over Sambal"), and news.

"Marcolo, my friend. I have word of the *Manual* that you seek."

"Yes! Yes! Gus — where is it?"

Gus seemed to shrink, deflated. "It is gone. Destroyed."

Jane and Elzabet began to weep. Sam, intending to console them, ended up joining in. Tinka looked furious. Marco seemed to have been struck dumb.

"What happened?" Tinka asked.

"The Deacon's House was taken with a fire-fight. Flaming arrows through syntei. Among the rooms burnt out was the Deacon's library, where he kept the sixteen volumes of the *Manual*. The books did not survive the heat. Not even as ashes.

"I know this Book has great significance for you, though as yet you have not told me why. I am saddened beyond measure to bring you this news."

So this was where their quest had ended. Their plans, over-complex, had bitten their own tails. Elza walked over to Gus, who looked distraught. "Gus, you weren't to know. We needed to get hold of that book to talk to the stars. To leave this world."

Sadruddin put out his hands and grasped hers. "To you it is a profound source of sadness," he said. "To me — it means that you and Marcolo will remain here. With me. So I cannot fully share your sorrow. But I do feel it."

"Perhaps you're right," said Marco. "Perhaps we were destined not to take the news of syntei to the stars. Who knows what harm they might have caused?"

Elza put her arms round both men. "I used to argue that, Marco. But I think I was wrong. And I don't believe in destiny, especially negative destiny. I don't know how we are going to get the news out, but we can't just give up!"

"However, Gus will be tired, and now is not the time to consider our next steps. Save one. Marco, Gus? Come with me. We have much to — uh — catch up on."

Perhaps out of tact, or not to seem too forward, Gus had not brought his toys.

They managed pretty well without them.

~~~

"Much has now become clear to me," Sadruddin remarked, during a quiet time late one evening, alone with Elza while Marco was running some errand or another. He seemed distracted, almost sad.

"You can tell me, Gus."

"Yes, Els'bett. You remember a Vain Vaimoksi who organised body-dividing performances and events in Shaaluy? The one to which I foolishly took Marcolo, who was overcome by fumes from the *kreesh* plant and seen by the Deacon's informants?"

Elza remembered it vividly. How could she forget?

"I thought she was Vain Vaimoksi." He sighed. "I was mistaken. Blinded by lust. She was Wevorin."

"*Ohhhh!*"

"Precisely. *All* illicit body-diving in Shaaluy was run by female agents from Wevory, using Vain Vaimoksi as cover. It was part of the cavern-dwellers' masterplan to destabilise the Church and take over the continent. Body-division was a way to select suitable persons for recruitment, and to groom them for eventual revolution."

She reached over and drew him close. "You were a recruit."

"Yes. I should have suspected. My position as Chaplain, close to DeLameter, made me an obvious target, a valuable dupe."

Elza kissed him. "Not a dupe, Gus. They recognised your potential as a political game-changer, and helped you to realise it."

Gus sighed. "That is one way to put it. But I still feel used."

Elza's mind went back to the morning her mother told her, with no warning, that she was assigned to a group of citizenship candidates bound for Starhome, with two days to prepare. "You're not the only one, Gus. What counts is what you make of it, not what the people who used you intended. You can't avoid use, but you can choose between feeling used and feeling useful."

29

Crowd Cuckoo Land

> Hear us, you who are no more than leaves always falling,
>   you mortals benighted by nature,
> You enfeebled and powerless creatures of earth
>   always haunting a world of mere shadows,
> Entities without wings, insubstantial as dreams,
>   you ephemeral things, you human beings:
> Turn your minds to our words, our aetherial words,
>   for the words of the birds last forever!
> —*Aristophanes, The Birds, from Alas, Poor Yorick: a Short History of the Performing Arts, University of Central Dool Press*

Shortly before dawn, Elza found Gus awake. Snuggled close, she murmured in his ear. "Perhaps you're right. Who needs Starhome? But, much as I adore your loving body, it really is a terrible shame that all the information in the *Manual* has been lost."

Gus moved sensuously under her hands — and froze. "Information?"

"Yes. We needed to know something written in your nameless Holy Book."

"To know? Not to touch?"

"Of course."

"But, Marcolo, he told me — he said he wanted to *lay hands* on the Book. You said you wanted to *get hold* of it. To talk to the stars. I assumed you needed it for some ritual purpose, some sort of prayer."

"Ah. Just a way to speak. We meant we wanted to know what was inside it."

"Then you both should have said so. That is different, and —" He shot out of bed, and began to pull on a robe.

"Gus, where are you —?"

He was gone.

~~~

The man was very old, downcast, and defeated.

"Why has Sadruddin brought this poor man all the way from Shaaluy?" wondered Jane, out loud.

"You will see," Sadruddin replied. He addressed the man. "You are Brzeska Umbleby Crookshank?"

The man was terrified. He whimpered and nodded in some kind of panic.

"You were a membrancer in the retinue of Deacon DeLameter?"

"Yes, but I never — I mean, not — I just did what priests told, I was not —"

"I have not brought you here to punish you for whatever the Church did to or with your mind, Brzeska Umbleby Crookshank." Using all three names, he showed proper respect. "I want something from that vast tenacious memory of yours."

The old man made a visible effort, and straightened. "Do with me what you will. I am the best membrancer in all of Qish."

Sadruddin found this answer satisfactory. "We will not harm you, no matter what you do or do not tell us. But —" He motioned to Marco. "Start your wrist membrancer. Yes, I know you have such a thing." Back to Crookshank. "Tell us of the *Manual*."

The old man gasped at this plain use of the forbidden word, but his professional instincts overrode his emotions.

"*Manual*. Vol I: Introduction and Overview. Vol II: Before Departure. Vol—"

Marco butted in. "Gus? Tell him to skip Contents and go straight to Vol XVI."

The words alone were enough of a trigger. "Vol XVI: Technical Appendices," said Crookshank, the words flowing out in a single stream-of consciousness brain-dump. "One: Schematics — Sab, there are many drawings, I can replicate them all if provided with charcoal and pa—"

"Activation codes for the rescue beacon," Marco told him.

"Nine hundred forty-six point twelve point four. Rescue Beacon Memoblock Activation Codes. Zot, zot, zot, zot, sput, sput, sput. Zot, zot, zot, zot, sput, sput, sput. Zot, zot, zot, zot, sput, sput. Blanco. Zot, zot, zot, zot, sput, zot, zot. Zot..."

Zot? Sput? Sam didn't want to interrupt, in case the old man's memory glitched. He held his tongue even when Marco started bouncing in excitement. Only after Marco stopped the old man and asked him to repeat everything, and then a third time to be certain, did Sam dare ask: "What the nanacurst skunt was all that about?"

Marco tapped his wrist. "Our ticket home, Sam. Seven-digit binary groups, Shaaluy style. Now safely on my 'comp."

"That's it?"

"So Crookshank says. According to Gus, he has an eidetic memory, never mistaken. So, if it's not the activation code, we really *are* trashed."

~~~

"I no longer believe the sky is full of angels," said Sadruddin, "but I am eager to hear the voices from the stars." An audience of the lowest Cavern-Dwellers was bad enough as an invitation to the Bad Fairy Godfather of demo trials, but when Gus invited himself, Marco felt doomed. He checked for the tenth time that all memoblocks, old and new, had been correctly installed and activated. He hesitated, then touched the startup pad, hoping not to repeat the previous fiasco.

Five red lights.
Five yellow lights.
One, two, three, four…
Five green lights.

Deep breath, push blue button. Wait while your life flashes before your eyes. Exhale. No flash-bang-cough-cough. His experiments hadn't been misleading: a bigger synte did do the trick. His metamaterial theory of syntelics might just be right, too.

The screen lit up.

Connecting to Starhome Rescue Service
We're getting there.
Connecting to Starhome Rescue Service
We're not getting there.
Connecting to Starhome Rescue Service

"What is happening?" asked Sadruddin.

Somebody's wrecking my concentration, but Gus was his friend. "There should be a precise resonance…," he started to explain, "Oh."

"Marco, my friend?"

He lifted the casing. "I had to connect this silvery thread through a synte," he said. "The synte died, and this part," he pointed, "lost memory. That is why we needed Manuel Volxvi. Why did I ever think *this* part would work near a synte? The tuning is so delicate…"

"Why not use a longer thread, with no synte?"

"I didn't," Marco kept himself from screaming, "*have* a longer thread!"

"*Ni porbleem*," said Sadruddin.

" — ?"

He spoke into his falasynte of office. "Andriolti, go at once, itself, to the Sacristy of Spear Parts. Bring me the Chaplet of Magog. Bring it now."

Two Mountains is lower than Krig Mountain, so his secretary climbed a lot of stairs. Finally, Sadruddin was able to offer the shining cable.

"Is this," he asked, "long enough?"

"More than long enough," gasped Marco, "and exactly the right type."

"While I install it," he said, "please can we clear the area of *all* syntei? Falasyntei, scrikkers, oriels, … as far as we can reach from here without trapping ourselves in this Cavern. Please!" He was happy to see Sadruddin smoothly organising his Wevorin overlords into doing what was needed.

~~~

Connecting to Starhome Rescue Service
Still a long way to go.
Connecting to Starhome Rescue Service
Marco ran his eyes over the screen.
Connected to Starhome Rescue Service

After an endless wait, a laconic voice said "Rescue. Who are you jokers? Are you aware that it's a criminal offence to abuse Central —?"

"This is a genuine call. We're stuck on a boondocks planet and we need help. Check the transponders."

There was a long pause. "Those are very old codes. Where did you get them?"

"From the Colony Vessel *Magog*," Marco replied. "We're survivors from Da Silva caltrop *Valkyrie*, bound for Starhome in training. We hit severe *k*-weather and got kicked prematurely into normal spacetime near Squill III. *Valkyrie* was in a decaying orbit and burnt up. We got away in the capsule and crash-landed in a swamp. *Magog* must have run into similar trouble, but we found its rescue beacon and activated it."

Wait while the Rescue Service's duty officer processed this. "We do have a *Valkyrie* on file, but you're not cleared to know where it went, or what happened to it."

"Of course we're cleared," Marco protested. "We were on it! It was *supposed* to go to Starhome. That can't be secret! As for what happened to it — we watched it burn up in the sky of Qish — sorry, Squill III — three years ago."

Another lengthy silence. "I can tell you what's public. *Valkyrie* did not crash three years ago, on Squill III or anywhere else. It visited Starhome, then went back out on a classified mission. Five months ago, its trainee team visited the Wada Cluster on R&R. They went back to a location I am unable to reveal, confirm, or even deny.

"*Who are you*? And where did you get those codes?"

"I just told you. From *Magog*."

"There's no CV named *Magog* in current files."

Marco laughed. "It'll be archived by now. You need to go back a bit."

"How far?"

"Sixteen to eighteen hundred years."

"One moment... Right. Colony Vessel 23, one of the earliest. Made successful landfall 1,698 years ago in the Nuh Wisp, now the core of the Secular Islamic Alliance.

"So.

"Who are you?"

There was a stunned silence, followed by a babble of incredulity and argument. They might not have expected a welcome with open arms, but being told that the Colony Vessel and its rescue beacon had never made it to Qish was insane.

"That can't be right," said Marco.

"CV-23 *Magog*, it says here. Bit of a *k*-storm en route, but no damage done."

Oh, Mother. "The records must have been corrupted —"

"Shut up. Who are you?"

"Samuel Grey Deer Wasumi, born on Wounded Knee," said Sam, like training roll call.

"Irenotincala Laurel, Wayland."

"Jane Bytinsky, Ebisu. Felix Wylde, Daikoku, was in our group, but... he died. A year ago."

"Elzabet, Hippolyta." Reflexes for facing officialdom surfaced. "*Lady* Elzabet of Quynt. Third daughter of Duchess Arabella."

"Marco Leontevich Bianchi, Inferno."

"All six of those names are on my list, here —" the officer began.

"So I should hope!" Marco butted in, relieved.

"— on my list of *Valkyrie*'s R&R group. Which arrived in the Wada Cluster one hundred and forty-seven days ago.

"Who are you? I won't ask again."

Good question, Marco thought. We're us, and so are they. *Valkyrie* went to Qish with us, and to the Wada Cluster with them. Who are us. *Magog* crashed on Qish, populated the planet, and it also went to the Nuh Wisp and founded a colony.

Weird.

But Qish *is* weird. Spacetime around Qish is weird. Could it be *that* weird?

Why not?

Somewhere inside his head, a network tipped into an attractor basin it had never explored before. "By the unpaid ghost of Emmy Nöther, it's the Da Silva identity problem! In an extreme form. A multiple focus makes multiple copies. *Magog* and *Valkyrie* got duplicated. So did we."

It was enough to convince *Marco*. Now to convince Starhome, or at least to unconvince one Starhomer of what he thought he knew. "You'll find this hard to believe, but I'm afraid we *are* the same people as those on your R&R list."

"—?"

"Only different."

"—?"

"It's a rare and obscure effect of Da Silva drives. Never before observed. It *duplicates*." Now we've got *two* world-changing technologies to present to the Concordat. If they'll listen.

Marco grasped desperately for a way to prove he was Marco, and found one. "There's an easy way to settle this. I loaded an entangled bank-access algorithm before we left. Let me authorise a cash transfer — "

"To me? Are you trying to bribe me?"

"Let it be to the Home for Retired Popes! It's just a test of whether the Bank of Inferno agrees that I must be Marco Leontevich Bianchi!"

"Why should anyone do something that crazy?"

Elza pushed Marco aside. "Because the third daughter of Duchess Arabella of Quynt, Keeper of the Royal Standard to Queen Francesca VII of Hippolyta, so requires, you unimaginative *male*! Fail and my mother will ensure you spend the rest of your drab life searching for exometeorites on the methane icecaps of Basilisk XIII!"

"Understood, your ladyship," the shaken official replied. "Ready to initiate cash transfer *attempt* whenever the gentleman is ready to authorise it."

Marco took over again. Elza slapped her hands together in satisfaction. *The old reflexes never really leave you.* She turned and saw the others' faces.

"What?"

~~~

The bank said Marco was Marco. Entangled access algorithms never lie. They can't, not without violating several basic laws of physics.

Similar checks confirmed four other identities.

The official remained privately sceptical, but this was way above his pay grade. He kicked it upstairs.

~~~

"*Now*, can you tell us what your records say happened to *Valkyrie*? Presumably your copy went on that mission Starhome Security was planning for us? What was it, anyway?"

"I can't answer those questions without higher authorisation. But it seems I can tell you that after the R&R break, the resumed mission had two survivors. Marco Leontevich Bianchi and Felix Wylde. They're recuperating here on Starhome."

Survivors? *Perhaps Qish really had been the easy option.*

~~~

It got easier after that. They transmitted their location and a formal request for rescue.

The next part would be harder. Starhome was provisionally convinced of their identities, but the Concordat's senior officials would not easily swallow the coming tale. Marco himself was having trouble with it, and he had more tale-swallowing practice.

He had written out his words to avoid slips. He coughed to clear his suddenly dry throat. "Starhome: be warned that the spacetime topology around Squill is dangerously distorted. We believe that both *Magog* and *Valkyrie* appeared at Squill III for the same reason. Their focal geodesics approached the planet too closely."

"Distorted? In what way?"

"That's a long story. In a way that wrecks Da Silva drives and duplicates ships and people. I'll fill you in later, if this connection holds. We're talking on very old equipment here. Beacons may have been built for the ages, but this one's already suffered some damage. Best to assume the link could fail at any moment."

"Understood. How close is too close?"

"Five megaklicks should be an acceptable safety margin."

You could almost hear the mental cogwheels. "I hear you, *Valkyrie*. But if we stay that far, *how do we rescue you*? Standard procedure is to sneak up as close as Da Silva allows, then send down reaction-mass tenders. However, those have limited range. For a near-normal-gee world — which yours must be, as you're alive to ask for rescue — even half a megaklick is pushing it. We could use a plasma drive heavy transport if you're willing to wait four thousand years, but there's nothing else —"

"No worries, Starhome. Listen up."

This, Marco knew, was where the Starhome officials would become convinced that their five ghosts had shown up from Cloud Cuckoo Land. He took a deep breath. "Not quite nothing. What about an asteroid miner? Do you have a Da Silva ship with a big enough cargo capacity to hold one?"

"Yah, sure. The *Real McCoy* can do that. But mineships are for low-gee vacuum. The miners sidle up on a big rock and float down on to the surface. A mineship would break up as soon as it reached the thermosphere."

"Yah, I know. But don't some miners use reaction-drive sample probes? To explore a target from long range? Five megaklicks would take about a week each way, but it's surely within operating range. And some can pick up rocks from planets. Don't the mining cooperatives use robotic planetary exploration tech?"

Beat. "Yah, they do. And asteroid miners are always available for hire. But — *Valkyrie*, you do realise that a sample probe has no life-support? And its carrying capacity is limited to five kilograms?"

Here goes nothing. "Yah. That will be ample."

"*Valkyrie*, your signal must be breaking up. I heard 'ample'."

"The signal's fine. We'll use the probe to send you a sample of local technology, and *that* will allow you to rescue us."

"Wha — Oh. Something that damps down the distortion?"

"Nah, it's what caused it."

There was a sustained silence at the other end, eventually followed by a strained "Please repeat."

Marco did. Then he added: "Don't try to understand now. This connection is untrustworthy and could fail at any moment. With no backup. Please: *just do as I say*. Stay well clear and send down a probe. I've already given you the coordinates. When we send it back, you'll be able to check that I'm not crazy.

"Confirm that you can do *exactly* as I ask, and then I can start on just how the trick is going to work. If we lose this link at that stage, it won't matter. But you need to know a lot about the local conditions, and some of it will sound implausible in the extreme. We find it hard to credit ourselves, and we've been immersed in it. For three years. So it'll take a while. Don't call any psychs until you've heard me out."

~~~

"I *know* it sounds crazy, Chief Scientist Tampledown. Just follow instructions — to the letter please, I really do know what I'm doing — and I'll prove to you that it's not. Or do you want to go down in history as the man who declined the offer of free matter transmission because he couldn't be bothered to try it?"

~~~

On a secure link, Jane talked to Felix, lost to her in the Dunelands.
Felix talked to Jane, lost to him in an accident that never took her.
The strangeness of it almost overwhelmed the joy.

Elza, Jane, and Sam struggled to come to terms with their own deaths, and failed. Not me, guv.

Marco talked to Marco. He was used to it.

~~~

"*Magog* beacon: be advised that your package is at Starhome. It will continue to be at the same gravitational potential as your location on Krig Mountain, as requested." The duty officer on the Rescue Ship spoke in the tone of voice you use to humour lunatics. Lunatic ghosts. It had taken a week to reach this weird orbit, and he was still burning fuel to maintain it, with the requested mad precision. A sinusoidal term allowed for the spin that kept this room comfortable for stan-gee humans.

"Understood, Starhome," said a Galaxic-speaking Dweller, at the Beacon.

"As requested, shutting down Da Silva drive and communicator in three seconds... two seconds... one second... *now*."

Invisible to him, the Dweller waved to the woman holding a falasynte at a safe distance, who relayed the news to Marco on the outside.

"Thanks. I need to fine-tune the gravitational potential," he told the others.

"You mean, gain some height."

"Yah, Elza. Sorry about the cold, but there's no long gentle slope inside."

The Starfolk on the ship, including Felix and the replica Marco, stared at the fist-size paper-wrapped disc returned by the probe. They had followed Marco's instructions and resisted the urge to unwrap or scan it. Marco hadn't wanted to risk premature poking at the interface; some fear of damage, but more his stagecraft.

Now, it started unwrapping *itself*. From the inside. The paper tore, revealing a featureless wooden hoop, into which it vanished. The hoop filled with unnerving whiteness. For minutes, nothing happened. Then white puffs streamed out, and the temperature in the room dropped. *Snow?* Some sort of refrigeration device? *Definitely Cloud Cuckoo Land. A bizarre hoax —*

Something more solid poked out from the disc, for all the world like a gloved fingertip.

"Potentials equalised," Marco quietly told his companions. He had walked gently up Krig Mountain, watching until snow fell through. They had followed him, with bags. They passed him the contents, in turn.

The thing that had poked, whatever it was, disappeared. Then the disc disgorged a tube, that unrolled to a wider hoop. A second, larger tube emerged from *that*, unrolled. Then another, and another, like Russian dolls in reverse.

Finally, a human head.

Marco, kneeling in the snow with his head down, eyed a row of feet. The eyes connected to them saw Marco's disembodied face, amid a hood of furry animal skin.

"Hi, everyone." He made a handstand, then dropped into the synte. Qishi gravity threw him up through the ship floor. Landing on his feet, he tried to look as though this was something he did every day. As it had been, lately.

Disembodied hands pushed a fur-wrapped bundle from the hole. He bent down and took it, cooing softly. A second followed. One bundle started wriggling and let out a wail. The other joined in.

Lomyrla sprang acrobatically from the synte and helped Marco unwrap, before the twins overheated in the sudden warmth. There was a pause while the Krig Mountain kasynte was turned, for access from below.

Tinka clambered out. Then Jane. Then Sam. Lady Elzabet of Quynt's elegant form climbed *gracefully* from a cosmic manhole.

Jaws dropping isn't close. Faces sagged like puddings.

The five escapees hugged Lomyrla and the twins and each other, and their carefully choreographed entrance came to pieces at an emotional breaking-point. Jane went to Felix, shutting out the rest of the universe. Marco watched Marco watch Elza and Lomyrla, as if hoping for smiles from beyond the end of the world.

The Concordat observers felt the storm of *Valkyrie* emotion, but froze in an equally ancient brain response: total incredulity. Reason told them there was no way to work a conjuring trick over six hundred and fifty-seven light years. Babies do not emerge from portable holes in a ship hull. The old lizard brain, honed by two hundred million years of evolution into a highly effective reflex Bayesian decision machine, knew it for a scam. Its prior probability was simply too low for any evidence to be credible, from eyes or ears.

Tampledown was the first to recover some of his wits. "You did tell us this has to be seen to be believed," he said. "And I have. And even now, I don't." He paused, overcome by a potent mix of disbelief and awe. "How did you guys *do* that?"

"Just exploiting a vegetable connection," said Marco.

"Where did the babies come from?"

"Did your mother never tell you?"

"Nah, I mean—"

"What's that thing clinging to her shoulder?"

"It's Rapunzel, my frog," said Jane, cradling the creature protectively.

"And what the Mother are those *eyes* doing, crawling over *you*."

"Looking at you," said Sam. "First Chief Scientist it's ever seen."

But now an eye had caught sight of the toddlers, and parts of the *skiti* poured out of his pockets to resume its endless game of chase.

Marco cut in. "I have to tell you my metamaterial theory, and why syntei come to pieces when the boundary circle is cut, like peeling a banana, some kind of minimal surface effect — yah, Tinka, sure, not right now. I was about to make the same —"

Tinka shoved him aside and stepped forward. "Star Pilot Class 4 Irenotincala Laurel reporting on behalf of Candidacy Group #87439, out of Suufi on an unregistered trajectory. One death, circumstances unavoidable, details to follow.

"We wish to report the discovery of a lost colony, descended from the passengers of CV23 *Magog*. Well, *a* CV *Magog*.

"We wish to notify you of the discovery of a radical new technology. The locals call the devices *syntei*. You just saw a small example of what they can do. After proper scientific study they will create a revolution in local and interstellar transportation — and much more. It seems they also create Da Silva duplicators. If we can tame that, it will create a second revolution.

"Our mission report will provide full details. Finally, we — oh, trash this formality. Rustle up five cups of coffee, please? We've not had any for three years. And some juice for Lomyrla." She gestured. "We brought our own stuff for the kids."

"Can we change orbit?" asked the duty officer, "This is costing reaction mass."

"Ah — *ni porb*-" said Tinka. "Yah."

There was a subtle shift in the gravity, then an outraged wail from a twin. "Oops," said Marco. "I think we just went below the working level of the napisyntei. I hope Rescue Ships carry startech equivalents."

"And *coffee*," said Tinka.

Tampledown stared at the scattered syntei. "If this stuff *really* does what my eyes just told me it did, I'll give you an entire coffee plantation. And you'll all be fast-tracked to full galactic citizenship as a matter of course, for services rendered."

By the looks on their faces, the five had forgotten their original objective. It no longer seemed to matter. But Tinka's slow doubletake was interrupted by a dull gonglike noise and a soundless voice inside her head:

#*Welcome to Starhome.*#

It was her wristcomp. The galactic grid had registered their presence, and they were back in touch with the data-nebula. From their faces, it was obvious that the others were undergoing the same experience.

"I want a meeting with your top karmabhumi experts as soon as you can schedule one," said the Marco in the *rhunka*-fur jacket.

"Count me in, too," said Marco. "Two heads are better than one. Well, they will be once Marco here has brought me up to speed about syntelics."

"Consider it done." Tampledown could move almost as fast as a pair of Marcos, once he'd wrenched his brain back into gear.

"Experimental facilities. Pion microscopes, lab assistants, supercomp access. You'll want an oversight committee. Set it up, just make sure it doesn't get in the way. We need all the brainpower we can get as long as no galloping dingbeaucrat tries to tell me syntei are impossible." Some of Elza's instincts must have rubbed off on him. "I want to test my metamaterial theory. You don't know how frustrating it's been piling up anecdotal observations with no suitable lab equip—"

Another gonglike sound. #*You have 1,293,446 unread messages.*#

Tinka looked at her companions. "You too?"

"Yah," said Elzabet. "Welcome back to civilisation, people." She paused. "Is there some way to delete all this junk *easily*?"

Marco was about to reply, but Marco got there first.

"*Ni porbleem*, Sabi."

Epilogue

> **Bianchi Identities. (1)** [*Pre-Concordat O.E.*] Symmetry properties of the covariant derivative of the Riemann tensor. **(2)** [*Contemp. Shm.*] The fundamental equations of the Magneto-Gravito-Karmabhumic Unified Field Theory, as derived by Marco Leontevich Bianchi and Marco Leontevich Bianchi using their metamaterial model for syntelic gravito-magnetic fuzzification. The identities take the elegant form
>
> $$\mathfrak{S}\{\Omega\} = \Theta^{\cdot\cdot}$$
> $$\mathfrak{S}\{\Theta\} = -\Omega^{\cdot\cdot}$$
>
> where $\mathfrak{S}$ is the normalised Quynt operator.
> —The Ptarmigan Dictionary of Mathematical Engineering

The Concordat

Learned that a monopoly on mahabhavium is not a monopoly on interstellar travel.

Old Earth

Learned the same, and reacted (as always) messily.

Marco Leontevich Bianchi

Led the Starhome Syntelics Institute until leaving for Qish, where they married Lomyrla Polo Koorbun and helped her raise their twin daughters Marcolette and Polonia. No further children. Appointed Joint Professor of Theoretical Syntelics on Dool (a synte-accepting planet), discovered Bianchi's Identities, the basis of mathematical syntelics.

Irenotincala Laurel

Mastered orbital synte matching, for spaceships under power, and adapted the U-bend glider principle to a system of syntelic mass transfer alternating with free ballistic motion to reach points with arbitrarily high gravitational potential within a star system: first implemented at Nazg, a giant solar system with large insystem trade. Refused an executive position in Tinka's Ladder (Universal Beanstalk Rfd.) to continue flying, and training pilots.

Gave a knife to her grandson when he went off to ballet school.

Jane Bytinsky

Offered Qish Anthropology chair at Starhome Syntelics Institute but resigned to return to the planet and found the Felix Wylde Memorial School of Medicine. Instituted a programme of infectious cures to eradicate the planet's main human diseases. Later founded and became Director of the Institute for Qishi Ecology, delegating administrative tasks in order to spend most of her time observing in the field. Disappeared on a field-trip to study the behaviour and habitat of Kriggian drift-orms. No body or other evidence discovered.

Felix Wylde

Accompanied Jane Bytinsky to Qish but failed to accommodate to her deeper sense of its cultures. *This* Felix hadn't been moulded by the violence of Qish; *this* Jane had, possibly too much. Became mildly reclusive. Created the first evolutionary genetically accurate tree of the planet's flora and fauna, but left cultural structures to specialists in network sociodynamics.

Samuel Grey Deer Wasumi

Returned to Wounded Knee to research his Amerindian ancestry, discovering, to his surprise, that the family legend was right: he was one-sixteenth Iroquois. Spent nine years as part-time advisor to Universal Beanstalk Rfd., specialising in field-testing new installations. Covertly visited Qish for longer and longer periods, seeking a simpler lifestyle. Subsequent whereabouts unknown, save for unsubstantiated reports of a large number of unusually tall children, with red hair tied in a single lopsided pigtail, in several secluded villages of Central Lamynt.

Lady Elzabet of Quynt

Commuted daily to Hippolyta (a synte-accepting planet) and made a fortune selling punctyle pants and more exotic body-dividing equipment, until stripped of her title by her mother the Duchess Arabella and jailed for fifteen months for subversion.

Upon release, had a dynastically improper daughter by the Marcos, and founded the Masculinist Party. One hundred and twenty years later this movement brought full male emancipation to Hippolyta, followed within a decade by equal pay for men, the overthrow of the monomatriarchy, a written planetary constitution, and the creation of a democratic government.

And that was when their troubles *really* started.

Augustine Tambiah Sadruddin

First Governor of the Shaaluin Province of the Wevorin Empire, a post that he held for seven years. Abolished all restrictions on bodily uses of syntei. With Irenotincala Laurel, founded Universal Beanstalk Rfd. Responsible for the first global wyzand network on Qish, and for linking the Squill system to other stars.

Lomyrla Polo Korbun

Accompanied by both Marcos, rejoined her family and the *khanatta*, finding the Concordat insufficiently exciting and missing the nomadic lifestyle. Despite well-meant fatherly advice to the contrary, married the Marcos in a unique ceremony, welcoming either or both on extended vacations from Dool, with their co-mate Lady Elzabet of Quynt.

With new funds, formed her own *khanatta*, which included effects like ossivore roars from below the seats, and visions appearing and disappearing in the air: much disapproved of by her bodyfather, but popular with the audience.

Drusilla Sybilschild

Refused rescue when the syntenet was re-extended to Vulcan's Anvil. Became revered as the Fishing Hermit, but acolytes learned to approach her in pairs.

Glossary

Deep, adjective: of a synte with a long synterior, and thus less tidal stress than a 'shallow' synte used only to transfer fluids or sounds.

Exsynte, verb, transitive: to syntelically egest (final 'e' silent).

Kasynte, noun (most Qish languages): apparent-space-manipulable aperture of a synte. Exists only while entangled with its **kantasynte**, the other aperture.

Kreesh, noun: you don't want to know. People go blind just thinking about the stuff.

Klòvij, noun: one thousand *vij* (see below). Approximately half a kilometre; exact measure varies with locality.

Qish, proper noun (most Qish languages): planet galactically listed as SQL7812-III.

Qishi, adjective, concerning or native to Qish.

Skint or **Sqint**, proper noun (most Qish languages): small monetary unit; usually about 75gm of copper, but sometimes debased with silver.

Strint, proper noun (most Qish languages): syntelic transfer of metabolic material.

Synte, noun (all Qish languages, final 'e' pronounced as in 'wet'), plural syntei final 'ei' pronounced as in 'way'): botanical Smale surgery of the meta-persistent karmabhumic hypersurface, requiring entangled meta-particles. Includes functional structures such as membranes, baffles, channels, etc. Evolved and bred varieties include:

>   **Brasure**: synte big enough for a human to wriggle through, barely.
>   **Chamfret**: synte a finger-length across.
>   **Dropsynte**: projectile-transmitting synte or kasynte, turning potential energy to kinetic.
>   **Falasynte**: bidirectional sound-passing synte or kasynte.
>   **Grubsynte**: synte or kasynte specialised for passing edible slurry.

Kolosynte: view-observation kasynte, kantasynte to an olosynte.
Koriel: oriel small enough to be carried.
Lopsynte: asymmetrical synte or kasynte.
Mamasynte. Used in Samdal to enable fathers to mother's-breastfeed.
Mismatch: synte with differing geometry of kasynte and kantasynte.
Napisynte: garment worn by humans without toilet training or cloacal syntei.
Night-synte: long-distance sunsynte lamp.
Olosynte: view acquisition kasynte, kantasynte to a kolosynte.
Orelsynte: unidirectional sound-transmitting kasynte.
Oriel: synte or kasynte large enough to pass a human quickly.
Punctyle: synte a thumb-joint across.
Slavestone: synstone adapted to control.
Specksynte: miniature olosynte (highly diffracting) or orelsynte. Natural ancestors transmit molecular signals undetected by Quishi science.
Spillsynte: large fixed watersynte.
Spysynte: inconspicuous information-transmitting synte or kasynte.
Sunsynte: sunlight-transmitting synte or kasynte, local or distant.
Syndial: wearable sundial, with a static kantasynte.
Synlight: sunlight transmitted through a synte.
Synstone: gut-anchored syntelic parasite.
Synsurgency: multiple hostile intrusion via synte.
Synthole: synte arranged for disposal of human waste.
Syntorch: portable sunsynte.
Syntrap: syntelic man-trap.
Syntube: small portable dropsynte.
Syntecannon: large dropsynte.
Syntehead: initial access synte, which other syntei and material can pass. Cf *bridgehead*.
Syntseed: seed syntelically linked to its parent plant.
Syntower: tall structure in a planar region, with stairs to reach a high wyzand.
Syntwell: deep structure in a planar region, with stairs to reach a low wyzand.
Wasynte: synte passable by aquatic creatures.
Watersynte: synte or kasynte specialised for high flow of water (fixed or portable).
Weathersynte: atmosphere-transmitting synte or kasynte.
Wyzand: synte or kasynte large enough to pass a walking human

Synte, verb (all Qish languages, final 'e' silent), reflexive or transitive: to syntelically relocate.

Syndept, noun (all Qish languages, modulo grammatical form): breeder, developer or cultivator of syntei.

Syntelic, adjective (all Qish languages, modulo grammatical form): related to syntei and the practice of their manipulation.

Syntelics, noun (Galaxic neologism, later adopted on Qish): related to the theory of syntelic manipulation.

Synthelics, noun (Galaxic neologism, later adopted on Qish): related to the theory of syntelic manipulation without dependence on living matter.

Syntenet, noun (all Qish languages): system of nodes, most with multiple kasyntei, whose kantasyntei are in other nodes.

Synterior: space between kasynte and kantasynte, which relative to their surrounding spaces is neither here nor there.

Vij, noun (all Qish languages): an arm's length, without the hand. (Compare classical English *foot*.)

Warning

This book is in part a work of fiction.
Not all the syntelic devices and methods described have been field-tested by a licensed Safety Inspector. Do not try them at home without expert supervision.

About the Authors

Ian Stewart was born in 1945, educated at Cambridge (MA) and Warwick (PhD). He has five honorary doctorates and is Emeritus Professor of Mathematics at Warwick University. He has published over 80 books including *Does God Play Dice?*, *Professor Stewart's Cabinet of Mathematical Curiosities*, *Why Beauty is Truth*, *Flatterland*, *What Shape is a Snowflake?*, *Nature's Numbers*, *Professor Stewart's Incredible Numbers*, *Seventeen Equations that Changed the World*, and the bestselling series *The Science of Discworld I, II, III,* and *IV* with Terry Pratchett and Jack Cohen. His new book *Calculating the Cosmos* will appear in September 2016 followed by *Infinity: a Very Short Introduction* in 2017.

His awards include the Royal Society's Faraday Medal, the Gold Medal of the Institute for Mathematics and Its Applications, the Public Understanding of Science Award of the AAAS, and the LMS/IMA Zeeman Medal. He was elected a Fellow of the Royal Society in 2001 and currently serves on Council, its governing body. His Letters to a Young Mathematician won the Peano Prize and The Symmetry Perspective won the Balaguer Prize. His app Incredible Numbers (Profile and TouchPress) wont the Digital Book World award for adult nonfiction, and he shared the Lewis Thomas Prize for Writing about Science with Steven Strogatz in 2015. In Pursuit of the Unknown has been chosen to receive the MAA's Euler Book Prize award in January 2017.

He delivered the Royal Institution Christmas Lectures on BBC television in 1997. The final lecture began by bringing a live tiger into the lecture room. He has made over 400 radio broadcasts and 80 television appearances.

His iPad app Incredible Numbers was listed among 'Best apps of 2014' on iTunes store, US and Canada 2014; AASL Best Apps for Teaching & Learning 2015; and won Best Adult Nonfiction App, Digital book World Awards 2015.

He has also written two science fiction novels *Wheelers* and *Heaven* with Jack Cohen, and the SF eBook Jack Of All Trades. He makes frequent radio and television appearances, including the 1997 Christmas Lectures. He is an active research mathematician with over 190 published papers, and works on pattern formation, chaos, network dynamics, and biomathematics.

He lives in Coventry, England.

Tim Poston is an interdisciplinary scientist, with a 1972 Mathematics PhD from the University of Warwick, England. He has since worked in universities from Brazil to South Korea, and in companies ranging from start-ups to GE, in sciences and technologies from ophthalmology to archaeology. Much of this work has led to books and other publications (87, with 2,148 citations on ResearchGate), some to patents (currently 26 issued, several pending), from search presentation technology to glyph rendering, calibrating magnetic resonance receiver coils, the 5-dimensional geometry of real binary quartics, vibration spectra of crystals, brain surgery planning, settlement patterns in archaeology, rod buckling, vision (human and machine), and 3D medical image analysis.

For the last two decades his chief concerns have been in the acquisition and analysis of medical images, and practical human-machine interaction; in April 2013 he joined Forus Health in Bangalore, exploring novel ways to analyse images of the eye with the practical goal of fighting blindness with widely deployable, affordable equipment.

In 2003, with Rebecca, his wife of 49 years (and joyfully counting), he published *Tales of Unexplained Mysteries,* fantasy stories for and about Singapore teens, of different groups and times.

In 2015 he impersonated Dumbledore's smarter older brother at Bangalore Comic Con, and gave a keynote at the Fifth Elephant big data conference.

He enjoys change and simultaneity quakes.

The two have worked together since the mid-1970s on a variety of research and writing projects, including their joint research text *Catastrophe Theory and Its Applications* (over 1000 citations on ResearchGate, with more every week).

More books from Ian Stewart and Tim Poston are available at:
http://ReAnimus.com/store/?author=Ian Stewart and Tim Poston

ReAnimus Press
Breathing Life into Great Books

If you enjoyed this book we hope you'll tell others or write a review! We also invite you to subscribe to our newsletter to learn about our new releases and join our affiliate program (where you earn 12% of sales you recommend) at
www.ReAnimus.com.

Here are more ebooks you'll enjoy from ReAnimus Press, available from ReAnimus Press's web site, Amazon.com, bn.com, etc.:

ROCK STAR - the sequel to THE LIVING LABYRINTH (coming soon)
WHEELERS by Ian Stewart and Jack Cohen (coming soon)

Deep Quarry, by John E. Stith

Manhattan Transfer, by John E. Stith

And Coming Soon from ReAnimus Press by John E. Stith:
All for Naught
Scapescope
Memory Blank
Death Tolls
Redshift Rendezvous
Reunion on Neverend
Reckoning Infinity

The Exiles Trilogy, by Ben Bova

The Star Conquerors (Collectors' Edition), by Ben Bova

The Star Conquerors (Standard Edition), by Ben Bova

Colony, by Ben Bova

The Kinsman Saga, by Ben Bova

Star Watchmen, by Ben Bova

As on a Darkling Plain, by Ben Bova

The Winds of Altair, by Ben Bova

Test of Fire, by Ben Bova

The Weathermakers, by Ben Bova

The Dueling Machine, by Ben Bova

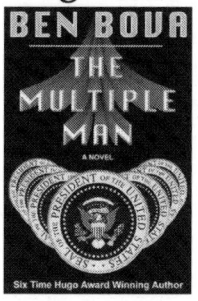

The Multiple Man, by Ben Bova

Escape!, by Ben Bova

Forward in Time, by Ben Bova

Maxwell's Demons, by Ben Bova

Twice Seven, by Ben Bova

The Astral Mirror, by Ben Bova

The Story of Light, by Ben Bova

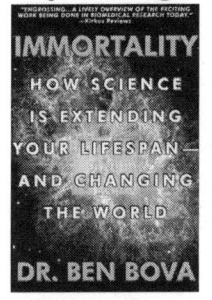

Immortality, by Ben Bova

Space Travel - A Science Fiction Writer's Guide, by Ben Bova

The Craft of Writing Science Fiction that Sells, by Ben Bova

Phoenix Without Ashes, by Harlan Ellison and Edward Bryant

Shadrach in the Furnace, by Robert Silverberg

Bloom, by Wil McCarthy

Aggressor Six, by Wil McCarthy

Murder in the Solid State, by Wil McCarthy

Flies from the Amber, by Wil McCarthy

Innocents Abroad (Fully Illustrated & Enhanced Collectors' Edition), by Mark Twain

Local Knowledge (A Kieran Lenahan Mystery), by Conor Daly

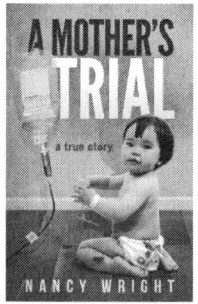

A Mother's Trial, by Nancy Wright

Bad Karma: A True Story of Obsession and Murder, by Deborah Blum

Siege of Stars: Book One of The Sigil Trilogy, by Henry Gee

Scourge of Stars: Book Two of The Sigil Trilogy, by Henry Gee

Rage of Stars: Book Three of The Sigil Trilogy, by Henry Gee

Printed in Great Britain
by Amazon